FUNERAL MUSIC

International cellist Sara Selkirk is apprehensive about the charity concert she is to perform at in Bath's famous Pump Room. It is vitally important to her as it is the first time she will have played in public since the death of her lover the previous year and she needs to regain her lost confidence. However, if she'd known what was to happen that day, she would have lost her nerve completely.

Sara's performance is overshadowed by the death of the concert's organiser, Matthew Sawyer. In the ensuing police investigation, many secrets are uncovered including a stolen needlework collection, an immigration racket, and a headmaster's adulterous affair with his secretary. What, if anything, do any of them have to do with Sawyer's death?

FUNERAL MUSIC

Morag Joss

WINDSOR
PARAGON

First published 1998
by
Hodder & Stoughton
This Large Print edition published 2005
by
BBC Audiobooks Ltd by arrangement with
Hodder & Stoughton plc

ISBN 1 4056 1017 4   (Windsor Hardcover)
ISBN 1 4056 2012 9   (Paragon Softcover)

British Library Cataloguing in Publication Data available

Printed and bound in Great Britain by
Antony Rowe Ltd., Chippenham, Wiltshire

For Tim and Hannah
and with special thanks to Phyllis

AUTHOR'S NOTE

Bath is rightly famous for having more than its fair share of finely preserved and well-proportioned citizens, many with pleasing frontages and classical features, but none of them appears in this book. While many of the places described are real, all the people and events are imagined.

In describing Bath's buildings I have tried to be accurate in historical and architectural detail and true to atmosphere. But, presumably lacking in prophetic acuity, neither the Romans nor any of Bath's later architects designed their buildings with a view to facilitating murder, its concealment or investigation, so I have adulterated one or two fine interiors with all the hidden rooms, passageways and back doors that my characters needed and for which I hope they are grateful. I admit I neither sought nor obtained planning permission but have been reassured that fictional alterations do not (yet, anyway) fall within the ambit of Bath's planning authorities.

I am indebted to Margaret Campbell for the valuable information and insights that I found in her book *The Great Cellists*. I would also like to thank the broadminded Head of Heritage Services in Bath, who remains alive and well, and the District Commander of Bath Police, whose custody I can recommend as pleasant and informative. Any errors I have made regarding cellos, cellists, thermal springs, police procedures or indeed anything else are, of course, my own.

Morag Joss

PROLOGUE

It was worrying, this much water. He wasn't used to this much water. His people were inlanders and had lived by a broad river which for a short season was as shallow as glass but for the rest of the year so dry that, walking across, he would get dust on his feet. And all this water might not be worrying him so much if he were not so far below, alone and in darkness, out of which came deep metallic boomings and slappings as if the ship were colliding with other ships, as if crates and containers were falling over or exploding around him. Holding tight to the knowledge that there could be no help for his terror that would not also include discovery of his presence, he tried not to see in his mind the steep salt sides of the Atlantic shouldering into the steel hull and the arrows of white foam shooting from the impact like arcs of powdered rock as the ship broke a path through the green boulders of the sea.

He closed his eyes, but found that the darkness behind his eyelids was equally comfortless. From the back of his mind he pulled out his fear of discovery and opened it again for examination. Its certainties loomed at him once more: a rough arrest, the bare theft, called confiscation, of his money, questioning, beating, perhaps torture, perhaps court, certainly back to jail. The crashing of the sea seemed sometimes near and sometimes far off, like the banging shut of cell doors along the prison corridors in which had always come, of course, the loudest and daily humiliation, the

1

slamming of his own door and the scrape of the lock. Early in his time there he had learned deeper humiliations, starting with the night when, expecting the banging of his door, he had looked up to see a dark figure blocking the doorway, a heavy, half-smiling guard who had paused, rubbing his crotch, before lumbering into the cell and closing the door. The terror of a few nights at sea below the water line subsided. This night would pass, and so would other nights. Majmout had been paid enough to provide him with enough to eat and keep him hidden, and he had said that during daylight it would be possible for him to walk about the ship, as long as he was careful not to draw attention to himself and went only where Majmout said. He had said most of the other hands would ignore him anyway; many of them brought a stowaway on board from time to time, either for money or to help someone in the family. Everything would be all right, even this first night. Could the next few hours bring anything that could not be borne, compared with the thought of more years in prison?

He listened for reassurance in the snoring of the ship's engines, surely not far away, and breathed in the fumes of oil and metal which he, not a sailor himself, took to be the smells of seaworthiness. He wriggled further down into the envelope of dusty sacks and felt their weight press on him. The cold of the floor was seeping into his shoulders and spreading down through his back, and although his body was chilled and stiff, his face was hot. He had not felt hungry all day, but he was desperate to drink. The fear that he might die of thirst swam into his mind and swilled there feverishly with his

2

other terrors: being discovered, or the great black buffalo of the sea somehow bursting into the ship. And yet another fear rose up in him. When he stopped to think about it, if Majmout knew how much money he was carrying he would probably heave him overboard and could easily get help to do it. He must keep his bag by him and make sure Majmout never got a chance to see what was in it. For as long as this voyage lasted he would need all the strength and cleverness he still possessed. For now he must rest, and if he kept his eyes closed he could almost believe that tomorrow would be better than today, if only because the morning would bring him one day nearer to dry land. But sleep was not possible, and all through the night-long crashing of the ocean against the bows, his horror of the huge, lurching sea clung so tightly round his neck that he feared it would strangle him.

Part One

Part One

CHAPTER ONE

Sara was breathing hard, partly from exertion but also with annoyance. It was not that the telephone was interrupting anything except that first, quiet moment when all movement stopped. It was more that she very much wanted it not to be her agent Robin, whom she was not yet ready to forgive, and was annoyed in advance in case it was. Her legs were shaking as she reached for the telephone. She was still sweating. As she picked up the receiver, the warm smooth plastic slipped through her wet hand, banged on the floor and bounced on the end of its coiled flex, spinning and clunking against the chest of drawers. Whoever was on the other end would probably think she had just hurled the telephone against the wall, so there was no chance of sounding poised and reasonable now. But it was not her agent, it was James. Only a little less annoyed, Sara tried to sound nonchalant which, being breathless, she found difficult.

'Sara Selkirk. Oh, it's you. What was what? Oh, nothing. I just dropped the phone.' She eased her shoes off without undoing the laces. 'I'm a bit out of breath, that's all. Just been out running.' She wiped her free hand damply down her chest.

'So, how are you getting on? Are you all right?' asked James. With the receiver crooked under her chin Sara leaned over and peeled away her stained socks. She sank on to the floor and sat with her legs straight out in front of her.

'Oh, I'm fine—a bit bloodstained.' She sighed, turning her feet to inspect the damage. 'But I'd do it again tomorrow. I enjoyed it.'

James was incredulous. 'Come off it, honeybun. You couldn't actually enjoy it, unless you were sick or something. Are you some sort of pervert, or what?'

'Oh, shut up. It's a wonderful feeling. I'll convert you one day. Look, when are we rehearsing? Not that I feel particularly keen.'

'This afternoon, at four. They're closing the Pump Room early so we can get in. We'll have to put up with them shifting tables and stuff, but it should be okay,' he said. 'Look, are you sure you're all right? You don't sound all right.'

'Yes, yes, I'm fine,' Sara said, flexing her feet. 'I suppose.' Her heart was still hammering but a little more slowly now. 'Four o'clock's fine, I suppose. If we must.' She was suddenly aware of a hurt silence at the other end of the telephone and kicked herself for forgetting. 'Oh, look,' she began.

'Well, yes, I am afraid we must. But you might remember that I'd rather be somewhere else as well. At St Michael's on Lansdown Hill, to be precise. Only I did think, once I'd said we'd do it, that we were committed, and I do think it's quite important for *you* to do it,' James said. 'And I don't *mind* putting you before Graham, but—'

'James, I'm sorry, really I am,' Sara pleaded. 'I'd forgotten about Graham's service. I know you wanted to be there. I am glad we're playing at the Pump Room. I'm really sorry.'

'Oh, no need,' James said wearily, and sighed. 'Look, *I'm* sorry. It's not your fault, it's just the clash of dates that's so fucking annoying. Anyway, Austin understands. And he couldn't get St Michael's on any other day.' He sighed again. 'It'll

8

be a good memorial service, with or without me. It's just so sad.'

'Perhaps you could send flowers.'

'Yeah, perhaps. Anyway, go and prick your blisters, or whatever turns you on. I'll see you this afternoon.'

It crossed Sara's mind as she sat down to practise later that morning that James really was putting himself out for her. Only a matter of days after he had persuaded her into this little performance and confirmed that they would appear, his friend Graham Xavier had died, and his memorial service arranged for seven p.m. on Friday, 13 June. Austin, worn down by months of caring for his partner, of watching him waste away, blind, emaciated but angry to the last, had explained patiently that it had to be then, partly to allow their many London friends to get down to Bath, but also because it was one of the few times that the church happened to be available. Sara recalled James's dismay. She had invited him to cancel their Pump Room date and play at Graham's service instead. But James had said sadly, better do something for the living, Graham would approve of that. She thought guiltily that she had better summon something rather fine, like proper gratitude to James, up from the cellar where her good manners lurked more or less unvisited these days.

As she played, her mind wandered away from Graham and back, as it frequently did, to herself. After all, Graham had been James's friend, and that was important, of course, but a *friend,* one of many. So Graham's death was a loss, but not sudden, not personal like the loss she had suffered.

9

Was suffering, she thought indulgently. Suffering, misunderstood and very, very peeved. She had begun to notice that the people who had been around her at the time, the few people who had an inkling of the reasons behind her sudden withdrawal from her career, were looking to her now for some progress in what they all regarded as a temporary abandonment of purpose. They stopped a little way short of asking outright: *Do you think you might be getting over it yet*? but that was what they wanted to know. Especially Robin, whose enquiries were becoming increasingly blunt: *Look, just when do you think you might be able to think about it*? Well, not now, not yet and certainly not if you ask. James avoided any clumsy direct questioning, but although he saw her every few days even he was now beginning to ask: *How are you getting on*? not just *How are you*? Probably not even his patience was inexhaustible. She would have to show James that she was grateful. But Robin could rot.

Because it would be a mistake to let anyone make too much of her first public performance in over a year. First thing this morning she had lost her temper on the phone with Robin after he had been deaf to the fact that the 'performance' was going to be less than half an hour's playing at a charity event. '*Well*, don't *be thrilled, Robin. Don't go on about it,*' she had said. '*James bullied me into it. No, it doesn't mean I'm able to take any proper engagements. I'm not ready. I don't even want to do this one.*' He had turned on her and declared that if that was truly the case, then speaking not as her friend but as her agent she should not be playing at all. If she bottled out again it would be disastrous.

She, while silently agreeing with him, had then childishly forbidden him to come. '*I wasn't necessarily planning to*,' he had said. '*I've got lots to do in London. Other people to look after, you know, people who actually like performing. People with careers.*' She remembered saying, '*Is that so? Well, I have one brief suggestion for you, Robin. And it ends in "off".*' And then she had, unforgivably, put down the receiver and stomped off on a three-mile run which had not cooled her temper.

She came to the end of her scales and realised, with the air vibrating round her in an angry thrum, that she had been bowing as if she were sawing Robin's head off. She stood up, placed her cello on its side and wandered over to the French window, but instead of stepping out to the garden she turned back to face the room. She liked the bare paleness of the bleached floor and white muslin, hung from black poles, next to Matteo's ebony Bosendorfer concert grand and the small dark chair and music stand that she used, but it had been more Matteo's room than hers. For the first few months she had avoided coming in here and later, as an excuse to go in, she had begun to see to it that there were always fresh flowers from the garden in the room. One day, finding an appalling slug slinking across the piano, she had felt her floral offering mundanely infested, exposed as exactly the sort of mawkish shrine-making that Matteo would have hated. Now she forced herself to use the room sometimes and to keep it bare. Only very occasionally now, when on the threshold and raising her hand to the door, would she suddenly miss the sounds of occupancy, the notes of the piano or Matteo's voice within, and the thought would come to her like the involuntary flutter of a muscle that he must have just wandered out to the garden for a moment. She conceded, looking round, that none of it was Robin's fault. I should ring him, she thought, because it is not his fault and anyway he is right. She did not want to play again in front of an audience yet, but worse, and what neither Robin nor James realised, was that she was approaching the concert not with the fear that she might not cope but with a flat boredom that was infinitely more terrifying in its implications than the most crippling nerves.

James's theory was that only when she started playing again would the old feeling come back, and that she would overcome what he called the Block. *'One sniff of the old greasepaint, you'll see, that's all it'll take,'* he had said optimistically and, as it was turning out, wrongly. She did not want to let him down so she would play the concert, but it would be with the same perfunctory deadness of heart that had first overcome her in Paris. She would have another forage in the manners cellar in the hope of unearthing sufficient humility to ring Robin. And then she rather hoped that she would be left alone.

In a mood of atonement she worked for the whole of the morning. It did not strike her until later that she had practised mechanically for over four hours with such technical precision that she could barely remember which pieces she had been playing.

*　　　*　　　*

Cecily Smith was idly considering liposuction when the bell went. With a sigh she jammed her shoes

12

back on, shoved her *Cosmopolitan* back into her desk drawer and trundled across the corridor to Derek's office, where she set up his coffee-maker almost as carefully as he would have done himself. As it went 'spleuch spleuch' she washed up his cup and saucer and straightened things on the desk, running her hand lightly over his bulging brown leather Filofax. Occasionally she tugged down her short black skirt which she had bought as the consequence of an article entitled 'The New Mini—You're *Not* Too Old To Wear It!' But she was. And Derek was too unfit to bound up the stairs, so when he swept into the room he was hot and panting as well as very large. Cecily, who knew the sound of his arrival at the top of the staircase, pumped her hair, pulled in her stomach and turned from the desk just in time to bestow upon him the picture of herself, the consummate headmaster's secretary, with a smile which she knew conveyed a certain readiness. Derek dumped a pile of manila folders on his desk, poured out his coffee and gulped at it twice, eyeing her dangerously. Putting down his cup, he led her by the wrist to the corner furthest from the windows and (considerately, she thought) wiped his hand across his lips before plunging his tongue into her mouth. Strange how coffee, so clean and delicious, is instantly transformed on a person's breath into a kind of bitter compost. Somehow she hardly ever minded, and seldom allowed herself to reflect that Derek's preferred order of stimulants these days was caffeine first, hcr second. Without ceremony his hands hoiked up the back of her skirt, sank under her tights and began energetically kneading her backside.

All was quiet around them, save for the far-off playground yammer. The others, to whom Derek referred as 'my admin team', would all be downstairs in the staffroom having their coffee now, motivated by either (Cecily was not sure which) raging thirst or raging discretion. She and Derek had roughly four minutes before they could expect an interruption from someone or other, a rounded-up band of bike-shed smokers or, more likely, a harassed junior teacher. Not daring to be too reckless they had learned, more or less, to wait for the sanctuary of Cecily's little house in Bath, but for now, in the corner among the box files, spider plants and back numbers of *TES*, they chewed hungrily at each other's necks with the promise of a proper meal later.

Over his shoulder Cecily looked through the windows down across the tarmac to the hall, the 'PE Complex' in Derek-speak, a ghastly seventies addition to a more subtly disastrous sixties building. Dispirited seagulls tottered on the asphalt roof. Below, dispirited clusters of children roamed the wire at the playground's edge. Beyond, a line of dispirited and widely spaced saplings drooped across implausibly undulating banks of municipal grass, where two dispirited dogs sniffed and trailed each other tediously. Behind rose the estate of medium-rise blocks on whose walls even the graffiti had assumed a weary air. She could not look at any of it for long without feeling her heart sag like the gusset in an old pair of tights. It was not hopelessly awful; of course there were many places worse, but it just seemed that no one who had ever had a say in how the place was put together had bothered to consider that human beings might need to enjoy what they saw around them. There needed to be things for the eye to rest on with pleasure, things that were perhaps, strictly speaking, unnecessary. Cecily thought of her new urn. She had just bought it from an overpriced and precious reclamation outfit in Walcot Street and, knowing she had paid more than she could afford for it, consequently loved it too much. She had planted it up with an expensive collection of trailing plants which, if they did as the packaging claimed, were going to provide 'a cascade of colour all summer long'. The urn now stood in her otherwise uncultivated front garden which was roughly the size of a door, but it looked well, in keeping with the rest of the terrace whose six houses all had Victorian ornamental bricks above the front sash windows and twiddly bits round the doorways.

Feeling brighter, for it was Friday and she would soon be driving home to Larkhall, she pulled away from Derek, who was pinker in the face and seemed to be feeling brighter too, although he still had not spoken a word. They both looked down sheepishly at his crotch while he tried to dispose of his erection by pulling down on it as if it were a recalcitrant door handle.

'You really turn me on,' he said, redundantly.

Cecily sorted her knickers and tugged down at her skirt.

'I like you in that,' he said, then added heavily, 'and out of it too. Just a few more hours, Cec.'

She was following his train of thought, which allowed her to overlook his use of his name for her. Perhaps it was silly and over-dignified to object, but her name was Cecily. She had even laughed when Derek once referred to her bedroom as the Cec pit.

Ha-ha, Derek. But he did so enjoy a pun, especially his own. She put up with the little things because she really did admire him, loved him really, for the way he kept at it, toiling away to elevate the unpromising young of unlovely south Bristol. And one day she would be able to give him the real, proper support he deserved, waving him off each morning in a fresh shirt and making their large house and generous garden a pleasure to come home to, while she would be happy and organised and well dressed and get her nails and hair done regularly and never have to worry again about the Visa bill or the mortgage.

'I'm really looking forward to it,' she said truthfully.

Derek's wife would be away running a course for infants teachers until Sunday morning so they had the luxury of a whole evening and night together instead of a few illicit hours snatched whenever Derek could plausibly claim to be at 'one of my meetings'. In nearly two years he had managed at least as many meetings naked under a duvet with Cecily as he had endured in a stale shirt under strip lighting with his long-winded governors and had grown adept, arriving home late and ragged, at steering his wife into indignant discussions on the iniquities of the headteacher's workload.

'Have you decided what you're doing for us?' Cecily asked.

Derek's voice took on the authority and mystery of a man who is doing dinner. 'Duck, I thought, with something. I'll see. Fruit, if there's anything interesting. And some cheese, I'll go to the Posh and see what they've got.'

What they always had plenty of at the Posh,

16

Derek's name for the Fine Cheese Company, his favourite shop in Bath, as well as dozens of cheeses, was a ruinous array of beautiful olive oils, and lovely breads to dip in the oils, and pots and jars of other lovely things marinading in oils, and even more little delicious things to nibble. He resisted none of it. Cecily, unable to afford it on her own, could not bring herself to discourage this generosity over food and still, despite the passing of two birthdays and a Christmas with only cards and nice dinners, kept hoping that the same impulse might occasionally spread over into other areas of their shared existence. She kissed her diet goodbye again and half-regretfully opened her accommodating heart to the prospect of a weekend with Derek filling her pretty Victorian house with his big, powerful appetites. There was always liposuction.

*   *   *

Sara had finished the rehearsal with James and was deciding, with bad grace, that she would have to kill time in town before the concert. It was already after five o'clock and they had to be ready at the Pump Room by half past seven. It would not be worth the effort of crawling back to St Catherine through Friday traffic to spend an hour at home.

'Lighten up, honeybun,' James said. 'You've got your frock in the car, haven't you? Come over to Camden Crescent with me. You can have a bath and a sit-down there. You should try to relax.'

Sara shook her head. She was restless, and the thought of two hours of James trying to be soothing and wonderful, but actually striding about his flat

17

singing his tuneless snatches from *Don Giovanni* or *Phantom of the Opera*, was more than she could bear.

'No, I fancy a walk. No, don't come. I've got a couple of things to do. Waitrose, that kind of thing. I'll see you later.'

'Well, you should really be resting. But anyway, don't forget your Chopin Liszt,' James trilled, 'and don't trap a finger. Remember the date. See you later.'

As she expected it to be at this time on a Friday afternoon, Waitrose was busy with women who were cornering recklessly round the aisles, their big hair apparently conferring upon them the sense of safety assumed by wearers of crash helmets. It was an infiltration of Hell's Shoppers, straight from the hairdressers', faces tight and pink from the drier, and wearing chains in most of the standard but inappropriate places: round the heels of their shoes, dangling from wrists, slung over arms as handbag straps and stretched round their uncomely waists. They did nothing to improve Sara's temper and not for the first time she wished she could fit on to her trolley axles some of those nice rotating blades that Ben-Hur found so handy.

Next to them, the Men Who Cook, browsing in their lovely putty-coloured trenchcoats and their tilted hats, were quite benign. They cooked, but for accolades and consenting adults only. They shopped, but usually for one meal at a time, never with children or a cello, and sufficiently seldom to consider fifteen minutes pondering eight different options of lettuce to be time well spent. They were often to be found hovering in the fruit and veg, having taken off just a little early from their

18

creative jobs in architecture, design or the media in order to put together delectably expensive food for little Friday night dinner parties. Once a promisingly attractive Man Who Cooks had asked Sara, who had happened to know, what one did with a daikon radish and had taken such an interest in the answer that she had known the question to be a disappointingly genuine request for information rather than a conversational opening. It had been disheartening to discover that she held rather less allure than a tuber; that Alistair Little had a lot to answer for. There was a bit of a Man Who Cooks picking over the nine varieties of wild mushrooms now, except that he was almost too old, about fifty. And he was really too fat but, being over six feet tall, was managing to carry it off quite well. But he certainly qualified on the basis of the trolley, which contained Barbary duck breasts, tarragon, crème fraîche, a Californian Zinfandel, Beaumes de Venise, chocolate almonds, unsalted butter, ripe South African plums, tiny red peppers and shallots. Several little paper bags from the Fine Cheese Company and a bunch of five perfect tiger lilies sat in the front. And now lots of wild mushrooms, chervil and fresh figs. There was something touching about this large, gloomy-looking man in his dark suit and Liberty tie, so thoughtfully choosing such obviously seductive food. I hope she appreciates it, Sara thought, knowing for certain that it would be a she.

She looked down into her own trolley. Cashew nuts, one French baton, a single salmon fillet and a bag of pre-washed salad. Food for one. She lost heart for shopping, and wandered out of the supermarket with her carrier bag, wondering where

19

in Bath, at six in the evening, time could best be killed without her going to a pub. She could go back to the Pump Room. She could find somewhere in the back to wait while the frantic preparations for the evening's dinner carried on around her, but the idea held no appeal. She much preferred the daytime calm of the Pump Room, the white-clad tea tables under the chandelier, the fountain where the water was still pumped up for a pound a glass, the window with its view down to the hot, bubbling bath below. And although one could no longer enjoy the diverting sight of floating invalids bobbing scrofulously in the healing waters, it was amusing to watch the happy trespass of the tourists, with their camcorders, phoney university sweatshirts and shell suits, upon the late eighteenth century gentility of it all. But the tourists had been booted out early today, because of the concert and dinner.

She dawdled up New Bond Street and paused outside Jigsaw. The laconic dummy in the window was draped in a turquoise tube which, understandably, she did not look particularly happy to be wearing. Sara, looking past the dummy and taking in her own reflection in the mirror behind, measured herself mentally and concluded without excitement that she could get away with it, if she wanted to. The colour might suit her dark hair and large greeny blue eyes, and the cut of the dress would not be too unforgiving over her hips which, although not large, were wider than the dislocated twin pelvic bones of the plaster dummy in the window. Her jeans were looser than they had been a year ago. The cambric shirt she was wearing was baggier. It was partly because of the running and, since she had joined the health club, also the regular working out, but it had something else besides to do with a growing indifference about most things, including food. She was not exactly disinclined to eat, but often had to remind herself to do so. In the same way, the prospect of trying on dresses in shops presented itself as a tremendous chore to which she would subject herself only when she felt she needed a new one. Which she hoped would not be in less than ten years or so.

'Hiya! Buying it? Great, isn't it? Are you getting it? It'd look great on you!' The sudden appearance at her side of tall, blonde, physical Sue from the health club was, despite the absence of oars and a helmet, like a one-woman Viking landing.

'Oh, God, you gave me a fright. No, I don't think so. It would be good on you, though,' Sara said.

Sue looked critically at the dress and gave her stomach a complacent pat. 'I might. Depends if Paul likes it. He hates shopping, though. They all do, don't they?'

'Do they?' Sara said, remembering some of Matteo's glorious extravagances. 'Look, are you walking up town? I'll go with you—I'm just dawdling. I'm on at the Pump Room later, but I've got a bit of time on my hands till then.'

'Oh, come with me!' Sue cried. 'I'm going to this great thing at the Assembly Rooms. The Healing Arts—it's an alternative healing fair. You'll love it! I've only got a couple of hours now. I've got to be back to do eight till eleven at the club. Aw, come on, it'll be really interesting. Aunt Livy told me about it. She'll be there; there's a proper opening at half six.'

'Is Olivia doing the opening first, then?' Sara

21

asked. 'I know she's coming to the Pump Room dinner at eight. Busy, busy, isn't she?'

'Nah, not really; she's got to be there, but she's only deputy director now. The new bloke's doing the speech, I think. Forget his name. You coming? Go on, it'll be fun. Keep me company. Paul's there as well. He's doing a bit of moonlighting in the kitchen, so I won't even see him. Come *on*.'

Sara opened her mouth to refuse, then hesitated. Why not go? She had plenty of time, because although the Assembly Rooms were close to the Circus, almost at the other end of town from the Pump Room, in Bath that meant a brisk twenty-minute walk at the most. Even if she left the Assembly Rooms as late as ten to seven, she could, by following virtually a straight line down through Milsom Street, Old Bond Street and going via Union Street into Abbey Churchyard, be at the Pump Room before seven fifteen.

Sue was already walking up towards Russell and Bromley at the top of the street, and Sara allowed herself to follow.

'You seem very "up" today,' Sara said. 'Things going well?'

'Dunno about "things", but Paul and me're having a good spell. All week, now,' Sue calculated happily.

Sara reflected that that was indeed a record. Sue's boyfriend worked as a waiter in the hotel, Fortune Park, to which the health club was attached. One afternoon the previous winter when the club had been almost empty she had found Sue weeping behind the desk and had got the whole blubbed story of how he could be terribly moody and sometimes very cold, 'like he doesn't want me around at all, and then it all changes and he's nice again, so I know he loves me really'. Not having met him, Sara had nevertheless pictured a shallow, local boy of limited intellect, fundamentally silly and out of his depth. In the same conversation Sue had told her that her parents were divorced and her father had since died. Her mother had had two more children with her second husband and now lived in Canada. She only really had her Aunt Olivia and her grandfather, Olivia's father, although she didn't really live with them any more. 'She works at the museum, my aunt,' Sue had sniffed. 'She's a curator, practically in charge. She's really nice.' She had been strangely consoled to find out that Sara already knew Olivia, and Sara suspected that since that day she had looked upon her as a kind of stand-in auntie.

They wandered up into Milsom Street. Well, since Auntie One was on museum duty, perhaps it would be a kindness if Auntie Two were to stand in and keep the child happy—admittedly a stunning, volatile, twenty-four-year-old child, who was now contentedly window-shopping at the lingerie shop with the eighty-quid knickers—and it would not kill Auntie Two to do something unselfish for once, after all.

'I really want to go to this. It's all about being *centred*, you see. I haven't befriended my inner child enough,' Sue told her earnestly. 'Have you?'

Sara was not sure how to reply to this and was glad, since Sue did not pause very long for her answer, that she did not have to. 'Oh, but of course you have. You're so together. Anyway, being centred. Mind and body. I'm sure there's a connection. I mean, doctors know nothing, do

23

they? *Nothing.'*

Sara murmured non-committally, enjoying Sue's happy energy without really having to listen. They walked on together and as Sue expounded on the 'latest findings' which proved that the ancient Egyptians had used pineapple tops as a hallucinogenic drug, or perhaps a contraceptive— Sue couldn't remember—Sara was wondering if she had somehow strayed into the teddy-bear and iron-candlestick epicentre of the universe. Almost every shop, except those purveying futons, posh underwear and Panama hats, seemed devoted to them. They ogled in the estate agents' windows along George Street and made their way into the Circus where, between the solicitors' offices and dental surgeries, the lights from several basement kitchens were already warming the area walls and casting a gleam on the glossy leaves of camellias and bay trees in tubs. This was clearly where the action was at this time of day, for the tall drawing rooms above were dark and their draped windows stared out emptily. Sara breathed in and smelled prosperity, speculating that a few of the Men Who Cook would be busy behind the kitchen windows, pacing the terracotta floors, opening the wine to let it breathe, presiding over their copper pans on their bottle-green ranges. Not so much 'the smell of steaks in passageways', more the smell of grilled goats' cheeses with a jus of rowanberries sprinkled with toasted pine kernels on rocket leaves with a raspberry and chive vinaigrette, she thought, but it hadn't got the same ring.

*   *   *

Derek had got away at a quarter to four by stalling an orthodontically challenged probationary teacher who wanted a chat, knowing that it would mean a miserable weekend for the poor sod who obviously wanted to share the shocking realisation that he was not sure he was really cut out for teaching.

'Dave, come and see me Monday morning, we'll get you sorted. Okay? See Cecily, she's got the diary.'

For good measure he had poked his head into the admin office on his way down the corridor and bawled a cheery and public, 'Bye, folks! Bye, Cecily, have a good weekend!'

He shot home. He did not take time to change. He stuffed a few things into a huge Marks and Spencer carrier bag: a shirt, jumper, cords, underpants, socks, spongebag. He rolled his favourite knife into his favourite apron and put those in too. He would have liked to take a decent lemon zester and his favourite sauté pan as well—Cecily's kitchen was naff—but it was smarter not to take too much; it cut down the chances of leaving something behind at Cecily's that Pauline might later miss. Not that she spent enough time in the kitchen to be entirely au fait with its contents, but she was an observant woman. He scanned the post and stuffed the one envelope addressed to him in his briefcase and took that too. Now he had to get over to Bath, do some shopping and with luck he could still be at Cecily's before six.

Shopping accomplished, Derek sat fuming, stuck in traffic on the London Road. Worse, he was stuck just outside a filthy pub from whose door an alarming-looking clientele trickled like a toxic spillage out on to the pavement corner. They

25

seemed to have dressed themselves out of dog baskets, with a bit of sleeve and cardigan here and two or three bits of trouser there, rather than complete garments, although their black boots, clinging up to mid-shin, looked whole enough. Most of them looked as if they might have been rolling in mud and were eyeing Derek as if they believed that he had pushed them in it. Despising himself, he locked the car doors. The *PM* programme chirruped on about league tables, incompetent headteachers and falling standards. Still exasperated but feeling more secure, he fished out the letter he had brought and opened it without noticing the postmark.

Suddenly the world changed colour. It was reelingly good news. The letter informed him that he had been shortlisted for the post of Director of Education and Cultural Services for the City of Bath and North-West Wansdyke. Derek's heart started to bang in his throat as he recalled the details of his application. He had applied for the job knowing two things: one, that he was a rank outsider and two, that he could write a damn good application when he tried. Although it had been five weeks since he had written it, it was easy to bring to mind what he had put because they were the things he had once believed in and had been bluffing about for years. He had referred to the need to balance consolidation with change, traditional methods with new thinking, and standards with opportunities; he had sprinkled about like hundreds and thousands notions such as diversity, enrichment, accountability, consultation, visionary leadership and fiscal prudence. The result had been a very digestible confection entitled

'Citizen 2001: Prioritising Educational and Cultural Needs for Bath and North-West Wansdyke into the New Millennium'. He could have been applying to be Secretary of State. He had played up his 'role' in the region as a professional educator with 'solid, hands-on experience', signalling his readiness to 'move into the strategic management sphere'. As a 'key figure' in 'culture and the arts', he had cited a number of small arts charities on whose boards he had rather grudgingly served. He had exaggerated both the scope and scale of two consultancies in the Midlands he had done eight years previously and had described his influence as an 'advisor' to a now disbanded theatre-in-education company in terms that were close to fraudulent. He had mentioned a book he was writing about arts education in England and Wales since the 1988 Act, omitting to observe that he had not actually started it, but had done most of the research and lost his notes when his hard disk crashed.

It was not so much an application as a visa, his passport out of his collapsing job in south Bristol and into lovely, elegant Bath (he dismissed the pub crowd as atypical) and the career he deserved. He belonged in Bath. He certainly did not belong in Bristol, and he couldn't stand much more of it. He had to get out. He *had* to get the job. He looked at the letter again. It gave no date for the interview, but said he would be contacted in the coming week. Meanwhile, the appointments subcommittee looked forward to the opportunity of hearing an outline of his vision for the authority's education and cultural provision for the next five years. That would be a doddle. Would he please note that the committee would be taking a special interest in his

27

plans for museums services, since the post for which he had applied, following recent restructuring, would combine the duties of Director of Education for the first time with overall responsibility for the museums function. Oh, God.

Cecily had got back only minutes before him. She had had Dave in tears for an hour and so had had no time to tidy up or change, and was not in quite the desired frame of mind for Derek's lavish groping in the hall. Nor was she flattered to learn the real reason for his excitement, nor charmed at the prospect of driving straight back into Bath to have a quick look at the costume museum before it closed.

'I've got to be completely prepared for this interview, Cec,' Derek said. 'Come with me. It won't take long. I've got to sound as if I know what I'm talking about and I'll have to get round all the museums, and I haven't got long. The interview could be the week after next. We could do the others tomorrow. Look, Cec, if I get this job, everything'll change. For us. It's what you want. *Please*.'

Derek so seldom said please.

CHAPTER TWO

Sara and Sue left the savours of the Circus and walked down to the Assembly Rooms which sat in stately amber splendour surrounded by the flat façades of Bennett Street. For a public building it was oddly discreet, with its main entrance at one side and nothing so obvious as posters of forthcoming events or intelligible signs as to its function. Suppose you were a stranger, or somehow just impermeable to the curious Bathonian intelligence that John Wood the Younger's Assembly Rooms (completed 1771) were now open to visitors and available for functions? If you were just skulking round in ignorance, looking for a way in, you might imagine the building to be the headquarters of some wealthy religious fringe, or perhaps a hugely upmarket private cinema. It was slightly irritating, Sara felt, as if you were just supposed to *know* that inside there was a fabulous costume museum as well as a suite of magnificent eighteenth-century salons.

They went in together through the surprisingly unassuming pillared entrance and into a crowded vestibule. Sara began to feel silly. Perhaps she should have taken up James's offer of a rest at his flat before the concert. The rehearsal had gone well, although it had not fooled either of them; she had managed to create some semblance of involvement with the music, but no more. They both knew she was cheating, but in the absence of the real thing there seemed to be nothing else she could do. The spark was no longer there. Technically, of course, she was superb, as good as ever, and that would satisfy most of the people listening tonight who would be local, well disposed and feeling charitable. It was an expensive invitation-only dinner and concert, a fund-raiser for the Bath Festival, so Sara expected that she would recognise about two-thirds of the people there. She would see the artistic director of course, impassioned and charming, as well as the festival's chief executive, perpetually worried about funding, and most of the Festival Trust Board, a motley but well-intentioned crew. Prosperous Bath business people with prosperous clients, strategically invited potential sponsors and festival patrons, as well as many other well-heeled and cultured Bathonians would be there. And the more active Friends of the Bath Festival, like Sue's aunt, Olivia Passmore, and several others Sara could think of, would probably not miss the chance to hear what they might (wrongly) think was to be Sara Selkirk's come-back concert. The thought that it was hardly a concert kept returning to her.

People were milling about in the vestibule as Sue got her name checked off and was handed several sheets of recycled paper and the inevitable badge. She moved out of the mêlée and leaned against the wall further up the hall to read down the events programme. The words 'workshop', 'sharing' and 'empowerment' were cropping up rather a lot, even for Sue, and while Sara was reading over her shoulder and trying not to feel supercilious, she saw the big man from Waitrose come into the foyer. As he was almost the only man and certainly the largest person in sight, he immediately seemed to fill the place up. He was with a woman, and together they had a tense, straight-from-the-office look. She was on the short side, carrying only a little surplus weight for her forty-eightish years and clearly not in the habit of asking herself if she might be wearing too much make-up. She was wearing plenty, and broadly speaking to good effect; her round grey eyes had been edged expertly in black which made her look rather sultry in a slightly dim sort of way. They were only just visible under her coarse fringe, which had apparently been

30

nibbled by something small and very hungry. The original colour of the shoulder-length hair could only be guessed at, because her rough bob had been so mercilessly streaked with bottled colours that it had a strange, defeated patina and curved flat over her head and under her chin like a low cottage roof of thatched aluminium. Through her hair she was peering with interest at the tables of leaflets.

'Can't make head nor tail of this,' Sue whispered. 'I'm going to ask.' She wandered further up the hall to a desk marked 'Enquiries' and was soon engaged in consultation. From her position against the wall just inside the vestibule Sara observed that a row was starting. The woman in the pay kiosk was agreeing with the big man that, indeed, there were several people here. Yes, she was saying, those people could go round the Museum of Costume in the basement because they were attending a private event at the Assembly Rooms on the ground floor, but the museum was actually closed to the general public from six p.m. It was now five past six, and no, they could not get into the museum until tomorrow morning unless they were participating in the private event, which they were not, were they? This was not going down well. Sara was wondering why these two people should be here at all instead of starting off their evening with a leisurely bottle of champagne somewhere. And since they were obviously together, obviously not married, and had the makings of a delightful and intimate dinner somewhere in the background, would not the most sensible place be in bed, as a postlude to urgent, passionate lovemaking? Given what Sara presumed were their other options, this consuming interest in historic textiles seemed not altogether healthy. But they really were taking it very seriously, or rather the man was, pointing out that as the premises were actually open, it was surely a little churlish to refuse them entry. His very loud and slow manner of speaking was in itself an insult, implying that he was a patient and forbearing man and she was a pitifully unintelligent woman. That he certainly was not, or that she might have been, was not really the point, and it was having not the slightest effect on the lady in the kiosk.

'Let it go, Derek,' his companion was saying quietly behind him.

'I have *no intention* of letting it go,' he said furiously, wheeling round at her. Perhaps they were married after all. But she wore no rings except for two God-awful nuts of turquoise and silver on her right hand.

'My name is Derek Payne,' he announced loudly, turning back to the kiosk and pausing as if he expected this information to produce some change of heart. Miraculously it did, or seemed to, for just then the double doors further down the passage behind the kiosk opened and a tall figure in evening dress emerged. Sara was momentarily taken aback, for in the gloom of the corridor the figure looked uncannily like Matteo. The black tie partly created the impression, but also the long legs, the swing of the walk and the thick dark hair, just for a second, unsettled her. The bright light of the vestibule did not quite dispel the impression for, also like Matteo, this man had such an air of professional confidence that immediately Derek Payne looked a little silly.

32

'And mine,' the tall figure said, 'is Matthew Sawyer. And I am the Director of Museums and Civic Leisure Resources.'

A second surprise: this must be Olivia Passmore's new boss. The big man Derek was allowing himself to be drawn to one side and Sara, overhearing the persuasive baritone of appeasement, guessed that he was being skilfully brought round. It would be fun to relate this little drama to Olivia. She would catch her at the Pump Room later, although if she saw her here they could perhaps walk down together. Olivia was almost a friend, more accurately one of those close acquaintances that are so easy to collect in a place like Bath. Sara knew that after nearly three years as Acting Director of Museums, during which the council had tortuously restructured all its departments, Olivia had dropped gratefully back into her post as deputy director when Sawyer had been appointed about three months ago.

Derek's little woman friend was shuffling awkwardly some distance away in the vestibule, picking up leaflets from the Healing Arts registration desk in an attempt to conceal her embarrassment. Sara suddenly felt embarrassed too, feeling that she had been much too obvious in her observation of events. It was not as if this couple held any real interest for her, it was just that having seen Derek in the supermarket it had been amusing to watch the episode unfold, and it was funny, that man looking for a moment so like Matteo, and being called Matthew. She moved away and rejoined Sue, who had finished deliberating and had signed herself up for the first evening session on effective mind and body

33

communication.

'Sounds brilliant. It's all about mind and body circuitry, how to talk to your body, get it to heal itself. Attitude, really. Being *aware*,' Sue said grandly. 'You interested?'

'Er, another time,' Sara said. 'Look, you go and find out about your natural healing circuitry. I'll just have a bit of a wander here, have a look at the stalls. You don't mind, do you?'

In less than half an hour it would be time for the official welcome, which Sara was certain would amount to a glass of warm organic wine, some turgid phrases from the platform and polite applause. Then she could get off to the Pump Room while Sue delivered herself up wholeheartedly to her—what had she been saying?—*simple light tapping on the skull to isolate the problem area and stimulate the brain*. She smiled. 'It's nice to see you really happy,' she said, touching Sue's arm. 'You must make it last, this time. Get that Paul to behave himself.'

'I'm going to do my very best,' Sue said seriously, and then sighed. 'I wish I could be like you. I'm so up and down all the time. I'd love to be more like you. You don't ever change, do you? You're always the same.'

Sara, giving Sue a smile which concealed how much this remark depressed her, made for the Ballroom. It was a relief to get away from all that young enthusiasm, and from the embarrassment of the episode in the vestibule. She worried that she might be turning into one of those barking, lugubrious spinsters who stare at people in public. She was going to have to watch it. If she wasn't careful she would soon be muttering in the street

34

and taking her clothes off in Waitrose. She wandered on, browsing desultorily at the stalls promising holistic massage enabling healing, psychic readings enabling spiritual growth, and something called overtone singing, enabling the finding of one's voice, which were settled in alongside palmistry, aromatherapy and authentic Guatamalan handicrafts. There was nothing, as far as she could see, that approximated to essential deep relaxation enabling international concert cellists to resume their careers, so she had to settle for some tea tree bath gel. She walked slowly across to the Tea Room. Sue was already there and in conversation with Derek Payne's woman with the problem hair.

'Hiya!' Sue yelped at her from several yards away. 'You'll never believe it! This is my landlady!' Sue beamed. 'My Monday to Friday landlady, I should say. Cecily! Sara! Meet Cecily, Sara. Cecily, Sara!' Cecily smiled without showing her teeth. 'Cecily's joining the thing tonight, just on impulse, aren't you?'

Cecily was trying to look relaxed. 'I just thought I might stay. Someone's picking me up later. There's something on organic hair treatments. And the weight-loss bits, I'd like a look at those. I'm only here by accident.'

Sara gave her an enquiring look which was supposed to convey complete ignorance of the circumstances of Cecily's arrival.

'I came with a friend. On another matter. But perhaps I should just go on a diet,' she added sadly. The big round eyes could look abject as well as sultry. Sara felt certain that Derek had gone off in a huff, having not got his way with Matthew

35

Sawyer. She had seen how short his temper was and guessed that he was easily peeved, although it was just possible that Cecily had been the one to be offended and make a stand, deferring their dinner and subsequent seduction until after she had salvaged some benefit for herself out of the earlier embarrassment. But she could hardly ask.

'Oh, *dieting* doesn't work,' Sue said, landing happily on the familiar ground of the conversation. 'You've really just got to stop eating *completely*, that's the only thing that works for me. Willpower's not a problem. I'll do anything when I really want to. Paul hates me fat. Anyway, there's a woman here who sorts the whole thing out with her hands. It's a mind-body thing; she lays on her hands and it kind of disperses all the fat. It's very gentle, apparently.'

'Really? That sounds amazing,' Cecily said, wide-eyed.

'Yeah, it is. I mean, you've got to follow this eating plan as well. Obviously. Loads of water and fruit, to eliminate body toxins. No meat or fish. Or coffee, or fat or sugar, *obviously*.'

'Oh,' said Cecily, wanly. 'It's a diet, then.'

'I sometimes wonder where my body toxins are,' Sara said. 'And what are they, exactly? How much do they weigh? I mean, could I get a test tube full? When I die,' she said importantly, 'I am going to donate my body toxins to medical research.'

Sue squealed with laughter. 'Oh, *you!*' she said, just as the hub of conversation in the room fell away.

'Now I don't intend to keep you standing here long,' said the man on the platform, whom Sara immediately recognised as the tall pacifier of

36

Derek. He had an unattractive, upper-middle-class accent of the kind which would have got him lynched in many parts of Britain although not, of course, in Bath. He introduced the 'ladies' with him on the platform.

'. . . the President of the Natural Healing Arts Association'—grinning, ample and kaftan-clad, Sara noted—'and my colleague Olivia Passmore who as deputy director of Bath museums is responsible, with me, for this wonderful venue.'

There was Olivia, obviously already dressed for the Pump Room, her short greying hair and strong features looking marvellous above a silvery-looking silk jacket. She was bound to be walking across town to the Pump Room afterwards, so they probably would go together, or would she have to go with Matthew Sawyer? Was that why he was wearing black tie?

'Now I'm just a simple chap who's worked in museums all his life, and I'm also jolly lucky because it's my job to run all the museums in this wonderful city. And that means I have the pleasant duty of welcoming you all here this weekend and I hope that you'll enjoy not only this very special building, but also the many other unique features of Bath. Now of course Bath has long been a centre of healing. Before the Romans, the prehistoric peoples hereabouts thought the hot spring contained the healing power of the goddess Sulis. So to them this was a holy place. Then the Romans came along and they were no end impressed, I can tell you. Now the Romans recognised a good idea when they saw it . . .'

Oh, God, Sara thought, exchanging a look with Sue, we're going to get the works.

37

'. . . and so there was a bit of a hostile takeover—har-har—and so generations of Romans also came to know this place as holy. Only this time the chap in charge, or chappess rather, was the *Roman* goddess Minerva. And by the eighteenth century . . .'

That's more like it, skip two thousand years or so, get to the point, she thought approvingly.

'. . . people were a little more prosaic and they flocked here in their droves. Now this was all on the basis of quasi-scientific ideas about the benefits of the waters . . .'

Then it started.

'. . . and it goes to show, doesn't it, that we never really learn! It's all a question of faith, isn't it? For here all you dear ladies are today, in the dying years of the second millennium, to tell us that with a drop of vegetable extract here and little massage there, we'll all be "cured" of whatever ails us! Extraordinary, isn't it? Just clutch your healing crystal—that'll be twenty pounds please—and breathe deeply! And large numbers of us believe you, much in the way that people have believed in the power of the waters here, and a whole host of other quackery, for the past two thousand and something years! And it's just as good for business as it ever was, isn't it? I don't need to tell you that it's *faith* you need, even today! And where, ladies, does faith end and superstition begin? I put it to you that superstition is simply the name we give to all those familiar articles of faith that have stood the test of time. Just look at today's date if you need convincing. Friday the thirteenth! We consider it unlucky, don't we? And we consider the spa waters to be beneficial to health. Two articles of faith, you see, of which we are equally fond and which are equally unsupported by fact—har-har!'

His laugh was inane and nasal. Sara, although in broad agreement with most of this, was aghast at his clumsiness. Could he really think that this was the time and place to outline such a robustly sceptical analysis of the nature of belief? The audience was not laughing, but staring back at him in silence. Sensing perhaps that all was not well, Matthew Sawyer attempted to lighten the message with humour.

'So, do venture out and see Bath's unique Roman Baths in the course of this weekend. That's if you're not too busy stirring your cauldrons and cooking up cures for all those little afflictions that we all suffer from! Actually, I have a little wart on my finger here—any suggestions?'

Sara heard Sue smother a snort and felt a panicky need to laugh. She looked at the ceiling. Had his audience consisted of less deeply relaxed and psychically healed people they would by this stage have been transformed into an insurgent, seething and disaffected mob. But, being broadminded and non-violent to a woman, this mob was doing little to convey its discomfiture to Matthew Sawyer. And he had not yet finished.

'Actually, I don't have any particular regard for the established medical profession myself and that is another reason why I am grateful to you, as representatives of the alternative healing lobby. The more active you are, the more full the GPs' waiting rooms will be! Personally I like the idea of keeping our doctors off the golf course with a few cases of prune juice overdose!'

He actually said '*orff*'. Sara brought her eyes down from the ceiling. She had been staring in

39

apparent admiration of the swags of laurels and berries which transversed its vast area, intersected with stuccoed garlands of palms and flowers, and after eight relentlessly appalling minutes of Matthew Sawyer, she knew every leaf. She had resolutely avoided meeting Sue's eye, knowing that to do so would have reduced them both to cackling wrecks.

Apparently stunned into a show of good manners, the audience did actually applaud, albeit thinly. How British that is, Sara thought. If you are roundly insulted by your speaker you must still of course clap, but you clap a little *less*. In a surprisingly muted hum of conversation the delegates moved gratefully to the buffet tables set out at the west end under the long colonnade of columns and pilasters, anxious to blot out the whole ghastly, misjudged episode with solid platefuls of samosas and salad. The squad of chefs and servers behind the tables was trying to impose some system against the tide of people, among whom were Cecily and Sue, pushing in staunchly with their empty plates.

'Get me a roll, could you?'

'Want some of this rice?'

'What's that, quiche? Yeah, a little bit. I've got feta, okay?'

Evidently the joint witnessing of a blatant act of self-destruction had been a deeply bonding experience. Turning smiling from the tables, Sara caught sight of Olivia at the far side of the room. She was standing with Matthew Sawyer beside a small side table and they were engaged in a tense-looking conversation. Sawyer looked rather angry, standing tall over her with his head bent stiffly towards her and his jaw ugly and tight. But it was Olivia who was doing most of the talking and, despite her size, looked much the more formidable of the two. She must be giving him hell for that speech, she thought. Wiser not to interrupt. Just then Olivia turned and marched towards the door at the far end, leaving Matthew Sawyer to gather up the two or three papers on the table and stare crossly after her. Sara decided not to go in pursuit of Olivia, and went to the Pump Room alone.

*   *   *

James had gone early to the Pump Room to warm up on the piano before any of the audience arrived. Sara could hear him on the Steinway as she came in by the Stall Street entrance to the new, functional side of the building. She paused in the small circular lobby and moved up against the wall so as not to be in the way of the traffic of caterers. Several halls and passages led into this lobby: one from the Pump Room itself, one from the offices and stores, and another which led from the modern stairs bringing visitors back up from the Roman Baths and into the Pump Room via the museum shop. From yet another passage came the smells, clatters and voices of the kitchens, and a procession of waiters and chefs who crossed the lobby every few seconds, bearing piles of plates and huge trays of food for the warming ovens of the Pump Room servery. The race was on to produce a four-course dinner for three hundred people, as well as to convert the demure teatime Pump Room into a dining room full of large circular tables set with candles, polished glasses, generous arrangements

41

of flowers and fruit and burnished silver chafing-dishes. And they had less than two hours in which to do it.

James was so good. Sara listened in admiration to the flow of his playing, as he played through the accompaniment to the first piece they would be performing, Mendelssohn's Song Without Words in D. As a very young man he had won several of the major international prizes for accompanists and Sara thought it a slight pity that he now did so much broadcasting, fronting the big televised music competitions and presenting radio programmes, rather than playing. But he was so good at that too: engaging, witty and articulate, and immensely knowledgeable without ever being intimidating. He was small, very dark and good-looking, with ears that stuck out noticeably and attractively. In all that he did and, indeed, all that he was, he seemed incapable of inelegance. He and Tom were by now an old married couple and lived partly in London, where Tom was based as an EU lawyer and had kept his house, and partly in Bath, which they both preferred. Tom's necessarily frequent spells in Brussels meant that James was often on his own.

Here he was now, coming through from the Pump Room calling, 'Och, it's yourself! All right now?' in his best Tannochbrae and planting a kiss on her cheek. He went off in search of drinks while she went to change in the small office which served as a dressing room. She dressed quickly, stepping into her wonderful Manolo Blahnik shoes, just low-heeled enough to allow her to play without getting in the way, and climbing into the stiff petticoat which gave the blue-black velvet dress such a supple and extravagant swing. It was by now second

42

nature to her to choose her concert dresses with a view to how they looked when she was sitting down, and this was a good one. It was almost demure at the front, cut high from shoulder to shoulder just below her collar bones. The waist was small and belted tightly with a broad band of brilliant blue silk, and the almost circular ankle-length skirt sank softly in folds to the floor when she sat down to play. At the back it was cut in a deep V almost to the waist, exposing most of her polished back. She fixed her face in a hand mirror under the atrocious light of the office. She could look the part, anyway. James called, 'Ye decent?' from the doorway and came in.

'You look very nice. Still working at the rowing machine, I see,' he said, watching with a glass of mineral water in each hand as she brushed and twisted her dark, ridiculously shiny hair up underneath a large diamanté and velvet clasp.

'Aye, it's not a bad wee frock, this,' she replied, pouting theatrically and dredging up for his benefit the never-forgotten vowels instilled in her at Glasgow Academy. '*You* look gorgeous. That new?'

'Oh, *this*?' James said mischievously, fingering the printed velvet waistcoat that he was wearing with a creamy white dinner jacket and dark blue bow tie. 'Georgina von Etzdorf. Present from Tom, actually. Och, no, I've had it *weeks*.'

Sara shifted her pile of clothes off the chair in the cramped office and brought her cello out of its case. Pulling the endpin out of the base, she rested it on the floor and then sat down and drew the familiar warm wood of the shaft against her shoulder. She tapped on the strings lightly with the fingers of her left hand, moved the folds of her dress out the way as she planted her feet and pulled the body of the cello between her knees. She tightened up the bow and with her head slightly tilted, tuned up. She shifted in her chair, blew lightly on the fingers of her left hand and played several scales, apparently without effort, repeating one or two difficult shifts for the left hand. She played them again very softly, then again with a rich sonorous vibrato which the small room could barely contain. Sara's instrument was the Christiani, a glorious Stradivari cello made in 1700, just as he was entering his Golden Period. Its celebrated owner Lisa Christiani had died in 1853 at the age of twenty-six, but in her short career had so captured Mendelssohn that he had dedicated to her the beautiful Song Without Words which was the first piece Sara was to play. Then she practised some broken chords, first smoothly and then staccato, allowing her bow to bounce regularly and lightly on the strings. She stopped, adjusted the tuning and sat in repose for a few seconds. Then she lifted the bow and played the opening bars of the Mendelssohn. Then she played twice through the fiendish scale passages of fast demi-semiquavers of Bruch's Kol Nidrei. She paused, closed her eyes and began the Schumann Three Fantasy Pieces Opus 73, the middle piece of their programme.

James saw that she was in danger of doing too much and tensing up. He nodded and smiled. 'That's good. Why not leave it to settle now? You'll be fine.'

She smiled without looking at him. She got up and placed the cello carefully back in its case. Then, taking their glasses, they went back out to

44

the lobby and descended the stairs which led down through the museum and out to the Great Bath.

They stood staring into the great rectangle of milky greenish water from which wisps of steam were rising. The open flares on the stone columns surrounding the bath underlit the colonnades, where a few people were already standing or strolling in the twilight. The flames cast their light upwards and caught the aloof stone figures standing on the Victorian balustrade above. Downwards, their glow touched the surface of the water, revealing the edges of the stone steps which descended into its depths. A breeze caught the water's surface, which rippled delicately with the slight guttering of the flares. Steam eddied upwards. As she always did, Sara tried and largely failed to imagine the Great Bath roofed over in hollow brick as it once had been, for to see the sacred water now held in its rough stone cradle, lit by torches and open to the summer night sky, intensified its watery magic. Generations of Romans had come to bathe, swap news, argue and do business here, and Sara knew that they had come to show off too, which put the representatives of moneyed Bath presently sipping their drinks under the colonnades in their proper context, as merely continuing an old tradition. But long before the Romans, the spring had been a place of pilgrimage and devotion. Sara wondered if it had been, when dedicated to the Celtic goddess Sulis, somehow more holy. 'Minerva is patron goddess. In her temple eternal flames never whiten into ash,' so the Roman historian had said. What had become of Sulis? The Romans, unnerved by a foreign, elusive deity, had simply superimposed one

45

of their own, the familiar Minerva, a goddess they could talk to, one who spoke their language, one whom they could capture and contain within the carved stones of their new temple. Sara left James's side and made her way over the lethally uneven flagstones to the edge of the water, crouched down and swirled her hand in its unearthly heat. She did not feel like talking, particularly. She looked out across the green pool where the reflections of the flares, against the darkening sky, trembled. Perhaps it was just the passing of time, these walls having borne witness to so much skulduggery, gossip, barter and supplication, which now made the place seem not hallowed, but over-exposed. The Romans, as was their way, had tried to articulate and quantify the spring's sanctity and, in so doing, had rendered it utterly secular. No ghosts of holy tenants were lingering here. It was the wind, only the wind, that caused the flares to shiver with such malevolent-seeming delicacy, and only silence that was in possession now. Again tomorrow, and the next day, and every day, people would come to the Roman Baths not to visit the ancient and sacred shrine of a pre-Christian deity, not any more to bathe for physical, let alone spiritual, renewal, but to be impressed by engineering. And that was the glory that was Rome. Sara rose, turned gingerly and returned over the stones to James, who stood patiently holding her drink. As she took it, an echo of cocktail laughter reached them from the other side.

*   *   *

About an hour after his public humiliation and two
46

minutes into his first glass of Cecily's plonk, Derek began to calm down. He had tried inwardly ridiculing the man: 'Oh, yes . . . *and I am the Director of Museums and Civic Leisure Resources!'* Oh, yes? Arrogant prat! Upper-class bastard! but it had not worked, because the man had not been ridiculous and Derek, knowing himself to have been the arrogant prat, found less than the usual comfort in not being upper class. It is a terrible thing, at fifty years of age, to be sufficiently embarrassed to blush in an empty room. He sank back on the sofa, a whale in a dolphin's shirt, rested his glass on the straining button in the middle of his high stomach and looked at the ceiling. What had made him go on like that? He had been swept along by the excitement of getting the letter, lost his usual reserve and had just let events run away. He drained the glass and refilled it. It was a sort of hidden Mediterranean streak he had, this occasional tendency to cast caution to the winds. Nothing wrong with being spontaneous now and then, was there? Sometimes it was best just to pitch in and reveal your hand. It was an impulse to which he had often succumbed where his secretaries were concerned. Well, not so much his hand as other parts of his anatomy, ha-ha, but it usually went down well enough. Oops, did he really mean 'down'? He had to admit it, he was a bit of a devil.

Halfway down the bottle he thought he might one day be able to go outdoors again, and around the time he was finishing it off he felt able to go over the conversation with Matthew Sawyer once more in his mind, trawling every word and nuance for a shrimp's worth of hope that he had not, with each syllable, shown himself to be a world-class, award-winning, twenty-two-carat, pompous fool. He was disappointed.

'Ah, well now, if you're the director, you're just the fellow I need. I'd like a word,' he had said, in the chap-to-chap tone that usually worked when he was extracting a favour from one of his junior teachers. The Sawyer guy had looked a bit surprised. Not as surprised as he would be when Derek got the job and introduced himself as the new boss, ha! But he had not got it quite in the bag yet, and he had felt it wise to acknowledge that he had rather turned up out of the blue.

'Is this a good moment?' He had slipped easily into his habitual talking-people-round voice. 'May I have just a minute or two of your time? I'd love to know'—he remembered dropping the volume confidentially at this point—'how things are going, generally. Running a museum, not easy, I'm sure. I'm in education myself,' he added, lest Sawyer think he was just some weirdo off the street, 'so I know.'

Sawyer had smiled wanly. 'Oh, indeed, yes. Difficult times, all round. Although I'm an architectural historian actually, by background. So, you're bringing a party. Education is a large part of my remit, of course. Terribly keen on school visits. Have you contacted one of my education officers?'

It had been Derek's turn to smile. 'Perhaps I haven't been clear. I'm not bringing a party. Of course my head of history might—she's quite an energetic girl—but so much depends on our parents. We're talking south Bristol here.'

He had sighed the sigh of the misunderstood and undervalued education professional, Blunketted, bloodied, bowed but unbeaten. 'No, you see, my

48

interest is more, well, strategic, in a sense. I'm interested in the general policy direction. Staff structures. Management style. Resources. Get me? How's the funding? Got a lottery bid in?'

The effect of this had seemed to ruffle the guy a little. Good.

'May I know your particular reason for asking?' Sawyer had asked, rather haughtily.

The pompous little creep was actually talking down to him, coming over all 'I'm an architectural historian and who the hell are you?' It was in his voice and Derek could see it in the supercilious lift of his upper lip. He had felt a surge of rage. He was only running a bloody museum, for God's sake. Who the hell cared, in the end, what happened to a few bloody artefacts? Of course they were important, but they were a damn sight less important than *schools*, which had real *people* in them, people like the hopeless sods that he had been trying thanklessly for ten years to do something for. His school was a damn sight more important than any bloody heap of relics, and running it was a bloody demanding job, a proper job, a job and a half, these days. But he must not say that. He *would* not say that. He had to keep his temper, but he would put this architectural snotty historian bastard in his place. Yes, he would keep his temper. He had even smiled.

'Look, I'm quite happy to be straight with you. Yes, I *do* actually have a very particular reason for asking, since you ask. Perhaps I am being a little premature, but there is a very strong possibility that I will soon be in a position to bring considerable influence to bear upon developments here.'

He had paused while Sawyer had simply raised

49

his eyebrows. 'Oh?'

Derek, feeling forced to continue, had leaned forward. 'Look, it's probably better to be straightforward from the start. Better in the end. You see, it might interest you to know that I have in fact been shortlisted for the job of Director of Education and Cultural Services.'

Sawyer's face had not changed in the short pause before he replied, 'Oh, really? Well, as a matter of fact, so have I.'

Alone in the half dark of Cecily's sitting room Derek sucked a mouthful of red wine through his teeth, moaning, and forced himself to relive his humiliation to its end. At that point Sawyer, still talking, had made a half turn and begun to lead him by the elbow back along the corridor towards the entrance.

'Yes, most interesting. What fun. Ah, the machinations.'

Back in the vestibule he had turned to Derek and raised his voice in a pitying drawl. 'You see, Mr . . . er . . . my dear chap, there's always a makeweight candidate or two for these education jobs. You know, some bright deputy head from somewhere ghastly, the inner city or the Midlands or somewhere. Unappointable, of course. Wheeled in to keep the councillors happy—education committee's always chocka with self-made bores. Wide field, national advertising, equal opportunities, can't be seen to plump for the Oxbridge fella straight off. But in the end'—Derek had noticed at this point that the woman in the kiosk had been joined by two others and that all three heads were staring gravely through the window—'in the end they'll get someone who can

50

speak the language, get on with the right people. Hearts and minds, d'you see? In a place like Bath? A *social* role. Calls for a certain . . . *background*. Got to be someone on the up. Fast track, do you follow? No job for a rough diamond. Or someone ten years off retirement. Wouldn't get your hopes up, old man.'

Then, as he had moved towards the wide front door and pulled it open, he had brayed with a hideous sound that could have been a laugh or a seizure. To Derek's disappointment, it had been a laugh.

'And the museum *is* closed. Cruel old world— dear me, yes. Well, cheerio!'

Derek sank the last of the plonk and burned with inarticulate fury towards the man and all that he stood for, socially, politically, professionally and, most of all—oh, very much most of all—personally. Hatred was making his palms sting. It rose up his arms and across his shoulders, warmed his huge torso, made his buttocks prickle and coursed down his big legs. All through his body his blood was beating like a ticking bomb. To lose this job, this one job, his only chance, to lose it at all, but to lose it to that—to *that*—But before he could decide what he almost drowned in a wave of heartburn.

Knowing that such rage was bad for him, he turned his mind to his erstwhile comforter, Cecily, and found no comfort. If anything, the recollection of what had then happened made him angrier still: Cecily following him out on to the pavement and pretending that she was more interested in that dieting rubbish than in their evening. She had insisted on staying, which would mean him coming all the way out again in a couple of hours to fetch her and them eating so late that he would probably be too full for their usual, unless he could persuade her to get on top. He stopped short of admitting to himself that that was mainly what he was here for. She was spoiling their evening and was behaving as if *he* were. His anger subsided into an impotent fatigue. He was tired of the whole thing. It had been a knackering week, all round.

He yawned, but he could not allow himself to relax completely yet. He had brought in his shopping but he was still in his suit and would not be able to change until he brought in the rest of his stuff from the back of the car. He had, as usual, parked it quite a way up the street, which was more discreet but also much less convenient. Also, he reflected, fairly pointless, since Cecily's neighbours must have seen him dozens of times using a key to let himself in. It was just as well she lived in Bath where nobody knew him. He could even go out in public with her here, not that they ever did much, a thing he would never have risked in Bristol. He would get his stuff in a minute. He would get started in the kitchen in a minute. He finished the dregs in his glass, lay back and closed his eyes. Just for a minute. But before the minute was up his mouth fell open, his hand relaxed, and the wineglass, tumbling gently off his stomach, landed softly beside him on the sofa.

*   *   *

They played the programme and followed it with two encores, a short Sicilienne by Maria Theresia von Paradis and the almost compulsory Swan by Saint-Saëns. Sara was taken aback by the length and warmth of the applause, which she knew to be both sincere and undeserved, and took her seat at dinner gratefully. James was placed on the other side of the table and apart from an exchange of platform smiles at the end of the performance there had been no other communication between them. She guessed he would say she had been 'fine', and in some respects she had been: her fingering agile and virtuosic, bowing fluid and assured, phrasing intelligently musical and her tone sweetly powerful. The man on her left, attacking his tartlet of mushrooms with hollandaise sauce, was telling her so, while she managed to shake her head, nod, smile and eat without really listening. Her mind wandered back to the summer school at Tanglewood in 1974 when she, a nervous wee 'promising' young cellist from Glasgow, aged thirteen, was giddily soaking up the experience of a masterclass with the legendary Piatigorsky, who had said: 'What really matters is how you will use your art as a human being in a productive life. Everything hangs together. You cannot be a stupid person and a great player; you cannot be a mentally unhealthy person and produce something of value in our difficult profession.'

At least she was not a stupid person, she thought afterwards as she made her way across Kings Parade in the dark, although it was verging on the mentally unhealthy not to have waited for the rain to ease off. It was pouring, and as she dodged the puddles, laden with cello, bag with shoes and petticoat, and her velvet dress on a hanger in a zipped cover, she regretted not leaving even earlier. She was going to be soaked just getting to the car in Manvers Street. She had left James lugubriously nursing a bottle of claret. '*Oh, come on, have another glass of wine. Life is a cabaret, old chum,*' he'd said. It was only ten thirty and it was selfish of her, she knew, but she had had to flee from the prospect of a morose eulogy from James about Graham. Half an hour ago when Olivia had come over to her table to say goodbye it had been quite dry, so even though she was walking, lucky old Olivia would have missed the rain.

When she had reached Medlar Cottage, bolted through the rain to the house and changed into her bathrobe, she brought the velvet dress out of its bag and noticed at once that its broad silk belt was missing. She was sure she had not dropped it, and realised crossly that she would have to go back to the Pump Room for it in the morning. But she would treat this as an exercise in good grace; she would get up early, miss the worst of the traffic and turn the necessity of going into Bath on a Saturday in summer to advantage. James was coming to supper and she would go to the fish market and the Fine Cheese Company and get something special. She would make a little occasion of it as a way of thanking him for this evening and for trying to get her going again. It was not his fault that she did not feel any further forward. And tomorrow might even be a nice day, she thought, switching off her bedside light at midnight and, in the dark of her room, enjoying for a moment the silence that followed the stopping of the rain.

CHAPTER THREE

On Saturday when Sara got up just after seven o'clock the day was bright, although clouds were gathering in the west over Wing-o-'the-Hill. She left the cottage when the morning shadows were still long and walked into the aftermath of a botanic bloodbath. It had rained again in the night and at dawn an unseasonable wind had swept through the valley, striking the massive crimson heads of all the late peonies in the garden with the swiftness of a cat's paw. Their petals lay across the paths like scattered feathers. Sara made her way up the garden, kicking the flurries of petals in her way, inflicting upon herself the pain of a closer inspection. Almost every one had been wrecked. They would only have had another week or so to go anyway, but the knowledge did not lessen her sense of violation.

She cruised into town in ten minutes, left the car in Manvers Street and was at the doors of the Roman Baths on the dot of nine o'clock, just as George, the chief security attendant, was unlocking them. He grinned at her.

'Whoah, glutton for punishment, you are. Can't you get enough? Last out, first in, I don't know. What's your problem?'

Sara pretended offence, a necessary part of the game she had to play with George, as she explained her errand. She had met George several times in the course of rehearsing last night's programme, since the Pump Room acoustics were atrociously difficult and James arranged a couple of sessions after hours, during which they had been able to work at getting a good balance. George had been asked to listen and report back from different points in the room, and in his new role as sound advisor he had become outspoken and pally to the point of banter.

'Leaving all your clothes behind, is it? I see. I 'spect it'll be in the office, then, but it's locked on Saturdays. Yes, I've got the key. Look, I was on till late last night and I'm a little bit behind this morning. Can you give me ten minutes till I've opened up below?'

'Sure,' Sara said. 'You go on. Don't hurry. I wouldn't mind a wander round anyway. I'll come and find you a bit later, shall I?'

George strode on ahead of her, unlocking doors, switching on lights and whistling good-naturedly as if (as it effectively was out of hours) the Roman Baths were all his, but that he did not mind a bit letting other people have a look-see. Sara hung back until, the whistling fainter and George out of sight, she had the place almost to herself. Three Japanese girls with backpacks followed after her and lingered happily on the terrace above the Great Bath to take endless photographs of one another beside the life-sized stone statues. Sara hung over the stone balustrade, marvelling at the steamy green pool beneath, and then strolled on into the half dark of the museum below. As she descended closer to the spring, the warm, humid air rose around her. She felt none of the cynical unease that she had felt round the Great Bath the night before. It was good to be in town so early. She might have coffee afterwards in the Pump Room and she would stay in town a little longer to do her shopping. She might go off for a run when she got home, just a couple of miles, or she might go out to Fortune Park for a work-out and swim instead. She made her way through the museum, enjoying a desultory reading of the earnestly informative wallboards.

She came to the part devoted to burials and stood looking down over a row of rough stone coffins whose engraved lids had become the biographies of long-dead people's lives. The carved stones told the stories of lost soldiers, mourned wives and the slave's little baby, who was 'freed' by its adoption into a Roman family. Had the young slave mother died? Or had the child simply been taken from her, becoming the property of the childless couple who owned the mother? Perhaps she, poor thing, had given up her baby in order to secure its freedom. Perhaps the child had been fathered by the Roman master. There was no way of knowing from the coffin lids which had so long ago closed over these people, and how little it mattered anyway. The baby had died before its second birthday. The suffering of these dead was over and now two thousand years had passed to quiet the bereaved. In all that time the sacred spring, never ceasing, had poured forth how many gallons?

She looked round mildly, hearing as if for the first time the background rush of water. She allowed herself to be drawn away from the coffins towards the source of the noise. It was coming from the Sacred Spring overflow which gushed straight out of the wall about twelve feet away, at the end of a wide tunnel-like corridor. Sara stopped and looked down its darkness to the light at the end.

The corridor led to a railing just in front of the overflow, which formed the only barrier between the spectator and the thousands of gallons of hot water that daily poured out of the wall. Under the spell of the sound, she walked towards the railing as the rush of water tumbled out at eye level and fell vertically for five feet before hitting rock below. She could see how the water slid in a deep, rusty sheet towards her and disappeared through a rough grille at a point directly below her feet. From the railing's edge she could almost, by leaning over the railing, have placed her hand in the hot powerful flow of water, if she were stupid in that kind of way; it would be easy to overbalance and tumble on to the rocks. This overflow arrangement, an arched brick hole in the wall, fed the water into the drain which carried it beneath the floor back to the main drain and eventually out to the river. The Romans could surely not have imagined that it would still be working, and people still marvelling at its brilliance, two thousand years after they built it.

The gauzy steam rising all around had basted every contour of the surrounding wall with mineral-heavy droplets, laying down particle by particle a bronzy, gingery crust round the brick mouth from which the water exploded, apparently stained with gold, as if from a bottomless reservoir of riches. Hidden spotlights played on the tumbling flood as it burst forth and bathed it with the luminosity of a miracle. Sara approached it cautiously, as she would an altar. Arresting as the sight was, the crash of water upon her ears was yet more stupefying. Breathing and tasting became the same thing in the roaring, tin-edged air. Sara felt the grip of dampness underfoot as she went on, silent and staring. She reached the rail. Then. Looking down. And the rush of the water almost drowned the scream, but in the orange light her head jerked up suddenly and she turned away. The water flowed on. But she had to turn back. Her eyes travelled down again into the wet glistening pool below where the body lay. It was so large and so dark in that small, bright space, in all that flowing, tumbling water. Those legs and arms, they were going all the wrong way; spider limbs, it was a huge, drenched, dead spider. She tried not to look again at the face. The water flowed on. She looked again at the side of the poor, stiff, dead face with its mouth open and soundless, while the water ran over it and over it like clear, flowing glass. It was all wrong, that face, which yesterday she had thought was Matteo's. Matteo's poor, dead, empty face. Move him. We must get him out of there. We must stop that face looking like that. Sara staggered away from the railing, and as her hands went up to cover her eyes, a hurrying, dark shape loomed at her out of the dark and enveloped her, as she stumbled, in its arms.

*   *   *

Numbness descended over the next few hours. Sara supposed that a number of practical things must have been done. She could recall people running, raised voices, and George practically holding her up and leading her kindly away, back up the stairs and across the high, echoing Concert Room. She had no idea how much time had passed, but she was recovering from the nausea and giddiness that had first swept over her, and had been able to field

59

the anxious enquiries. Yes, she would be all right just sitting here. No, there was no one at home they could contact. She was now sitting in the Smoking Room, one of a number of smaller rooms off a corridor which ran alongside the Concert Room. The room was steadily filling up. The three Japanese girls were there, as well as a dozen or so people who must have come into the baths after them. One or two were still holding guidebooks and they sat in groups of three or four on the chairs round the walls, talking in a dismayed kind of way. The door opened and George came in again, followed by three of the junior attendants, the two souvenir shop assistants and two entrance desk ladies. Sara watched in silence as the sight of people in uniform inspired one of the tourists to ask what on earth was going on. George shook his head. He hardly knew. A fatality appeared to have occurred. He had telephoned for the police, who had arrived almost immediately and gone straight to the body. They had ordered a cordon round the building and had stationed officers on all four sides of it. No member of the public was to be admitted, and no person inside the building was to leave. George had been instructed by a police officer to find a suitable room in which an enquiry and preliminary interviews could begin. Having shown them into the Drawing Room next door, with which they had seemed satisfied, George had then been sent to round up any remaining visitors and escort them, with all the staff, to the Smoking Room. That was all he knew.

More police cars had drawn up; from the Smoking Room windows they could see out to Abbey Churchyard where one stood with its blue light circling and flashing and from whose open front doors the on-off, whish-crackle of the radio could be heard. A woman detective constable came in and all conversation stopped. Everyone was being asked to wait for the time being. She apologised for the inconvenience and hoped that it would not be for too long. They waited.

The WDC returned shortly afterwards and asked if there was a kitchen where tea could be made. The two shop ladies left with her, glad to have something to do. They came back with two trays. It seemed slightly profane to give a welcome smile to a cup of tea under the circumstances, but most people did, and the low hum of conversation resumed as the cups went round. George brought a cup to Sara and sat down beside her.

'All right now, love?'

'That man in the water. It was the man who did the speech last night at the Assembly Rooms, wasn't it? Matthew Sawyer.'

George nodded solemnly and Sara went on, 'I feel awful. I laughed at him. We both did, my friend and me. Last night it all seemed funny. I just thought he was embarrassing, didn't know what he was dealing with. I can't believe he's dead.'

The door opened and the WDC returned.

'We have to interview everyone who was in the building when the body was found. For most of you, all we'll need from you today is your personal details and a statement saying where exactly you were in the building when the alarm was raised. I'm sorry you've had a wait, but we shouldn't have to keep you much longer.'

More tea. Another officer came and took names and addresses. Sara sat on, white and quiet, relieved that nothing except sitting there seemed to be expected of her. She watched as gradually the numbers dwindled, as the tourists were ushered next door to give their innocuous details and peripheral knowledge of events, and then allowed to go. She realised that some of them would eventually look back on the day as a faintly enjoyable one, that for some of them, like those two Americans in lemon cashmere sweaters, the episode would become no more than an extra bit of spice in their travellers' tales. Boy, is England ever violent! Did we ever tell you what happened on our trip in '97? Sara was envious, for she felt changed, once again caught off-guard by events, by death. Without meaning or wanting to, she had once again strayed into that different territory, where simple pleasures and unambitious hopes for a good day seemed not just slightly indecent, but ludicrous.

'The poor sod,' George was saying, 'probably just got up this morning as usual. Thinking he's going to have another perfectly ordinary day, and it turns out to be his last, his last ever. The last day of his life. Probably just toppled over the railing, hit his head and that's that. It's a thought, innit? Unbelievable.'

As she spoke Sara saw again the Assembly Rooms, the audience of women, the platform and the tall man of the night before, floundering through his disastrous speech.

'George, he *didn't* get up this morning as usual,' she said quietly. Involuntarily, she saw again the gangly, soaked body and the dead face. 'George, he was still in black tie. He must have been there all night.'

Detective Sergeant Bridger did not get up when the WDC, who ushered Sara from the Smoking Room, opened the door and showed her next door into the Drawing Room. He gestured her to a chair and, unaware of the irony, asked if she minded if he smoked. Or rather, he waved his packet of Silk Cut at her and said, because he was dealing with a member of the general public and was meant to ask, 'Don't mind, do you?'

'Actually, I do.'

She did not care what he thought. He was quite unforgivably unattractive. He was wearing, presumably in pursuit of the hard cop effect, a pair of Gap chinos, a dark blue militaristic bomber jacket, definitely of mixed fibres, and a slightly loosened thin tie of brown suede. Sara was sure that the strain showing on his face owed less to a tense all-night stake-out than to the fact that he'd had to forgo his doughnut down at the station that morning. Bridger knew her type too. Educated cow, one of them lippy, neurotic man-haters.

'Oh, dear,' he said with mock concern, consulting his list. 'Right then. Well, Miss—oh, I beg your pardon, I see it's *Muzz*—Selkirk is that, let's hope we won't be too long then. I'm afraid I'm gasping. Terrible habit, I do realise.'

He put away his fags and produced a Snickers bar from his pocket. Unwrapping it and taking a bite, he then made his second mistake.

With his mouth half full he said, 'So, with a name like that, would I be right in thinking you hail from north of the border, then? Cold up there, isn't it? Never been, myself. Prefer the sun.'

63

Sara stared back steadily with a look which she hoped conveyed her exasperated boredom with the subject of Scottish weather. Bridger decided to abandon any attempt to be friendly, and instead went into his highly trained professional, got-a-job-to-get-on-with-here mode, running yellowish fingers through his pale hair as if he expected to find something interesting in it. Sara tried to work out why she felt so antagonistic towards this man, who was a policeman, after all. He did look young and she couldn't exactly blame him for that, but he had one of those ratty faces and the kind of slight and probably hairless white body that she found revolting. Whippets had the same effect on her. Looking round, she felt a surge of annoyance at what he had already managed to do to this once tranquil and elegant room. Various flower arrangements had been lifted from their proper places and stacked with obvious impatience on a long Regency bench along the wall. The deep windowsills and three semicircular side tables were already filling up with police detritus: folders and papers, a lap-top, a mobile telephone and a box of computer disks. A desk, surely borrowed from one of the other offices, had been shoved under the windows. The room was already more chaotic and grubbier than it need have been. Sara was willing to bet that Bridger expected the WDC to keep things tidy, wash up discarded teacups and so on, and that she, all power to her, steadfastly didn't.

Now he was being brusque and efficient. She related, in answer to his questions, what she had done since her arrival at the Pump Room that morning. He quizzed her about the evening before and she went through it all in detail, beginning with her afternoon rehearsal, right up until when she had left the Pump Room, in the rain, at ten thirty. She told him about Matthew Sawyer's speech.

'It was disastrous. He was so rude and dismissive, as if he had no idea of what was important to those people. He must have upset them very badly. He certainly embarrassed me.'

'And you're saying that more or less the whole audience was annoyed? Did you see anyone who seemed particularly upset?'

'How could I tell? Anyway, I left just after that.' She paused. 'I only saw one person speak to him afterwards. A colleague of his, Olivia Passmore, the deputy director. No, I didn't hear what was said. I suppose you can find that out from her, can't you?'

She was damned if she was going to give any more help than that. Olivia would be sure to be on the list of people to be interviewed. Anyway, it was none of her business to speculate on what they might have been talking about. It was their business or, more accurately now, Olivia's. She felt a sudden, tender pity for poor, clumsy Matthew Sawyer, whom she had never even properly met. Bridger was drawing her back to the finding of the body. Why? Why go over it again? He is doing this to torment me, the little reptile, she thought. She answered mechanically.

'As I've told you, I was looking round the museum. I was just waiting till George could open up the office where I'd left my belt. I was the first visitor in. I simply walked up to the railing in front of the overflow. I saw the body lying in the water. I realised who it was. The water was running over his face. The mouth was open. His legs and arms seemed all . . . all over the place. I must have

65

screamed. George grabbed me. That's all I remember. It was very upsetting . . . Matthew Sawyer was like someone else I . . . I once knew.'

She stopped. She did not think she was going to be able to say any more without crying, but she had to know.

'How did he die?'

Bridger paused. The press would be told in a couple of hours anyway; the statement had already been prepared. He picked up the sheet of paper from the desk. He shouldn't say anything, but it would be a pleasure to watch her take it.

'Pending the forensic pathologist's full report, a preliminary examination suggests that the deceased sustained fatal stab wounds which are not thought to have been self-inflicted,' read Bridger, running his tongue over his caramelly teeth, well satisfied.

CHAPTER FOUR

Sara could not free her mind from the grip of the day's events. It had started to rain by the time she left the building, refusing offers of help, and drove home, forgetting all her plans, intent only on getting back to the comforting privacy of the cottage's thick walls. She rang James.

'So you see, because of all this, I haven't bought a thing. I'm so sorry. I was going to go to the fish market. I've got salad. There's nothing for pud. It was going to be a treat. Oh, James, I'm really sorry. What about cheese? What are we to do?' she babbled, transferring her anxious need for the restoration of some sort of order to the state of the larder, where it could at least be acted upon.

James interrupted. 'Will you stop that? I will tell you what we are going to do. I am going to do some shopping, then I am coming straight over. You are to do nothing until I get there, except perhaps make yourself some tea. Hold on.'

And although he thought it would probably do her good, he reflected that it would not be quite the thing to suggest that she soak in a long, hot bath.

In the lateness of the afternoon the wind got up again and it turned cold. Sara gathered some of the fallen peony heads and floated them in a wide glass bowl. She brought in a few logs and lit the fire, and then made tea. Afterwards, she coaxed herself upstairs. In her oversized bathroom which doubled as a dressing room, she ran a deep hot bath, pouring in most of the tea tree bath gel, and stepped in, gasping in the intense heat. She groaned and slid under the water, then surfaced, reached for her Floris bath oil and tipped in a decadent quantity, enough to extinguish the scent of tea tree. For a long time she lay absolutely still in the hot, aromatic water and felt some of the day's taint wash from her. Much later, wrapped in a bathrobe, she rested for a moment in the large cane rocking-chair where she sat to dry her feet. She thought of Matthew Sawyer's widow and children, assuming that he would be married and a father. Her own experience of his death was now effectively over. She had nothing to do now but recover from a momentary shock. For Mrs Sawyer, it was only beginning: the pain, fury and bitterness, followed by loneliness and long, long sorrow. She covered her face with her warm and water-wrinkled hands.

James arrived in perfect time to make large kirs for them both. He let himself into the kitchen and by way of announcing his arrival launched into 'Ma in Espana', just as Sara was coming downstairs in a cloud of stephanotis, barefoot and dressed in grey silk Indian trousers and a man's collarless white shirt. She was pink and extremely shiny and James, thinking that she looked like a very large baby, judged that this was how she might need to be treated. He saw that a damaged look had returned to her beautiful eyes.

'In da capo mode, I hear,' she said. 'Leporello has landed. Don't you ever get tired of *Don Giovanni*?'

'Probably not as tired as everyone else does. Come here, honeybun,' James said, kissing her forehead and wrapping his arms round her. 'Poor baby. You know you shouldn't really leave the door unlocked like that,' he said, rocking her gently.

'This is the country,' Sara said. 'Don't be so *Londony*.' She gave a shuddering sigh. 'I'm so glad you're here,' she muttered into his chest. After a moment's silence she drew away and said, 'You saw him last night, didn't you? At the dinner, in the Pump Room. He did look a bit like Matteo, didn't he?'

'A bit. Only a bit. Come on, here's a drink. Do you want ice in that?'

He wanted only to make her feel better after her horrible experience and like all unconsciously charming people he did not realise how much this was accomplished merely by his presence. He stationed her at the table with her glass and a bowl of olives while he worked happily in the big high kitchen. He enjoyed moving around in its generous space, reaching for the spoons and herbs hanging from butcher's hooks, putting things he had finished with out of his way. Sara watched, recognising the same impeccable, technical ease that he brought to the keyboard. His movements were simple. There was none of the impassioned throwing around that so many musicians went in for, believing the audience expected it. He directed his energy straight into what he was doing, and focused only on that. Consequently, whatever it was, whether a piece of music, a story he was telling or even, as now, a salad, it contained no jarring element or empty gesture but had a kind of honest life that arose from the deep concentration he gave it. He used his hands perfectly. He seemed to establish a harmony with the things he touched; he got out chopping boards without banging them about, he did not drop and then tread on peeled cloves of garlic and he did not rip the skins off onions as if he were tearing brown paper off a parcel. As he started on the potatoes, Sara thought he was the only person she could happily watch using a knife. The kirs went down quickly and James made more. Partly from the wine, partly from James camping things up and partly from a need to relieve the day's tension, they got a bit giggly. They took in trays of food to the drawing room and ate off the low table round the fire, while the cat lay on the hearth, stoned on Whiskas.

'Want mustard? It's got beer in it,' James said, helping himself. 'I say, isn't this frightfully Famous Five? Look, heaps of lettuce, *pommes savoyarde*, wild boar sausages, some olives and yummy French bread, lashings of Cabernet Sauvignon. Not to

69

mention a murder. Rather a gruesome puzzle, what? Of course it's not funny,' he added, answering Sara's look, 'but I wonder what it's all about? The speech got anything to do with it?'

Sara snorted that he had certainly upset people very badly, but nobody could be driven to *murder* because of it.

'Ah, but,' James intoned portentously, 'it *seems* impossible, but all kinds of things *seem* impossible, don't they? Ancient echoes. What about those curses that people used to throw into the bath? Chuck us the guidebook.'

He leafed through it.

'Listen to this. "May the person who has stolen from me become as liquid as water." No, *listen*. "May my enemy sink like lead." "May the goddess Sulis afflict him with maximum death." See?'

Sara stared with mocking, goggle-eyes and went, 'Oooh-oooh!'

'No, listen, it's all very powerful stuff. It *is*. Don't you think there could be a link?'

'Well, Watson, there could be, but I'm not sure Bath CID will go for it,' Sara said.

She regaled him with a scurrilous account of Detective Sergeant Bridger and James, suddenly an expert on police procedure, said, 'Oh, but he's very junior. He certainly won't be in charge. They'll have to interview all the museum staff, at the Assembly Rooms as well as the Pump Room, and the caterers, as well as everyone who was at the do last night. That's well over five hundred people, for a start.'

'But why?' asked Sara. Suddenly it seemed serious again. 'Surely they'll find whoever broke in without going through all that? They must have surveillance cameras. Or someone may have seen him get in, or heard him. He would probably be drunk, about to trash the place. I bet it was just some drunken yob with one of those combat knives.'

'Think so? I mean, you arrived first thing and George was opening up as usual. He obviously hadn't come across a break-in or any malicious damage. He must have found everything just as he expected it.'

'Well, yes, I suppose so. Including the alarms,' Sara added. 'The alarm is set every night by the person locking up. George, or whoever's opening up, switches it off. If it hadn't been set, he would have been in a bit of a state this morning. But he was perfectly relaxed.'

'Well, who *was* locking up last night?' James asked. 'Because if they locked up in the usual way and set the alarm, whoever it was either left Matthew Sawyer, or Matthew Sawyer's body, inside.'

'But it was Matthew Sawyer who was meant to do the locking up,' Sara said. 'Olivia mentioned it when she was saying goodnight. So what then? Who actually *did* lock up? The murderer must have done it.'

'That's if the alarm was set. Suppose George was behaving as usual because he wasn't surprised to find the alarm switched off? Because *he'd* done the murder? Oh, but wait, no, because if he'd done the murder and left the alarm *off*, so that the police would think the murder was done by someone who *didn't* know how to set the alarm, then part of that trick would be acting all surprised when he "discovered" the alarm off in the morning. So he couldn't have done it. Could he?'

'Don't. You're getting me all confused,' Sara said, sniggering. 'Anyway, I think it's all horrible. When I think of the last people going off home, never thinking of what they were leaving him to. You stayed till the end, didn't you? Looked like you were enjoying yourself, anyway.'

'You know me. Hate to leave before the party's over.' James raised his glass to her archly before drinking from it. 'I'm still wondering *why* he was killed. Not burglary, by the look of it, or vandalism. Must have had enemies.'

'One enemy at least,' Sara said firmly, 'although I can never understand how people's feelings run so high. I mean, in the *real* world—'

'Ha! You mean in your sheltered little world, don't you?' James said, more abruptly than he intended. 'You don't know what goes on, you don't really. People aren't always what they seem, you know.'

Sara gave him a look of pitying sarcasm. 'Oh, right. I get it, we're back in gay paranoia land, are we? No, wait, perhaps Matthew Sawyer was an underground drugs baron. Or a pimp. Both. Christ, James—'

'Cow. You *don't* know what goes on. It's not paranoia, there's a lot of real homophobia out there and it's not all yobs gay-bashing on a Saturday night in the provinces. There's a lot of it under the surface.'

'So you think Matthew Sawyer was gay, do you?'

'I'm not saying he was gay, am I? Not that being gay and homophobic don't often go together.'

'Oh, don't get started on that. Anyway, I think we should leave it to the police.'

James said mischievously, 'You mean you're going to ask the splendid Andrew what he thinks. He might even be conducting the case.'

Sara shot James a look. 'There's no need to be nasty about him, just because he's a policeman.'

'The world's first cello-playing policeman,' James said slyly. 'And I'm not being nasty about him. I just question his motives for pestering you, and getting you to teach him the cello, that's all.'

'There's nothing to question. How would you feel if you'd been stopped from learning the piano just when it was getting interesting? Because your parents thought it was time to get proper qualifications and a proper job? He was just made to give it all up and he's regretted it all his life. He could have played professionally, only he wasn't encouraged. It's a criminal waste of talent.'

'He fancies you.'

Sara scowled.

'And what about your motives for taking him on? Is it really his talent that's so interesting? He's very good-looking, of course, but don't tell him *I* said so—he'd be horrified.'

'Anyway, he's not a policeman, he's a detective,' Sara said, 'as you perfectly well know. Detective Chief Inspector.' She added, as an afterthought, 'You're just jealous, because you fancy him yourself.'

'I do not intend to dignify such a scurrilous suggestion with a reply,' James sniffed. 'And as usual you're missing the important bit, which is that you, the world-class concert artist, are actually *giving lessons* to PC Gorgeous. And don't get me wrong; he may well be worth teaching, but whether or not you should be spending *your* time doing it, instead of thinking about getting back to playing a concert or two, is open to question. In my view.'

There was a silence.

'And there's his little wifey to consider, isn't there?'

Sara sighed. She knew that after Andrew had lost the battle over his music studies and joined the police, he had been easy game for Valerie. They had married when they were both twenty-three and henceforth Andrew's life had shrunk to a preoccupation with the mortgage, parentcraft classes, police exams, his in-laws at every other Sunday lunch, forays to Mothercare, instalments on the suite, the microwave and camcorder, and regular spats with Valerie on all of these topics. Most of this he explained the first time he had come to see Sara. He had not told her until he knew her better that it had been after one especially bad row that he had gone out and spent their holiday fund on a cello, having the previous Christmas sold his old one, under pressure, so that they could buy the kids a computer. Valerie was still giving him grief about it but he had reached a point when he just had to play again, and Valerie was going to have to lump it.

'His little wifey is his business,' she said.

'Okay, okay,' James said. 'Maybe your motives are entirely pure. But he did kind of manipulate you into teaching him, didn't he?'

James could be so irritating. She wasn't going to explain it all again, how Andrew had simply needed lessons, and when he had read in the *Bath Chronicle*, which had run a feature on her, that she had come to live near Bath, he had written her a sort of fan letter. He had introduced himself, told

74

her that he had all her recordings and said that he did not suppose for a moment she would consider teaching him. She had written back acknowledging the first part of the letter, failing to state categorically that she did not take pupils. Then he had simply rung up and asked when he could come and meet her and get her advice. She had not been surprised to find that the attractively gentle voice was attached to a strongly built, fair-haired, brown-eyed man a year or two older than she was. But she had been surprised at how musically he had played despite many years' rust on his technique, and how very strongly he had resisted the idea of approaching any of the other people she suggested about lessons. 'But I don't take pupils,' she had said.

'I don't charge him,' Sara said, staring defensively at James, who was sipping smugly from his glass. It was hardly the point. Andrew had written again. And then telephoned. By this time he was being so reliably surprising that she, ridiculously flattered, had relented. The thought had entered her mind that she would much rather that this amusing, insistent man with his gentle way of getting exactly what he wanted were in her life, rather than out of it.

'Look, it's only once a fortnight or so. And I like him and I like teaching him, so you can stop looking at me like that. If he is on the case, he'll probably have made an arrest by now. How complicated can it be? Give me another drink. Didn't you get any cheese?'

'Of course I did,' said James, still looking smug.

CHAPTER FIVE

The next morning, despite a slight hangover, Sara drove out along the London Road between the high walls of the Batheaston town houses. She stopped for a paper at Dennis and Maureen's shop where, to her surprise, news of the corpse in the water and her involvement in its discovery had not yet arrived. Then she turned left up towards Bannerdown, where the Roman road ran straight along the top of the hill towards Colerne and the sanctuary of the health club at Fortune Park.

As Sara came through the double doors into the club she saw that Sue was on the desk and that her happy mood of two days ago had flown. It was almost an achievement, the way she managed to look so depressed in her sharp little up-and-at-'em fitness instructor outfits, although this job was often combined with being the club receptionist and waitress. Her perfect athletic body was dressed and immaculately accessorised today in expensive aerobics kit, yet her face betrayed a life again quite devoid of fun.

'Hello there,' Sara said, annoyingly bright.

Sue tried to raise a smile.

'Oh, dear. Paul?' Sara asked.

Sue nodded. Her voice was barely a whisper. 'Not what you think—not a row or anything. He's being questioned about . . . oh, God, it's awful . . . about . . . oh, God, a murder! At the Pump Room. The police rang up here. He's gone into Bath police station, and the whole game's up! He's been found out and it's over. He won't be able to work here any more!'

Sara wanted to say several things at once, one of which was that if Paul had committed the murder then there were surely going to be more pressing and serious consequences than the loss of his job. She deferred her exercise without complaint, took a stool at the bar among the potted palms and old copies of *Country Life* and sipped coffee while she listened. She managed with a little difficulty to tell Sue that she had been there, that she had actually been the one to find the body. Sue was suitably aghast but it deflected her only momentarily from her own woes.

'No! God! Ugh! Ghastly! Really, *poor* you. Ghastly! So anyway ...'

As she carried on things began to make sense. Paul had been working at the Assembly Rooms on Friday afternoon and evening, preparing and serving the vegetarian buffet. And that was the problem. Paul should not have been there, because moonlighting was strictly against his contract at Fortune Park. The management's line was that they paid their staff to be alert and on the ball and they did not want anyone going off doing functions in their off-duty hours and then showing up the next day to serve breakfast, half dead with fatigue. So their contracts forbade it. Sue had once pleaded for special permission to run an aerobics class outside the health club and been turned down.

'He was only doing it to get on a bit,' Sue said. Sara murmured understandingly. 'He's wasted as a waiter, you see. He's a chef really. He's really good, he's half French, his mother was French, he trained over there at his uncle's restaurant. He wants to be a chef, only he hasn't got any formal qualifications and he could only get taken on here as a waiter. It's practically impossible to move up in the kitchens here, not from being a waiter. It's like the army, everyone in the kitchen's got a rank, and even the juniors have got to have degrees, just to slice the vegetables. He'll never get a start here. So he's been doing a bit for Coldstreams, you know, the people that do the food at the Pump Room and the Assembly Rooms and wherever. The Guildhall as well, I think. He's been assistant chef sometimes, at some of the functions. It's vegetables mainly. He did meringues the other week. But it's proper cooking. And he's careful, he only takes on the hours he can manage on top. Now he'll get the sack. It's so unfair! We need the money. He's trying to save so we can get a flat together.' Her face crumpled.

'Look, don't assume the worst. You never know, maybe the management will be sympathetic. They might even help when they know why he was doing it. Maybe they'll even help him with training. Or maybe Oliver Coldstream will put in a good word for him with his boss here, explain it all.'

'He's hardly ever seen Mr Coldstream. And he'd never even seen Matthew Sawyer at all, and just because he was *there* he's got the police asking him questions, and he'll probably lose his job. It's so *unfair.*'

Sara did not know what comfort to offer. More people had come in and the pool was now busy, relatively speaking, with three or four children and their dad and a couple of ladies. Sue had to be on hand to do lunches. Sara changed a little reluctantly into her running kit and jogged off alone out of the back door of the club. Circling her

78

arms as she went, she trotted sedately round the outside of the walled garden that separated the club from the hotel, and joined the narrow service road that led down the side and round to the front of the hotel, which had originally been an exquisitely pretty manor house. It was homely but imposing, with its gabled upper windows, pillared entrance and semicircular apron of lawn. But the guests' BMWs parked directly in front of the long windows did nothing to enhance the façade, and presumably also impeded the view from the public rooms down the avenue, a straight road between high beeches, which ran for more than a quarter of a mile from the lawn in front of the house down to the main gate. Sara plodded along under the trees, her legs heavy. Yesterday's events had taken more out of her than she had thought and she was not yet enjoying the run. There would be no stopwatch today, just the two-mile circuit down the drive, out and round by the edge of Colerne and back in to Fortune Park by the rear entrance.

The even pace of running always helped her to think. So he was stabbed. How is it that such a tall man, probably quite strong, could end up in the water? She concentrated on getting her breathing to come evenly as she thought about this. He could not easily have been overpowered and pushed over the railing, unless his attacker were stronger than he was. But if he were hurt, or already dead, his body could have been tipped in easily. Was he stabbed in the back, then, and tipped over into the water? Those long legs would have acted like a lever. Perhaps 'not thought to be self-inflicted' is police code for stab wounds in the back. She had seen no knife, but perhaps it had been under the

79

water, or lying around somewhere. The police would want to find that. Her legs were getting warmer now. Don't murderers always get rid of the weapon? The body must have been there all night. Perhaps he wasn't married, then, because his wife would have contacted the police when he didn't come home after the dinner, surely? Probably divorced. She had reached the end of the avenue now and she turned left out on to the pavement towards the crossroads on the edge of the village. The way ahead rose slightly with an angle of incline that was practically imperceptible if you were walking, but running, even at this gentle pace, you felt every contour. She ran on the spot for a few paces and again circled her arms extravagantly in an effort to loosen up her breathing. She set off again, lifting her knees more deliberately. Now the pace was coming more easily. She quickened her stride and felt her body relax into an easy rhythm of breathing and moving that she knew she could keep up for an hour or more. Wonderful.

Out of the shelter of the avenue the landscape opened up too. In the fields on either side of the high road along which she was running, the new wheat was sighing and soughing in the breeze which blew out of a huge, exhilarating sky. The sun came and went with the clouds but the wind itself seemed to carry light. As she ran on with her hair whipping her face, Sara recalled the ploughing and sowing of the black fields on a squally March day, when grit had been blown into her eyes and mouth by gusts which had lifted the seagulls away like paper bags. And months before that, when she had ventured out heavily track-suited one winter morning, out of a solid sky the wind had suddenly begun to throw out fistfuls of sleet which had rattled around her on the empty road, across the iron topsoil and swirled into the dark field corners. Today there was such brightness in the silky wheat, the banks of cow parsley and the far-off glinting, low roofs of Colerne. In another few weeks the air would be sharp with wheat dust and stray chaff and the fields brittle with stubble. She had lived for months like this, now. Months of being patient, allowing her fatigue to lift, developing her stamina, reclaiming her energy, practising and practising, hoping for some change in her playing that still had not come and that she could not force. And as she was waiting, practising, running round and round, things were planted, they grew and they were reaped. If nothing changed she might be plodding between these fields in her track-suit next time round, watching the snow and waiting for the spring.

As she breathed and ran steadily, she thought back to the events of Friday and Saturday. At the Assembly Rooms I saw Matthew Sawyer, Olivia, Sue, of course, and Cecily and her odd man in the foyer. Derek something. I left there just before seven, got to the Pump Room maybe twenty minutes later. Saw James, then changed, warmed-up, had a drink. Played at eight for twenty-five minutes, well, thirty with the encores. Who was at the Pump Room? Olivia, she turned up about quarter to eight, left early, almost before dinner was over. I chatted to her before she left. I didn't dare mention the scene at the Assembly Rooms. Don't even know if she saw me there. She left a minute or two after ten; she said she had to get back to say goodnight to her dad before he was settled for the night. He's housebound with a nurse now, and Matthew was in charge of locking up, she was just a guest. 'I'm off duty,' she said. 'Being deputy has its compensations.' He was covering the Pump Room, George was due to lock up at the Assembly Rooms. I didn't notice Matthew Sawyer until almost after dinner, about quarter to ten. I suppose he was behind the scenes somewhere, or still at the Assembly Rooms till then. He didn't have a table, just went round and chatted to people, with puddings and coffee. I left at half past ten. Pissing with rain. Said goodnight to George, on the door. Plenty of people still there, James included. He stayed till very near the end, he said. Forgot to ask him last night when he did leave, and who was still there. Who *was* last, before Matthew Sawyer? Maybe the murderer just waited till he was the only one left. Maybe he was hiding. And what was it George said: 'Last out, first in?' Well, I wasn't the last out. Whoever *was* last must have done the murder. No, could have done it. Where have I got to? Nowhere. Just been running round and round and round, story of my life.

She absolutely would not speculate any more. She would put the whole thing right out of her mind. She jogged back to the health club entrance feeling invigorated if not enlightened. In the gym she stretched out her legs and back and spent ten minutes whirring back and forth on the rowing machine. Most of the rest of the club's clientele had abandoned themselves to lunch by the time she was ready to swim, so she had the pool almost to herself and drifted up and down, hypnotically slow, stretching and floating between strokes. Then, physically tired, she gave herself up to a pleasant weariness and read her paper on a lounger by the side of the pool.

CHAPTER SIX

'Andrew, a horse could play that better.'

Sara had not meant to sound quite so brutal, but since the only point of Andrew's lessons was to help him achieve a half-decent standard, she had resolved to keep him up to the mark. She could safely dismiss James's suggestion of an ulterior motive for taking him on, because it was of no relevance at all that Andrew's body had struck her again as exceptionally finely made. She could hardly be expected not to *notice* how long and muscular were his thighs, straddling the cello. Of course she was aware of how intelligent and strong was his face, but she was unmoved. It was central to her role as his teacher to notice these things; they were part of the visual information that she relied on to help him improve his technique or concentration. James should know that, but next time she saw him she would tell him anyway.

Since he had arrived Andrew had said not one word about the murder or the enquiry. He had postponed his usual Monday lesson until Tuesday 'owing to pressure of work', and from a brief factual report of the Pump Room murder in Monday's *Chronicle* Sara had learned that he was indeed working on the case. And now here he was, saying little and playing so atrociously that Sara felt something close to alarm. She had regained her own equilibrium since the events of Saturday

83

mainly by convincing herself that the killer would quickly be arrested. She had expected Andrew to bound in today metaphorically wagging his tail, and instead he was carrying in his jaws a bloodied offering of unresolved, unexpected death, and dropping it at her feet. An atmosphere of threat eddied all around them. He was so pointedly *not* talking about the murder that he was managing to do not much of anything else either.

He sighed, put down his bow and leaned his cheek against the wood. He loved it up here at the very top of Sara's garden. They were in the hut, Sara's summer music room, a little garden house made of dark green painted wood with windows on either side and large double doors which opened right back, allowing you to sit either in the hut looking out, or on the little gravelled space in front with its low wooden balustrade. As well as two chairs for playing on and a rather disgraceful chaise-longue, there was a rickety table and some spidery wicker basket seats, with faded green cushions, for collapsing into. Hanging from chains in the pitched roof were two storm lanterns. The hut stood camouflaged in the shade of a huge pine tree and was as private as an eyrie. Up here you were invisible, untouchable. Andrew looked down through the mass of lavender bushes to the old climbing roses which twisted in full flower through the fruit trees, over the roof of Medlar Cottage and across to the valley and the lime tree meadow.

'I know. Sorry,' he said, without moving his gaze from the hillside. 'I know I'm playing badly. I was determined not to bring it up, but I'm in charge of the Pump Room case. And I know that you got caught up in it.'

He paused, still staring out. At seven o'clock on this evening in June, the valley was lit in bright sunshine. Black and white cows idled under the trees in fields that were wrinkled with the ridges trodden by generations of their hoofed ancestors. The new grass was washed in a chalky, early summer green. You half expected Bo-Peep to skip into view.

'Valerie doesn't think I'll be up to it.'

'Oh, I'm sure she does,' Sara said casually. 'Is it, er, going well?'

'No, it isn't, as a matter of fact,' he said.

'But don't you know most of these people? Your yobs and vandals, I mean. The regulars. Surely it's one of them you're looking for?'

Andrew pored over the Fauré on the music stand with apparent absorption, but he was a poor actor.

'What does Valerie think?'

'I don't discuss these things with Valerie.' He started the piece again and his tone brought to mind a cat whose tail has been stood on.

'Stop, *stop*! God, stop that noise. Look, you'll probably reel in the lout who did this in no time.' She added softly, 'I *hope* you will. The whole thing's making me feel . . . unsafe. You will, won't you?'

Andrew put down his bow again. 'I'm sorry. I really can't discuss the enquiry. But it's not one of our regulars, I can tell you that.'

'All right then,' Sara said deliberately. 'I understand. But if you just told me how you knew it wasn't, that wouldn't be *discussing* it, would it?'

Andrew played a little, considering. 'All right then, in complete confidence. Matthew Sawyer was lying dead in a locked building, with the alarms set. The person, or people, who left him dead must have locked the building and set the alarm after them. Still, not your problem. Sorry. Shall I try this again?'

'Start again from the beginning. Breathe with the phrases. Think about where you want them to go. And listen.'

'Sounds easy, doesn't it? The music, I mean,' he added, frowning over the Fauré.

As he played Sara said, 'But isn't it easy? You just round up all the people who know about the alarm and eliminate them till you find the one who could have done it.'

'Done that. Nothing. Look, Sara, I'm really not meant to discuss this.'

'Well, try to concentrate on what you're doing with that cello, then. What do you mean, nothing?'

'Nothing. They're transparent. Decent, respected museum employees, and nothing that even begins to suggest a motive. And they've all got alibis.'

To Sara's irritation, Andrew's playing became momentarily convincing. Then he put down his bow again.

'All right, in *confidence*. Two of the attendants were off duty. One of them, Jack, was taking part in a pub quiz at the Centurion in Twerton. He was there all night and dozens of people can vouch for him. Colin was at home with his wife. They've got a new baby. And all that evening and most of the night it was ill, so Colin rang their GP at ten o'clock for advice and again at half past twelve, when he called him out; they couldn't get its temperature down. George Townsend, the senior chap, was on duty, of course. He did door duty at the Pump Room until ten to eleven, then he went over to the Assembly Rooms to lock up and relieve Andy who was there on his own after Matthew Sawyer left the Assembly Rooms to check out the event at the Pump Room. Andy's new, he's not an authorised key-holder yet. George relieved him just after eleven. Andy lives with his mother and she had a friend round. He got home at quarter past eleven and drove the friend home at half past. He came straight back home and locked up at ten to twelve, made a cup of tea for his mother as usual and brought it to her in bed. Then he went to his own room. George locked up the Assembly Rooms at about ten past eleven and was home at about twenty to midnight. He went straight up to bed. His wife was there already.'

Suddenly he seemed to remember himself. 'I shouldn't have told you all that. Forget I did.'

'You're welcome to tell me things if it helps.'

Andrew gave her a meltingly grateful smile, but said nothing.

She went on, 'Well, since it's clearly out of the question to expect you to think seriously about Fauré today, do you know exactly when Matthew Sawyer died?'

'That's another problem. The time of death is never easy to establish exactly, as you probably know. We do know he didn't drown. There was no water in the lungs. He had stopped breathing before he fell in the water.'

'What about rigor mortis? Can't you tell by that?'

'Not with any precision.' He paused. 'What *is* it about this view?'

87

'Oh, it's just old-fashioned,' Sara said. 'There's no big road, no pylons. The fields are all different shapes, and they've left the trees. I keep expecting to see a young John Betjeman in grey flannel shorts swinging on a gate, catapulting pigeons, don't you?'

Andrew was silent. 'Rigor mortis,' he went on, 'is really a chemical reaction in the body after death. The temperature surrounding the body can affect how quickly it happens. There isn't, I'm afraid, a great deal of precedent which helps us establish the onset and progress of rigor in a body left in hot running water, but it could have speeded it up. In any event, it doesn't wear off completely for several hours after that, sometimes even a couple of days.'

He turned to look at her. 'What do you mean, John Betjeman? Certainly not John Betjeman. William and the Outlaws, maybe.'

'Okay, William and the Outlaws, pursued by Violet-Elizabeth Bott. So what have you decided about the time of death?'

'Well, rigor had almost completely set in when the body was examined, which was shortly before ten o'clock. Which was, as you'd be aware,' he said ruefully, 'about forty minutes after you first discovered him. Sawyer was seen alive at eleven forty-five the night before, when the last of the catering staff left. Two lads, who left together and were both home within half an hour. Given that, the pathologist says death could have occurred any time from about midnight to five in the morning. Rather a wide margin. He reckons that the body lying in the water the way it did *could* have accelerated the onset of rigor by several hours, but it's a guess as to how much. Supposing the water did speed up rigor, but only minimally, he could

88

have been killed within minutes of the last people seeing him alive. If on the other hand the hot water accelerated it significantly, which is possible, he could have been killed as late as five o'clock in the morning. The stomach contents don't help either: in this instance, they were well digested. Metabolic rates are too variable for us to conclude anything. The water doesn't exactly wash away the evidence, but it obscures it. It's a real curse.'

Andrew went on. 'You saw the body in the water, under the floodlights. You told Bridger he looked sort of yellow, like the colour of the water. There's a gold filter in those lights, you know. I saw him in the mortuary, afterwards. The stab blows were mainly to the back, eight of them, made with a knife at least ten inches long. One in the right shoulder and another on the right upper arm. He was stabbed from behind and almost certainly swung round to try to defend himself. The one that punctured the left lung was the fatal one. But I've never seen anything like it. The blood had been washing out of him all night, with the water just running over and over him. It all just . . . pulsed away. Like raw meat under a tap. It's so nice here,' he said, breathing in the warm mixture of old wood, sun-baked cushions and lavender, before adding sadly, 'Valerie's after a patio.'

Sara was silent for a moment. Neither the warm hut, the flowers nor the view would provide safety from the picture that Andrew was holding up before her. 'Have you found the knife?' she asked.

'Nope. It was most likely a kitchen knife. There's no sign of it, and the keys that Matthew Sawyer had are missing, of course. There's more than one set, naturally. George Townsend had the other set on

89

Friday night, and there's a master set in the Guildhall safe. Each set of keys contains the keys for *all* the museum buildings. It's reckoned to be easier to keep track of three big sets than several separate ones for different buildings.'

Andrew had been speaking quietly and carefully, plotting aloud all the known events of the night. Up in the creosoty, scented peace of the hut, he was talking and simultaneously searching in his words for the bit that was not quite right, the bit that could not be right, the single little thing that would give him a start in the enquiry. He dug his feet hard against the wooden floor and drew his bow in a single discordant swipe across all the strings of his cello.

'Damn it, there's nothing to get hold of in this case. George Townsend took his set of keys with him to the Assembly Rooms and locked up there at about ten past eleven. And then he took them to the Museums Service general office in the Circus and put them in the safe there. He says sometimes he takes the keys home with him if he's back on first thing in the morning, but on Friday he didn't because Mr Sawyer was locking up the Pump Room and bringing his set of keys back to the Circus too, and he would have noticed if George's keys hadn't been in the safe, so he played it by the book. Only of course Sawyer didn't deposit his keys. They're still missing. On Saturday morning Colin had to take the master set from the safe to open up the Assembly Rooms. He said he assumed Mr Sawyer had gone off home the night before with the bunch of keys still in his pocket, and that he would be bringing them back later. Wasn't for him to complain, Sawyer was the boss.'

90

'The murderer wouldn't hang on to the keys, surely?' Sara murmured. 'Or the knife either. I mean, you'd get rid of anything that associated you with what you'd done, wouldn't you? *Now*, can we play some Fauré, please?'

She began quietly to play the Élégie in C Minor. Andrew watched and then lifted his bow and joined in. His tuning was less certain, his phrasing half-hearted. It was a depressing sound.

'Try to breathe through these phrases. Right through, don't be mean with them. Make it *sing*, Andrew, not whine. That's better.'

She stopped playing and looked out across the garden as Andrew carried on.

He said, 'It would still be helpful to find them.'

'I thought you didn't want to discuss it? Listen, *listen*. Your pitch is slipping under. Brighten it. That's it.'

Andrew played to the end of the phrase. 'We've done the routine search of the drains. Nothing there, which is no surprise—keys and knives would be too heavy to get carried along. Naturally I want to drain the whole place, but do you think I can get permission? Oh, no, up pop the council's heritage committee. "Unacceptable risk to this unique and irreplaceable monument, to upset the flow of the spring and divert the water." The boss, the District Commander, had to agree we won't do it unless we have a "sound reason to suspect" that the search would yield something. And I haven't, not yet.'

'Mind you, if it was me, that's where I'd chuck them.' Sara was scrutinising his fingering. 'The keys. They might never be found. And they'd be close to the body. In a locked building. Not that I'm interested.'

Andrew snorted. 'Fine detective you'd make. How would you do it? You *might* chuck the knife in after you'd used it, but not the keys. Either you've got the keys from Matthew Sawyer before you stab him, or you stab him and take the keys off him afterwards. You've still got to get out of the building, haven't you? Suppose you lock the door to Stall Street first, from the inside, then you'd have to go across the Pump Room to the main door into the Roman Baths on Abbey Churchyard, right? Then you set the alarm in the box which is inside a panel just inside the doorway, lock the panel, leave and shut the door and lock it behind you. So you're *outside* with the keys, aren't you? So how on earth could you dump them in the bath, Einstein?'

Sara looked at him witheringly. 'Easy. After you set the alarm and lock the door behind you, you just walk round the corner on to Kingston Parade and climb up on the wall of the terrace. The street level outside is much higher than the bath, so the wall on the outside up on to the terrace is not high at all. And there are even ridges cut into the stone. Once you're up there, you just have to throw them up and over, so they clear the terrace and the balustrade. You just lob them over and splash, there you are. You're still flat, by the way.'

Andrew went on playing and gave a clever smile. 'Haven't you forgotten something? You've just set the alarm, right? All the area round the Great Bath is alarmed. You'd have bells going off all over the place.'

Sara paused. 'Sure? Is the *water* alarmed? Sure, someone walking anywhere *round* the bath would set the alarm off, but what about something just landing in the water? Seagulls don't set it off. There's always a seagull or two around there, standing on the statues' heads. The alarm doesn't go off every time a bird comes down to the water, does it? So either they're not big enough to trigger the alarm, or the water is not alarmed at all. And so I'd have thought a bunch of keys *could* be flung into the bath without bells going off everywhere.'

Andrew played on to the end of the Élégie without replying, and finished it with eloquent, unhurried musicality. Sara, about to exclaim that he was really getting somewhere with the piece, was interrupted.

Andrew was grinning. 'Do you mind if we stop there? I think I can dress that up into "sound reason to suspect". So must dash, I've got a Roman bath to drain.'

Halfway down the path he turned back towards Sara. 'You're wonderful, you know. I can't thank you enough. I'll let you know if we find anything.'

He had turned away, and was anyway too far down the path to notice the movement of her lips as she said, half to herself, 'Oh, please. Please don't. Don't tell me.'

CHAPTER SEVEN

Derek's afternoon was dragging. He had agreed to take Year 8 for geography so that the head of geography, Mrs Higgens, and her sidekick Philips could get an early start with the Year 9 field trip to the Brecon Beacons. As he saw them off at lunchtime he had felt nothing but envy that they

93

were getting three days away from school, even if it did consist of four nights in a youth hostel with a troupe of hormonally demented teenagers and was beginning with a three-hour drive up the M4 in a packed minibus with testosterone running down the windows.

He was tired. His groin ached with anticipation at the thought of his forthcoming weekend with Cecily and his head ached at the thought of the two and a half days he still had to get through before it could truly be said to have arrived. He resolved to make it a better weekend than last which, all in all, had been a fiasco. He was still reeling from a sense of relief at having got away with it all. The police had come round to interview Cecily on Monday. They'd said they were interviewing everyone who had been in the place that Friday and they'd got her name from the delegates list. Clever old Cec had convinced them she knew nothing. It was niggling him a little that she had had to mention his name, but then, it was no secret that he'd actually been to the Assembly Rooms. After all, he'd given his name to Sawyer (who would have more than a stiff upper lip by this time, ha-ha, and serve him right), and anyway, at least three other people had seen him (be made to) leave. He could even, if it came to it, admit to Pauline that he'd been there. Just *being* there didn't amount to adultery, after all. Not that it would come to it. Nor did he foresee any great difficulty in keeping everything that had happened later in the evening entirely to himself. He was safe. Nevertheless, there would be no more going out in public with Cecily. Really, he should cut down on the visits. In fact, the whole thing would have to be reviewed, when he had time to think, which was not now.

It was only Wednesday. He had always hated Wednesdays, especially the last lesson, by the end of which he usually felt shipwrecked and adrift on an unending and dangerous week. He had always hated geography. And he hated Year 8, from whose room emanated the unmistakable aroma of mucky kid, a disgusting mixture of wet dog and stale cake. As he opened the door Derek discreetly lifted his sleeve to his face in the hope that a vestige of that morning's Eau Sauvage might linger there and sustain him.

He called them to order, a thing he did effectively, being several times larger and more intelligent than any of them and also the headmaster. He discouraged the word headteacher. Thirty-eight specimens of south Bristol's *jeunesse dorée* looked at him expectantly. Higgens would have set them something to do, not that she, he or they expected that this meant that they were really going to do it.

'So, what have you been doing with Mrs Higgens?'

Obscene sniggers.

He tried again. 'What has Mrs Higgens left you to do?'

Silence. Bewilderment. Outrage.

'*Do*, sir? Aw, sir, 's nearly four o'clock, sir!'

Derek sighed as the mayhem of protest rose around him. He folded his arms. He really could not be bothered.

'Sir, sir, we got a sheet, sir,' came a sole, craven voice. Good. You could always rely on there being at least one crawler. Half the class groaned and the other half hissed hideous threats of reprisal to the informer.

'Right, thank you. Now, let's have a look at this sheet. Have you all got it?' A proportion of the class waved the sheet in lethargic surrender.

'What is the country on the sheet? It is a continent, in fact,' he added quickly, pre-empting any, Ooh, sir! Mrs Higgens says it's a *continent*, sir! Does Mrs Higgens know *more* than you, sir?

'Sir! Sir! Sir! It's Africal, sir!'

Derek sighed again. He should be used to it by now but it could still catch him unawares, the Bristol accent. When he had first come to this school ten years ago, taking up his first, and as things had turned out, his only headship, he had been taken aback when the caretaker had said, 'Ah, good ideal,' when Derek had proposed some minor change to the litter-picking rotas. Hardly the province of an ideal, he had thought, before the caretaker had added, 'I'll see to it tomorral.' But he *had* had ideals then, a real vision, and nowadays he could barely see further than the end of the lesson.

The class broke into two opposing camps.

'Snot! S'Indial!'

'Course's snot! S'Africal!'

Derek said nothing. On a good day, he was just pallid with the boredom of it all. On a not so good day, perhaps in assembly when he was about to lead the whole fucking school in some listless prayer, or at his desk, hearing the janitor (my site manager) explain that half a hundredweight of paper towels had blocked the toilets again, he could feel a sort of dry sobbing going on somewhere inside him and he would have to take a deep breath to prevent his whole body from cranking publicly under the weight of his unhappiness. But on a *bad* day he could see quite far enough ahead, thank you. He could see right ahead to the forthcoming OFSTED inspection in November, which might very well consign his whole dog-eared school and all its chewed-up staff and its spat-out youngsters to the bin marked 'Failing Schools'. What could he do, what *more* could he do between now and then, to give each child a turn with the books he had to share with three others, to stop Miss Cross teaching art history with black and white photocopies of the paintings, to get the head of maths off anti-depressants and back into his classroom? On a bad day the hot, incoherent soup of rage and shame that simmered inside him rose to a fast rolling boil, making him windy and irritable. People knew to keep away. There had been a time when Cecily, with her adoring availability, had perked him up on bad days, but after a time compliance as even-tempered and unvarying as hers had become irksome to him, as had the hints that she might be expecting something more permanent to develop from their liaison. She had even come close, once or twice, to mentioning that she was short of money. Good God, if he helped her with money, what would that make her? What would it make *him*? Cecily just couldn't help being a little shabby. The only real balm for his bad days now came from the prospect of getting another job before he was suspended after the OFSTED disaster. He could still, just, conceive of a sweeter life for himself beyond the boundaries of south Bristol, but he hardly dared to. Now that an opportunity in Bath, that parallel universe of prosperous gentility and nice buildings, had beckoned, he was not going to let it go. It would be his. He would make it his. He was seeing to it.

'It is, in fact, Afric*ah*,' he said. 'The continent of Afric*ah*. And what is the name of the country shown over the page? One of the countries of Afric*ah*?'

'Sir! Sir! Sir, *Kenyal*, sir!'

'Keny*ah*. All right, what can you tell me about Keny*ah*?'

After this Year 8 dried up, but with determined coaxing, Derek managed to evince from them the fascinating news that like many countries in Africal, Kenyal was a tropical malarial areal.

CHAPTER EIGHT

On Friday Sara got back wet through from her run to find a message from Andrew asking her to call him back on his mobile. Over the crackle he said there were two things, and he was coming over to discuss them. From the tone of his voice it was obvious that neither of them was Fauré's Élégie in C.

'But I've just been out running and I'm soaked. You don't mean this exact minute, do you? I've got to shower.'

'Oh, no, not this exact minute. You've got, oh, about fifteen, I should think,' he said, and hung up. When he arrived he asked if they could go up to the hut. They made their way up the long zigzagging path which crossed the orchard, bordered the wide lawn on the left of the cottage and then, continuing to rise, ran between the banks of lavender bushes above. At several points a number of smaller paths joined the main one: these led from the lawn, from the line of hazelnut trees which formed the boundary on the far side and from the large pond surrounded by corkscrew willow and irises at the other. The air was heavy with the scent of the sun on wet petals and damp stone. Sara fastened back the wide double doors of the hut and they sat in the wicker chairs looking out at the sodden hillside and the six lime trees, heavy and bright with rain. Andrew spoke without looking at her.

'I find I can think up here, and I wanted to go over a few more things with you. First, though, thanks for the help with the keys and knife. We got them, although it took until this morning. They were in different parts of the bath. So it's possible—likely even—that they were thrown in from different points which means your theory might be right. Forensic's looking at them, but they're unlikely to tell us much. It'll be in Monday's *Chronicle*, but I wanted to let you know first.'

'You shouldn't have bothered. It doesn't concern me, you know, just because I found the body.' She turned to him. 'Look, Andrew, I'd rather forget all about it. You should come here to play the cello, not to talk about the case. I can't help you. I don't want the case taking over . . . all this. Here. All this is . . . private.' She waved an arm vaguely. 'This is my place.'

He took her by the wrist and replaced her arm in her lap.

'I understand that you'd rather forget all about it. But you won't, you know, any more than I will. You can't. I'm talking to you now as . . . just me.

99

Not as a police officer. But I can, and I will, if you'd prefer it that way. But, Sara, please'—he took her arm again and gave it a gentle shake—'please help me? I need your help.'

Sara did not look at him. Andrew paused, his hand still on her arm, seeming to find the next bit difficult.

'Sara, what was your impression of Detective Sergeant Bridger?'

Sara gave a short laugh and turned to face him. 'Frankly? I thought he was a sexist prat. He assumed things. He stereotyped me. He was also profoundly ignorant.'

Andrew looked weary. 'Off the record, I'd have to agree. We've still got a few of his type, not many now, thank God.' He sighed. 'I've been going over the reports of his first interviews. And by the way, if I tell you this, it's strictly between ourselves. I could be in trouble otherwise. Understood?'

Sara nodded.

Andrew went on. 'Bridger thought it was pretty suspicious that you own your house—in an extremely desirable location, he said—and are so extremely well dressed when you are single and "don't have a proper full-time job" and wonders if this unexplained prosperity could somehow have a bearing on the case. Worth following up, in his view.'

Sara gave an ashamed laugh. 'It's my fault. I couldn't help it. He asked me if I did "this cello-playing stuff" all the time. He didn't think there'd be that much call for it. And I said, no, because I was taking a break for the time being, and I just played the charity thing to help the festival. Then he said, "I suppose you'd have to be *really* good to

100

make a living at it, so it's what, more of a hobby then?" And I said, "Yes, I suppose you could say that, although I do get paid *sometimes*."'

Andrew exploded with laughter.

'I'm ashamed of myself, really. I was piqued because he'd obviously never heard of me, and I had no right to be. I'm a brat. He said he didn't go for the highbrow stuff himself but he quite liked that fat bloke, that Italian, what was his name, Nessun Dorma.' She smiled. 'And I said yeah he was quite good, funny name for a bloke, though.'

She paused and watched as a wood pigeon, startled by Andrew's laughter, took up and off from the shelter of an apple tree.

'I suppose now I've obstructed the police in the course of their enquiries and I'm going to be handcuffed and shoved in the back of a police van. I'll be eaten alive in Holloway, I hope you realise.'

'That's the least you deserve. I'll see to it you get a good going over down the nick as well. You *are* a brat.'

'Look, I really didn't mean to cause trouble or hold things up. If I have, I'm sorry.'

'You haven't, don't worry. Actually it's helped, because it was only because I know you that I could see what a hash he'd made of interviewing you. And I really enjoyed being able to tell him that your inexplicable prosperity arose from the fact that one of your concert fees would amount to about a third of his annual salary, and that it would be an unusual month if none of your recordings cropped up on Radio 3.' He paused, smiling again. 'I'm not *absolutely* sure he'd heard of Radio 3.'

He grew more serious and it crossed Sara's mind, as it periodically did, that she could not go

101

on indefinitely living off royalties and repeat fees. She would have to ring Robin.

'So, I've been going back over the people he saw, and some of them I'm seeing myself now. It's possible he's been missing things. I only found out from Olivia Passmore, for example, that you and she know each other. He spent barely fifteen minutes with her and ticked her off as spinsterish: a workaholic with ageing father. He thinks she's a strong suspect.'

'Why on *earth* does he suspect her?'

'Oh, he's a tabloid thinker. Unhinged by having to go back to being number two when Sawyer came on the scene. Frustrated, neurotic, bitter, trapped by dependent relative. He'd practically written the headline. You know the sort of thing: SPINSTER'S FRENZIED KNIFE ATTACK.'

'Oh, typical. Oh, God, Andrew, how can you work with this person?'

'No, it doesn't convince me either. I went round to see Olivia Passmore on Sunday afternoon, and unhinged is the last word I'd use to describe her. Bridger had been to see her in the morning. But how true is the workaholic bit, would you say?'

'Oh, she is very clued up and good at her job, but you shouldn't reduce Olivia—well, you shouldn't reduce *anyone*—just to that. There's much more to her. Her father is Edwin Passmore.'

'Right. Er, just remind me?'

'The horn player. Really brilliant. Years and years ago—he's in his eighties now. But a fabulous player. He's been ill for years with emphysema, and Olivia looks after him, and there's a resident nurse now. She's never been married. I think it all falls to her. She's got a niece who works at Fortune Park.

102

You know, where I go to swim. Sue's called something else, Olivia has a married sister. Sue's heavily into aerobics and the body beautiful. Olivia's a music lover: she loves the festival and does things for the MBF. You know, Musicians' Benevolent Fund. That's how I met her.'

'And what about her job? Was she jealous of Sawyer, do you know?'

'Oh, absolutely not. You know she ran the whole museum service for quite a while. Well over two years. She said to me once she couldn't wait to be free of all the hassle. She's a curator, a conservator. She takes care of objects, textiles, mainly. She wasn't interested in running shops and tea rooms and party bookings and security and all that. She was glad to hand over to Sawyer. Didn't she tell you all this?'

'Yes, of course.'

'Yes, well. There you are. That deals with Bridger's little theory, doesn't it?' She added indignantly, 'And what the hell is "spinsterish" supposed to mean, anyway? She's got such style. Don't you think she looks fantastic? I don't just mean the clothes. There's a poise about her— strong, knows what she's doing. I really admire her, actually.'

'I can understand that,' Andrew said, recalling the unembellished elegance of the woman. 'Inner calm. She is quite beautiful, in an Eleanor Bronnish way. What's wrong with her?'

'What do you mean?'

'Well, when I went round I had to wait for ages before she came to the door. Then when she took me up to the drawing room she was having trouble with the stairs. Same thing coming down. Bad legs

103

or something.'

'Well, she seemed perfectly all right last Friday, as far as I noticed. Maybe she's got rheumaticky knees or something, that just flare up. It was wet that weekend, and the damp brings it on, doesn't it? Or she may just have been up at the top of the house, where her dad is. Or in the loo. It's up on Bathwick Hill, isn't it? They're all big houses.'

'It is big. Yes, you're probably right.'

'Well, then. I hope you're going to leave her alone now.'

'And then there's George. I'm interested in George. He's what Bridger calls "salt of the earth", of course. He may be. But I don't go for all that shocking-business-Constable, anything-I-can-do-to-assist-the-police-sir crap. Phoney. I don't like forelock-tuggers.'

'Oh, you're being unfair. All right, he's a bit of a cheery chappie, but I'm sure it's genuine. He's just always been like that. And he's been in that job for *years*. He's not suddenly going to top his guvner, cor lumme, is he?'

'S'pose not. I can't see why he would. But, Sara, I'll get nowhere if I get hung up on motives. Anyone can hide a motive and we could spend for ever looking for one. The fact is that this murder had to be done by someone who could lock up and set the alarm afterwards. That means that Olivia, George and his band of assistants—Andy, Jack and Colin—are the chief suspects. Sticking to facts, you see? Someone's alibi will break, and then the motive will emerge. I *hope*, because the forensic evidence is unlikely to be sufficient for a conviction.'

He paused. 'Sara, this is a big enquiry. I've got

twenty officers on it. There are hundreds of people to interview, and almost any one of them, at this stage, could be guilty. You do understand that I have been talking in the strictest confidence? I mean this, and I'm warning you: share this with anyone else and I will have you banged up for the rest of your natural.'

'Trust me,' Sara said lightly, laughing.

'Sara,' Andrew said, 'I am serious. I probably shouldn't have said anything. In fact I would be in big trouble if it came out I had. I could even have put you in danger. Look, you are not to let on to anyone—*anyone*, Sara—that you know anything about the police enquiries. Keep all this to yourself, for your own sake but for mine as well. We don't know who the murderer is, and whoever it is would naturally be interested to hear anything about our lines of enquiry.'

*   *   *

That evening, Olivia rang.

'This is terribly short notice, but I just wondered if you'd be able to come to supper on Sunday? I've been meaning to ask you for ages and I just thought with this awful thing with Matthew . . . it must have been so awful for you and I'm sure you're fine, but, well, I thought of you on your own and maybe it would be good to get together. Sue and Paul are coming. Would Sunday do? Oh, good. Sorry it's such short notice. Oh, yes, very informal.'

CHAPTER NINE

Dunsmore Park Road was a left turning off Bathwick Hill, and Dunsmore Place, where Olivia lived, was a left turning a few yards further up off that, so that Olivia's house, the end one on the right side, 'afforded a fine view' as an estate agent would have put it, down over the city. A similar row of houses stood opposite on the other side of the road and the two terraces stood facing each other in a state of benign stand-off, separated by the road and surprisingly long front gardens. Just past Olivia's house, the road turned almost ninety degrees back down towards town, giving the house the benefit of a strip of extra garden which ran down the right-hand side and was separated from the back garden by a wooden fence and gate. The disadvantage of having road on two sides was negligible, since the piece of road running along the other side of the high garden wall was a cul-de-sac which ended in a row of lock-up garages used by Olivia and her neighbours. The spur of Dunsmore Place ran back down to meet Bathwick Hill, and contained three pairs of newer semi-detached houses made of reconstituted stone, a car-wash and a few shops.

Sara saw, when Olivia opened the door, that her poise was a little precarious. Her eyes were glistening, and she seemed somehow in a hurry to appear relaxed.

'Thanks so much for coming early,' she said quickly, taking Sara's offering of garden flowers. 'Oh, thank you, how lovely. I thought we could just have a drink before Sue and Paul come. What will you have: red or white? Or there's gin.'

In the upstairs drawing room, wineglasses, bottles and bowls of nibbles were already stationed. This was not quite what Sara had been expecting for a 'very informal' supper, nor did it seem at all like Olivia, who had always seemed more the kind of person who would take you into the kitchen and shake bits and pieces into bowls as you talked. Not that it mattered, for the room was so lovely. It contents were entirely, conspicuously un-Georgian and yet were exactly right in their setting. Olivia was a modernist, and was also, as she explained when Sara remarked on the beautiful uncluttered space, a fiscally determined minimalist as well. Meaning, she said, that she could not afford much of the kind of thing she liked, and she would rather have one glorious pot than three undistinguished ones. And there, standing between the two tall windows, was the glorious pot, a slim-hipped floor piece whose frenzied grey on white patterning looked like the pencil scribbles of a precociously gifted toddler. Showing both originality and restraint, Olivia had not filled it with birch twigs or dried grasses. There were other things too: a pair of Brangwyn lithographs, a wide circular dish of black glass with flecks of yellow swirling in its vortex, and a pair of amazingly comfortable chairs, really leather slings hung between ingeniously balanced steel tubes. The room had the controlled air of a small and exquisite gallery, with Olivia its exacting curator. Every object in it was worth not just looking at but pausing over, and because they were arranged sparely and without ostentation there was a still, almost modest quality about it.

107

Sara felt rather crass about some of her greedier statements at Medlar Cottage, such as the Spode ewer in the window on the landing, that she had crammed with wheat and lavender. She resolved that she would review all that pastoral nonsense, get rid of a few cushions.

As they sat down she noticed that Olivia's gin had brought a pink edge to her high cheekbones, and she looked very tired.

'You must have had a ghastly week,' Sara said gently.

'Oh, I have. It's been really, really dreadful. I can't tell you,' Olivia said. 'The police closed the baths and actually drained the whole place to search it. It's an *appalling* risk to the building. I've been so worried. And I've lost count of the number of calls I've fielded from furious members of the public. And I've had the Tourism Bureau on my back going on about projected loss of revenue, as if I could do anything about it.'

She rubbed her fingers up her forehead and into her hair, as if to shift all the worry out of sight. 'And Coldstreams are losing business, and it turns out their contract with the council isn't clear about compensation. The Assembly Rooms are pretty chaotic too. A lot of the staff double up at the Pump Room, you see, and they're being called away to talk to the police all the time. So we couldn't even keep the costume museum shop staffed on Wednesday and we had five parties in. And then when the police decided to drain the Great Bath, someone had to be on hand to prevent them damaging anything. I had to supervise the whole thing.'

'You're open again to the public though, aren't

you?'

'Oh, yes.' Olivia sighed. 'We opened again yesterday, although it's pretty difficult for everyone. They need a firm hand at the moment. I suppose it's my job to look after morale. Suddenly, I don't feel equal to it.'

Sara, thinking that a firm hand was almost certainly what they would be getting, said, 'You never think, do you, when you read about a murder in the paper, about all this sort of thing: all the disruption, so many people being affected. At the most, you might wonder about the dead person's family. Not their colleagues, or friends, let alone all the other people further down the line somewhere. Did Matthew Sawyer have a family, by the way?'

Tears collected in Olivia's eyes as she nodded. 'Three children, the eldest fourteen. It's *awful*.'

'Were they together? I mean, I saw him on that Friday and he was in the same clothes the next morning, when I found him. He couldn't have been home that night, but he wasn't reported missing. I wondered if perhaps he was divorced.'

Tears were running down Olivia's face as she shook her head. 'No. Annabel had taken the children to her parents for the weekend. They live near Swanage. It was her father's seventy-fifth birthday. Matthew was meant to be going over on the Saturday. There was going to be a big party, marquee, everything.'

She wiped at her face. 'Oh, Sara, I'm sorry. I've got over the main shock, but when I think of them all—what it must have been like for them. And such a pointless death. For no purpose whatsoever.'

She shook her head and swallowed some of her drink. 'But look, tell me about you. Are you all right? You must have had a terrible shock. You know Andrew Poole, don't you? Don't you teach him or something? He came here, you know, last weekend. What does he think?'

Sara was pretty certain that she had never mentioned Andrew to Olivia. Had James been gossiping?

'How on earth do you know that?' she asked, hoping that her bright enquiring smile disguised how defensive the question made her feel.

'He told me himself. At first I thought he meant he knew you just as a name, by reputation, but then he said something about finding the body being a terrific shock for such a sensitive person, for an artist, he said. I believe he used the word fragile. I must say I didn't quite recognise you. But what does he think?'

Sara saw the slightly sardonic look that people who are well into their third gin cannot conceal.

Olivia emptied her glass. 'I mean, do they know who they're looking for?'

'Oh, Andrew doesn't say much about it to me. He comes to play music, he never discusses work.'

Olivia was looking at her calmly.

'I only talked to Bridger, after I . . . you know . . . found him.'

Olivia rose to top up Sara's wineglass and pour herself another gin.

'Never mind. I'm sorry to raise it; it must still be upsetting to think of it. I didn't expect you to know anything particularly. Just generally, I thought you might have heard. Who they might suspect, for instance. *Are* there any suspects yet?'

She paused as she sat down again. 'I'm not just being curious. I have a job to do, and the longer it takes for the police to catch the murderer, the harder it is for me and all the staff. It's *them* I'm sorry for. They all feel under suspicion.'

She gave a rather superior laugh. 'I do myself! I've told Andrew Poole, of course, that I got back here that night at half past ten. I went up to see the night nurse and look in on Dad and then I went straight to bed. But I still feel as though I'm a suspect.'

Sara demurred, searching in her mind for a change of subject.

'How's Sue? She was awfully worried about Paul's job at Fortune Park. Is he all right?'

'Oh, that's all blown over, according to Sue. She does get put out by things; she overreacts. They ticked him off for working on the side, but he's not going to lose his job. They'll be here soon; they're often round here, actually. I suppose you know she's renting in Larkhall now, but she's still got half her things here.'

She paused. 'Sara, I want to ask you something. You may not want to answer; if not, it doesn't matter. But I'd be grateful if you could.'

'What is it?'

'Well, when I asked you about suspects, I was really hoping you might know something, whether—look, I know this sounds awful—whether the police think George might have done it.'

'*George?* Are you serious? You don't think *George* did it? George has been there so long! And he's such an old sweetie.'

Olivia interrupted. 'No, no, of course not. Of course *I* don't think he did it. But I'm worried. I just wondered if . . . you know . . . I mean, the police have spoken to him.'

'Well, they've spoken to everyone, haven't they? I mean, I *suppose* they have by now. He was at the Pump Room that night, wasn't he?'

'Oh, he was, yes. That's why I wondered. Not if he did it, not at all, but if he might have seen something.'

Sara looked blank. Olivia went on, 'George was on door duty at the Pump Room on the night of the thirteenth. He was supposed to leave there before eleven to get over to the Assembly Rooms to lock up. Well, not just supposed to, in fact he did. Then he took the keys back to the office at the Circus. I just wondered if he might have gone back to the Pump Room for something and perhaps seen . . . something.'

'Why? What makes you think he might?'

'Well, it's really just how he's been since it happened. I mean, he got an awful shock of course. We all did, but most of us are getting over it. We have to. George isn't. If anything, he's been getting worse since it happened.'

'What do you mean?'

'Well, if you didn't know him you might think nothing of it. He's obviously trying to go about as usual, but he's preoccupied, very moody, not at all himself. He literally can't look me in the face. Something is definitely bothering him. And I just thought, maybe he saw something. And whatever it is, I wonder if he's told the police.'

'Have *you* mentioned this to the police? Shouldn't you?'

'No, I haven't. Because it might just bring them down on poor old George and, anyway, I may be completely wrong. But George is a great fan of yours. He loves an excuse to talk to you, and I just wondered if he'd mentioned anything. You know, if he was worried about something. To do with the case.'

But Sara hadn't seen George since the day the body was discovered.

'Anyway, shouldn't you just encourage him to tell the police anything? You're acting director now, aren't you? So you could just have a quiet word with him yourself.'

'Well, I can see I'll have to,' Olivia said, a little snappily. 'Although it would have been useful to have your help. But heaven knows, I'm quite capable of dealing with things on my own by now.'

'Oh,' said Sara quickly. 'Was that the door?'

Sue and Paul had gone straight into the kitchen downstairs and when Olivia and Sara joined them, they were already unpacking carrier bags on to the circular table that stood in the bay of the window at the front of the high room. Great swags of blue and white striped material hung at the window and there was a cheery busy Lizzie in the middle of the table. The kitchen end of the room was arranged practically, with wall cupboards on two sides mounted above cupboards and worktops, one of which, running along the back wall of the room, contained the sink. Above it was a large framed print of floppy leeks on a rumpled blue gingham cloth. A smart hob took up most of the worktop opposite, which had been built out from the wall to divide the room and form a three-sided workspace for the cook. A panelled door in the back wall was ajar and through it Sara caught a glimpse of a desk.

'Oh, well done, Sue, he'll love those,' Olivia exclaimed, as Sue unwrapped a dozen or so freesias and began trimming the stems with a kitchen knife.

113

Sue pulled out three or four blooms and laid them down. 'You have these, Livy.' Sniffing the rest she said, 'He loves the scent, especially now he can't get down to the garden. I'll just take them up and say hello. He's got vases upstairs, hasn't he? Shall I take up his whisky as well?'

'No, I'll bring it,' said Olivia. 'He likes me to.' She smiled happily. 'He's an old shocker, really. He'll want you as *well*, not *instead* of me. You can meet the new night nurse. He likes her.' She looked at her watch. 'Let's go up now; he'll be wanting to nebulise in peace in a little while.'

They left the scent of freesias behind them. Paul answered Sara's raised eyebrows.

'Nebulise,' he said slowly, in a hypnotically attractive, faint accent. 'It's a machine called a nebuliser; it opens up the tubes in his lungs so he can breathe. There's a glass tube of liquid you put in, then he has to put this mouthpiece in his mouth and breathe in. It doesn't take long but the machine is very noisy.'

As he spoke he made his way across the room and through the panelled door. He reappeared a moment later with a small vase in the shape of a classical urn. The body was a rich deep pink colour and the little gilt handles on each side were worn to a dull gold. Sara perched on a stool, watching him from the dining room side of the hob worktop.

'It doesn't sound very nice. How often does he have to do that?'

'Every four hours or so. He'd be dead without it.'

'Poor him. Poor Olivia.'

He placed the flowers in the vase where they looked natural and perfect.

'What a lovely vase.'

114

Paul smiled, pleased that she had noticed. 'French. Late eighteenth century. Probably made between 1780 and 1795. I deal a bit in antiques, actually. French and English.'

He tidied away the freesia stems, discarding also the rubber bands, leaves and wet cellophane that Sue had left. The simplicity of his movements, the long hands, the choice of absolutely the right vase and the unfussed, pleasing result reminded Sara of James. Another artist. And a heterosexual one with a divine bottom, she thought, as Paul turned to the sink to put water in the vase. She finished her drink, reminding herself that he was actually attached to someone else, and, moreover, to a twenty-fourish, blonde fitness instructor next to whose body hers would probably look like a bag of spanners. And don't forget, antiques or no antiques, that he's a waiter, the inner voice warned, and that you're a snob. And a sick old woman, it whispered, working out that if Paul were about thirty, that would make him six years younger than she was.

'Is that Olivia's study in there?' she asked, nodding towards the panelled door.

'Oh, yes,' he said, a little surprised. 'Haven't you been here before? Sorry, I tend to treat the place as home.' He paused. 'Come and have a little look. Olivia's got some wonderful things. Not hers, of course, the museum's; she does quite a bit of work here. She won't mind, she likes people to see. If you get her started, she'll keep you there all evening.'

Feeling a little intrusive, Sara followed Paul into the room. Curtains were drawn across the French windows.

115

'It's for the light levels,' Paul said. 'She often has textiles here. She's cataloguing some shoes at the moment. Here.'

He stepped over to the desk where a deep-sided grey cardboard box sat among piles of papers. He lifted the lid and carefully pulled back leaves of tissue paper. 'Acid-free box and paper. Look. But don't breathe over them, or touch them. Moisture, you see. Finger acid.'

Sara stepped forward and peeped in as if she were leaning into the pram of a sleeping baby. In the box, standing upright, was a pair of pale green silk shoes with tie fastenings of fragile, frothy ribbon.

'Also late eighteenth century. English,' Paul said. The heels were sharp and high and the toes narrowed to an agonising point, but it was the tiny scale of the feet they had been made to fit that struck Sara most. She thought of her own feet, not as now in her beloved Missoni sandals, but in huge cushioned trainers and thick white socks, pounding along her five-mile circuit round the lanes of St Catherine's Valley. The owner of these shoes, a teetering doll, might have been just about able to mince once or twice round Sydney Gardens before collapsing elegantly at tea and going home in a sedan chair. She looked at the shoes in silence, wondering if their owner had died old or young. The last time she had worn these shoes, did she know it was going to be the last? Or had she just heaved them off her feet with a sigh, after stepping it out all evening at the Assembly Rooms in a matching pale green silk gown, with no thoughts in her head but relief for her pinched toes and the next day's morning calls? Now the shoes in which

116

she had danced her quadrilles and cotillions, leaving behind the stain of her heels, were simply historically interesting, ultimately more memorable than their owner. But the greatest eloquence of empty shoes, Sara thought, is to tell us, as if we didn't know, that all it comes down to in the end is the running of trivial errands.

Paul carefully wrapped the tissue over the shoes and replaced the lid. Sara followed him back out to the kitchen and went back to her stool while he opened the fridge in search of another bottle of wine. He found a whole poached salmon on a platter. He took it out, peered at it and made an irritated noise with his tongue. 'Chilled solid! What is she thinking of? It should have been out of there an hour ago. *Chilled* fish—just *awful*. There is no flavour in fish *chilled* like that.'

He looked as if he might spit on it. Was he going to throw a chef's tantrum? No, he was fetching things from cupboards. He was going to throw egg yolks in a bowl and did so, separating them flamboyantly with one hand, showing off.

'Mayonnaise?' asked Sara.

'No, *sauce rémoulade*,' he said, Frenchly.

'Oh, good,' said Sara, not flinching. 'That's the one with capers, gherkins and parsley, isn't it? Shall I chop? Are you using anchovy essence or mustard, or both?'

He was impressed, as she intended him to be, and rewarded her with a look of amused surprise and a smile which revealed annoyingly lovely teeth. He fetched her a chopping board and, unwrapping a length of canvas on the worktop, selected the smallest knife from the roll.

'You can use this. Be careful, it's very sharp.'

117

An intimacy surrounds any two people preparing food that will end up in the same dish, and Olivia's reappearance a few minutes later, albeit in her own kitchen, was felt fleetingly by all of them to be an intrusion. She gave a broadminded smile at Sara and Paul's communion over the chopping board.

'I showed Sara the shoes, Olivia,' Paul said. 'You don't mind, do you?'

'No, that's fine,' Olivia said. 'Since you know how to handle them. Aren't they wonderful?'

'Lovely.' Sara smiled. Olivia began to lay the table around Sue, who had followed her in and was sitting languorously eating olives. Sara looked up, feeling guilty even for her purely mental piracy of Sue's man, and deftly sliced the top off her finger.

'Bugger it! Ow! Oh, *shit*. Sorry!' she said, trying not to drip blood into the little pile of chopped parsley. She slipped clumsily off the stool and looked round wildly for kitchen paper, shoving her free hand into the pockets of her dress for a handkerchief, simultaneously reassuring everyone that it was a stupid and unimportant scratch and realising that it was her fingering hand and that if she had removed the whole finger pad it would affect her playing. Oh, God, couldn't *somebody* find her a handkerchief? She was aware suddenly of Paul's long, slow-moving hands taking hold of her wrists. He gently removed her left hand from the grip of her right and without inspecting it, wrapped a white tea towel round it. He led her, still by the wrists, over to the sink where the cold tap was already running, pulled the hurt finger under its flow and held it there.

'Take a few deep breaths,' he said quietly.

She did as she was told, and after a minute the

heat in the throbbing finger subsided into an icy anaesthesia. She said brightly, 'I'm fine. It's fine now, thanks.' Paul released his hold on her wrist and stood, watching.

'It *was* sharp, wasn't it?'

'I warned you.'

She turned the finger slowly under the water. She would lose a flap of skin, that was all. She apologised again, pulling her hand away to dry it. Immediately all the pain flooded back into the cut. Blood welled out and plopped into the sink.

'Keep it there,' Paul ordered, drawing her hand back under the rod of water whining from the tap. 'You'll have to keep it there a while, until it runs clear.'

'I'll get a plaster,' said Sue, who had come over from the table and was bending into a drawer.

'It needs a proper bandage,' Paul said. Sue came round and stood on the other side of Sara, staring at the finger dangling under the fall of water.

'No, a plaster,' she said. 'A plaster would be better.'

Sara was aware of a hissing noise which was coming from between Paul's lips.

'And *I* say that it needs a proper bandage,' he said slowly.

Olivia had a green plastic first-aid box open on the worktop. 'Here's a bit of gauze. If you fold it it can go under one of these big plasters,' she said, hitting on the compromise. Sue and Paul exchanged a look over Sara's head that made her want to duck.

'I can do it,' Sara said, hoping to pre-empt any squabble over the privilege, but succumbing easily to Paul's insistence that he could do it better than

119

she would herself.

At supper it was a relief when the conversation turned from interesting injuries and recommended treatments to the now mundane topic of the murder. Sara endured the by now tedious trading of hypotheses and counter-hypotheses, which was always accompanied by the reiterating of everyone's alibis. It was strange how people felt the need to do that. Almost everyone she had spoken to had, sooner rather than later, and unprompted, delivered the statement that exonerated them personally from all suspicion. 'Well, of course *I* . . .' was usually how it started. Sue, well, of course, had left the Assembly Rooms that night at a quarter to eight and arrived nearly fifteen minutes late for her late shift at the health club. She had locked up just after eleven and then gone over to Paul's place, a bedsit in the staff quarters in the grounds of Fortune Park, where she was staying, as she usually did, for the weekend.

'I've got my place in Larkhall now, but I'm not usually there at weekends,' she said. 'It's Cecily's house and I'm more the lodger, only she's having this thing with this married man.' She sighed. 'So it's agreed, I make myself scarce at the weekend. Stupid, that, really, I think. Never works out, does it? I don't think so, anyway.'

She looked at Paul, who appeared not to be listening. 'Anyway, he's there at the weekend, usually. Sometimes just for an afternoon, sometimes longer. Suits me to keep away, anyway.'

She smiled winningly at Paul. 'Suits *us*, doesn't it?' Paul gave a faint smile. 'Even with our shifts. There's always a bit of time together. We were both working that night, I remember. Paul got in just before one, didn't you?'

He nodded. 'We finished early in the Assembly Rooms so I went over to help with the desserts at the Pump Room. I left to come home just after eleven.'

'But it's only about half an hour out to Fortune Park, isn't it?' Sara asked.

'Oh, yes, by car it is. But I take my bike in the summer. It's an hour and three-quarters, then.'

So that's how he got that butt.

Sue was talking again. 'Bad enough in the summer sometimes, though, isn't it? You got soaked that night; your hair was wet. It *poured*, didn't it?'

Olivia gave Paul a surreptitious coded glance at which he rose obediently and refilled glasses, while she left the table and returned with an overcrowded cheeseboard. She had obviously briefed him beforehand to look after people's glasses, which seemed a little intense for a supper party for four people. Or perhaps he was just accustomed to playing host for her. He had certainly known where everything was kept in the kitchen cupboards, and had turned out the *sauce rémoulade* and some fairly ritzy salads to go with the salmon in the same mesmerising way that James had worked in Sara's own kitchen. As they picked at the cheese Olivia still seemed anxious and Sue lapsed into silence. It was as if Paul were the holder of initiative for the whole household. He was the source of energy, Sara supposed, a kind of battery, without which the other two would simply run down and stop. Across the table Sara was able to look properly at him. His hair fell in thick brown skeins over his head and was so long Sara guessed that he had to tie it back for work. He had a long nose of interesting Gallic near-ugliness, but his face was dominated by his extraordinary green, almost unkind eyes. He looked back at her. They were feral; Sara was live meat, and he was considering whether to bite her in half now or play with her for a bit first and bite her in half later. She was convinced that he knew precisely the effect he was having on her, including the moments following the cutting of her finger when in the confusion of pain, embarrassment, fright and mess, there had been a fragment of joy because he was touching her with such care. He was quite unreasonably sexy. We are simply not designed to withstand such men, Sara thought, looking over at Sue.

How did she cope? She certainly worked hard to look the way she did. Her skin, suspiciously golden against her white T-shirt, looked marinaded and lightly oiled, ready for grilling. She wore delicate gold jewellery: a tiny chain with a minute something on it—possibly an 'S'—and three or four meagre rings. Like her blondeness, her jewellery was pretty and feminine in a High Street way, but her shiny health would have suited bold, ethnic things, bright enamelled bangles or a heavy beaded collar. Her thin, strong body was a model of aerobics-moulded loveliness, the contours of her pared-down haunches looking convincingly Californian for a girl from Corsham. But all her strength was physical, concentrated in her confident muscles; she conveyed no other power. It was as though her will were an injured cat hiding in a deserted building. Her black eyes were windows with broken panes. What at first had seemed in her to be mental vacancy was really dereliction.

Olivia's over-organised menu moved on smoothly to the finale of strawberry pavlova. She had worked hard for them. Sara wondered why she had gone to the trouble of inviting her at all, since she was obviously so tired and things at work were clearly more than enough for her. Was it really a concern for Sara's well-being? Olivia had not really enquired about her beyond what politeness dictated. And she was surely too sophisticated to harbour any cosy ambitions to 'get the young people together', not that Sara regretted that she had. Over coffee in the beautiful drawing room, she concluded that perhaps Olivia was simply responding to an instinct to gather people round her after the outrage that had occurred in their midst.

Remembering how tired Olivia had seemed, Sara rose to leave before eleven. She noticed that Sue and Olivia, coming downstairs to see her off, brought the used coffee cups with them, keen to have done with the clearing up and have the evening over. They said goodbye at the front door and turned back towards the kitchen. But Paul walked with her down the path, into the cool, private peace of the summer night. Sara was deliciously aware of him close behind her, near enough for his arms to reach round her waist, for him to bend his head to brush his lips across the back of her neck.

'Well, goodnight. Thank you for looking after my finger,' she said, turning.

Paul took her hand as if to check the bandage, then turned it over gently and kissed it.

'No fee,' he said, not letting go.

Sara looked at him, knowing that the

powerlessness of her hand in his was signalling to him her willingness to succumb. He gave her fingers the merest, gentlest squeeze and kissed her hand again lightly, this time for much longer.

'In fact, I think you might benefit from another consultation.'

Sara withdrew her hand.

'Oh, I'm sure you'd have *much* too long a waiting list,' she said, rather loudly. 'Goodnight, Paul.'

*   *   *

By the time she reached home, Sara was feeling not just slight triumph at having withstood Paul, but also a warm self-congratulation that the shock of Matthew Sawyer's death was ebbing peaceably out of her life. So it was a new shock to discover that the one message on her answering machine was from Tom in Brussels, saying, in a voice at first barely recognisable as his, that he was catching the first flight back in the morning. James had been arrested.

CHAPTER TEN

Sara parked atrociously in the forecourt and barged into the police station in Manvers Street, ready to be as loud, insistent and abusive as was necessary to get hold of Andrew and put him right about the outrage, the *ludicrousness* of James's arrest. The station constable rolled amiably over to the glass partition and gave Sara a smile of such naked pleasantness that she faltered at once. They must train them to look like jolly uncles, she thought wildly; underneath he's a corrupt little bastard.

'Good evening, madam. That your car just now? I believe you've left your headlights on. Now, what can I do for you?' he asked, still smiling. It was no use. Every molecule that went to make up the well-brought-up and socially effective Sara Selkirk understood that if someone is nice to you, you have to be nice back.

'My friend, I have a friend who's here, he's being kept here, there's some sort of mistake. James Ballantyne. I *must* see him. No, wait, is Chief Inspector Poole here? Can I see him? Andrew Poole? Please, it's very important. There's been a mistake.' Inwardly, another Sara Selkirk, a mentally dislodged fishwife, was screaming, *You bastards, you've got my poor sweet friend here; let him go, give me back my friend who has done nothing wrong. Oh, how dare you, you idiots, you bastards . . .*

The station constable shimmied off cheerfully, leaving Sara to wait in the faggy wood-panelled lobby. Time passed, punctuated by the occasional exchange of voices in the office behind the partition and the sounds of doors and feet. Then the station constable was back, beaming through the glass.

'Sorry to have kept you waiting.'

She heard the sound of a door being unlocked from the far side of the lobby and sprang up. So it had been easy after all. Obviously, just a misunderstanding. James was about to step through the door, sheepish, grateful and glad to be

125

going home. Her relieved smile fell when Andrew appeared. Under the strip lighting of the lobby his face had a pitted, buttery pallor and Sara reflected with dismay that she probably looked the same to him.

'Mr Ballantyne has been told that you are here. He has been informed, however, that you won't be able to see him this evening. I'm sorry, Sara, there's no more I can do.'

'Andrew? What are you *saying*? You've got to let him go! Why is he here anyway? You've made a mistake! Why don't you just let him go?'

'Sara, Mr Ballantyne has been questioned about a serious matter. Yes, to do with the Matthew Sawyer case. No, I can't tell you what. He is being held overnight and will be questioned further in the morning. His, well, partner—is that what he is?— will be here in the morning and legal representation is being arranged. He can't be allowed to see anyone tonight.'

Sara was open-mouthed. 'I don't believe I'm hearing this. What's all this sudden Mr Ballantyne claptrap, Andrew? This is James we're talking about here, Andrew, *James*. My friend. You've *met* him. You *know* he hasn't done anything. Come on, he's a pianist, a musician, not a murderer. Look, I want to see him. I'm here to take him home.'

Andrew sighed with exasperation. 'Sara, please try to get this straight. I'm doing you a favour even telling you this much. In ordinary circumstances the officer here would just have been sent to tell you to go home and come back in the morning. But I'm telling you myself. I'm sorry, but you can't see James tonight.'

'But why not? I *want* to see him! You're not

listening—'

Andrew butted in angrily. 'Christ, Sara, will *you* just listen! It makes no difference that he's your friend, *or* a musician. If he's guilty, I don't care if he's Herbert von bloody Karajan. I'm going for a conviction in this case, and I don't give a damn if your precious friend has to put up with a night in the cells in the process. You may like to know that there is reason to suspect that he has already lied to the police.'

'My God,' Sara said, her voice low with venom, 'I don't believe this. Can't you see how wrong you are? You're just *wrong*! You're being a fool. An absolute *fool*. And I'd been thinking you really were . . . *something*. I was thinking, poor Andrew, wasted like that, all that creativity, all that music, wasted in a job like that. And you understand *nothing*. I've been so stupid. You're just—'

'Yeah, I'm just a big, nasty old policeman, is that it?' Andrew said bitterly. 'Well, I'm sorry to disappoint you. Go home, Sara. Go home. I have work to do. Goodnight.'

Sara drove miserably to Camden Crescent, her head exploding with the discovery of Andrew's brainless, mistaken unreasonableness and his I Am a Hofficer of the Law attitude. She parked outside the flat. The whole of Number 11 was in darkness. For no very sound reason this infuriated her further. She wondered how long James had been in police custody. He must have been allowed to make the telephone call to Tom some time this evening, presumably quite late, if Tom had not been contacted in time to catch the last flight. He was an hour ahead in Brussels anyway of course, which did not help. It was now half past twelve.

127

The whole night lay ahead and she could do nothing for James until the morning. She drove home.

* * *

Tom kissed Sara drily on both cheeks and led her to a bench in the lobby of the police station. Outside it was a golden morning but the fluorescent tubes on the ceiling had not been switched off and still emitted a sick blue film of light that was so perturbing it was almost a noise.

'I got here at seven,' he said to Sara. 'James didn't even ring me till yesterday evening. They'd questioned him all yesterday afternoon with the duty solicitor there. I've got hold of someone from Thrings and Long who'll be here at nine. Their main criminal cases chap. They can't question him any more before then. But they won't let me see him, even briefly.'

'But why have they got him here in the first place?' Sara said. 'I just don't see why he's here at all. What's he supposed to have done?'

Tom gave a slow sigh. 'It's his own fault. I still don't really know why, but he gave a false alibi for Friday the thirteenth. He told the police I rang him at about half past eleven and that we chatted for nearly half an hour.'

He shook his head. 'I didn't. And if he'd stopped to think about it even for a second he'd have realised how stupid it was to say I had. The police rang me to verify it. And I've made a statement.' He gestured helplessly. 'I'm a lawyer, for God's sake. I can't possibly, *possibly* give false information to the police, in any circumstances. Even these,' he

128

said, before adding hopelessly, 'I don't think James quite understands that, even now.'

'What a crazy thing for him to do. I mean, even if you had lied for him, they could easily check to see if the call had been made, couldn't they? I don't get it at all.'

'Of course they could. No, I don't get it either. And nor do the police, obviously. When they pressed him about it, he came up with some other story about looking in on a friend after he left the Pump Room. Wouldn't elaborate. He can be so stubborn. And then later on he backtracked again and now says he went straight home and was there alone from eleven thirty onwards. Perhaps we'll find out more when the lawyer gets here. But I don't understand any of it—it's a mess.'

'What can I do? Is there anything?'

Tom looked at her despondently. 'You are so sweet. But no, apart from magicking an alibi out of the air, no, not really. There's nothing. You were sweet to come, but look, you go now. I'll ring you later.'

Sara left the police station, crossed the road and wandered hopelessly along Henry Street with nowhere to go. She found herself outside Marks and Spencer, went in and picked up a basket, not sure what she was doing there but dimly aware that if she was going to do some unnecessary shopping then the food department was a better place than many in which to do it. In fact she was quite hungry, not having bothered with breakfast, and a big, reliable egg and bacon sandwich might help her to think.

CHAPTER ELEVEN

The possibility did not occur to her until a little later, and of course it couldn't have been the sandwich that did it. But driving out of town up over the top of Lansdown to avoid the Monday traffic, she had seen it and remembered. Graham Xavier's memorial service at St Michael's. And as she waited for the lights to change, she also remembered how, at the end of that evening at the Pump Room, she had left James drinking mournfully on his own. In truth, she had been unwilling to see how upset he was. Perhaps now, she thought, pulling over to park, she could be of some use to him.

She looked up towards the church. It stood on the very top of Lansdown Hill, at the fork where Lansdown Road led off on the left towards an undeclared little Vatican of private schools, tennis clubs and depressing houses in prosperous taste, and where Richmond Road on the right rose towards Charlcombe, almost as well-to-do but, by virtue of its muddy lanes and airy views, rather less stupefyingly nice. The church façade was stained a deep Victorian black from the cars and buses which coughed up the hill before dropping a gear, almost at the foot of the church steps, and burning off to the left or right, but above the door the stone paled and the high pointing spire was light against the clean sky.

Inside the door, almost a third of the nave had been sectioned off and carpeted in bright blue and looked, at first glance, like an underfunded

130

kindergarten. Floor mats, probably useful for prayer and meditation as well as for the Mothers' Union yoga, were stacked in a corner. Three trestle tables of papier-mâché models and children's paintings, in which bearded men and rainbows featured prominently, lined one side. On the other, posters depicting the smiling beneficiaries of various Third World 'projects' spoke of outreach and global community. Everywhere, display boards bawled about the relevance and dynamism of the Church today and invited everyone, but everyone, to get to know their vicar and the pastoral team, whose scrupulously informal portrait photographs grinned out in a collective rictus of quite terrifying Christian welcome.

Sara escaped swiftly through the glazed partition doors into the proper gloomy church where at least she could feel unworthy in peace. But it was not empty; she made out a dark, rather solid female figure near the altar, deadheading the flower arrangement next to the pulpit steps. The grey-haired woman half turned round from the flowers, gave a faint nod and smile in Sara's direction, and turned back. Sara hoped the woman would carry on ignoring her, because although she wasn't at all sure exactly what she was looking for here, she knew it wasn't one of the parish flower team.

'I'm, er . . . just looking,' Sara said, moving towards one of the stained-glass windows.

The woman was concentrating on the flowers. 'What? Oh, yes, do. You carry on.'

After a moment she asked, without turning round, 'Are you looking for anything in particular?'

'Well, I was wondering,' Sara went on. 'I mean, it's nothing *particular*. I think there was a memorial

131

service here ten days ago, for Graham Xavier.'

'Oh, yes, I remember,' the woman said. She stepped back from the altar step and looked at the arrangement. 'How does that look to you? Have I gone and made it all uneven on the left?'

'No, it's fine. They're lovely. Do you, er . . . do all the flowers?'

The woman burst out laughing, and came towards Sara, reaching out her hand. 'No, I just get told off for fiddling with them. I'm the vicar. Maggie. How do you do. I took Graham's service. Were you there?'

'No, I didn't know him. But a friend of mine did, and this friend, well, he couldn't make it to the service and, I'm not sure, I think he may have come here later on, on the same night. And I need to know if he did. Actually'—Sara looked hard at Maggie, unable to predict the effect of her next words—'he's sort of in trouble. It's the police who need to know.'

Maggie raised her eyebrows and nodded. 'Really? Well, if you're not in a hurry, come on over to the vicarage, and I'll see if I can help.'

*   *   *

Both Maggie's instant coffee and study were hideous, but within ten minutes Sara was so dazed with gratitude that she had no spare capacity to notice either.

'No, I didn't really *see* anyone in the church that night.'

They were sitting in shabby chairs in a slightly damp room so stuffed with papers and books that there was hardly enough room for their feet.

132

'But I heard someone. It was my turn to lock up. I was a bit late going over, nearly quarter past midnight. I always go in through the vestry and through the church, and lock the front door from inside. That way I can see if anyone's kipped down in the front.'

'But could you tell who it was? I mean, was it someone's voice? What did you hear?'

Maggie shook her head and laughed. 'Some people would have freaked out. I had just got to the outside door leading into the vestry when I heard the piano. The one at the back of the church. It's a grand, terribly out of tune though.'

'What did you do?'

'Well, my first reaction was to barge in and stop it, thinking it was kids or something bashing about on it. Then I realised it was being played properly, so I slipped into the vestry very quietly, because then I thought, you see, that it must be our organist practising something for Sunday, and I didn't want to disturb him. And then I realised it couldn't be our organist, not in a million years.'

'Why not?' Sara sipped some of her acrid coffee from the thick stoneware mug with IONA etched on it in lumpy letters.

'Well, I'm no musician, but the playing was just too *good*. Our Rodger could never play like that, bless him. And it was *what* was being played. Rodger's a traditionalist you see, even Lord of the Dance raises his blood pressure. And this, well, this was just about every song from *Cabaret*.'

'You're sure? What did you do?'

'Oh, I'm quite sure, I saw the film four times. Anyway, I opened the door from the vestry into the church, really quietly. There were lights on, but you

133

can't see the piano from there. And then I'm very glad to say that something stopped me from barging in. I just listened for a bit and then I remembered something from the service. One of Graham's friends had talked about how he'd always been crazy about Liza Minnelli.'

Sara hardly dared breathe.

Maggie went on, her voice very quiet. 'Then that really sad one started, and it was almost like she was there. And I remembered the words: *"All the odds are right in my favour, something's bound to begin, Maybe this time, maybe this time, maybe this time I'll win."* Remember?'

Sara nodded and Maggie looked up.

'I'm no musician, but I could feel the words, it was almost like the piano speaking. And I reckoned that whoever it was, it was someone who had something to say, something for Graham. There was such longing in it. I didn't want to interrupt, so I just waited. Then when it stopped there was a little pause, and then I heard footsteps going back down the aisle to the front door. So I stepped into the church and I saw the back view of a man. Dark hair, with prominent ears. Not tall, and in a white jacket and black trousers. He didn't see me.'

'Maggie, *thank* you. I can't tell you, you're a saviour. Will you come and tell this to the police?'

'Well, I will, of course,' Maggie said, rising with a sigh. She beamed at Sara. 'But *I'm* not the saviour, actually. I do hope you'll come again. We're open on Sundays.'

CHAPTER TWELVE

She had not planned to go to the Pump Room. But the woman in the dry cleaners was saying that Sara's dress would not be back until after five o'clock. Surely, Sara protested, Wednesday was Wednesday whatever the time, and they had said Wednesday. Oh, but they had meant after five. It was not yet half past three.

'Haven't you any shopping you could do?' the woman asked patronisingly, as if Sara were barely fit to be at large and might be incapable of filling an hour and a half without guidance.

She did not much feel like shopping, so when she arrived at the Pump Room an hour later and in need of tea she had acquired only an oversized white cashmere jersey (half price), some huge, fresh langoustines (very slimming), a Cadillac pink lipstick (to go with the jersey) and three copies of the *Big Issue* (guilt). As she entered she could hear above the tinkle of teaspoons the trio on the platform, swinging laboriously through a medley of airs from Gilbert and Sullivan. George was stationed on his high stool just inside the doorway.

' 'Ello, my darling,' he said, routinely lascivious. 'You'll have a bit of a wait today, I'm afraid.'

Sara looked in dismay as a party of two dozen or so Japanese tourists were ushered in past the queue and took their pre-booked places, occupying nearly half the seats in the room. Four waiters strode back and forth around the choreography of small, dark, nodding heads, as jackets and cameras were settled on chair backs, tablecloths were fingered and the flowers pointed out as real. Plates arrived. Cups, saucers, spoons, knives and napkins followed, as did tea, milk, jam, scones, sugar and cream. After several trips to each table, the waiting staff eventually left the tourists furnished with all the arcane trappings of the English Cream Tea ceremony. Except the instructions. A little tentative nibbling began amid much sniffing of the cream and peering into teapots. Finally, an elderly lady recognised the obvious link with cappuccino and, showing some leadership, planted a healthy dollop of thick cream in her cup, where it floated greasily on the surface of her tea. Undeterred, she lifted her cup. The others followed, and soon they were all sipping appreciatively at their frothing teacups, leaving moustaches of clotted cream on their upper lips and nodding happily in time to the 'Lord High Executioner's Song' from *The Mikado*.

'Aw, would you look at that, Gawd love 'em,' George said. He looked kindly at Sara. 'Looking for a cup of tea? Look, I'm just off on my break, soon as Jackie comes. You fancy a cup with me up the back? It's not very smart, but I won't charge you too much.'

When Jackie arrived to take George's place a minute later, she followed him with her bags as he swung through the throng of visitors entering and leaving by the revolving door of the Pump Room. Between here and the entrance to the Roman Baths further along was a wide, wood-panelled corridor with a slippery floor, tiled in a bold black and white geometric pattern. On one side large windows looked out on to Abbey Churchyard. To the right was a solid wall, on the other side of which was the Ladies and beyond that the Concert

136

Room, where visitors queued and bought tickets for the Roman Baths. What George meant by up the back was a mystery.

Suddenly, he broke into a run. Still following him, Sara looked ahead towards Colin who, on duty by the Roman Baths door, had a young girl by the shoulder. She was dressed in a dishrag of a skirt with black leggings, at least two T-shirts, and a jumper knitted out of ends of wool. Her nose was pierced in four places and her dreadlocks were orange. A skinny dog trembled on the end of a string tied to her wrist and a clapped-out-looking baby dribbled into a sling round her neck. She was shouting in a pathetic mixture of pleading and invective, 'Aw, don't give me this, man!' followed by, 'Uptight bastards, I just want to change my bloody kid, don't I, you fucking uptight bastards!' Young Colin, agitated and unhappy, was trying unsuccessfully to placate the girl.

But George was an old hand. He had attended every Interface with the General Public in-service training course that the council had ever run in his thirty-three years of employment and in a matter of seconds he summoned everything he had ever learned on the subject of Confrontation Management, and ignored every word. He shoved his way between the girl and Colin and thrust his jaw in her face.

'*Right*! Right, Colin, if you would just step outside and hold the door open, please,' he said, without taking his eyes off the girl. Colin obeyed. George grabbed the barking dog by the jaw, silencing it, and swung it round so that its muzzle was pointing towards the door.

'Now, young lady, perhaps you'd like to take

your canine friend and your offspring off the premises?' He shoved the dog forward. The dog squealed as it was propelled through the door and the girl stumbled after, protesting, very nearly falling, still attached to the string. George sauntered out after them. The busker playing his bagpipes by the railings stopped as the knot of people around him turned to watch the unscheduled performance. On the pavement the girl turned, her mouth twisted to deliver another stream of abuse, but George got in first.

'Get right out of here, you piece of filth. We don't welcome your sort of scum in here. So you take your stinking baby and your stinking dog out of here. Now. You hear me? And don't come back, or I'll get the police.' The girl was crying quietly as she walked away, her lips stroking the top of the baby's downy, impassive head. The piper struck up with 'Show Me the Way to go Home' and a wave of laughter rose from the crowd. Change was rattling into the busker's hat as George marched back inside, rubbing his hands.

'Can't stand those filthy junkies,' he said affably. He turned to Sara. 'Come along then, I'm gasping for me tea.'

George, old George, dear old George was ugly with petty triumph, cheered and revitalised by bullying that sad creature out on to the street. Considering the matter satisfactorily closed, he went on ahead to the foot of a tiny staircase, its entrance cut out of the panelling on the corridor wall between the Roman Baths and the Pump Room doors. Sara followed silently. She had never noticed the little door before. George went up first, explaining that the stairs led up to the gallery of the

138

Concert Room, where the musicians used to play. About halfway up, the stairs branched out to the left and another four steep steps led into a room of the same length and width as the corridor below. She had never even known the room was there. Both it and the contents had a forgotten air; presumably once a too-long, too-narrow, inconvenient office, it had been abandoned and then quietly, unofficially requisitioned as a den for the museum attendants. There were no windows; the room was lit by fluorescent strip lights hung from the ceiling and one old anglepoise lamp. In a far corner was a deep sink with one tap and no draining board, and the floor was covered with a red carpet that had had odd rectangles cut out of it here and there, obviously to fit round long-departed office furniture. Pubic-looking underlay curled indecently from the edges. There was a notice-board studded with faded holiday postcards, cartoon cuttings, a few typed lists and a dusty First Aid notice. The room was slightly chilly, despite an ancient electric fire with a brown, illegal-looking flex, around which were grouped various small tables on which lay ashtrays, scattered newspapers and a Bush radio, and an assortment of chairs looking like squatting fugitives from the council's office refurbishments of yesteryear. George, after a moment's hesitation, offered Sara what he apparently considered the best chair. It had a modernistic frame of chrome tubing that had been bent into a series of twisting shapes, resulting in an oval base to which the circular seat and curved arms were attached by a single steel stem. Sara discovered, sitting down, that whoever sat on it bobbed idiotically every time any weight was

139

shifted. The seat was upholstered in a greyish lime herringbone material, probably of interest to a sixties' textiles design historian but best overlooked by anyone else.

She was still burning at the humiliation of the girl with the baby.

'Was she doing any harm, George? Babies have got to be changed, after all,' she ventured, bouncing in her chair. 'Looking revolting doesn't make you a bad mother, necessarily, does it? We can't all be Jane Asher.'

George turned round from the tray where the kettle and teapot sat among the mugs, spoons and biscuits on a small table whose surface was whirled with ringed stains.

'Bloody junkie. Nipping into the Ladies to shoot up. I hate them. It's the ones with kids that really makes me wild. What's she doing with a baby? You think she'll be looking after it properly?'

He brought tea, offered her biscuits out of the packet, and stirred two sugars into his mug before sitting down on a grubby Ercol chair with brown paisley stretch covers.

'My own daughter turned into one of them. First she's off to Glastonbury; that's fine, we said, just don't get into anything. That was it. She's into the lot. Goes off doing that travelling, gone over four months, then rings up. In a mess, broke, boyfriend gone off, wants to come home.'

'How old was she?'

'Nineteen, at that time. Working at BHS before that. Did a lot of dancing, ballet and tap. Twenty-four now. Well, I wasn't having her back home. Her mum's soft, forgave her and that. Gave her money and all sorts.'

140

'Is she all right now?'

'No, she's ruined herself. Can't get a job of course. She's got MS now; all to do with that drugs nonsense. Oh, she says, there's no connection, none at all, but you tell me, a healthy girl, medals for dancing, goes off, gets into all the drugs and boom, two years later she's falling about all over the place and she's got MS. Can't tell me there's no link. I won't have her home. She did it to herself.'

He slurped at his tea and sighed. 'I needed that. Yours all right?'

'George, that's terrible. Five years later, and she's ill, and you haven't forgiven her for four silly months?'

'That's what the wife says. You're all soft,' he said breezily. 'How's your cup?'

In silence he topped up their mugs from the dull metal teapot. The sounds of buskers rose from Abbey Churchyard. Sara was uncomfortable, not at the thought of their remoteness from the hub of people below them, nor even the slightly sinister hideousness of the room, but because she suddenly knew herself to be sharing it with a stranger. A stranger, she recalled, who was a prime suspect in a murder case. In a slight panic, she cast around in conversation looking for the George she knew.

'Thanks. So, are things getting back to normal for you now? Open again, busy?'

'You could say so.' He took another biscuit. 'Quieter at night. We've had cancellations right, left and centre for the evening functions. Can't say I'm sorry. We never used to have that many, years ago. Toga parties, of course. Different now.'

Suddenly he looked tired. He must be over sixty, Sara thought.

'What was Matthew Sawyer like to work for?' she asked. 'It must be hard for you, whatever he was like, to have him killed like that,' she added.

'He was better than some. I've seen them come and go, of course.' He looked hard at her. 'The ones I can't stand, they're the ones comes in and tells me what's what before they've been here ten minutes. I've been here longer than they've been born, some of them. Mr Sawyer was one of them.'

He dunked a biscuit and let it collapse into his mouth like a sugary avalanche. 'Trying to prove himself. Rubbed certain people up the wrong way.'

He swallowed. 'To tell you the truth, he was on my back. Giving me some hassle. Mind you, don't you think *my* conscience isn't clear. As a matter of fact I'm the only one with witnesses. I left here at ten to eleven the night he was killed, and there were people who saw me go. Mr Sawyer says he'll lock up the Pump Room, and will I go over and do the Assembly Rooms. So off I go, locks up just before quarter past, take the keys to the safe at the Circus and I'm off home. Get there at twenty to twelve.'

'But what sort of hassle?' Sara asked. George ignored the question and leaned forward.

'Not that anybody can back me up on that, strictly speaking. My missus had gone to bed when I got back, she was asleep. So I took a bit of an opportunity, know what I mean? Stayed up watching a video. You know?'

He gave her a watery look. 'Not the sort of video the missus would care for. She's not a broadminded woman. She woke up when I went up later, quarter to one, and she says, "What time is it?" and I says to her, "It's the usual time, time I was in bed; go back to sleep." So when the police come round and ask her when I got home she says usual time, half eleven or just after.'

Sara did not wish to dwell on the subject.

'I just left it, you see? Because I *was* home by the usual time, see? Saves hassle.' He gave a guilty snigger.

'But what sort of hassle were you getting from Matthew Sawyer? He hadn't been here all that long, had he?'

George breathed in slowly and sighed. In the few seconds this took, his features fell a little and she saw that in repose he had the face of a troubled tortoise.

'I suppose I don't mind telling you. You're not really staff, are you? Won't make no difference telling you. See that notice-board? See where there's a clean patch? Well, there was an important sheet of paper there one time, put up there years ago. By me.'

Sara looked to where he was pointing, and saw the patch where something had been on the board so long that the hardboard had darkened uniformly around it.

'What was it?'

'Hold on, I'm getting to that. About a month ago, that sheet went missing. None of the lads took it; well, they wouldn't. I was very, very upset. No one had the right to come in here and help themselves like that.'

George leaned forward in his chair, held out the palm of his left hand and stabbed at it with the forefinger of his right, emphasising his next words.

'That sheet was important. That sheet had all the names of all the people that does lock-up duty

143

or is allowed to hold keys, that's from the director down to my lads, and next to the names it had all the codes on it, for the alarm. Six-figure numbers.'

'On the notice-board?'

'Yes. We got this new system put in, oh, must be six years ago. And we all get a different code, so there's no passing on the number and the wrong person getting hold of it.'

'Isn't that fair enough? I mean it sounds fair enough. Quite sensible.'

'Sensible! Bloody daft. First off, there's people forgetting their codes right, left and centre, and every time they have to go off down the office at the Circus and ask to have the safe opened for the master sheet so they can check it again, 'cos they're not meant to write it down. The people we get here, they're good at the job but they're not intellectuals, know what I mean? So the whole thing's a pain.'

'Well, yes, a right pain. But it would only be like remembering a phone number, wouldn't it? Couldn't they do that?'

George snorted. 'With a different code for each building? I'm not saying it was impossible, I'm saying it was a right bloody pain. No consultation, nothing. Just here's your numbers, memorise them, get on with it. We didn't even get to choose our own numbers, so's you could put in your birthday or something, to remember it. Got up my nose, that did. Unfair on my lads.'

'So you wrote all the numbers down?'

'Yeah, I wrote them down for my own benefit, because after a while they're all coming to me to help them, because the Circus doesn't like it, them all trooping in there. So I get the lads and I say,

144

right, the numbers are going up here and you sort yourselves out. After a while of course we all get used to the system; no one's looked at that sheet for years. So they're all up there, the lads' numbers, the director's, the deputy's, and it goes missing.'

'God, how worrying. What did you do?'

'I didn't do nothing. What's the point? I don't hold with these alarm systems anyhow. I know plenty people that's got alarms, they get burgled same as everyone else. In my time there's never been a break-in here anyway, alarms or no alarms. Waste of time.'

George paused while Sara drained the teapot into their mugs and brought him the bag of sugar.

'But, George, if all the numbers have been here all that time, dozens of people could have memorised a code, couldn't they? I mean, I'm here. You must have other visitors.'

'Well, not often. No one else comes in here much, just the lads. I mean, look at the place. But it wouldn't make no difference. See, us and some of the Coldstreams blokes, we'll do each other a favour now and then. On a late shift, sometimes one of them'll lock up for us, if one of us wants to get off. You have to give them your code for that, get the key back off them next day. Only now and then, mind. And then we'll slip their kids into the museum for nothing. Anyway. So, weeks after this thing goes missing, Mr Sawyer summons me to see him. And guess what?'

'He's got it?'

'Right. He's been in here, seen it, rips it down and then waits to see if I'm going to go confessing to him. That's what annoys me. "I'm very disappointed in you, George," he goes, "as a key member of the team, that this was on the board in the first place and that you did nothing about it when it disappeared." Oh, all very formal.'

'Oh, George, that must have been ghastly. After all the years you've been here.'

'Well, right, him half my age and here ten minutes. Waving the bit of paper in my face. And then he says he'll give the matter further thought. Says he'll consult with colleagues and decide whether he will start the disciplinary procedure. That means Miss Passmore. He asks her about everything, seeing she was in charge before; she knows more than he does. And he will inform me of the new code changes that will be necessary. And that's it.'

'What did you do?'

'Well, I says nothing. I reckon all I can do is just go by the book, keep smiling, show willing, until he comes back to me. I'm thinking I might weather it, I've been here so long. And that was on the Wednesday.'

'The eleventh? Before he was murdered? Oh, how awful.'

'Yeah. Then two days later; boom, he's dead.'

'Have you heard anything since?'

'No. But I don't know if that's because he didn't get round to doing anything about it or if Passmore's going to do it and is just too busy since the murder. I keep thinking she's going to spring it on me, the old dragon.'

'I'd have thought, though, George, if he had told her about it she'd at least have done something about the codes by now, wouldn't she?'

'Maybe. I can't very well ask, though, can I?' He smiled weakly, optimistically. 'Oh, it'll come out in

146

the wash. Forget I told you. Fancy another biscuit?'

*   *   *

Sara left the Roman Baths unrefreshed by George's hospitality. Making her way mechanically through the pigeons, buskers and visitors in Abbey Churchyard, she went into the abbey without letting herself think. She needed to sit down first. The cool of the abbey made her pause to breathe in deliberately, and slowed her pace down the long central aisle. She entered one of the front pews, sidled along to where it met the stone pillar and sat down, feeling its solid chill against her side.

Well, thank you, God, she thought, looking up, thank you for that. Thank you for showing me that someone I thought was a nice, friendly man with a kind word for everyone, always happy to do a person a good turn, is actually a resentful, unreliable and heartless idiot who watches mucky videos on the quiet. Makes me feel a whole lot better, that does. Was there any limit to the extent that she could be wrong about people? It must always have been there, George's cheerful cruelty towards others, like the pathetic young girl and her baby, and his disappointing, broken daughter. She continued to stare upwards. At the top of the stone trunk against which she was leaning the branches of the fan vaulting radiated up and outwards into the roof where they joined, stretched across and then closed into the tops of the pillars opposite, the struggle between lift and gravity held in resolution by their exuberant, virtuosic symmetry. Some phrase about architecture being frozen music came back to her. Her eyes followed the arching pattern which was repeated with glorious effortlessness down the length of the nave. She felt duller still. In their many exchanges of pleasantries she had picked up snatches of George's opinions on a number of subjects, from Pakistani cricket to monetary union, and she could now see the style of smiling bigotry in them all. His reasoning faculties were a set of keys with which he locked out all points of view which were at variance with his own and he no doubt set great store by never changing his mind. And he could be a murderer.

The abbey had grown quiet. Sara looked round and saw that there were only a few visitors left and two women kneeling at prayer. A verger was pottering about in one of the side aisles, shifting prayerbooks. She could hear footsteps somewhere ahead and above her; someone was climbing up to the organ loft. Papers were shuffled. Then a few ragged chords parped out, followed by a silence in which the harmonies sagged and died. Someone coughed. Then, after a fraction's pause, from the high loft the opening Allegro of Bach's Trio Sonata in C Major splashed out and down in a shower of weightless drops into the open lap of the abbey nave. Sara felt a sudden rush of excitement that made her want to laugh, or applaud. Only Bach could do this, make you feel you had been only half alive until this moment, pull you into the dance, lift you and take you as high as the roof, right up to where you could drink from the music's spring and be filled with a few bubbles of his crazy joy. Yet the sonata, requiring total independence between the hands and feet and revealing instantly any faltering of rhythm or fingering, was one of four that had been written by Bach with the deadly serious intention of furthering his son's organ studies. It was impertinent, that much brilliance. And this organist was playing well enough to bring the music to life, thereby concealing its true difficulty. It flowed on, the little sounds dancing out across the transept like drops of light, darting through the melodic web that the organist's feet and fingers were spinning to and fro on which to catch them. Sara had the sensation that she had unknowingly been suffering from some sort of deafness and that with this glorious noise she had suddenly woken up to find that her ears were working properly. She knew she had a recording of this somewhere; she must dig it out. Andrew would love it.

Then, without warning, the organist began to lose it. One note slipped, the one behind it tripped and then all the little fluting drops slowed into solidity, took weight and form and were finally caught and held swinging like a necklace of rare, trapped insects. The music stopped. For a moment the whole shimmering construction hung in the air before the fragile web, the clinging drops and all their brightness dropped away into nothing and evaporated into the dark of the empty choir stalls. Above in the organ loft the organist blew his nose with a hoot like a trombone, conveying the message that he was just practising and not to expect him to play the rest; the next bit was *really* difficult. Sara's dismay deepened as she remembered that there would be no more shared pleasures with Andrew, over Bach's trio sonatas or indeed anything else, unless she patched up her row with him. She had not spoken to him since Sunday night in the police station, and the longer it went on the harder it would become. Her thoughts returned to George.

149

This crass behaviour over the security codes. She pictured Matthew Sawyer finding George's list of numbers on the notice-board. The new director, still finding his feet, discovering that the whole system has been confounded, and had actually been vulnerable for years and years, because the long-serving, trusted chief security attendant didn't hold with alarms. Alarms which must have cost thousands to install, and which he, by his stupidity and almost single-handed, had rendered laughably useless. On balance, she admired Sawyer's restraint. It was decent of him not to have sacked George on the spot. Could he have been such a bad boss? George seemed even now to have no qualms about what he had done. His reaction had been one of simple annoyance at what he saw as interference. Sara wondered if George's sacking were still a possibility. Had Matthew Sawyer had time to discuss it with Olivia before he died and was she planning, when time permitted, to throw the switch on the disciplinary procedure? It seemed unlikely. Olivia's concern over George's behaviour since the murder had been real enough; she had been genuinely mystified and worried by it. She could not have been told. Sara rested her cheek against the pillar and breathed in a resinous, damp smell as heavy as all her grounded prayers. She thought about George's alibi. Before this afternoon she would have dismissed the possibility of George, kindly old George, ever committing a murder, but now, having seen another side of him, could she be sure he was incapable of such a thing? He might be not only capable of it, but also a supple and convincing liar.

But if his story were true, it explained his shifty

behaviour towards Olivia since the murder. George had just told her the very thing that Olivia had wanted to know, and which she had refused to help her find out. Did that mean that she should now tell Olivia what George had confided? George had not sworn her to secrecy. But he would certainly land in trouble, would possibly be sacked if she did, and he could have only a few years to go before retirement. He would not get another job, and what about his pension, his lump sum and all that? On the other hand, this question of the security codes would surely help Andrew with the case. He still had not been able to explain conclusively how Matthew Sawyer had come to be lying dead in a locked building with a set alarm and the keys inside, or, more importantly, to draw from that anything that led him nearer to finding the murderer. The alarm box was being analysed by the 'electronics people', but Andrew was dubious about what, if anything, they would be able to discover from it. Sara saw clearly for the first time that Andrew's apparent zeal in detaining James was probably a sign of desperation to get somewhere with the case, rather than the blind stupidity she had taken it for. And James had anyway been released without charge and was today going off with Tom to recover for a couple of weeks, so really, that whole episode seemed to be over. In all fairness, she could not go on blaming Andrew for it. He was, after all, trying to find a murderer. And he was unlikely to welcome the news that almost anyone connected with George's team or with Coldstreams in the past six years could have casually got to know a security code, or could, without being noticed, have made it their business

151

to find one out. But she would have to tell him. Dammit, she was going to have to apologise.

When Sara was gathering up her bags and making her way back down the aisle the music began again, but she did not pause. Outside in the late sunshine the pigeons had almost reclaimed Abbey Churchyard and were strutting about, casting long shadows among the plastic and paper carrion of litter. Shops were shutting. The ice-cream parlour staff in their perky hats were hosing down the sticky paving stones around their tables and stacking green plastic chairs and tables. Women from offices crossed the open square of Kingston Parade with food bags from Marks and Spencer. They hurried past exhausted tourists who lolled gratefully on the benches, surrounded by their carriers of fudge, tea caddies, funny mugs and scented candles, feeling their retail fever subside. High in the spire the abbey bells were chiming six, which was when, Sara realised, across town, the sodding dry cleaners closed.

CHAPTER THIRTEEN

Paul watched from his bed as Sue got dressed. She knew he was watching her. And he knew she knew, because without once looking at him she was moving as if he were filming her. With her back to him she dropped the bath towel and walked with a slow swing over to the sports bag which held her clothes, turned side-on to him and leaned very slightly into it, tilting her bottom outwards and revealing the curve of her spine. One of her best

152

lines. She sat on a chair with her knees together and her legs at a pretty angle in order to pull on her knickers. Stretching both arms behind her to do up her bra, instead of looping it round her waist and first fixing the hook at the front as she would have done if she had been alone, she arched her back just enough to show how redundant the garment was on her high, small breasts. She sat in her gleaming white underwear to brush her hair, knowing she looked like a lingerie advertisement and hoping that by gazing out of the window as she brushed she also looked touchingly vulnerable. Paul wanted to hit her. It was not just the vacant face. It was the way that she was always contriving some effect on him, staging pathetic little *tableaux vivants* and succeeding only in infuriating him with her obviousness. Why couldn't she behave naturally? These days (or had it been always?) every look, every gesture, every statement of hers seemed to be part of some strategy to provoke in him a reaction, the show of feeling that she wanted from him. He knew that at best he demonstrated only the kind of uninvolved affection he might show an engaging cat. How sad it was that she went on sitting there in her broderie anglaise, hoping that her display of herself would move him to love her, not realising that with every premeditated turn of her golden head and swish of the brush she was driving him closer to contempt.

If it were just a matter of looks, of course there would be no contest. But he would never be able to explain it to her; Sue would be absolutely baffled by the idea that there could be any more to the attraction of one person to another than physical beauty. She would wonder how on earth he could

153

be in love with an older woman, and one who didn't even work out. It would be to her an inexplicable betrayal for him to fall in love with a person whose nipples didn't stand to attention in preference to her who, in her own phrase, made the best of herself. She would look upon it as a form of blindness, which perhaps it was, or a sort of mistake, which it was not. It was the only real and precious thing that had ever happened to him.

Now her little bits of jewellery were going on. She spent only pocket money on jewellery. He knew she was waiting for him to buy her the serious stuff, the ring. He was still staring in her direction, but thinking of the one he loved, speculating about her body. What would she look like naked? Heavier than Sue, bigger-breasted, older, with none of Sue's oiled, muscular plasticity. She would be natural, apricoty, French. He remembered seeing her in a vibrant blue-green summer dress with thin straps and he recalled her soft shoulders and the dip just above her collar bone which he had longed to touch. He found it easy to imagine the warm skin of her body, the heavy tilt of her pale breasts and her round stomach. She would smell of cedar. It was a dangerous train of thought with Sue in the room. Beneath the duvet his penis gave a subversive lurch and he rolled over luxuriously as his stomach let out an extravagant rumble. Now Sue was being attentive, standing dressed with her hands on her hips, asking him maddeningly if he would like her to make some coffee, or should she just pop back into bed and they could make something else? Coffee, please, he said, pretending to be sleepier than he was and realising that he would never get the credit for being just honourable enough to turn down her other offer.

While she was busy in the tiny kitchen next door Paul got up, pulled on the jeans that he had left on the floor and stepped outside through the French windows. The sting of gravel on his bare feet, then the prickle of the grass and the breeze on his bare shoulders made him want to pee. He walked gingerly across to the washing line under the chestnut trees, the morning air pricking his nose in a way that he liked. He could hear birds. He was waking up, and as he now began to think of her with his whole, thinking mind, the full knowledge of his predicament mingled with his physical longing for her. He always thought about sex first thing in the morning and for quite a while now it had been a welcome torment to think of it with her. He had met her just when his interest in Sue was waning. Sue had been sweet and he had been lonely, but he had exhausted all possibilities with Sue within months. But now he had met *her*, and she had moved him in a way no other woman, certainly no younger woman, ever had or could. Within a very short time he had realised that he loved her, and thinking, mistakenly, that this fact simplified everything else, had told her so in a panicky, ardent rush that had genuinely surprised her. He had been sure that his revelation gave her pleasure, although she had not consented to becoming his lover. She tried half-heartedly to talk him out of it in that flattening English way that was so easy to see through. She said that he should think of his girlfriend; if he left her on the strength of this 'silly crush', she would not consent to see him again. So she was playing it dignified for the time being. He admired her for it.

155

She had no children and never would have now. He was thirty-one. His mind slid again to her body, its ripeness all but blown over, its life-giving potential unfelt, the quiet, mothering part of her reduced to a whisper. He ached to wrap himself in her, rock her out of her smooth habit of reciting a serene rationale for everything in her duty-laden life. She knew that her coolness was driving him wild, but she would not allow herself, and him, the pleasure of being thawed. She insisted that his feelings for her were based on pity, and would pass; he should settle down with Sue. They both knew that she did not really mean any of this, that no amount of English sensibleness would talk away the turbulence they both felt; he wanted only to touch some long-embedded nerve in her that would let her shout aloud her disappointment with her life. He wanted to hear her say that she needed him, as they both knew she did. He would melt her. He would make her love him as he loved her. For the first time in his life he had found that he was prepared to wait. Sex, of course, he would continue to have with others while he waited; it simply added to the frisson with which he anticipated it with her. One day. For now, the knowledge that it would happen was enough.

Sun slanted through the chestnut branches overhead. He tugged his warm T-shirt off the line and he felt where it was sticky with the sap that had dripped from the trees. The faint smell of soap powder as he pulled it over his head reminded him of Sue. Think of Sue. She was the one deserving of pity, really, walking out now with their coffee cups, in her shorts and sandals, smiling up at the sun. She was all summer, golden and young, yet her approach across the catwalk of the grass was like the coming of frost.

He took his coffee, smiling, and braced himself for conversation. It was his day off. Sue was on duty in an hour, and she was bound to open brightly with some suggestion about meeting up for a quick jog or a sandwich during her shift, anything to break up her interminable day when she could not know for certain what he was doing. He had to pre-empt her.

'Can you do me a favour this morning? Give me a lift to the station? I've got to go to London,' he said, as breezily as he dared.

'Oh. *Oh*. You didn't say anything about going. What for? Of course I'll take you,' she added, anticipating his impatience. 'I'm just surprised. I didn't know. Is it, um, anything interesting? Why you're going?'

'It's interesting. But I haven't any more to tell you than that. Not yet. Okay?' He knew this to be unsatisfactory, but with the right smile, which he now turned on her, it would do. She was such a sweet person, really.

'Ooh, be all mysterious then,' she said playfully. 'See if I care. Want some toast?'

She had learned that it only made him angry if she pestered him and they drove more or less in silence to the station in Sue's old car. Paul used the inherent difficulty of saying goodbye in cars to good effect and kissed her on the edge of her face with the side of his mouth. Sue drove back feeling only a little more alone than she had when in his company. Face it, she told herself, it's over. No, it isn't, she said back. He's going through some kind of crisis and needs you with him. He just can't say

157

so. Of course he's scared of commitment, he's a man. But he's still here, isn't he? Remember how it was at the beginning. One day he'll realise what a great thing we've got going and he'll surprise me.

Sue had always loved best the stories that ended 'and he just swept her off her feet'. For the rest of the day she stood by her man, incubating the hope that Paul was in London on some business to do with their future together: an interview for a proper chef's job, getting them a flat, maybe even choosing a ring. If he would only come back with just one lovely, wonderful surprise that would show her how wrong she was to have been quietly losing hope in him. 'It's a solitaire. Do you mind having just one diamond, darling?' Even flowers would do, anything, just one sweet, touching, silly gesture that would prove to her that he loved her, perhaps even as much as she loved him. 'They're gardenias, darling. And now you need a wedding dress to wear with them.' All that was needed to dispel instantly the long shadow in her, the sad suspicion that he never would take proper care of her, was just one glorious Hollywood ending. But so far he had never even called her darling.

*   *   *

Later, when Sue had begun to wonder which train Paul would be coming back on, Sara sauntered into the club.

'Fancy doing a run?' Sue asked. 'Nothing strenuous, it's too hot. Just the short one, down the drive and round?'

'Sure,' Sara said, knowing that a run with Sue meant uncompetitive companionship and

158

encouragement to show a bit of pace when she needed it. It was no hardship to listen to the latest in Sue's love life; in fact she had to admit that now that she had met Paul it was all rather riveting. For Sue it was restful to have a running companion whose pace was more sedate than her own and who often noticed things along the route, and it was also a way of getting out of serving coffee to those club members who supported the idea of exercise in principle but so often felt, on balance, that it was altogether better for them to lie by the pool in a bathrobe.

'It was nice to meet Paul properly,' Sara began, as they made their way down the drive. 'At Olivia's,' she added. 'How long have you known him?'

'Nearly two years. Almost since he came here. He worked in Bristol first. For a few months.'

Talking while you were running required short sentences. Sue was dimly aware that she was choosing only the words she needed, giving her answers efficiently, and perhaps saying more than she really meant to. Sara had often noticed that the act of running, in separating you from the normal world, made your language plainer, your position clearer.

'But you don't live together, do you?'

'Not properly. He's only got the one room.' They were close to the end of the drive. 'But you know it's not always easy.'

'Well, never was, was it? You told me he was moody. How're you doing? I'm not too bad today.'

'Fine. Got these new trainers. Should be good, they were sixty quid. Lost my others. No, I mean, he's been going off.'

'How do you mean? He walks out?'

159

'No, no. He just goes off. At weekends. Only sometimes.'

At the end of the drive they turned right to do the short route and continued along the road where the narrow pavement followed the boundary wall of Fortune Park. Sue dropped back and, in single file, conversation stopped. After two or three minutes they reached the end of the wall, which turned away from the road at ninety degrees and stretched back towards the hotel. A bridle path ran along the far side of the wall under a line of trees and Sara turned from the road on to it, running gently on the spot as Sue caught up and joined her.

'He's got friends in Bristol. His mates, he says. It's only sometimes. I suppose I shouldn't mind.' They jogged on side by side.

'God, I'm tired,' Sara said. 'We're about halfway, now, thank God.'

'Yep. You're doing great. You should try zero-balancing—releases more energy.'

'Hmm. Maybe. I could go astro-planing at the same time.'

They ran on, cooling under the trees.

'No, seriously. Anyway, Paul. The thing is, he always goes over there, they never come here. So I've never met them.' Sue hesitated. 'Sometimes I think he's got someone else over there. I get all upset.'

I bet you do, Sara thought, and felt sorry for her. She could imagine Sue in a state of near hysteria, her nice manners abandoned in a storm of fear, rage and bewilderment.

'But I don't think he has, really. He's gone to London today. Don't know why, think it may be about a job.'

160

'That would be exciting. Would you mind moving?'

'Oh, no, I'd like it. I want us to get a flat anyway, a proper place together. Even if we stay here we'll probably manage it—by Christmas. I keep saying to him.'

They ran on in silence for a while.

'Look, we're here. There's the gate.'

They entered the grounds of Fortune Park by the gate in the boundary wall and ran on along the bark path that wound through the woods. There were many of these paths, artfully made to wind and wander among the trees. There were benches here and there, and through the trees they could see glimpses of the hotel on the right. Staying out of sight they jogged on before clearing the woods behind the buildings and coming out on to the gravel of the tiny overflow car park at the back of the health club. Here they halted. They had been running for only twenty minutes, not a difficult run for either of them, but there was as always a moment of shared triumph at the finish.

'Good one,' Sara said. 'Thanks. God, I'm hot. You swimming?'

'No, I'll have a shower at Paul's in a bit,' Sue said, nodding towards the detached stone house under the trees on the far side of the car park. A covered walk of about sixty yards through its front garden led to double doors with the sign 'Fortune Park Spa Hair and Beauty' above. She prised her key out of her shorts pocket.

'Is that where he lives? I thought that was the beauty salon and hairdressing place.'

'It is. They've got the two main rooms on the ground floor and one room upstairs. But round the

161

back it's converted. Paul's room is downstairs and there are outside stairs up to the two other staff rooms. He's got his own little bathroom. It's nice. No proper kitchen, but it's not bad. Come and see. Fancy a coffee?'

Sara, her face resplendently pink, knowing that her legs needed waxing, accepted, reassuring herself that there was no chance of running into Paul. Sue led the way past a line of rhododendrons round to the back of the house where French windows and a solid back door gave on to a square of grass under the chestnuts. Round the far side of the house a wooden staircase stretched up to a small door at first-floor level. They went in by the main back door into a small square hallway which was almost filled by Paul's bike and a line of laden coathooks with an assortment of trainers and wellies underneath. The door on their left was Paul's room and next to it a doorway led into a small basic galley kitchen. Sue pointed at one of the two doors opposite.

'That's the way into the salon. The girls used to make coffee in the kitchen, before it was converted, but they've got their own place now. That door's kept locked. That other one's the bathroom.'

They took their coffee into the large bed-sitting room and sat in the two rattan armchairs.

Sue waved an arm. 'I've just rearranged it all. I read this thing about feng shui and realised at once why Paul and me kept going wrong. The energies in here were *completely* blocked.' She frowned. 'Course, it takes a while for the new energies to flow. But it's a bit better. Although he shouldn't have the flowers. And I keep telling him about the blue. Still.'

162

Sara looked round. Although some of Sue's clothes (and none of his) were draped over a chair at the bedside, it was definitely Paul's room and not Paul's and Sue's. It was essentially simple and orderly. A portable television stood on a low black circular table in one corner. There was a double bed in the other corner, covered with a dark blue heavy cotton bedspread. The shelves which ran along one wall above a long, built-in chest of drawers contained mainly books: food and cookery classics—Larousse, Escoffier, Michel Guérard, Elizabeth David—but also many others, the drawings of Degas, one on the Incas, another on the cave paintings at Lascaux. The book-ends were simple cubes of black marble. There was a modern clock with no numerals and two or three ethnic sculptures. Instead of proper curtains, several dozen yards of striped ticking had been ingeniously draped and stapled to a pole that ran almost the length of the wall, and were now pushed behind two heavy iron hooks that had been set into the wall at the sides of the French windows. In front of the window was a small square table with a cloth of the same ticking on which stood a tall glass jug of deep ultramarine containing several sprigs of philadelphus. It was grown-up and male and altogether consistent with Sara's impression of Paul, yet there was something else, something that, although familiar, she could not quite identify.

'Oooo, look at the time!' Sue suddenly squealed and got to her feet. 'And I said I'd be back at four. Look, I'm just getting under the shower for a second. No, don't go.' She had already picked up a towel and was on her way out of the door. 'You stay and finish your coffee. Shan't be a tic.'

163

A few seconds later Sara heard the noise of the shower. She got up and went over to the bookshelves and picking a book almost at random opened it, not out of interest in its contents but to see if there were some inscription or some other little tantalising insight into its owner. But there was nothing, not even his name. As she replaced the book she wondered idly what his handwriting was like. It was just as she was reaching up to the top shelf for the book of Degas drawings that she heard the voice say, almost in a whisper, 'How's the finger?'

She spun round to see Paul laughing in the doorway of the French windows. Before she could say anything he had crossed the threshold, slung his black denim jacket on the bed and stopped in front of her, his thumbs hooked over the front pockets of his jeans.

'What an *honneur, madame,*' he said, bowing slightly, his green eyes not leaving her face.

'Sue's in the shower,' Sara blurted. 'We were running together. She asked me for coffee. She's just had to dash off and have a shower.'

Paul took in the background shshsh and his face broke into a sarcastic smile of disappointment. 'Tcha! And I thought perhaps you had come to see me. For a consultation and possibly even . . . further treatment.' He was laughing at her embarrassment. And without being in the least furtive, he was looking steadily and thoughtfully at her body.

Sara cursed herself for being caught in her clinging, sweaty running clothes and with a greasy face. Just how hairy were they, her legs? And she knew, without looking down, that the coolness of

164

the room had made her nipples stand out under her thin vest. Oh, please, God, please let them be level, she prayed.

'So, we'll have to find a more convenient time, won't we?' he said, still amused.

She knew better than to reply. She stared straight back at him and with one hand slowly moved her damp fringe off her forehead with a gesture of dignified disdain. At that moment the shower stopped abruptly and Paul moved over to the door.

'I'm back!' he called, which brought a muffled 'Ooooh' from the bathroom and a moment later a drenched and delighted Sue skipped into the room, wrapped in a very short towel. Sara made her excuses and went back to the changing room at the club, blazing.

CHAPTER FOURTEEN

The next day, unable to put it off any longer, Sara telephoned Andrew to apologise. He apologised back and admitted it had been difficult to detain the friend of 'someone he felt close to'. But now, if she had a moment to listen, he had other things to worry about.

'What? *What* happened to your instrument?' asked Sara eventually.

'Natalie,' said Andrew dully at the other end of the telephone. 'Natalie happened to it.'

It was the drained voice of a man whose anger is spent.

'The youngest; she's five. She decided to post all

her Polly Pockets into my cello. What? Oh, they're little miniature plastic doll things. Then she couldn't get them out, so she decided that the cello was their own little house with a funny curly door. So to make it prettier, she decorated it with felt tips and wrote POOLY POCIT LIVS her on the front. Then she gave them their tea. Half a packet of crisps, a Milky Way and a carton of Ribena. And a yoghurt. Blackcurrant. Straight in.'

'*No!* You mean she actually poured all that . . . inside?'

'Oh, yes.' He sighed. 'And after tea, what do we do? Well, we have our bath, of course. So in went two milk bottles full of water and most of her My Little Pony bathtime bubbles. And three Dewberry bath beads from the Body Shop.'

He sounded half strangled. 'And then it all lay there soaking in until I found it. Valerie was doing a cookery video in the kitchen with headphones on. Says it was my own fault for leaving the case open.'

Sara considered that it would be both heartless and pointless to suggest that there was some truth in this, and it was anyway out of the question that she would ever side with the unspeakable Valerie over anything.

'Don't worry. Get it over to Avon Strings in Bristol, they're in *Yellow Pages*. They'll do a good job. You can use my Peresson till yours is ready,' Sara said, still anxious to make amends for their row. 'You'll love the sound, it'll blow your head off. Andrew?'

She hesitated. 'Can you come this evening? I have to talk to you about the case again. No, nothing to do with James, something else. And I know I should stop you discussing it and actually it

166

is none of my business, but I *feel* involved now, in a way. And I'd like to help. Help you, I mean.'

*   *   *

Early the same evening, with no cello to carry, Andrew rode his bike up to Medlar Cottage. There was precious little time in ordinary circumstances to get a bit of exercise and with the Sawyer case refusing to break he had been working late most nights. He reviewed the past few days. They had interviewed everyone who had been at the Pump Room and Assembly Rooms, close to five hundred people now, and scanned over thirty hours of closed-circuit television pictures from the only two shops in Stall Street that had security cameras. They showed only the shop doorways and a few metres of pavement and had so far turned up nothing of significance. Then there was the new information about the alarm which wasn't exactly helping. James Ballantyne had turned out to have an alibi that he hadn't even known about. Bridger was being petulant, trying to fly in the face of the facts, claiming that they should have put more pressure on him. Bridger was pitifully inexperienced. He was only gradually realising that this enquiry was par for the course: unexciting, filled with dogged, repetitive routine and, so far anyway, yielding nothing. They were just going to have to interview people all over again, check alibis, look at security footage again, and just keep at it until something broke. There would be something. And as long as this weather held he would use the bike to get to Sara's. After what Natalie had done (and with something horribly

167

close to sly approval from Valerie) he was not going to risk taking the Peresson home with him. It was so like her to offer to lend it to him, and it would be wonderful just to play it. It was the Peresson she was playing on that recording of the Dvořák concerto he had, the big, modern, steel-stringed instrument that she used for the big romantic repertoire. He did not understand why she did not seem interested in playing in public any more. When he thought about it, it worried him, but then so did the thought that she might at any moment resume her concert career and ditch the lessons. He hoped she would not mind his still coming to play without practising in between. It still helped him improve. And now she was even offering to help with the case. Of course he shouldn't be discussing it with her, but someone in his job needed a sounding board, that was understood. And if it couldn't be your wife, why shouldn't it be someone else you could trust, like Sara? She was an amazing woman.

Even more amazing than he had realised, after she had told him about her conversation with George. They were sitting in the shade in front of the hut ready to play, but had not yet sounded a note. As he listened he gazed out, noticing that the lime trees and hedgerows in the valley opposite were darkening into a deeper green and the dark purple buddleia that overhung the path to the pond at the other side of the garden was now in full flower and surrounded in a flicker of butterflies. His bow rested on his knee.

'And you see it's quite awkward,' she was saying earnestly. 'Olivia on the one hand asking if I can winkle out of George anything that he knows, then

168

he goes and tells me all this, probably needing to tell someone who's not one of his colleagues. It might be the end of him if Olivia finds out, and on the other hand, it's quite important for the case that *you* know all about it. So here I am, shopping George. Matthew Sawyer was going to discipline him, perhaps even sack him over the security breach, and Olivia was meant to have been told about it. And you see anyone, just about anyone who went in that room, could have memorised an alarm code. And then there's the thing about his alibi.'

'This may help,' he said. 'Sort of. Because I've got news for you, too. I've heard back from the electronics people. The code that was used to set the alarm that night was Matthew Sawyer's own, and it was set at two forty-five a.m. Two forty-five fits in more or less with what the PM report gives for time of death: between midnight and five o'clock. We have to suppose that he was killed at, say, half past two or minutes after. I had been puzzling over how the murderer could have got Sawyer's code out of him. Coercion sounds obvious, but there was no sign of any struggle, no sign that suggested Sawyer wasn't taken completely by surprise. And if Sawyer hadn't been forced to tell his murderer the code, that seemed to offer us a choice between a corpse or a ghost setting the burglar alarm. If we now know that his code was not as confidential as it was supposed to be, it's more plausible that someone else was able to use it. But of course the problem of who becomes *more* difficult.'

'And you've got another problem, haven't you? You said he could have been killed between midnight and five o'clock. Supposing he *was* killed just before the alarm was set, at around half past two. What then was Matthew Sawyer doing all that time between twenty to twelve when the last person left the Pump Room and the time he was killed? Chatting with the murderer? It doesn't take three hours to lock up. So, suppose instead he was killed nearer to midnight. Why then would the murderer hang about until quarter to three? Why, in any case, did the killer bother to lock up at all? Why not just nip out of the door, or climb over the balustrade of the terrace and jump down on to Kingston Parade? Forget about the keys and locking up altogether. If you think about it, locking up and setting the alarm gained nothing.'

'I know. Nobody was going to discover anything before the morning, in any case. It's not as if anyone would be likely to try the doors in the middle of the night, not for any legitimate purpose at any rate. But George's story is interesting. I'll have to talk to him about it, you know, and I'll have to find out a bit more about his er . . . viewing material. I expect it'll turn out to be top-shelf stuff. If it was anything really hard core I can't see him telling you about it. I'll have to see Olivia Passmore as well. It's pretty unlikely Sawyer told her about George. She would have told Bridger, wouldn't she, at the very beginning of the enquiry. He went into all the building details—doors, locks, alarms and all that—right at the start. And I doubt very much that she'll do anything about it now. I'll recommend she gets the crime prevention lot over and she can go through the whole security management issue with them, without making a scapegoat out of George. Even though,' he added with a smile, 'he probably deserves it.'

He went on. 'It's a pretty safe bet that the murder took place nearer three o'clock than midnight, although the problem of the hours in between remains a problem. What we've been doing, of course, since we found out that the alarm was set around three in the morning, is going over everybody's statements again and concentrating on what people were doing not around midnight, but three hours later. Although, of course, every single one of them says that they were safely tucked up in beddy-byes.'

He suddenly looked terribly tired, as if he'd like to be tucked up there himself.

'Andrew, when did you last eat?'

'Oh, I had breakfast. Well, a banana in the car. And someone got me a sandwich about two,' he said absently, 'but come to think of it, I didn't get a chance to eat it. I'm okay though.'

He pulled the cello back against his shoulder and checked the tuning dolefully.

'Come on,' said Sara. 'Food first, art second. It'll wait.'

They left their instruments in their cases in the cool of the hut and made their way back down to the cottage. Sara heated an iron skillet and pushed the langoustines around in blackened butter, into which she squeezed the sizzling juice of a lime. Andrew, following her directions to the fridge and larder, brought bread and salad to the table, found garlic, oil and vinegar and made a dressing. They sat opposite each other and ate with their fingers. The effect of food on Andrew was immediate and visible. As he pulled the shells off and sucked on the meat, he went on talking. The cat cruised the

171

legs of their stools and dived greedily on the tail ends Sara dropped for him.

'I've been working on piecing together Matthew Sawyer's movements before he died. Quite a busy bloke. You never think of people in that sort of job being rushed, do you? Seems all very calm and sedate on the outside, a museum.'

'As in, "Is that a proper full-time job?"' asked Sara, pulling off a piece of shell and licking her fingers languorously.

Andrew watched her thoughtfully. 'Yeah, well. Anyway, I saw his wife. And I spent a long time with his secretary. He had a busy day that Friday. I can't help admiring the bloke, working that hard when he probably didn't need to.'

'What do you mean?'

'Loaded, on the wife's side. She is a Bowman. Old man Bowman was in property. Made a packet in the eighties, sold out and retired to Dorset. The Sawyer family do very well out of it: children in private schools, lovely big house on Sion Hill, bought outright. She doesn't work, she does lunch, swans about. They couldn't live like that on a museum director's salary—"Matthew's pittance", she called it.'

'What about the secretary?'

'Oh, a gem. She took it very hard, apparently, couldn't come in to work for three days after she heard the news. She rated him very highly.'

'Aha, a whisper of intrigue? A jealous mistress?' Sara said. 'Have we got a *crime passionel* here?'

'Trust you. You meet Mrs Trowels in the flesh and see if you still think so.' He paused to finish his langoustine before taking another. 'She's in her late fifties, weighs at least fifteen stone. All right,

172

all right, I'm *not* saying only young thin people have affairs. But her desk's covered with pictures of her cats. She knits for Mr Trowels. She refused to go to a hen party for one of the girls in the museum shop because they were going to some "disgusting" show in Bristol. What did she call it—the Chesterfields, would it have been?'

'Chippendales?'

'Right. And for her, loyalty to the boss is part of the creed. But it does seem that he could be difficult to work for. A gentleman, but inclined to overreact, she said.'

'So what about that Friday then; what was he doing?'

'Morning taken up with a meeting; some local charity he was a trustee of. We've looked into it. Nothing to do with the museum at all. The Terry Trust. It's to do with the disabled—mobility grants, that kind of thing. According to the trust secretary it was a routine meeting, nothing unusual, but I've asked for the minutes. He gets to his office in the Circus about one o'clock, has a sandwich at his desk with a cup of coffee, made by Mrs Trowels. Sees the post, answers a couple of letters, then he goes round to the archives at the Victoria Art Gallery. Something he was working on. All the museum's archives, records of acquisitions, provenance, storage, display details and so on are kept there. All on paper, outgrown their space by miles, apparently. I went to see it. Sawyer was trying to make sense of it all, trying to get to grips with exactly what was in the collections. I've found out, you know, that there are acres of boxed artefacts belonging to the museum stored all over the place. This archive is the only way of finding

173

out what is where, if you're new. Part of Sawyer's remit, when he was appointed, was to get some of these things out of storage and on display, things that nobody has seen for years, possibly ever.'

'I'd heard that,' Sara said, 'Olivia told me. The councillors on the museums board tried to bully her about it years ago, when she was in charge. They criticised the museums service for withholding all these so-called treasures from the gaze of the local tax-payers. The *Chron* took it up—remember?' She slipped off her stool and went to the larder and returned with more beer and a dish of tiny tomatoes.

'Well, haven't they got a point?' Andrew said, opening two of the bottles and decanting them into their glasses.

'Well, except that the council kept very quiet about the fact that they'd squeezed the museums so tight that there was no money to employ extra curators to research new exhibitions and build new displays. Olivia came straight back at them with that. And she told me that the stuff in storage is a pretty mixed bag. Laundry lists, quite literally, and a collection of button hooks. Dreary watercolours by Bath ladies. Enough fans to start a hurricane. Hardly the hidden treasures of the nation.'

'Anyway, Sawyer was going through the archive gradually, getting to know what there was. Rationalising, he called it. He was very keen on order, according to Mrs Trowels. She approved of that.'

'So did he make much progress that afternoon, "rationalising"?'

'It seems he did. He sent a handwritten memo to Olivia Passmore's office at the costume museum

174

from the art gallery, via the internal mail system. He was very methodical; he photocopied it and had the copy sent back to Mrs Trowels at the Circus for filing. I made a copy of the copy for you—here.'

He stood up, reached into his back pocket and pushed a piece of paper across the table to Sara.

Memo

To: OP (Ass Rms)
From: MS   Fri 13 June

Re: Hackett Request

Have located whereabouts of above (paint)! Quite a story! Only Q. of time before more located/ lost — MS requires urgent updating. What do you know re this ??
May we discuss At AP ?

'Brisk,' she said. 'Shocking writing. Not even clear what he means. Wrote it in a hurry, I'd say. What *does* it mean?'

'Mrs Trowels explained it to me. In the archive there's part of a catalogue of a collection called the Hackett Bequest. Sewing boxes and what-not. Needlework tools, silver scissors, thimbles and such. Only the bit of catalogue survives. The actual collection was destroyed in 1941 when a bomb hit the back of the museum offices in the Circus. Everything in the basement was destroyed, either by the bomb or by water, including the Hackett Bequest. The original handwritten catalogue survived. I think it was kept somewhere else. Obviously Matthew Sawyer had tracked it down in the archive, and found it in a bad way. He wanted to get some conservation work done on it, that's all.'

'And Olivia saw the memo on the Friday afternoon?'

'Yes. She confirms the Hackett Bequest details—that was common knowledge. It was nothing new to her, this story about the lost bequest, but she wasn't sure if Sawyer had heard it. Presumably he had, or had got part of it. He was obviously quite excited about coming across the catalogue fragment. And the catalogue did need rebinding, she said. It would have been done within the next six months anyway; they have a system for checking the state of things in the archives. The memo seems to have been pretty unimportant, to her at any rate. She didn't even keep the original. Anyway, after he'd finished in the archives and sent the memo, he went over to the Roman Baths and

Pump Room—he often did that, just looked in on staff, "walking the job", he called it—and then went back to the Circus.'

'And I bet the sainted Mrs Trowels made him his tea?'

'She did. He got back at about half past four. He asked Mrs Trowels to ring to see if Miss Passmore would be free at quarter to six for a short discussion, and she said she would. And he was at his desk at quarter past five when Mrs Trowels went home. She popped in to take away his cup and say goodnight. She says his DJ was hanging on the back of the door. He must have changed soon after and gone over to the Assembly Rooms for his meeting with Olivia Passmore. She says he was there just after quarter to, and the kiosk staff saw him come in too.'

'And I saw him a little while after that. He came out of an office—Olivia's, I suppose—and talked to some people in the vestibule. A man and a woman. I met her later on; the man went off.'

'Yes, I'm sure we've got the names of everyone he spoke to from then on, until the last of the staff left the Pump Room at twenty to midnight. He saw them off at the Stall Street door. In all that time he was never alone, except for some time back at his office, and walking between there and the Pump Room.'

'When was that?'

'Can't be precise to the minute about that. But he left the Assembly Rooms about half an hour after he'd made his welcome speech. He was in the Tea Room all that time, talking to delegates. We know he chatted to a group of three or four of them and said something about going back to his

177

office, it was a great time to catch up because it was completely empty then.'

'Do you think it could have been someone at the convention, you know, prepared to kill him for what he said about natural healing? Only if it was, following him back to the office and doing it there would have been simpler, wouldn't it?'

'Yes, if the murderer knew that that was where he was going. But it's stretching it a bit far, isn't it?'

'Probably, but some of them take it very seriously. And there *are* people who are capable of anything if they're sufficiently worked up.'

'Yes, but don't forget the weapon. A kitchen knife. You wouldn't keep one on you, just in case you felt the need to kill someone.'

'Have you found out where the knife came from?'

'We've found out all we can. German-made, sold widely, department stores, specialist kitchen shops, singly and in sets. Yes, they're sold here. And in Bristol, of course. The kitchen shop in Quiet Street does its sales totals by the week and we know that four knives of that type and make were sold in the week before the murder, and three in the week following. The murderer may have bought a knife in advance, you see, knowing what he, or she, was going to do with it, or, more likely I think, gone out afterwards and bought a replacement for the knife they used, so that it wouldn't be missed. Most were card transactions and we've checked them all out. As you'd expect, nothing of interest to us, because the murderer would almost certainly use cash. A total of four were paid for by cash, two in each of the two weeks, but there's no way of following them up. The staff don't remember who bought the

178

knives. It's a busy shop. None of the Coldstreams staff, either at the Pump Room or the Assembly Rooms, has replaced a knife or missed one. Not one of them specifically recognises the actual knife that was used, it's too familiar a type. No help there. So, we know that Matthew Sawyer rang his wife from the office at seven fifteen, told her where he was and said he was staying for an hour or so. She says that he always used to say "an hour or so" and it could mean anything from an hour to nearer two. But Sawyer was at the Pump Room at nine, after dinner had started.'

'Doesn't get us any further, does it? And it's exactly two weeks now.'

It didn't. But when they went back up the path in the fading light and played the middle movement of the second Haydn cello concerto in the hut under the slanting shadows cast by the storm lanterns, Andrew felt inexplicably optimistic, delighting in the full-throated, deep singing of the Peresson cello. It was almost dark when they dowsed the lanterns, closed the hut and carried the instruments back down to the house. Sara followed him out to his bike and stood brushing the flowering tips of the huge rosemary bushes through her hand as he unpadlocked it from the railings by the gate.

'Mind you lock up, now,' he told her almost tenderly, reluctant to leave her standing there alone. He was much later getting home than he had said he would be and he told Valerie that he had had to nip back into the office after his lesson. It was the first time he had lied to her without actually being unfaithful.

179

CHAPTER FIFTEEN

By the flaccid whump of the door closing and the sigh of the bag dropping on the hall floor Cecily got an inkling that Sue was depressed. Or perhaps, being depressed herself, she was simply more attuned to other people's misery.

'In here,' she called and went to put on the kettle. Sue dripped into sight and slumped in the doorway of the kitchen, seeping deprivation. Cecily took one look at her, put back the coffee jar and took down the instant chocolate, leaving the painted tin of Charbonnel et Walker, Derek's 'proper cocoa' which she happened not to like, untouched. She made two large mugs of chocolate with extra powder and, sighing, stirred some gold top milk and two sugar lumps into each one.

'Bring those,' she said, pointing with her nose at a packet of chocolate digestives, and carried their mugs through into the sitting room. Sue obeyed and followed, her feet performing a little collapse with every step, and fell into an armchair. They sipped in tandem, each staring into the cold fireplace.

'Oh, *God*,' whispered Sue, rubbing her eyes so hard she seemed to be mashing them. It was the first word she had spoken since she arrived. 'I shouldn't be here. I wish I wasn't.'

'Oh, now, Sue, don't,' Cecily protested. 'Don't say an awful thing like that. You're young and beautiful. Have a biscuit. What you're feeling now will pass, you know. It *will*,' she said, silently hoping that what she was feeling would too, despite being no longer young nor ever exactly beautiful herself. Attractive, maybe. Once. Sue stared at her.

'I meant here. *Here*. In the house. It's the weekend. You know—your boyfriend, the arrangement?'

'Oh, I see. Oh, well, that's a relief. I don't have to lock up the aspirin then.' She tried a bright smile, then sipped miserably at her chocolate. She took another biscuit.

'It doesn't matter, not this weekend. He's with his *wife*.' She said 'wife' in a voice like a swishing blade.

'Oh, *God*,' said Sue. 'And Paul's in Bristol, with God knows who.'

It was twenty past three on Saturday afternoon. It is a depressing time in itself, twenty past three. Twenty past three is about the time, Cecily reflected, when it dawns on you that all those useful things that you vowed to achieve when you woke up determined to be brave about being dumped for the weekend will not be achieved, because you have dithered sluttishly through the day. The oven is still black and sticky, the kettle is still encrusted with limescale, the bed lies unmade, you still have not flossed, and your eyebrows, because you have still not had a proper look for the tweezers, still look like two brown caterpillars about to mate on your forehead. Yes, it is around twenty past three that you find yourself staring hard into the truth that you are such a slattern it can hardly come as a surprise that you have been dumped in favour of a bright, groomed, smiling, competent *wife*.

She had got up with brisk discipline. Today would be like a day at a health farm, only at home,

181

and hers would have the added feature of a few heroic domestic victories as well, like the oven. And she would bravely remove all the little dead lobelias and geraniums that she had planted up lovingly in her urn a few weeks ago and which had sadly and inexplicably died. She must have overwatered them, but just in case there was something wrong with the compost, she would replace it and start all over again. But the main thing for today, this book said, was to learn to treat herself as if she were a celebrity. Celebrate the Celebrity Within You. That way, you would enhance your self-esteem and soon other people would start to notice and treat you better too. Celebrate your inner self, and get acquainted with the celebrity within. She knew how to do it, she had read the whole book twice since she had bought it at the Healing Arts thing, along with all the organic vegetable and fruit-based skin, hair, nail and body preparations she needed to lard herself up for a forty-eight-hour orgy of relaxation, toning, moisturisation, energising and balancing. It said to start by wearing loose comfortable clothing. She had got dressed in one of Derek's huge T-shirts which had had the effect at first of making her feel small inside it, slapped some cleansing cream on her face and gone down to fix a healthy breakfast. She had whizzed up a chopped apple, a banana, an orange and a tin of peaches in the Magimix and produced a pale orange porridge that had tasted a good deal better than it looked, when it was helped down with a dollop of yoghurt and a couple of spoonfuls of honey.

Feeling too full to tackle the oven, she had plodded up to the bathroom to remove the face cream and embark on the day's beauty therapies, starting with her hair. Despite having to swathe her head in an old towel which now had more orange and brown blobs on it than a leopard, and wear horrible little plastic gloves like the ones doctors put on when they are about to shove their fingers where they oughtn't to go, she managed to uphold her inner celebrity pretty well. She maintained it even as she slopped the glossy gravy of the organic dye lotion into her hair and carefully combed it through, hoping, as she had hoped with every hair colour she had used for the past thirty years, that this one would be The One. The one that would make men under thirty turn and stare after her, the one that would make Derek startle and say, *Why, you're beautiful*, the one that would give her hair the colour, shine, health and bounce that it was *meant* to have. The hair that would have got her a degree instead of a secretarial diploma, the hair that would not have let her be dumped by her boy husband after the second miscarriage in 1970, the hair that would have seen to it that the body it was attached to was an eight-stone, five-foot-nine model, instead of the rounder, shorter specimen that she actually inhabited. Cecily's last skirmish with a hair colourant (Honey Ash Blonde) had left her hair looking whitishly rubbed out, curiously like the surface of limed kitchen cupboards. This one, she was confident, would restore some depth, a bit of soul.

Not daring to risk dripping through the house, she sat upright on the bathroom stool for the required twenty minutes, cursing that she had forgotten to bring up a *Cosmo* to read. Then she spent another fifteen minutes with her head upside

183

down in the basin and the pads of her cheeks puffing uncomfortably up round her eyes, groping blindly for the taps in her efforts to sluice the stuff off. Eventually, after filling and emptying the basin seven times, she decided that the straw-coloured water that ran off her head was as clear as it was going to get. In her bedroom with the hairdryer, Cecily pictured herself emerging with the sort of gleaming curtain of hair that goes with those laughably perfect teeth in the shampoo adverts, the kind that make you worry that hairdressers are in league with dentists and working together in secret to create a master race. But the finished effect was as if the limed kitchen cupboards had been vandalised with Marmite.

The book did not say anything about dragging alarmingly generous tufts of your own hair from the plughole or scrubbing the brown tidemark off the basin but, when these little details had been seen to, Cecily reckoned she was due for a sit-down and some deep breathing. Quality time, to think positively about some aspect of your life that you want to change, the book said. Like, maybe, not getting so worked up about hair colourants, or clearing fat greying headmasters out of your life, she wondered. But it had been impossible not to let her mind dwell on the trim figure, the naturally dark, burnished head and the solid career of smug, married Mrs Payne. She had pulled out the only photograph she had of Derek, the one of him in a suit holding a fountain pen that he'd had done for the school brochure and moped over it. There was none of him and her together.

From that point she had not really risen from the sofa again, except to fix lunch which was meant to be a light salad (no mayonnaise), wholemeal toast and a soft-boiled free-range egg. She fried it instead and had it with oven chips. She spilt ketchup down the T-shirt, which was now making her feel huge. And shortly after that Sue had arrived, and Cecily was finding it oddly comforting to be in the company of a fellow dumpee. The photograph of Derek lay curling gently on the table beside the biscuits, old copies of *Cosmo* and the stupid book.

Sue was saying, 'Paul went off to Bristol again. He said it was to do with this antiques thing that he's got going with this bloke in Paris. We had a row, so I went round to stay at my Aunt Livy's. She was out and there's these workmen all over the place, installing this thing. And the day nurse is on at me every five minutes: can't I make them their tea and watch them with the paintwork, my grandad's not very well and she's got his diarrhoea to see to. I couldn't stand it. I wanted some peace and quiet. It got on my nerves, so I came here.'

'Was it a bad one—the row, I mean?' Cecily asked gently.

Sue gave another long sigh. 'He was in London the other day, wouldn't say what for. I was hoping it was to do with, you know, us. Him and me: a job, or a course, or *something*, so that we could be together properly.'

She looked into her mug and swirled the dregs around. 'It's my fault. I was expecting too much. Anyway, he didn't say a word when he came back. That was on Thursday. Then today he hands me a little package. It's in a Harrods bag and I can feel it's a box. I forgot to give you this, he said. It's only a small thing. Well, I was over the *moon*. I thought,

185

Oh, how *sweet*, he's waited till the weekend.'

'What *was* it?' Cecily asked breathlessly.

Sue continued to stare into her mug. 'I suppose it's quite funny in a way. I was that thrilled, he couldn't understand why. I thought it was a ring.' Her eyes filled with tears. 'And it was a pair of Donna Karan trainer laces.' She paused. 'They're nice. As laces. But that's not the point, is it? So I just burst into tears and he got mad with me. And he just refuses to discuss it: won't say we won't ever get married, won't say we will. And then he says don't forget he's going to Bristol today and won't be back till tomorrow. He said he'd told me. He hadn't, though.'

There was silence. They felt the crushing weight of twenty-three minutes past three. Sue reached for a biscuit. Cecily leaned forward and pushed the photograph of Derek across the table. Then she leaned over and picked a pine cone from the top of the basket that filled the fireplace and began thoughtfully pulling it to pieces.

'That's him, that's Derek. He's having a party tonight. Or his wife is. He's doing the cooking,' she said flatly.

Sue, with her mouth full, tried to look sympathetic.

'You know she's been running these courses? No, I never really told you, did I? Well, it won't do any harm. He's my boss. She's an education adviser, and she's been running these courses for teachers. That's why Derek and I have managed to have so much time together.'

Sue nodded.

Cecily went on, 'They're finished now except for the assessment, so she's giving them all a nice little

186

farewell supper and Derek's doing the food. She expects him to.'

'Well, he's got to then, hasn't he? He hasn't got any choice. He'd probably much rather be with you.'

'I don't know. He likes all that mein host bollocks, and I think half the time he pretends she makes him do things. And the weekend before last wasn't too good. We had a row on Friday night at the Assembly Rooms and he stormed off. He was meant to be picking me up later but he didn't. I had to get a taxi back and the house was empty. I was furious. I was soaked through so I just had a bath and went to bed. I left him a blanket on the stairs. God *knows* where he went off to—he never really said. We made it up in the morning. We went shopping. Only for him, as usual. But everything was okay after that, or I thought it was.'

'Well then,' Sue said, without confidence.

'You know, I think I'm just fed up with it all. I'm still angry with him for wasting our time like that, when we don't have much. He's just fooling around. He used to say he hated weekends with his wife, but he's obviously looking forward to this one. The bastard is doing a fork supper for forty fat fucking infants teachers rather than spending the night with me, and he's *looking forward* to it.'

She tore at the remains of the pine cone. 'Picture it, them all simpering into their Frascati and congratulating her because her husband's in a pinny: *"Oh, aren't you lucky, I don't think mine even knows where the kitchen is!"* Ugh.'

She seized another pine cone and ripped it in half. 'Do you know, last week he actually consulted me about the menu? Did I think they'd want bread

187

as well if there was a pasta salad.'

'Incredible,' Sue said, shaking her head. She reached for her own pine cone and began systematically taking it apart.

'Yeah. Then I volunteered to do a pudding, and just for a second, not only did he think I was serious, he nearly accepted. *"Oh, would you really have time? Perhaps a trifle?"* he says. And I said sure, it wouldn't take a minute to grind some glass.'

Sue snorted bitterly.

Cecily went on, 'And then he went huffy with me for the rest of week. *He* went huffy. So yesterday, last thing, I told him he could make his own fucking trifle,' adding in a small voice, 'in front of the chairman of the governors.'

In the silence that followed, she looked despondently at the little pile of brown dusty shreds that had accumulated in her lap.

'I don't want a lot, you know, nothing that other people don't have. I'd just like'—Cecily turned two huge, tear-filled eyes to Sue—'I'd just like to be *secure*. He said he'd look after me. I thought that meant he'd be leaving her. He *knew* I thought that. Just a bit of security—it'd be so nice. Not to have to worry. That's not greedy, is it?'

She waved unhappily in the direction of the urn outside, in front of the sitting room window. 'Things like that,' she said, sniffing, 'little things. Going to the garden centre now and then. Being able to spend a bit, without panicking afterwards. Doing things together. It's not a lot, is it?' She sniffed angrily. 'S'not going to happen, though. And after all I've done for him! When I think of how I've helped him, how he said we'd be together. God, the things I've done for him!'

188

Sue was grinding the remains of the pine cone into powder. She was beginning to feel the warm, comforting feeling that comes from hearing that someone else has been every bit as craven and undignified over a man as one has been oneself.

'Just look at us,' she said. 'We're pathetic. All because of two bloody men. I could kill them. What shall we do?'

Cecily looked back at her, deciding. 'Only one thing *to* do,' she said stoutly. 'Have another pine cone, and I'll get the glasses.'

CHAPTER SIXTEEN

On the last day of June Andrew arrived at Olivia Passmore's office with a fairly clear idea of how he was going to handle her. By nature or perhaps by background, he was inclined to be intimidated by genuinely charming women like Olivia, if he was honest. His mother had not been like that, and the closest Valerie ever came to charm was when, in order to get something from him, she oozed with a shallow sweetness so cloying that he realised he preferred her quotidian crabbiness. So he could sometimes find himself a little nonplussed by the cared-for air of elegant women, how they smiled, their self-possession, the gracious poise with which they glided through conversation. He had observed some of those qualities in Sara when he had first met her, although now that he knew her better and had seen how often she burst out laughing, how bright and surprising she could be, he was less in awe of her. Her fantastic musicianship, her genius were, of course, part of her, but they were not *her*. She was also a woman. She had that warmth that real women have; well, beauty, in her case. He was, he didn't mind admitting, getting very fond of her, although he should not be thinking about Sara now. As he waited in the vestibule of the Assembly Rooms with a rather sulky DS Bridger in tow, he pulled his mind back to the minutes of Matthew Sawyer's last charity meeting, which he had received yesterday, and the interesting little bit of information they contained, perhaps the thing they had been looking for. Olivia Passmore would call for firm handling and all his concentration.

'Right, Bridger, you're my bag man today,' he said. 'What I want from you is notes and no interruptions. Use your eyes, not your mouth. Got that?'

Olivia Passmore's office in the Assembly Rooms managed to be very full without quite being untidy. There was too much in it: a large desk overlooking the high window, two heavy break-front bookcases, one with books and files, the other with numerous small grey boxes, and a grey filing cabinet. It was a dark room. On this June morning a green-shaded library lamp on the desk was switched on, casting a yellow, studious rectangle of light on numerous papers on the crowded desktop. In an attempt to create a quieter, informal space for discussion, two very low upholstered chairs and a small coffee table had been placed in one corner. Olivia waved Andrew to one of these, while Bridger stationed himself on a hard chair against the wall.

Sunk in one of the low chairs, Andrew felt as though he were sitting in a sports car much too small for his long legs. He said, looking round,

'The office of a busy person, I see. I won't take up too much of your time.'

Olivia gave him a faint, gracious smile. Her chair fitted her much better; her sitting posture even flattered her legs and slim knees. 'Things *are* busier,' she said. 'Taking over as acting director again, and in the circumstances; it's much worse than before, as it was all so sudden. It's rather cramped in here now but I decided to stay put. I couldn't bring myself to move back over to Matthew's office.'

'Why not?' Andrew asked, raising his voice and speaking directly. 'It must be rather awkward, as you've got Mrs Trowels over at the Circus. Don't you need her here?'

'It would be easier, but we manage. She comes over every morning and afternoon. And there's the telephone. No E-mail yet, unfortunately.' Olivia gave a faint, disappointed smile. 'Now,' she went on smoothly, 'how can I help you?'

'I'd like to go over some points again. Let's start with the Terry Trust. I gather you had an application in. Would you talk me through that?'

'Oh, yes,' said Olivia. 'Oh, I'm sorry, how rude of me, would you like some coffee?'

Without waiting for his answer she got up and picked up the telephone on the desk. For the next few moments she absorbed herself in the business of arranging for coffee to be made and brought to them. Andrew looked at the hand that held the receiver, noticing how slender was the wrist revealed by the elegant falling back of her cream silk sleeve. It was a smooth, long hand, but was it quite steady?

'The Terry Trust,' she began, when she had

191

replaced the receiver and sat down. 'Well, my father is over eighty, and not very mobile. He has emphysema, the result of childhood tuberculosis. Other problems too, his stomach isn't good. We converted the top of the house for him a few years ago and since then he's got much worse and can hardly manage the stairs. I applied to the Terry Trust for help with a stairlift. They turned us down.'

'That was recently, wasn't it?' Andrew said smoothly, wondering if it was a little odd that the half smile had not moved.

'Yes, it was, very. I'm sure you know that Matthew was a trustee. The Friday morning before he died he was at the trustees' meeting when my application was being considered, so that afternoon I asked him about the decision. He was reluctant to tell me at first, he said that I really should wait to get the board's letter. Then I knew, of course, and he had to confirm it. They weren't going to give a penny.'

'Did he say why?' Andrew asked, still watching her face.

'I got it out of him, although he would much rather have left me to find out by letter. They had taken the view'—Olivia took a deep breath—'that my father's condition made him an "inappropriate recipient" of help from the trust. And when I asked Matthew what that meant he told me that going by the medical reports my father's prognosis was so poor that the outlay on a stairlift couldn't be justified. He pointed out that my father needed a full-time day carer, and now a night nurse as well, and said that he would be better off in a nursing home, and it was "unrealistic" to carry on keeping

192

him at home. We have to pay for all his nursing care privately, you see. There's nothing on the NHS unless he goes into one of those awful care homes and sells the house. And he suggested that the burden of having him at home was *already* too great.'

She paused. 'He wasn't being sympathetic. And he didn't mean financially. He was warning me.' She hesitated and looked directly at Andrew, her eyes calm and candid.

'Please, do go on,' said Andrew. Her face still had not changed. She was still wearing the studied, serene half-smile with which she had greeted him when he arrived.

'The day before, the Thursday, I'd had to take the day off because the day carer was ill and the agency took till lunchtime to find a replacement. So Matthew had had to cancel a meeting he'd set up with me and the council's Director of Personnel for the morning. He was rather annoyed.'

A light tap on the door was followed by the arrival of coffee, brought on a tray by a woman in glasses. As she set it down some coffee slopped from the pot on to the tray and the woman gave a terrified gasp.

'Oh! Oh, I'm *ever* so sorry, Miss Passmore.'

She was dismissed with a glare and an irritated 'That'll do, thank you,' from Olivia. She poured. As Bridger lumbered across and helped himself to three biscuits, she recomposed her face.

'What he didn't understand'—even through the restored half-smile, Olivia sounded quite fierce— 'is that my father will never, ever go into a nursing home. Have you seen those places? Do you think Matthew Sawyer would ever have any of his family

193

in one? Not, of course, that money would be any obstacle in *his* case.'

She paused, and went on quietly. 'I have given my father a promise that he will stay at home for as long as he wants to, and that we'll manage the expense. And we do. Please do help yourself to sugar.'

Andrew swallowed some coffee. 'It must have been quite a blow, not getting the stairlift?'

Olivia looked back at him. 'Actually, no. A grant would have been a great help, obviously. We do get whatever help we can. The Musicians' Benevolent Fund have been wonderful in the past, and there are other bits of help available. But in fact we're going ahead with the stairlift anyway. In fact we had the men in at the weekend. The grant wouldn't have made the difference between getting it and not; it would just have made it easier.'

'But you must have been rather angry and upset with Matthew Sawyer that afternoon, Miss Passmore?' Andrew said, neutrally.

'Oh, I was,' Olivia said, a little brightly. 'Of course I was. I wouldn't try to deny it. But I didn't have a reason for wanting him dead. I had nothing to gain by it. The Terry Trust's decision was already made, and as I said, the grant wasn't essential anyhow. Matthew was rather ungenerous about my having to take time off, but I wasn't particularly worried about that. I've been employed by the local authority for over twenty years and they can't go getting rid of people because they have frail relatives, you know.'

A slight frown appeared on her face. 'I liked Matthew. And you know, I'm a little too mature to go stabbing someone in the back out of pique, just

194

because they've upset me.'

'And the meeting that you were meant to have on the Thursday—the one that was cancelled because you had to take the day off. What was that to have been about? Was it mentioned when you met here on the Friday afternoon before he died?'

'No, it was some personnel matter and we were going to reschedule. But on the Friday he came to talk about other things. The Hackett Bequest, which you heard about from Mrs Trowels, and to be briefed for the welcome speech he was giving.'

'Ah, yes, the Hackett Bequest. Would you just remind me?'

'The Hackett Bequest,' Olivia said patiently, 'was a collection of sewing aids. Boxes, needlecases, pincushions, bobbins, tape measures, scissors, that kind of thing. There were three or four châtelaines as well. There were about five hundred objects in all, some of them extremely rare. As you know, the collection was lost in 1941.'

She paused, as if she hoped that were enough, and Andrew's silence indicated that it was not.

'Lots of the museum's collections were taken out of Bath during the war for safekeeping, but some had to be left. The bomb in 1941 in the Circus destroyed the basement and all the records and objects in it, including the Hackett Bequest. A copy of the catalogue was housed in the Guildhall archive though, and that survived, except for the five end pages. So we know exactly what the objects were. These things do happen sometimes. There wasn't much anyone could do. So after the war the collection was quietly de-accessioned.'

'What does that mean, exactly?' Andrew asked.

'It's to do with the way a museum manages its

195

collections. The bequest was made in 1910 and the museum accepted it as a gift, rather than on permanent loan, which is commoner now. In 1910 they obviously weren't worried about having the money to carry on curating things indefinitely, in perpetuity. So the bequest was accessioned: given an accession number which means that the museum would always be able to locate it, identify it and so on. And there is an obligation to have accessioned items properly described, recorded and conserved to professional standards and not sold or otherwise disposed of. A museum can de-accession things, reverse the process in other words, if for example something is destroyed. De-accessioning removes the accession number from the record. It's a legal proceeding, and is always minuted; a museum can't just get rid of things it doesn't want any more, not easily. In the case of the Hackett Bequest, it was the only thing to do. The collection had been destroyed by enemy action, so there was no point in keeping the Hackett Bequest accession number open when the collection no longer existed. It was tidier to write it off by de-accessioning it. The catalogue was conserved of course, for the purposes of scholarship.'

She interpreted Andrew's silent absorption of this information as a reproach and again her face assumed the pleasant half-smile.

'It wasn't a cover-up, or anything like that. It's all in the minutes. There were no surviving members of the family to take any interest, and there was no public objection; the bequest had never, as far as I know, been on display anyway. So it was never missed.'

196

'And you said, I think, that the whole story was more or less common knowledge within the museum. Then why was Matthew Sawyer so excited about finding the catalogue in the archive? Excited enough to send you a memo from there, rather than wait till he got back to his office?'

Olivia's slight smile did not waver. 'Well, I've always assumed it's common knowledge. Most people who've been here any length of time know about it. Matthew did "find" the catalogue in the archive, but it's not as if it were lost or anything, he just came across it in the course of one of his afternoons. He's been in there regularly since he arrived, getting to grips with the collections. He wanted to computerise the whole thing eventually. It's possible Matthew hadn't heard the story, but that would surprise me. He was very good at finding out things. Very thorough. But he wasn't *excited* about finding it, he simply wanted to get the paper conservator on to it as soon as possible, I suppose. I'm in charge of the conservation departments, so he wrote the memo to me.'

'And you discussed the conservation work when he came to see you at the end of that afternoon?'

'Yes, that's right. Although the murder put it right out of my head. I didn't get down to speaking to the paper conservator until this week, I'm afraid.' As was only polite, her smile became a shade apologetic.

'Well, better late than never, I'm sure,' Andrew said. 'Did you discuss any other matter with Matthew Sawyer that afternoon?'

'No. Except that I briefed him about the group he was going to address at six thirty. The natural healers. They've had their convention here three years running, now.'

'And is it your impression they'll be booking again next year?' Andrew asked impassively. 'I gather he didn't go down too well. And you'd briefed him?'

Olivia groaned patronisingly. 'Poor Matthew. I'll never know what possessed him. You'll have heard from all those irate delegates, I suppose. He did say some silly things. Yes, I had briefed him, but he didn't seem to have taken anything in. Sudden stage fright, perhaps. We'll never know.' Again the smile of polite disappointment crossed her face.

'Not from him, certainly,' murmured Andrew, looking at her dully. 'One last thing. Did you by any chance discuss a security matter? A security matter that concerned a member of staff and a serious breach of procedure?'

Olivia scanned Andrew's face for a clue as to what he was talking about. 'No. Do you mind telling me what you mean?'

'George Townsend?'

'George? No, we didn't discuss George. Why should we?'

'So George wasn't discussed at all?'

'No. Look, is George in trouble? He was one of the last people off the premises that night. He was locking up here. He didn't . . . surely . . . ? Has he said anything?'

'Nothing, at this stage, that leads to the murderer. We've had to double-check his alibi. There was a minor problem with it, to do with a little clandestine home entertainment that he went in for; I won't go into it. It didn't get us any further forward with the case. That's what we'd all like, isn't it, something that leads us to whoever did

198

this.'

'Of course. It's an awful business.' The silence which followed signalled to them both that the meeting was over.

'Well, thank you.' Andrew rose to go, wondering if the slight brightening in Olivia Passmore's eyes was a sign of relief. 'You've been extremely helpful,' he said, and had nearly reached the end of the dim corridor that led to the front entrance before he asked himself if he really meant it, and just who, in the end, had been handling whom.

Part Two

Part Two

CHAPTER SEVENTEEN

In the city the freshness of June thickened charmlessly into full summer. Privets and cotoneasters in the parks and gardens darkened into the menacing opaque green of old nettles and grass underfoot whispered like sand. Tall nameless weeds that thrived by being copiously peed on by dogs and cats sprouted along cracked walls and at the feet of lampposts, proffering seed heads weighted with clusters of succulent black aphids. Rubbish bins were overflowing by mid-morning and by early afternoon stank and buzzed with wasps. Daytripping senior citizens from Wales ambled along the pavements three abreast in lightweight cardies and wide shoes at a pace that was fractionally faster than glacial. Backpackers as sedate as camels shed their loads on every crossing and street corner, pausing to read maps, check contents of their bum bags and say wow at buildings. Normally unaggressive Bathonians banked up in scores behind on the pavements and trained their burning eyes into their backs, willing them telepathically and unsuccessfully to shift. Judging it too hot to negotiate passage in either Welsh or Dutch they would then smile insincerely as they stepped around them into the melted ice-cream slicks which shared the gutters and doorways with dropped cones, wooden forks, polystyrene trays and homeless people. Car parks were clogged from early morning. Lorries, delivery vans, cars, tour coaches, roof-racked campers and open-top buses hissed, squealed, started and stopped through town in a grey shimmering film of hot diesel exhaust, juddering forward at the whim of traffic lights whose changing colours were almost invisible in the glare of the sun on their filthy bulbs.

By mid-July no one pretended any longer to be enjoying the weather. Everyone was too hot, sick of strawberries and bored with barbecues; people imagined themselves asthmatic and grew animated about the pollen count and the ozone layer. They exchanged remarks such as 'Warm again today,' in tones of mutual pity. A toddler went missing from Victoria Park and turned up fourteen miles away wandering, mute, and covered with cigarette burns. Two boys of eleven who had gone fishing by the canal disappeared and eight days later their bodies were unearthed from a shallow grave by a dog called Rhona. The *Bath Chronicle* ranted about communities torn apart and launched appeals for information. It ran updates on the stories daily, along with bulletins on air quality and features on inexpensive summer cocktails, alfresco dining and skin cancer. On the inside pages it reported briefly that Matthew Sawyer's inquest had been opened and adjourned. Andrew was no further forward with the case and considered it a small and ironic mercy that most people seemed to have forgotten about it, the combination of summer diversions, worse mysteries and the deaths of children driving it from their overheated minds.

Annabel Sawyer took her children out of school a week early and rang Detective Sergeant Bridger. 'We're going to Umbria at the end of the week. I've taken a villa. I can't hang about all summer waiting for a date for the inquest to reopen. You can let me know, I suppose. I *suppose* you'll want the address, just in case you get any further forward. Although you haven't done too well so far, have you?'

At the other end of the telephone Bridger was finishing his Mars bar as she went on, 'There's no telephone. My parents are coming too, and the nanny. We all need a proper break; we'll be away at least six weeks.'

It was Bridger's first day back after a fortnight in Malta with his mates and he was still relaxed. 'That sounds just the ticket, madam,' he said, 'but I'd like to just pop round for an update before you go.'

There was an exasperated silence.

'I've been away myself. Need to get through the pile of stuff on this desk. Not worth going on holiday really, is it, it's all waiting for you when you get back. Anyway, Thursday morning suit you, Mrs Sawyer? The seventeenth? Just like to go over where we're up to, see if we can see the way ahead and work backwards from there. See you about half eleven then, madam?' he added jovially, certain that he was great with widows.

Thank God, anyway, for a reason to get out at least once from this baking office and away from those useless security tapes from Littlewoods. As if endlessly watching footage of two teenagers snogging in a doorway, two staggering drunks, both regulars, holding each other up, and a manic nocturnal jogger going round and round was going to get them anywhere. Andrew Poole just kept saying that he wanted them found and brought in, they had to have seen *something*. Well, it had been easy enough to question the two drunks and, of course, useless. He could have told Poole that in the first place. And if he ever managed to identify these other characters they'd turn out to be useless too, and that would be another God knew how many hours wasted and nothing to show for it. And that farce with Olivia Passmore, going over the stuff all over again. *'Use your eyes, not your mouth.'* Oh, yes, sir, three bags full, sir. All that rubbish about something being wrong with her legs. He'd got a proper eyeful (use your eyes, right?) and they'd looked all right to him, not half bad in fact. Well, fuck it. He was going to do some proper police work. She was quite attractive, that Annabel Sawyer, for her age. She might offer him lunch.

CHAPTER EIGHTEEN

Tetchy was not the word, but it was the one Sue used to excuse herself.

'No, I'm sorry, I'm a bit tetchy today. Sorry. Of course you can change your order. Bagel instead of baguette, cream cheese and smoked salmon with dill dressing not the beef, but you do still want the mayonnaise, sorry, the horseradish. No butter. And salad. With tortilla chips but no dip. Right. No problem.'

She could have ground her back teeth into powder, fed up to them as she was. The lady who had suffered such indecision over her lunch had now strolled over to the poolside and was blandly piling her hair into a swimming hat covered with rubber dahlias. In a few minutes she would be swimming up and down with pursed lips, keeping her earrings dry, while Sue argued with the hotel kitchen about the changed order and failed to convince them it wasn't her mistake.

It was Paul again, of course. He had been to Bristol again on Sunday. He had not said a word about what he'd been doing there but she knew it would be the antiques again. Honestly, they were taking over. His room and hallway were filling up with horrible things, chairs, mirrors, a washstand, all dark and really *old*, and playing havoc with the energy rhythms. Feng shui was right out of the window now. It was now Tuesday, and so far this week he had already worked a double shift and despite the trouble he had got into last time had taken on another job for Coldstreams. And why? Why was he working so hard and what was he doing with all the money? He never spent much on her and they never went anywhere really nice. He had always agreed with her that they should both save 'for the future', only when she came to think of it he had never quite said what he thought that future was. With this last row, she feared that it might not even include her. At one time, months ago now, he'd more or less gone along with her plans. He'd let her believe they were his plans too. A flat together. Moving away to get jobs. There had been a bit of talk at one time about wanting to start a restaurant, which had subsided into just running one and lately had not been mentioned at all. She had even suggested that he use some of his savings to do a degree in catering, which, along with her promise to help support him while he did it, had been greeted with polite scorn. She was beginning to suspect he hadn't saved a penny. If he would only talk to her, but he seemed to be, if anything, even more remote. Was there someone else?

She sighed and gave herself a trial squeeze in the

midriff. She had been practically living on iced tea and exercising like a racehorse for over two weeks to try to make up for that Saturday with Cecily and she was only now able, just, to look down at her stomach without shuddering. It had started with the hot chocolate. Looking back, the rest had more or less crept up on her, and that was why constant vigilance was so important. After their second bottle of wine, with which they'd demolished Cecily's entire store of crisps and nuts, they'd gone to the fridge and decided that a tiny bone of pecorino cheese, some furry pesto and a few leaves of floppy chervil provided no sort of answer to their need for serious comfort, added to which all that sort of stuff had reminded Cecily of Derek. So they'd rung for pizza and ordered not quite the biggest with as many extra toppings as they could fit on and eaten it all, surprisingly fast, with another bottle of Spanish red. Sue had then fallen asleep on the sofa (she still wasn't sure how long for) and awoken to a crisis. There was nothing for dessert! She clearly remembered wandering up the street with Cecily soon after this, lurching into JVC News and buying two large tubs of Häagen-Dazs and a frozen pineapple cheesecake. They had both found this funny at the time. On the way back, they had decided to celebrate properly and anyway, the fresh air had given them an appetite and the pizza, in retrospect, had been rather small and a long time ago. So it had been really funny to stumble back through Cecily's door bearing three warm brown paper carrier bags with oil-soaked bottoms as well as the ice-cream, the cheesecake, a Goldie Hawn video and two more bottles of wine.

They had been giggling as they unpacked the

tubs from the bags, discarding the saffron yellow dripping lids, and stacked up across the coffee table a line of aluminium dishes precariously full of lamb tikka masala, chicken pasanda, beef korma, vindaloo prawns, naan bread, turmeric rice and poppadums. A blob of food landed on Derek's photograph and gave him a yellow eye-patch and a head bandage. That had been funny. Then it had been a great laugh to sprawl on either side of the table stabbing into the dishes with forks and fingers and swigging the Fitou from tumblers. They had even laughed at the movie. It was some time afterwards, after the cheesecake and the wine but before the ice-cream that Cecily had heaved herself towards the kitchen muttering that the double pecan fudge chocolate ripple needed something to go with it. She had returned waving a brown liqueur bottle.

'Amaretto,' she sniggered, 'under the shink. I knew I had it,' and uncorked it incompetently, tipping it unsteadily towards Sue's glass. Nothing had come out at first, and Cecily had peered up it like a pantomime pirate. Then a slug of oily caramel had appeared at the neck of the bottle and dropped with a soft plod into the bottom of the glass, where it sat like a well-sucked toffee.

'My God,' said Sue, peering into it and breathing in the vinegary smell of ancient almonds, 'how long have you had this?'

Cecily replied, swallowing a belch, 'Oh, a while. Shmeant to keep. Shtoo expensive to drink all in one go.' Scanning the label, she said, 'I mean, somebody paid three pounds nineteen and six for thish. Jusht wants diluting. Where's the lemonade?'

Sue smiled at the memory. Cecily was so great.

She wasn't letting that Derek walk all over *her*. Sue would take a leaf from Cecily's book and face up to Paul. She would make him talk to her, get things out in the open. Whatever was going on with Paul, it would be better to know. Be out with it, whatever it was.

For some reason this brought her mind back round to Cecily and the end of that evening, whose shaky closing sequences she viewed as if through a faulty projector. She remembered wondering dimly why Cecily was shouting into the loo—who could be down there at this time of night?—and finding that the soothing tiled wall on which she was just resting her cheek for a moment was the bathroom floor. That was the bit she most hated to dwell on, so it was with mixed feelings that she was interrupted by the dripping return of Dahlia Head because she had not yet, she suddenly realised, rung the kitchen.

CHAPTER NINETEEN

He had learned that the best restaurants were the Bofinger and Chez Paul in the Bastille, La Méditerranée and Le Bistrot de Paris in St-Germain, and sometimes, in the middle of the day, Juveniles or Aux Bons Crus. It was inconceivable that he would ever actually eat in them, and although he had grown almost content with his baguette-based diet he could occasionally, loitering outside, feel angrily and hungrily excluded. The last two places could be hazardous, because the stockbrokers and bankers who frequented the restaurants close to La Bourse were less likely to linger afterwards on the pavements and, being Parisian, were never entirely lacking in vigilance. And they could be disappointingly light on cash, although good for watches, lighters and the plastic cards which he knew how to sell on. At this time of year, the best harvests were still the brasseries where tourists gathered, and the best time for picking was after dark when they emerged with full stomachs and swimming heads into the night, careless on dinner and atmosphere. He was scornful of the joy they felt at being in Paris and was sometimes aware, even as his fingers were slipping into bags and hooking their wallets, that he was robbing them of this, too.

Le Marais, where he was now, was no good for his purposes. From his bench in the garden in the middle of the dark square he watched, through the plane trees, as the waiters in long aprons from Ma Bourgogne passed among the outside tables under the colonnades, bright in the light beaming out from the interior. There were plenty of tourists here as well, of course, but most of the diners would be the young and fashionable inhabitants of the apartments hereabouts who would be wise to his type and infinitely more experienced in the ways of the city than he. He felt a rush of anxiety to be elsewhere, anywhere that he would feel less conspicuous and foreign.

He was nervous, although the man he was meeting was supposed to be reliable. Not that any guarantees came with that kind of information. But he had learned that there were ways of getting out of France if you had the money and knew the right people, and now after two months working the streets and the tourist spots he had got enough together to get to England and even to get by in London for a while. In England, he'd been told, there was plenty of casual work for cash and little trouble from the authorities; here it had been impossible to get any sort of job. Everywhere he went, even for waiting or kitchen jobs, he had been expected to sign things, things to do with the minimum wage laws, and how could he do that without immigration papers? And he had made the mistake of lodging with some of the other West African Wolof people in a cheap, crowded boarding-house in Montmartre where he had discovered, too late, that police raids were common. So his name and his illegal status were known, and he had been lucky to escape arrest and deportation.

The message had been to be here at midnight. There were to be no names; the man was simply Le Fournisseur, the supplier, while he himself would be addressed as Le Client. It was simply a matter of business: the price, the arrangements, the deal. What would he look like? From which of the garden's four gates, lit only by the white globes hanging from black, wrought-iron posts, would he approach? Le Fournisseur was obviously experienced and careful. He checked again that he was on the right bench. He had been told to stand facing the equestrian statue in the middle of the garden in the Place des Vosges, find the bench that the horse seemed to be looking at, and to wait there. It had been easy, because the horse's head was turning sharply, to identify this bench in the south-east corner, but he detected in the instructions a practised method of avoiding any confusion in mistranslation of left or right.

Looking across the garden once more towards the restaurants under the colonnades surrounding the square, his eyes picked up a movement among the heads of the people dining at Ma Bourgogne. A heavy man was standing up and removing the napkin from his throat. With a nod to the waiter, he was crossing between tables and moving alone into the darkness on the edge of the pavement, where he hesitated, waiting for a car to pass. Now, as Le Fournisseur crossed the road towards the gate and entered the garden, his eyes were coming to rest firmly and unmistakably on the bench and on himself, Le Client, waiting under the gaze of the cold bronze horse.

CHAPTER TWENTY

'Ah, Sara, Sara, forgive me for not getting up.' The frail, amiable voice came from behind the rose bushes. As instructed by Olivia, Sara had come straight in by the garden door. She followed the wavering parallel lines in the grass to the point where they disappeared on to a patch of lawn behind a mass of thick flowering Albertine and saw at first little else other than a generous bottom encased in tight grey cotton. Serena had parked Edwin's wheelchair and was now leaning over him, tucking a mohair blanket in around his legs. Edwin's white head darted out around her ample sides and he beckoned at Sara encouragingly with a flat brown hand as big as a paddle.

Serena straightened up and turned round as she

reached them. 'Well now, here's our important visitor!' she exclaimed to Edwin. 'We've been getting very excited, haven't we? Very impatient to show off our new stairlift and get out to the garden! Right-oh,' she said comfortably, 'no worries, okay? I'll pop off and get you some tea. Would you like that?'

She looked as if she might squeeze their cheeks between her thumb and forefinger. Sara replied, in the surprised tone that seemed necessary despite its being four o'clock in the afternoon and tea the very thing she had been invited for, that that would be lovely. They watched Serena's progress back across the grass to the house.

'Tedious cow,' Edwin said, pulling off the blanket and adding in a loud voice, 'Australian, you know! She can't help it!' although the effort brought on a wheezing cough.

He waved Sara into a garden chair next to him and said, 'Forgive me, I shouldn't say such a thing, but she does ask for it. But we haven't even properly met. But I know *of* you, of course. I've got your Elgar concerto. I think your playing is . . .'

He frowned slightly as he considered what to say, pausing just sufficiently long for Sara to feel a wave of worry that he didn't like it.

'Extraordinarily warm, sensitive. Nothing flashy, but romantic,' he said, smiling at her with a blue-eyed, intelligent look. 'In exactly the right spirit for the piece. The only way I ever want to hear it.'

'Oh, I'm so pleased,' Sara said, delighted. 'I've got all your baroque recordings. That Handel piece, "Eternal Source of Light Divine". It is simply wonderful. That long, long counter-tenor melody, then the trumpet answering. It's sublime.'

'Good, good,' Edwin said, nodding. 'That pleases me very much. I did always love Handel. Oh, my, but counter-tenors. Aren't they stupid? No, that's unfair. *All* singers are stupid.'

'Oh, really? What about cellists, then?'

'Oh, bone-headed and cloth-eared, most of 'em,' Edwin said, laughing. 'Present company excepted, of course. No, actually, my dear, I hope you didn't mind being summoned. When I heard you'd been here to supper I was rather cross with poor Livy for not bringing you upstairs so that I could meet you. So I got her to ask you to tea.'

Sara detected the imperiousness of the long-term invalid.

'And it's very kind of you to come.'

'It's a pleasure. And you've just got your stairlift, I hear, so you can entertain in the garden. That must be lovely. I love my garden.'

'Bloody marvellous, I can tell you. Olivia knows how I love the garden. She is bloody marvellous, my Olivia, goes through a lot. Thinks I don't know.'

Edwin smiled beatifically, then seemed to fade. He took a laborious breath and his eyelids drooped. He smiled weakly at Sara and said, 'Hang on. Just a minute.'

He reached back and with one hand picked a coil of curved clear plastic tubing from a hook on the handle of his wheelchair. Sara realised that his hands were not especially big at all, but only seemed to be because his wrists were so wasted. Under his clothes his body was terribly thin; his long legs, sticking out and meeting at the knees, were like two poles draped loosely in gabardine. The tubing led to a black metal cylinder propped up on a stand behind the chair. Expertly he

215

attached the two curling ends at the other end of the tubing into his nostrils and hooked the loops round his ears. It looked a little like a toy stethoscope, and a bit daft on his long, dignified face. He breathed in and immediately brightened.

'Ridiculous bloody set-up,' he grumbled. 'Oxygen. Can't go long without it. But I hate to meet someone for the first time with half a mile of tube wrapped round my face. Vanity, no doubt.'

They were interrupted by the arrival of Serena with a tea tray. Sara noticed with pleasure that there were only two cups, so Serena would not be joining them. She wanted this charming, funny man all to herself for a while longer. She said, 'I'll pour, shall I?' giving Serena time enough to glint with goodwill and encourage Edwin to 'manage' one or two of his favourite biscuits. When she had gone, they sipped at their tea for a while. Edwin surveyed his garden, and, waving from his chair, pointed out some of his favourite plants.

'That's a Cyprus rock rose,' he said, 'with a scent like crushed sweeties. Do you like it? Old Serena, she likes the lavender best. Old-fashioned, she says, that's what she likes. She's from Sydney, you know. Doing Europe. Bath's a revelation to her, of course.' He chuckled. 'She went to see that film, *Emma*. Raved about it. Oh, I said, borrow it. It'll be in the bookcase.'

He began to snigger and some of his tea went down the wrong way. As he recovered he reached out to touch Sara's arm and said, in a voice high-pitched with mirth, 'And you know what she said? She said, "Oh, is the book out already?"'

Edwin's wholehearted and malicious pleasure in Serena's mistake was infectious; they both shook

216

with laughter. They talked on. From time to time Edwin would pause and let his eyes close for a few seconds. Then he would open them and say, 'Go on, go *on*,' impatient with his own fatigue. He told her reliably scurrilous stories about his days as a baroque trumpet player: foreign tours, unpopular conductors, memorably good, and bad, concerts.

'Oh, God, Munich. Before the war of course. We dragged the entire wardrobe into the corridor. Funny at the time.'

After a while Sara said, 'I've brought my cello. I wonder if you might be in the mood to listen to something?'

Edwin gave her another beautiful, blue-eyed look, full of gratitude. He had knotted his handkerchief in the corners and was wearing it on his head, in defiance of Serena, who had brought out a ridiculous sombrero for him.

'Oh, *would* you?' he asked, like a child. 'Would you really?' He paused, looking at her carefully. 'Dare I ask, perhaps, for one of the Bach cello suites? I would love that.'

Sara was stricken. 'I don't play those now,' she said. 'I haven't . . . I can't . . . I mean, is there anything else? I really haven't played those for a long time.'

'I know,' Edwin said quietly. 'I do know, and I think I understand. I just think'—he paused—'that the time comes when we have to go on, you know, somehow. I thought perhaps here, it might be possible, not really a performance, only me. But never mind, anything would be lovely. You choose.'

As she hesitated he went on, 'I do so love those pieces. It's not, in a way, *playing* that they require, is it? It's *living*. In performance, you have to live

217

them. I always think they are . . . a little glimpse of eternity. Does that sound stupid?'

Sara shook her head. 'No, I think you're right. And that, of course, is the difficulty.' She looked away. 'I would like you to hear one. I could try, if you'll forgive any lapses. It really has been a long time. I haven't played them since Paris. You heard what happened? I think word got round.'

Edwin smiled and, nodding slowly, looked at her so kindly she thought she would cry. 'But never mind. Just never mind,' he said. 'You'll be all right.'

And so Sara brought the instrument out to the sunny garden and planted herself a way off in the shade of an overgrown lilac bush by the garden wall. Edwin stayed where he was, tucked up in his blanket again, surrounded by his beloved rock roses, and turned his face up to the sun. At first Sara's playing was so soft that she did not even drown out the noise of distant brakes as a bus trundled down Bathwick Hill, but Edwin did not mind. It reminded him where he actually was, and so only increased the wonder of it, that he at eighty-four, with his lungs played out and the rest of him rotting quietly in a wheelchair in a dusty city garden, should yet be in paradise. He had always supposed that time was meant to stand still at such a moment, and was finding that it wasn't. It was ticking on, and every second was sweet, finite and precious. For this little while he was feeling the slowing pat-pat-pat of his existence measured out not in daily pain but in the gentle beat of the sun on his tired temples, in the passing of each easy, flower-filled breath and in the wise and wordless cadences of Bach, played by that beautiful girl with the shining hair.

He was smiling as his eyes closed. 'Yes, we do have to go on, you see, even when it seems impossible,' he said, as the music drew to its end.

He opened his eyes and called softly across the grass to her as she approached and took her seat beside him. 'The gift! It does, in the end, all come down to the gift. If you have a gift but cannot give it, then everything'—he waved his great hands in a vague circle—'everything becomes blocked. There is a boulder in your stream. Until you move it, you cannot give, nor can you receive. You understand. The time does come when you find it moves. Of course, you still miss him. Of course. But you will move it, one day.'

Sara turned to him. 'I don't know what to say. Except that I wish I'd met you long ago. I've known Olivia for a while, and yet this is the first time we've met. And it's been just . . . so . . . lovely. May I come again?'

But there was no chance to say any more. Serena was bustling back towards them. It was nebuliser time again and Edwin, more tired even than usual, agreed that it was time to go back in. Suddenly everything was focused on the physical task of getting Edwin, wheelchair, rug, tubing and cylinder back inside. Sara helped, clumsily, following behind Serena who was pushing the lumbering chair, wheeling the oxygen cylinder on its little stand, holding up the tubing to keep it from being trapped under the wheels. The entourage made its way up the slope into the back of the house, in by the French window and across Olivia's study. This time the curtains were drawn back and the desk held only two or three large heavy books and a telephone. Serena wheeled Edwin from the study

219

out into the kitchen and from there into the hall to the foot of the stairs.

'Isn't it clever?' she said to Sara, stabbing down the wheelchair brake in front of the stairlift. 'No worries. Three men here for an entire weekend getting it put in and guess who got to clear up? Not that I mind, it makes such a difference, him getting out. Now, let's get you in the seat.'

The raising of Edwin from the wheelchair and the transfer to the little folding seat installed on its track against the wall was achieved.

'Quite a nifty little contraption, eh?' said Edwin triumphantly to Sara. A safety bar like a small aeroplane table was unfolded down in front of him and clicked into place. He pressed the button on the edge of the bar.

'Now watch this!' He glided slowly upwards for a few seconds and with another press of the button, stopped with his legs dangling.

'Ha! Wonderful bloody set-up!'

'You're a lucky fellow, aren't you?' said Serena, folding the mohair blanket. 'What these things cost!' She turned to Sara. 'You wouldn't believe it. There are three flights, you see. Up here to the drawing room and Miss Passmore's room, Sue's old room and the spare above that, and Edwin and my room right at the top. We thought we'd had it when the Terry Trust turned us down, didn't we? But Miss Passmore got round it somehow. No worries.'

She beamed at Edwin, waiting patiently in the little seat. 'You're a very lucky fellow.'

'Ah, but we don't worry about the cost, do we?' Edwin said grandly. He winked down at Sara. 'The gift. A gift of love, an offering of love. Not that I know anything, of course. Rum set-up if you ask

220

me, but I'm not complaining.'

And then, bestowing a royal wave as he ascended, he hooted a little breathlessly, 'Churchill, that was the fella! Remember Churchill?'

CHAPTER TWENTY-ONE

After her tea with Edwin, Sara contrived to keep out of town and in the shade. In her pond high up in the garden the waterlilies flowered and the newt family swam with the goldfish around the stems of brilliant yellow water irises. Screened on one side by high bamboo, she set up a huge calico umbrella over the table and chairs at the pond side and tied the hammock between a pear tree and a corkscrew willow a few feet further off. When James arrived he found her almost encamped. Books and old papers had collected under the table along with two sweaters and a pair of gardening shoes. On the table was a tray with two or three plastic mineral-water bottles, several glasses, a brown banana and a citronella candle in a flowerpot.

He came up the garden, hooting a bit of Mozart and then breaking off to call, 'Ach, where the hell are ye, ye daft witch?' She hooted back from the hammock. He climbed the path to the pond, rustled past the curtain of bamboo, and then paused to get his breath back and take her in. She certainly looked all right, loose-limbed, brown and dressed in rumpled white cotton and lilac espadrilles. Her hair was piled up under an unglamorous hat, her face was shiny with sun cream and James was pleased to note that she was looking after herself to the extent of bothering with earrings.

'It's lovely not going out,' she said complacently. 'How are you? How's Tom? How's the outside world? How was Brussels? And the seaside?'

'All fine,' said James, collapsing languidly into a chair. He sighed expansively. 'It's lovely up here, isn't it? Tempting not to go anywhere at all.'

Sara smiled. 'I was just thinking, before you came, that it's because of you I'm here at all. Remember?'

James smiled.

Old friends do not have to relate their remembrances to each other, Sara thought, it is enough just to check occasionally that we still share the same ones.

While waiting for him to arrive, she had allowed her mind to wander back to the time when she and Matteo had first met. Their careers were both taking off and how wonderful they had been together; it had been all mutual support, understanding of the absences, no jealousies. Matteo, made for glamour, had loved the itinerant life of an international conductor, moving between airports, hotel rooms and concert halls. In fact the life was not glamorous at all, yet he had managed to make it seem so. He had thought it amusing that in one two-month period they had only been home together for two days, but had managed twice to meet for a few hours, once at Heathrow and once when in desperation she had flown on from giving a concert in New York to hear him conduct in Chicago. Her plane had been delayed and she had arrived too late for the concert. She had checked in

222

to their hotel, exhausted, at two a.m. He had flown on to San Francisco at seven.

That was the summer two years ago that she, egged on by James, had persuaded Matteo that they should give up the London flat and buy Medlar Cottage. She had found it with James one weekend when she had gone to Bath to discuss a concert series that he was programming for the South Bank. They had gone for a walk in St Catherine's Valley and it had been extraordinary, to drive only two miles from the poised creamy stone and magnolias of James and Tom's flat in Camden Crescent and come upon St Catherine, all ancient pastures and hedges. High on the hillside, just across from a wide sloping meadow with six gracious lime trees, stood the long cottage of Bath stone. It was surrounded on all sides by over an acre of wild garden, while the narrow lane which led through the valley to St Catherine's Court ran below the wall of the front garden just like, Sara said, the hem on its skirt. She had been telling James of her unease with the pace of their life, and the For Sale sign on the drive had convinced her that London was the problem. James had been swift to agree.

Matteo, having stipulated his need for a large studio in which he could study scores and make as much noise as he liked, had been happy enough to go along. He defined a home as the place where you keep your favourite CDs, so that the London flat had been as much home as he needed. He had not observed that for Sara there was something more at stake. The wish to 'get out of London', being the only reason they could give each other for the move, became their only mutual ground.

They had moved into Medlar Cottage one September weekend. The cottage had been quickly and cheaply prettified by its previous colour-blind owners. It was just possible to believe, surveying the drifts of dog and cat hair that had collected along the skirting boards and under the radiators, that in their nine years of occupation they had not owned a vacuum cleaner. Woodlice clustered in scores under the orange Formica in the kitchen, while mouse droppings adorned the cupboard tops and larder shelves. While Matteo had had hysterics and flounced off back to Europe and the States on a string of engagements that would make it 'impossible' to return before Christmas, Sara had dragooned legions of roofers, plumbers, joiners, builders and decorators. She got a mobile phone so that she could check up on progress when she was travelling. She carried swatches and paint cards everywhere in the way that new grandparents carry baby photographs. Looking back, she was appalled at what a bore she must have been. At the time, she had felt as though she were fighting for the survival of everything. She could not have borne it if Matteo had continued to prefer the penthouse-suite-gym-Jacuzzi-room-service way of life instead of being lured back to the warmth of a proper home. She bought gallons of sludgy paint and acres of handwoven and handprinted fabrics, bought dubious bits of furniture at auctions and had them stripped, limed, waxed, stencilled. She installed wood-burning stoves, restored open fireplaces in the bedrooms and covered the floors in pale, prickly sisal. She went to Jermyn Street for the bathroom taps and towel rails, prowled the reclamation yards of Bath for wall sconces and a

Belfast sink. She bought log baskets, kilims, glazed jardinières, and employed a real designer to make the Shaker kitchen. They got to know her well at Mulberry. In three months, she spent nearly two years' earnings. She had been, in retrospect, a little extreme.

James was trying not to scrutinise her too obviously. 'You do look unbelievably relaxed,' he said, 'but I'm here to pluck you from your Arcadian idyll. I'm taking you to lunch. Go and get changed. Put on some proper underwear.'

'You're not taking me into town. I'm not going into town,' she said, stretching. 'It was mobbed on Tuesday. I'm not going into Bath before the end of August, unless I've got a cattle prod. Let's go over to Fortune Park. We can have a swim as well; they'll lend you something to swim in.'

In the car he said, 'Are you all right, Sara?'

She looked out of the window for a time before speaking. 'Of course. More to the point, are you? What *was* all that about the alibi, James?'

James looked straight ahead. 'Oh, something and nothing. Nothing. I'll tell you some time. All over now. Thanks for what you did.' Changing the subject he said, 'Heard from Robin?'

She squirmed. 'No. I suppose I should ring him, only it's a little . . . humiliating. I suppose, really, I'd better apologise.'

'If I were you,' James said quietly, 'I should.'

'Maybe I will,' she said lightly, wondering what he had heard and damned if she would ask.

After a few moments' silence, she tapped her forehead. 'But you see, I can't get his death out of my mind. There has to be a resolution, somehow. It was such an outrageous, unnecessary death.'

James gave an understanding murmur.

'I mean, think of the poor man, his . . . unquiet spirit. And somebody is responsible. Somebody is walking about with Matthew Sawyer's blood on his hands. I don't want to, but I have to . . . just, *attend* to it, in a way. I need to see it settled—one way or another. It's hard to consider anything else as very important. Do you see?'

So that's the lie of the land, thought James. So that's what we're talking about. Unwise to try to get her off the subject or broach any other, and at least she seems genuinely relaxed. We'll just go along. Sara changed the subject for herself.

'I can't help hoping that Sue's off duty today. Sue—you know, Olivia Passmore's niece. Works at the health club. Blonde. She's got this waiter boyfriend who keeps upsetting her and I keep hearing *all* about it, I don't know why. At least she won't try to take me running. It's too hot to run.'

The glass doors which surrounded two sides of the swimming pool had been opened wide on to the garden and most of the health club clientele were outside basting gently in the sun, turning themselves regularly to ensure even cooking. Loungers, little tables and umbrellas dotted the grass. Inside, the pool was deserted and Sue presided sulkily at the bar. James made straight for the water, while Sara was waylaid, obedient to the special freemasonry between women which interpreted Sue's bravely raised eyebrows and her meek 'Iced tea, Sara? On the house?' as a real hope that she would stay a moment. She needed a sympathetic ear, which Sara would give, and probably some stout advice, which she would not. It would anyway be a waste of breath to suggest she

226

leave him. A woman like Sue never would. Once condemned, a woman like Sue would simply await demolition, and then, emotionally destroyed, would wonder what she should have done to avoid being reduced to such rubble. It was harder for Sara to admit to herself that she enjoyed hearing about Paul and Sue's gladiatorial spats, imagining his rages and his silences, during which he would be sure to look sullenly, petulantly magnificent.

Sue was forthcoming with the whole story and interspersed it with frequent self-deprecatory wails about how it was probably all her fault, another speciality of women like Sue.

'I've been having a rotten week. I got a right ticking-off on Tuesday. One of the members complained because she had to wait nearly an hour for her lunch and it was my fault. I told her she should stop chopping and changing her order and it might come quicker. And I had a row with Paul this morning and he lost his temper. I said when were we going to get a flat, and he said he didn't know, and he didn't know what was going to happen and not to stick around waiting for him. He said go and get some other guy to give you what you want. You won't believe what he said to me, Sara. He said he didn't know how to make me happy! It was my fault. So I said look, I'm sorry. Because he really does love me, you see, I know that. Why else would we even be together? It's just very stormy. We sort of left it there. And then I said look, let's have a really nice weekend, do something really nice. I said I'll be finished tomorrow night at eleven, we could go to Cadillacs. But it was no good. He just gave me that look again, that smile he gives me when he's doing something and doesn't want me to ask him about it or complain. Oh, but Bernard's coming, he says, all reasonable. I told you he was coming this weekend. Well he had, give him his due. So there was nothing I could say because I'd just forgotten.'

She wiped the marble bar top viciously.

'Who's Bernard?'

'Oh, it's Bern-*arr* really, he's French. I said I suppose you'll be with *him* all evening then, in one of his pubs. He calls them "perbs", Bernard does. He likes our Eengleesh perbs.' Sue paused a moment to allow the huge but elusive power of her wit to be appreciated.

'It's nice, this,' Sara said, looking into her glass of iced tea. 'Got any more lemon? Sorry, *who*'s Bernard?'

'Oh, he's an antiques dealer. He comes over from Paris every two or three months. There's something quite creepy about him. He stays at the hotel. Paul's got a little sideline going with him and so of course it's handy for Paul; he's making quite a bit, so of course *he* doesn't mind him coming. It's only *me* thinks he's a nuisance because Paul's always tied up when he's here, going to the *perb*, seeing dealers and stuff. It's probably my own fault—I encouraged it at the start. That was when I thought that Paul was getting some money together for us.'

Sara sighed in sympathy and got up, walked round to Sue's side of the bar, picked up a saucer with lemon slices on it and returned to her stool. She stirred two slices into her glass.

'So they're partners, then? English and French antiques? You sure Bernard's not smuggling fags or something?'

'Oh, sorry, I meant to do that. Nah, it's antiques. Bernard's been coming a while now. Paul met him the first or second time he was here. He served him in the restaurant. He was nice to him, helped him translate the menu. Paul's good like that, when he's in the right mood. When someone's eating on their own. He says people on their own tip better. Anyway, this Mr Rameau was the last person in the bar when Paul was finishing, and he called him over, just to thank him and bought him a drink. He just wanted to rabbit away in French to somebody. And he tells Paul why he's here and it turns out he could do with some help with it, you know, with the language and whatnot. God, I wish I'd seen what was coming. Paul was really pleased about it at the time. So was I.'

She began flicking a damp tea towel over the bar top with aggressive, quiet regularity.

'He had this big Renault van full of French stuff, little things mostly—rugs, mirrors, pictures—and he had all these dealers in the Cotswolds he was going round to and selling stuff to, and other bits he was getting auctioned in Bath. Then he'd buy a vanload of English stuff to go back with that he could sell in Paris. He's got this shop in this posh square. What is it, the Place des Vosges. Paul was impressed with that. It's like having a shop in Knightsbridge apparently.'

The flicking of the tea towel went on.

'Paul must know a lot about antiques, then.'

'He does now. He didn't to start with. Bernard just took him along to help him bid. His English isn't bad but in an auction it was hard to follow the prices. Anyway, the whole thing worked brilliantly. Bernard got about double what he'd get if he sold

229

the French stuff in France and the English here. That's what he told Paul, so it was probably even more. More than pays for the trip, anyway, so now it's a regular thing. When he's in Paris Paul scouts for him here, talks to the dealers, so Bernard doesn't ever waste a trip. He cuts Paul in on the deals now.'

She sighed again and the flicking of the cloth became lethargic.

'I wondered once or twice if it might lead to a proper job. A partnership or something. If he'd like to do that instead of cooking. I wouldn't mind.' She added wearily, 'I'd love to go to Paris. Have you ever been?'

'What? Oh, yes. I used to love Paris,' Sara said. 'But I haven't been for a long time.' There was a pause. 'Look, I really hope it works out. I'm sure it will.'

'Yeah. Well, thanks. Sorry. I mean, it's not really about Bernard, is it? I shouldn't go on.'

Sara took her leave and went to join James. She swam up and down, considering that no, it really wasn't about Bernard, it was about Sue's lack of instinct for survival.

*   *   *

They pounced on a pair of loungers the moment their charred and blinking occupants rose and stumbled back to their rooms. Sue made sure they got their lunch promptly and brought it proudly a few minutes within a half hour of their ordering it. They were appropriately grateful and Sue went off smiling. Bernard or no Bernard, she had worked out that when her shift tomorrow finished at eleven

230

she could just wait at Paul's for him to come back from his pub crawl with Bernard. He would be not drunk exactly, just easy-going with beer and she would be able to stay the night and then hang around a bit in the morning to see if there was going to be any time together on Saturday. That's what she would do. Not in a clingy way, of course.

James said, 'So what's the latest, then? Andrew keeping you up to date?'

'Not at all,' Sara said, with her mouth full. It was not only a day or two since she had been out, but more than that since she had spent longer in the kitchen than was necessary to collect something that could be carried up to her haunt by the pond and eaten in her fingers. She was wolfing down her posh chicken and mayonnaise sandwich with trimmed crusts, and a properly dressed salad of yellow, red and green peppers sliced into strips like long needles, relishing the way that everything on her plate had been thoughtfully selected for colour, texture and taste and the whole combination skilfully executed and beautifully arranged—by somebody else.

'He comes to play the cello. And anyway, he's been very busy with those other cases: that baby from Victoria Park and the canal boys. They really got to him, you know. It does to all of them, not just the ones who've got children.'

Her mind went back to the evening about ten days ago when Andrew had phoned to say that he would not be able to make it for his lesson at seven thirty, but he still very much wanted to see her and he hoped it would be all right if he came late. He had arrived well after nine o'clock, white, tight-shouldered and haggard. Reminding herself that she was his music teacher and that he had only come to play the cello, she had resisted an urge to hug him. He had refused a drink. He had avoided looking at her and she had felt quite disproportionately hurt. Only after half an hour's playing, exchanging brief remarks to do with the music, had he paused. Then he had told her mechanically about the discovery of the boys' bodies that afternoon and Sara had listened, in horrified silence. How fatuous it was to think that a hug, or a glass of wine, or even music, or any solace of human devising could give comfort against the truth that Andrew had that afternoon been forced to see; that there were people, at least one person, who had derived gratification from stripping and tying up two little boys, raping them, pushing sticks into their lacerated anuses, beating them round the head so that they could hardly breathe and could no longer see through the swollen tissue and bone fragments that had once been their faces, before finally placing a bootlace round their necks and pulling it tight, so that the veins in their eyes exploded and their blackening tongues swelled up from their throats and lunged out between their stretched blue lips before they died. Because that was what somebody had done.

By the time Andrew had finished speaking his voice was hoarse. Sara, unable to stand his untouchability any longer, had placed her hand on his, still saying nothing. And when the story appeared in the next day's *Chronicle*, he had gone on, it would simply say the only thing it could say, that the boys' bodies had been found, that they had been sexually assaulted and strangled, and that the families were being comforted by relatives. It

232

would not say that in fact there could be no comfort for those people, now or for the rest of their lives. When he had risen to leave, Sara had said, 'I wish there was something I could do.'

And Andrew had simply replied, 'Ah, well now. But there isn't. Mind you lock up now.'

James was saying, 'What about the Sawyer case, though? It's no less important, really. A murdered man, a murdered boy. Two murdered boys.' For a few moments they pondered miserably on this.

'But one thing you can be sure of,' James continued sadly. 'It takes just one sicko like the canal boys' killer to bring the anti-gays out waving and shouting. Put all the poofs on Alcatraz. Castrate the pansies. It used to make me angry. Now I just get depressed.'

'Is there much of that?' Sara asked, 'I mean, locally? Isn't a place like Bath fairly enlightened?'

'Oh, my dear,' James said, in his Lady Bracknell voice, 'oh, we are *so* enlightened in Bath. We are *so* broadminded. We fully accept that being "like that" is not a vice, it's a misfortune. It goes with being artistic. We can even tolerate one or two of them at our parties, as long as they're well diluted among our other friends who are the ones we rely on to uphold proper family values.'

Sara had to laugh.

'It's different when it looks as though there might be more than half a dozen of us, though.' He paused. 'I don't know if I should tell you this, but anyway, if Andrew's not telling you much about the case, it won't matter. I happen to know that Matthew Sawyer was pretty anti-gay himself. You remember Graham?'

'Of course I remember Graham. How's Austin

233

coping?'

'Oh, all right, more or less. The thing is, a couple of months before Graham died, Austin tried to organise a benefit for Buddies. Loads of people, *everybody* was going to come. They booked the Tea Room in the Assembly Rooms; it was going to be a concert and then a bit of a party. It was just about coinciding with Graham's birthday, which everyone knew would be his last. He was determined to be there if he could.'

'What happened?'

'Well, Austin rang up the Assembly Rooms about a fortnight before to ask if there were any display boards there that they could use. And when they were sorting out all the arrangements, like how many wheelchairs and things, they asked him what the charity did and he told them: you know, befriending Aids and HIV patients, helping them, being there. And four days later he got a letter from Matthew Sawyer saying he's sorry but he has to cancel the booking, there's been an administrative error and the Tea Room is no longer available.'

'And that couldn't just maybe, possibly have been true?'

James gave Sara a pitying, sarcastic look. 'Oh, *please*. Oh, sure, it could have been true. But he wouldn't speak to Austin about it, wouldn't take his calls. So decide for yourself.'

'Yes, I see, it's pretty obvious, isn't it? Despicable. Didn't Austin complain? I mean, there are laws against that sort of thing.'

'Are there really? Look, darling, you're being a little naïve. Austin had a disabled, blind, but very articulate and angry partner, they both knew he was dying, and there was the shop to run. And who would he complain to? Some retired lady on the council with a perm and a handbag? A great use of his time.'

Sara felt as if Austin and Graham's struggle, because it had been invisible to her, was partly her fault.

'So now you know,' James said bitterly, 'why I gave a false alibi. I was just scared.'

'James, why?'

'Because somebody pointed out Matthew Sawyer to me at the Pump Room that night and it brought back the whole Graham story, that's why. I thought about how bloody homophobic people can be, sometimes the ones you don't expect it from. So then he gets killed. And I think we all know the police's reputation in the homophobia department, don't we? I mean, I could have done it, couldn't I? Stayed until I was the last, or hidden somewhere. Or even gone home and changed, and come back and slipped in, and done the bloody deed.'

Sara stared at him.

'And because, as you found out, I didn't go straight home. I felt so sad, as if I'd let Graham down, like I'd spent the evening with someone so prejudiced against him. I just wanted to play something for him. So I walked up to the church and played him his favourite tunes. Just like that, simple and private, only less private than I'd thought. I was very grateful you produced that vicar and got me out. You were bloody clever to think of it.'

'I still don't really see why you wouldn't tell the police where you were.'

'Look, when I brought supper round that night,

235

the day you found the body, we talked about it practically all evening. It was clear then there was no obvious reason why anyone would want to kill him. So I knew the police would be looking hard at anyone with *any* motive. Like a peevish old queen, for example, whose friend had recently been grievously insulted by the dead man. Better still, a peevish old queen with no alibi who's on the radio and the telly; extra points for arresting a minor celebrity.'

'All right, but why wouldn't you even tell Tom where you were?'

James looked a little shamefaced. 'I didn't want Tom to know how much Graham's death affected me because I'd always said Graham was just a casual friend. And the fact is that Graham and I had a fling about five years ago. It was over, it was part of the past, and Austin never knew and neither did Tom, and it would have hurt them both a lot to find out. And Tom would have been on to it at once if he'd known I went to the church. I had to tell him in the end of course. Afterwards. He's okay about it, thank God.'

Sara nodded.

'So when the police came round on the Sunday I'd been awake most of the night worrying about it and I just found myself telling them a whole heap of crap about talking to Tom on the phone on Friday night. Needless to say, I hadn't thought it through from Tom's point of view. And I'm a lousy liar. They weren't convinced for a minute.'

'Oh, James,' Sara said, 'you poor darling. You must have been desperate. I wish I'd been there. Did you have to talk to that awful Bridger?'

'Oh, yes, I had Bridger several times.' James

looked at her with mischief. 'In a manner of speaking. Eats a lot of chocolate, doesn't he? He won't have his own teeth much longer, the rate he's going.'

CHAPTER TWENTY-TWO

Ever since the supper party Cecily had been sour to the point of insubordination. Not that he did not appreciate that it did not do, in 1997, to bandy words like insubordination about. And anyway he knew he could hardly come the heavy boss now, nearly two years on, having put matters between him and Cecily on a more intimate footing within two months of her arrival. But then, swift to give himself his due, he had always made it quite clear that he was married, so there *was* something unwarranted about her sudden lack of tolerance of this fact. He had been spoiling her, he realised, giving her too much of himself. He had been too generous, that had always been his trouble. And she had been behaving very badly for a while, but he had been determined to keep on the right side of her for the sake of peace, as well as for the very nice sex he hoped to continue enjoying with her. All right, mainly for the sex. But that had been up until now. Sourness was one thing, a thing he could even, up to a point, ignore.

But this was something else. This made things rather different. With this latest trick she was showing herself to be not just sour but dangerous. It made him sad to do it, but he was going to have to let her go. He was not going to let her do him real damage, not after all he had already had to do to get this far. She could still be his secretary, of course, at least for the short time left that he would need her. But the other thing would have to stop. Because it was only thanks to the fact that he was such a good proofreader that it had not gone off for printing like that. That, and because he had happened to find it lying around. His was the only school in south Bristol that had a prize-giving now, although of course it was not called that any more. It was a Celebration of Achievement, and it was this afternoon. The chairman of the board of governors, two councillors, the Community Liaison Officer from Asda (or Asdal, as he had learned to think of it), the new electronic organ whose purchase they had sponsored, along with the piano, Mr Quinnell his head of music and the entire school steel band would be sharing the platform with him, and the hall would be full to bursting with pupils, staff and almost as many parents. So it did not bear thinking about what would have happened if the programmes that were to be placed on every seat had read:

Musical Interlude: The steel band and Mr Quinnell
on   **The Headmaster's**
                                   organ

Address: and piano:
will play and conduct h   is short
medley of music from Britain   and
to the School: around the world.   **'Thin**
king About The Future'

She had done it on purpose, of that he was sure, although when he had challenged her she had had

238

the nerve to be as furious as he was. She had pretended she was having trouble with her columns.

'They keep going wonky. It's this useless machine. And of course I would have noticed it before it went to the printers, only you took it off my desk before I'd had a chance to look at it properly,' she had hissed, stabbing at the space bar and hardly taking her eyes from the screen.

So he had not got very far with that. Thinking it over and particularly remembering the sex, he had then pretended to find it funny, and in a public display of magnanimity in front of his admin team had even shown it to his deputy, teased Cecily about it and signalled in every way he could that he was an easy-going kind of guy. Hell, he had a sense of humour. After three days of being great about it, it had had the desired effect, reminding Cecily of how much fun he had been in the early days. She recalled how his tempers and black moods then had been rare, special occasions: his to indulge, hers to understand and theirs to cherish, by commemorating their passing with a relieved and grateful fuck and a good dinner. In the end, of course, she had come round. When no one else was about he could now playfully nip round behind her and squeeze her tits again, taking care to use the words she preferred, like 'touch' and 'breasts', if he murmured anything in her ear while he was doing it.

It was a relief to have the loose cannon safely chained to the deck once more. He had the interview coming up, and Cecily could spoil it for him in a big way if she decided to get silly and bitter about things now. There was just this one afternoon, the last Friday of the year, to get through and that would be a doddle. He had done so many. He had let Cecily skive off for the afternoon so as to be sure of her good mood, and as soon as he could get clear he would pick up a bagful of things for dinner and get over there for the night, where he intended to drive home just what an easy-going guy he was and make quite sure of his reinstatement in her affections. Cecily did not know it, but this would be their last time together. He did not want the relationship to end with any kind of cloud hanging over the question of his virility (she *had* done it on purpose); he would give the bitch short and thin, only long and thick, and as many times as he, and more than she, could comfortably manage. Three, minimum. Then there would be only two more days next week during which he could easily avoid seeing her alone, what with lots of meetings and other end-of-term nonsense, before breaking up on the twenty-second, leaving him enough time to prepare for his interview on the twenty-third. And then it would be hoorah for the holidays. Even if she were rash enough to try to ring him at home, with judicious use of the answering machine he could avoid speaking to her all summer, and by September he would be clear anyway and starting the new job. Kinder in the end.

When Detective Sergeant Bridger telephoned the school he got the answering machine, which he thought odd for half past two on a Friday afternoon. He knew they could not have broken up yet. He would just get over there.

As 'Tulips from Amsterdam' plinked almost imperceptibly into 'Yellow Bird' Derek sat smiling on the platform, privately enjoying some Thinking About the Future of his own. But the steel band's medley was drawing to a close, so he carefully folded up his mental picture of Cecily stepping out of her knickers and filed it away for later. It was time to concentrate on the Headmaster's Address to the School. As the applause was finishing he reached into his inside pocket for his notes. Not that he needed them, really, because Thinking About the Future was substantially the same as Our Way Forward (1993), Fresh Horizons (1994), Learning to See Ahead (1995) and New Perspectives (1996).

After more than twenty-five years in teaching Derek was a more than adept public speaker, but no longer remembered what it was like to feel equal or inferior to his audience. It had been at least two decades since he had been nervous enough to worry about whether or not what he had to say was of any interest to anyone. He had also accomplished the knack of speaking while his mind was on something else, and was capable of memorising minute details of the room he was in—how many light switches and windows, the colours of ceilings and so on—while forgetting absolutely everything he said a few seconds after he had said it. By means of some invisible osmotic process, most of those compelled to listen to him found themselves equally in the grip of a strange fascination with fixtures and fittings and afterwards trapped under the same blanket of swift-acting and permanent amnesia. As he rose to speak he was aware only of the first of these facts.

With his first sentence he observed to himself that you hardly ever see kids' eyes any more, or

241

even their eyebrows. What you see is fringe, and that is what makes it more difficult than it used to be to know if you are getting through (as if you cared) even when, as now, most of your audience is actually facing you and not obviously engaged in any activity other than listening, apart from gum chewing, shoving one another a bit, scratching their rank polyester armpits and squinting amiably through their hair. He thought fondly of the half-dozen or so farewell cards on his desk, with their sincere and laboriously expressed gratitude to A Brilliant Headmaster, and the sweaty, sentimentally addressed offerings of Quality Street and Milk Tray which had been trickling in all week, delivered by this year's bashful and lumpen leavers. Kids. Snotty, shuffling, unobservant, inarticulate kids who could still, despite how he resisted, inspire these sudden stabs of love. Derek felt himself about to address a flock of mainly good-natured ruminants.

'Well, how nice to see the whole school together on this very special occasion.'

One side of the hall was composed entirely of windows, and looking out over the children's heads he was aware of a car drawing up and parking in one of the staff spaces across the playground. A police car. Great timing.

'Thank you, face the front please. We are all, at this point in the school calendar, looking forward to the holidays. Aren't we?'

Smiling at the surging 'Yes!' that growled from everyone in the hall, notably the staff lining the back wall, he wondered which and how many of the Year 10 boys had just been rounded up and what routine delinquency they were guilty of this time.

'Six weeks of freedom to look forward to!'

His eyes tracked the progress of the skinny plain-clothes officer and his colleague from the car to the open double doors at the back of the hall, where they were being intercepted by Alan, his bright deputy. *Good lad, Alan.*

'But just before we are all set free for what seems this long, long time, let's just think a little bit more about that for a minute.'

Some firm arm-folding going on down there. Alan's looking a bit fazed. What's going on?

'Now, most of you will be coming back to school in September (groans). Back to a new year, new subjects perhaps, new teachers, new demands, new challenges.'

Alan and this plain-clothes guy keep turning and looking towards me. Alan's shaking his head, got a hand on the guy's arm. Quite right. If it's me he wants, he's going to have to bloody well wait.

'And for those of you leaving us this year, the real challenges are just *beginning.*'

What the fuck is going on now? Alan is actually having to restrain the guy. And how am I supposed to get on with this, with all the kids craning round to see what the fuss is about?

'Yes, fine now, just turn round, turn round, would you. Thank you, thank you. Yes. *Now*, yes, thank you. *Now.* What does the future hold for us? That can sometimes be a frightening thought, can't it?'

This guy's unbelievable. Actually walking up the hall now. Come on, Alan, keep up, keep up. Does he think he's coming on the platform? Alan's waving at me. What?

'Because we can never know for certain exactly

243

what is going to happen next, can we?'

He's asked for it.

'For example, I have no idea who this gentleman is or why he's here, but I'm sure he'd like to come up and explain why he's had to interrupt our celebration this afternoon?'

God, he's skinny, half my height. A rodent. The kids are enjoying this. Fuck, so am I!

'Do, please, step right up. Be my guest. And what can we do for you, Mr . . . er?'

Make a monkey out of him.

*   *   *

Sitting in the police car later as it pulled away Derek reflected that perhaps this had been a mistake. He was numbly wondering what the hell he had done to deserve this, as well as how to react. What is the appropriate response when a plain-clothes police officer barges into the most public event in the school year and from the platform asks you if you'd mind answering a few questions in connection with their enquiries? In retrospect, the decision not to switch off the microphone had not been a good one.

'Well, goodness me, it seems I am a wanted man,' he had said, but the laughter, especially from behind him on the platform, had been nervous. Just as he was beginning to realise that he was actually going to have to leave the platform, indeed the building, accompanied by the police, Alan had appeared at his side and taken over. Ambitious bastard. From the tone of his voice he could tell that he was rubbing his hands as he said, 'We apologise for that slight interruption, ladies and gentlemen. I'm sure Mr Payne won't be er . . . detained, if that's the word, *very* long. Well, boys and girls, I'm sure after Mr Payne's unexpected departure, we can all come up with some really *fresh* and *new* thoughts about the future . . .'

*   *   *

Andrew rang Sara.

'Sara?' He sounded like a boy. 'Very busy. I'm expecting a call on the other line. Bridger may be on to something. He's spoken to Annabel Sawyer again. Apparently she came across some letter that Sawyer got the day he was killed. He'd been shortlisted for a job. She didn't think it was important but Bridger got on to the council and thinks he's found something to go on. He's got a match with one of the other candidates and a name we've already got—someone at the Assembly Rooms. I'm letting him have his head. I probably can't make the lesson today, but can you manage Tuesday next week? Shall we fix the time later? No, don't bother, I'll call you. Good to hear you. 'Bye.'

She had barely managed hello.

CHAPTER TWENTY-THREE

'Let's just go over it again, shall we? If you'd just tell me again what you told me at the school, starting with why you were at the Assembly Rooms in Bath on the night of Friday the thirteenth of June,' Bridger said, in control and oily. 'That's exactly five weeks ago today.'

245

Derek sank back in his chair and sighed, trying to swallow the sort of rage that he had long been in the habit of giving full vent to. After nearly an hour's interrogation in his office at school, against the ecumenical cacophony from the hall below of seven hundred voices with steel band accompaniment raised in Celebration of their Achievements, they had driven him here. They were sitting in Derek's blond living room, meticulously done in Pauline's favourite shades of biscuit, with cushions, picture frames and book spines (Pauline's 'little points of interest') in dark green. It was already after five. The police car was parked outside in the drive and his neighbours would soon be rolling past on their way home from work. They would assume that poor Pauline and Derek, such a nice, *professional* couple, had been burgled, and a spate of solidly middle-class anxious enquiries would be sure to follow, so for them, but mainly for Pauline, Derek would have to concoct a convincing story. Some invention concerning a delinquent kid at school would be easy enough, but he would have to work at it to furnish a reason why the police wanted to talk to him at home rather than at school. Then he would have to remember whatever he said. He reflected that adultery was indeed a wearing business, probably more trouble than it was worth. He was in a very awkward position, he had to remember that, but if he was careful not to antagonise PC Plod here, he would get away with it and Pauline need never know. The thought of Pauline brought a surge of anxiety and another burning wave of indigestion, but he reminded himself that for the moment she was safely out the way, up at the last session of her weekend course, doing their assessments. Thank God for that at least. He would be through with this lot soon and then there would be nothing to stop him getting over to Cecily's as planned. She was expecting him within the hour. He swallowed another chest-prickling, silent belch and sighed again.

'I went to have a look round the costume museum, in connection with the professional matter I have already mentioned.'

'And that would be?'

'That I had been shortlisted for a job which included overall responsibility for the running of the museums,' Derek rattled off. 'I wanted to refresh my memory, get an impression of things for the interview. When I got there I was told that the museum was closed to members of the general public and I was annoyed, because the place was literally full of people, and they could easily have let me in.'

'So you complained, I gather?'

'I objected, yes. And Matthew Sawyer appeared from the back somewhere and I talked it over with him.'

Derek pushed out of his mind the memory of his embarrassment. 'I only spoke to him for a minute in a corner of the entrance hall. Yes, I was alone when I spoke to him and no, we weren't overheard so far as I know. No, as I have already said, I was not alone when I arrived at the Assembly Rooms, but my companion was very taken by the Natural Healing convention and was halfway down the hall looking at leaflets.'

Bridger looked across at Detective Constable Heaton on the other side of the room with raised eyebrows, which conveyed that Derek's story had so far failed to impress. DC Heaton stared flatly back from the oyster Dralon armchair, embarrassed not by Mr Payne (his was an old, old story) but by the tone Bridger was taking. There was an uncomfortable silence.

'I've already said this, but I suppose you want it again,' Derek went on, his lips dry. 'My companion was my secretary. We are . . . very close, out of school, that is. My wife often works at weekends, so Mrs Smith and I had gone to the Assembly Rooms together.'

'No need to underline it, sir. We have Mrs Smith's statement that she gave to the police officer who interviewed her at home on the evening of'—Bridger leafed slowly back through his notes—'Monday the sixteenth of June. She told the officer that you made a brief enquiry about opening hours and left the building. Didn't quite tell the whole story, did she?'

'I'm sure she considered the question of my forthcoming interview as a matter confidential to myself,' Derek said. 'She is a very discreet woman. She was protecting me.'

'Protecting you, sir? Protecting you from what, exactly? From being identified as a suspect?'

Derek sighed in exasperation. 'No, of course not. Look, I've explained. We were . . . close. She and I were spending the evening together. Yes, all right then, the night. Look, is this relevant? I've already told you how I *did* spend the evening.'

Again he struggled to control his temper. It wasn't good for him, all this rage. Again a noxious bulge of heartburn surged in his chest and he stirred unhappily in his chair.

Bridger said, without moving, 'Let's just have it again, sir, if we may.'

There was going to be no short way out of this. Derek knew he must not hiss as he spoke, but the recollection of this part of the evening still made the bile rise in his throat.

'Mrs Smith decided that she would like to stay for the convention evening. I myself did not wish to do so. So we agreed that I would return to her house—yes, as I have already told you, 5 Bladud Vale, Larkhall—and return to pick her up at ten thirty. It was not a row, but I was, well, disappointed. I did not wait to discuss her decision at length. But it was not what you would call a row. It was only a little . . . acrimonious.'

He gulped dyspeptically, rubbing the flat of his hand slowly up and down his breastbone. He must concentrate. It was essential to convince them of the next part.

'I got back to the house round about quarter to seven. I brought my briefcase and shopping in but forgot to pick up the carrier bag with the rest of my stuff from the back seat. I parked quite a way up from the house so I didn't go back for it straight away. I meant to do it later. I just sat down for a minute first with a glass of wine. Then I was going to go and get it so that I could change. I wasn't planning to get started on dinner before about eight, so I had a bit of time to unwind. Well, I actually had a few glasses of wine, it had been a very tiring week, and then I fell asleep. I suppose I was just very tired. I hadn't eaten since lunchtime and I suppose I did drink rather a lot on an empty stomach. When I woke up it was after half past ten.'

'And you had promised to pick up your "lady friend" at half past, had you?'

Derek nodded, wondering fleetingly if Cecily could accurately be described as either.

'So when I woke up and realised the time I just picked up the car keys and ran. It was late enough already, and we hadn't eaten or anything. Anyway, I was about halfway along Camden Crescent when it dawned on me that I really shouldn't be driving. I mean, I felt quite sober but I probably had too much alcohol in my bloodstream. In my job you can't afford to take risks like that, not that I would want to anyway.'

He did not add that he had also realised at once that the loss of his licence after a drunk-driving charge in Bath late on a Friday night would take some explaining to Pauline.

'So I had to park the car on Camden Crescent and leave it. I walked the rest of the way to the Assembly Rooms.'

Bridger yawned. 'In the rain, would that be, sir?'

'Yes. I got there about quarter past eleven. There was a bloke locking up and he said a woman had just left to walk down to the rank at the abbey to get a taxi. It sounded exactly like Cecily. So I walked on down to see if I could find her, but she must have got a cab straight away; there was no sign of her. And then I remembered about my bag which was still on the back seat of the car. There were things I needed in it. I decided to walk back to the car and get it.'

He did not mention that by that time he had felt apoplectic with anger towards Cecily and that after following her halfway round town he was damned if he was spending the money on another taxi just so

250

that he could screech up seconds behind her when her taxi drew up outside number 5. He was wet through anyway and couldn't have got any wetter. He would walk and it would be her fault. Let her worry. Let her drop dead.

'When I got back to the car the bag on the back seat had gone. It was missing.' He sighed. It did sound implausible.

'And yet the car had not been broken into, sir?' Bridger asked, disingenuously. 'Amazingly enough.'

Derek coughed. 'I've told you. I had left it unlocked. By mistake, in the hurry, and in the wet. I just forgot to lock it.'

Patiently, he again went through the list of items missing from the green Marks and Spencer's bag and again Bridger stopped him when they came to the knife.

'And you didn't think to report any of this to the police then, sir, the "theft" of valuable items, not even the "theft" of a dangerous, eleven-inch, steel kitchen knife?'

Derek sighed. Of course he had not reported it, and Bridger knew why.

'You just went out the next day, I think you said, and replaced it from Kitchens in Quiet Street. Using cash. And we've noted that you also used cash that morning to buy a pair of corduroy trousers, a checked shirt, a cotton sweater, toothbrush and razor. So that Mrs P would be none the wiser? Very thorough of you, sir.'

Bridger grinned at Heaton. 'And going back to the previous night, you got back to 5 Bladud Vale at, what time was it?'

'I've told you. Some time around one.'

'And Mrs Smith is unable to confirm this, I

251

believe you said?'

'Mrs Smith, as I have told you, was taking a bath. She was playing music very loudly in the bathroom when I got back. She does that when she is feeling at all . . . tense. She had left a blanket on the stairs, which I took to be an indication that she did not wish to be disturbed. So I slept on the sofa.'

He did not add the little detail, the tiny satisfaction that had rounded off his unplanned and rather untoward evening. When he had got back, bursting for a pee, to find that Cecily had barricaded herself in the bathroom with Marvin Gaye on full blast, he had marched back out into the front garden and urinated savagely into her urn.

'So all in all, you didn't get quite the evening you were hoping for then, it would seem,' Bridger said. DC Heaton gave a little smirk, of which he was instantly ashamed. 'Anything to add at this stage, sir?'

Derek dumbly shook his head, which was beginning to ache. 'My wife . . .' he began, turning towards Bridger in an appeal from one man of the world to another and in this instance futile.

'I heard later from Mrs Smith about the murder. I was quite upset. But I didn't know him. I only spoke to him for a minute, about the museum opening times.'

'So you are confirming, are you, sir, that you didn't know that he had been shortlisted himself for the job you were going for?'

'No, I didn't know,' Derek almost barked. He rubbed his hands roughly over his face as if to wash away the lie. 'Look, even if I had, does anyone ever want a job badly enough to kill off the opposition?

252

In your experience?'

'Thank you, sir. Now, that knife you bought. In the kitchen is it, sir? If you'll just show DC Heaton where to find it, he'll bring it along, and then we'll just pop over to the station and see if we can flesh out a few of the details.'

Derek's despair was too deep for further speech. As he left the room, DC Heaton seized his chance.

'Sir, don't you want to arrest him? None of this'll be admissible evidence if you don't arrest him. It's not like you're letting him stay here, is it? He could claim unlawful detention. You need to arrest him.'

'Let me handle this, Constable. There's nothing wrong with the odd short cut, when you know where to make it. Go and get the knife.'

When Derek and DC Heaton reappeared a moment later, he said breezily, 'Right, sir. Just a few more questions down at the station, if you don't mind. In the hope that we can eliminate you from our enquiries, sir.'

CHAPTER TWENTY-FOUR

The man kept his eyes closed. Opening them seemed to hurt more, and there was nothing to see anyway, just the roof of the van. Still he couldn't stop shivering. It was bad, very bad. And he had no idea where he was or for how long they'd been travelling now, since he'd been picked up at the specified point, handed over the cash and seen it counted, and been told roughly to lie down and keep out of sight. In the dark, Le Fournisseur had not noticed that he was ill, nor was he the type to care, unless it was going to stop him getting his money. The van had stopped maybe half an hour ago, and the man had said only, 'Don't move', and then climbed out, banging back the door so hard that the pounding in his head had got even worse. Then silence, except for birds. This was not a city. He could not be in a city. Even if he was near a park he would be able to hear people and traffic. He knew even without ever having been in London that this could not be where he was now, and that the man had lied to him.

The man was back. He must be standing just outside next to the van, just on the other side of this thin metal wall. There was someone with him, another man, also French. They were talking in French. He was supposed to be in London, that was what he had paid the money for. He might not even be in England. Panic hit him somewhere in the stomach with a hot, gripping rush of pain. He wanted to cry out, but only a groan came. He felt his lips. He was so thirsty. Outside, they were talking about him.

'He's ill. He can't go tonight, he'd collapse on the road and get caught. How should I know if he was ill when we left? What's it to me?'

'He can't stay here. If he can't go tonight, he'll just have to stay in the van, there's nothing else for it. Look, you know I don't like this anyway. It's got to stop, this part of it.'

'Don't start, for God's sake. Look, he can't stay in the van. What if he throws up or something? I've got valuable stuff in there. Come on, we can get him into your place, can't we? It's only for one night. Tomorrow I'll dump him in Bristol and that'll be the end of it. Come on, Paul.'

254

'*My* place? Oh, no. Absolutely not. Not my place. You must be mad. It's far too dangerous. Anyway, what about my girlfriend? She's always coming round, even when I'm not there. What am I supposed to say to her?'

'Paul, it's one night. You can say something, tell her you're ill, say you've got an upset stomach. Something. Look, if we try to keep him in the van and he gets worse someone will hear him. Or he'll bang on the door to be let out. He's a difficult bastard anyway. He stowed away on a cargo ship to Bordeaux, been in Paris about two months. Immigration got on to him. Okay, so he's ill but it's only flu. He's still tough, and I don't want trouble.'

'Bernard, I swear this is the last time, you hear me? Try this again and I'm out of the whole thing. Forget the money, forget the whole bloody thing, it's too dangerous. I'm not interested, okay? Are you listening to me?'

'Yeah, okay, okay. It is, you're right. Last time. We'll just do the antiques. Look, I'm agreeing, okay? But we've got this bastard on our hands until tomorrow, and we've got to keep him hidden somewhere. It'll have to be your room. There's nowhere else, is there?'

There was a short silence.

'Fuck you, Bernard, and fuck him. Okay, because he's ill, that's all. Not to help you. It'll have to be my room. We'll come and get him later, in a couple of hours, after the salon's closed. And you'd better be ready to give me extra for this, you bastard.'

The voices faded, the men were walking away. So his name was Bernard, Le Fournisseur, the man with the fat yellow fingers. The other one sounded

255

younger. So he was going to have to wait at least another two hours with his thirst, his aching face, his pounding head, his numb limbs. He was in the wrong place, too ill to move, and they hated him. They would soon realise, if they had not already, that it would be easier to kill him. That was what Bernard would want, and Bernard carried a gun. Maybe the younger one would want him dead, too. He stirred and felt the rough canvas of his bag against his thigh. They would get all that, too. He had been a fool to let Bernard see it. They would be talking about him now, deciding where to do it, what to do with his body, sharing out his money. He whimpered into his hands and tears ran from the corners of his tight shut eyes and rolled into his hair.

When he heard the wrenching screech of the van door opening he realised that he had no strength to defend himself but still enough energy to feel terror. He opened his eyes and raised his head, sobbing. But it was not Bernard, it was the other one, Paul. Paul leaned forward into the van and stared at him over the stacked chairs, the tea chests and boxes, then turned round and hauled in a big soft-looking bundle. So he was going to be suffocated. Then he would be stuffed into a bag and dumped somewhere to rot or be eaten by dogs. He shrank back into the corner where the floor met the cold metal wall of the van and stared helplessly, his breathing short and wheezing. He was too weak to sit up or to scream.

'Here. These will help.'

They were blankets. Three soft, wool blankets, and there was also a pillow for his head. He must have brought them from his own bed. He must have put himself at risk to bring *him* blankets and a pillow. The man was crouching beside him, spreading them over him like a mother. Now he was ashamed of his tears and the incoherent thanks which came painfully from his thick, dry throat.

'I've brought you some water,' Paul said, placing a full plastic bottle beside him. 'I'll come and get you later, then you can eat, if you want to. You'll be able to rest properly. You'll be all right. I'm sorry.'

And then the man Paul was gone. And left in the dark of the van, he first drank some of the water. Then, wrapped in the blankets, he found that his shivering stopped long enough to let him fall asleep.

CHAPTER TWENTY-FIVE

As the taxi drove off Derek let himself in through Cecily's front door. She came into the narrow hall to greet him, and not kindly. It was too dark to see his creased and exhausted face properly.

'You're exactly'—she peered at her watch—'seven hours and eighteen minutes late.'

'Don't,' he said faintly, leaning against the wall with his briefcase in one hand, holding up the other in submission. 'Please, Cec. I'll explain. I've only just got away. I've been with the police. About the Sawyer murder. They grilled me, then they made me stay while they checked everything I told them. Took hours. Chief Inspector Poole says I'm lucky there's an insomniac in Camden Crescent who saw my car being ransacked. It wasn't my fault. Don't start. Please.'

To his surprise she did not, not straight away. She turned away.

'I had a takeaway,' she said, 'and now I'm going to bed.' At the foot of the stairs she said, 'I don't know if you're hungry. There's nothing in the fridge. You said you were cooking. I don't know where you were, I don't know why you were late, I don't know why you didn't phone. I don't know why I don't throw you out. In the morning I would like an explanation. And some decisions. About us. Don't wake me when you come up.' She turned and went upstairs.

Derek's aching heartburn had subsided and a headache pulsed in its place. Although he was starving, going out again for something to eat was unthinkable; he felt too exhausted even to stay upright much longer. Dumping his briefcase on the sofa, he wandered into the kitchen, collected a glass, a corkscrew and a bottle of Chianti and took them back to the sitting room, opened the bottle and swigged heavily from it before filling his glass. He prised off his shoes, returned to the kitchen and opened the fridge. She had been inaccurate. There was not quite nothing in the fridge. There was low-fat spread, oil-free salad cream, two tomatoes, half a lettuce and a soft cucumber end. Derek's personal view of salads was that about five times a year, and only when in Italy or France, a few choice leaves served as useful little boats for a good oil and garlic dressing. In all other circumstances his contempt for salads extended to the people who ate them. In the door of the fridge he found a plastic tub containing the curdled watery remains of reduced-fat cottage cheese with (which only added to his disgust) pineapple. Cottage cheese he

258

did not even regard as a foodstuff. Deep inside him his annoyance, thick, hairy and foul-smelling, yawned, got up, stretched, turned round and lay back down like a dog before a roaring fire. He shut the fridge and went back to the sitting room to damp down the flames with Chianti.

Stretched out on the sofa he sipped his wine and thought hungrily and wistfully of the fridge at home. Pauline always kept their fridge well stocked. There would always be good cheese, probably pâté or decent ham, olives, butter. Eggs. Bacon. Bread. Tins of anchovies in the cupboards. Chocolate biscuits in their tins. *Chocolate*. Suddenly, he remembered. Oh, may blessings rain upon Sharlene Hanrahan and Darren Harper, whose two boxes of Quality Street were in his briefcase. With trembling hands he whipped round the numbers of the combination lock and the catches snapped open. Taking a box in each hand he tipped their contents on to the carpet in front of him and spent a relaxing minute or two hunched over his hoard, picking out the ones he did not much like and then, with the toffees, coconut fudges and coffee creams safely de-selected, he set to.

Later he carried the empty bottle, his wineglass and about three dozen sweetie wrappers out to the kitchen. His headache was no better, but his blood-sugar level and consequently his temper had improved. He felt just about communicative enough to tell Cecily all about his terrible afternoon and even worse evening as a murder suspect, in at least as much detail as it would take to arouse sufficient sympathy for her to countenance the advance of his slightly chocolaty

259

fingers between her thighs. She might even want a
Quality Street, he thought wildly, picking up the
left-over sweeties and dropping them in one of
the boxes on his way upstairs. He clicked on the
bedside light and sat down heavily on the bed. He
undressed as noisily as possible. She could not be
asleep now.

'Fancy a toffee, Cec?' he said, shaking the box.
No answer. Obviously she did not like the toffee
ones either. 'Coffee cream?' He waited. She did
not stir. 'Coconut fudge?' he sniggered. Oh, she
was so picky. He climbed clumsily in beside her
motionless form, which remained quite still as he
rubbed himself perfunctorily against her wrinkly
bottom. She clearly intended to keep up the
pretence of being asleep, and she was wearing
seersucker pyjamas. Damn her, he thought,
popping the last four toffees into his mouth and
chewing lasciviously before dropping the wrappers
on the floor and turning out the light.

*   *   *

It was still dark, and he was at once aware that
what had woken him up was pain. Pain in, or near
his chest, where he could feel his heart hammering.
Turning slightly he felt it again; the tearing, raw
sensation in his left side, near his armpit. Oh, God,
a heart attack. Please, not a heart attack. He stirred
and he felt it again. *Pain.* Blood was thumping
through his temples and banging in his throat. He
tried to move his left arm and the pain came again
and left him panting. His arm was pinned to his
side, and now he was not sure if it was really dark,
or if he simply couldn't see. He knew that even if

the pain allowed him to sit up he would drown in a giddy, sick and swimming whirlpool. He cried out with what felt like his last breath, which was now coming in frightened gasps. Oddly, even while Cecily's white and tousled face was staring over him, during her agitated talking into the phone and as she was struggling into clothes, there was a detached and unsurprised part of him watching, knowing that he'd been heading for this. And all day he'd thought it was indigestion. He tried to turn and raise his head and the pain swept round him again. No mistaking it now. How long would it take? He couldn't move his arm. As he lay, the faintness in his head came in waves and his fifty-year-old heart clamoured beneath its flesh cloak of seven surplus stones. Oh, God, is this dying? Keep breathing. Don't try to talk. Oh, God, a heart attack. No wonder, no bloody wonder, right at the end of the year, and after a day like today. He would not be able to keep on breathing. He shifted his weight and the pain in his left side tore at him again before he lost consciousness.

CHAPTER TWENTY-SIX

Being Sue's listening ear had begun to feel like a heavy responsibility. Really, the proper and only substance of telephone calls around midnight, unless between lovers, should be hospital admissions, stranded travellers, and breakdowns. Automobile, not nervous, unless absolutely in extremis. Calling at ten to midnight with an invitation to meet for coffee in town next morning had not fallen into even the last of these categories, however brave the sentiment and brittle the voice.

'I'll tell you all about it when we meet,' Sue had said last night, and then proceeded to tell Sara most of it there and then. 'You weren't in bed, were you? Oh look, I really *hope* you weren't having an early night. I had to talk to someone. I'm here at Aunt Livy's, but she's not here, not down here with me, I mean. I think she must have gone to bed. Well, look, I'll just tell you *briefly*. I went round to Paul's when I'd finished work tonight. I was going to wait for him. But he was there, there was a light on, and the curtains were all shut. He *never* shuts the curtains. So I went up to the French windows and he'd locked them. And he *never* locks them. So then I banged on the door and he came, and he said he was ill. Well, he was trying to look ill, but he wasn't. He wasn't ill earlier on. He wasn't ill at all. And you won't believe this, but he wouldn't let me in. He actually refused to let me in. He'd got someone there.'

She had paused to give Sara room to absorb this and produce the appropriate outraged response.

'*No*. Oh, Sue, I am *sorry*.' She was thinking, the *bastard*.

'He'd *got someone there*, I'm sure of it. So that's it, Sara. I mean it. That's *it*. And do you know what? I'm not even angry. I'm calm. I'm really, really calm. And that's *it*. He's had it.' She took a deep breath.

'And so I came here, and I've had a proper think now, and I thought what I'll do is, tomorrow I'll go shopping in town and do Something For Myself. I'm going to get a new track suit and I'm going to get it tomorrow and get really fit and take proper

262

care of myself and sod him. I've got this book my landlady lent me, how to treat your inner celebrity. You just decide what your type is and then you do all these things it tells you. Makes *tons* of sense when you read this book. So I'm going to make tomorrow the day I drink eight glasses of water, to clear the body of toxins. And I thought it'd be really nice to see you and have coffee—well, water probably—and just have a nice day and not think about him at all. Do you know, I'm practically over it already. I've *decided*, Sara, I've really decided. And I'm *really* calm. *Stuff* him.'

A slight screech had come into her voice and Sara heard her start breathing slowly in through her nose and out through her mouth, the way therapists tell you to.

'Well done. You have a good night's sleep and I'll see you tomorrow. Pump Room at eleven,' she had said.

*   *   *

And so now here she was, pleased to have secured a table in the Pump Room, albeit one rather too close to the trio pounding out a reduction for piano, violin and cello of the Trout Quintet, and waiting for Sue. She had walked down through Northend before it got too hot, caught the Badgerline bus into town, browsed in the music shop and bought a re-released CD of one of Edwin's early recordings with a hilarious early photo of him, lugubrious and slick-haired, on the front, which she was looking forward to teasing him about. She had strolled round a watercolour exhibition in the Victoria Art Gallery. It was

263

pleasant to feel unencumbered by the car-parking deadline, a little like being on holiday in a foreign city. She pushed the sudden thought of Paris from her mind as she saw Sue coming towards her, laden with the spoils of a morning's fearless shopping. She was beautiful, aglow with the triumph of acquisition. Sara thought benignly that she looked so great striding across the Pump Room in her expensive sunglasses that she could be forgiven for not taking them off before she got to the table.

'Hiya! Mmwaw! Mmwaw!' she exclaimed, leaning over and bestowing extravagant air kisses on either side of Sara's face, before landing theatrically in the chair opposite.

'Whoof! Sorry I'm late. Look at *this*.' She stretched into one of her bags and pulled out a fistful of pale grey fleecy cotton. 'New track suit. Maroon piping,' she said. 'I got fed up without one. I had another grey one, but I lost it somewhere. I thought it was at Aunt Livy's, but anyway, it wasn't. I lose track, I've got stuff all over the place. I should get it sorted out. Maybe I will, now. I may have left it at Fortune Park. Anyway, it's not there now. It could have been nicked, only you don't like to think of stuff getting nicked from there, do you? Meant to be a bit classier than that, really, isn't it?'

She burbled on as Sara ordered coffee. 'You see, the Paul thing, and the track suit. They're kind of related. I mean, I've just gone along wondering if any of it'll turn out. I've done everything Paul wanted. Didn't matter what he wanted, I did it. Anything. I just believed whatever he said.'

She reflected. 'I can see now how wrong I was. He's just strung me along, you know? And suddenly I've got fed up, see? Just so fed up I'm thinking, right, enough. If he wants to get someone else to do everything he wants, I'm thinking, well, Paul, you just sod off and I'll just go and buy myself another track suit. And I just wish I'd done it earlier. Seen it. It's all to do with self-esteem. Empowerment. Celebrating You. Know what I mean?'

The new-found power within her was making her babble. Coffee arrived.

'I'll pour, shall I? Are you having anything to eat? I'm starving. Screw Paul, I'm going to get fat.'

She craned round looking for a waiter, but instead her eyes rested on some point of interest near the door. She turned back to Sara confidentially.

'There's a bloke in the queue,' she said in a quiet, puzzled voice, her chin inches from the tablecloth. 'No, don't look now, I'll tell you when. I recognise him from a photograph. I'm sure it's him. Remember Cecily, my landlady? He's the boyfriend, only he's married. He's supposed to be spending the weekend with her, that's why I went to Livy's. Only he's here with someone else. Him in the shirt and suit trousers and brand-new trainers. He does look strange.'

'That's extraordinary,' said Sara, when Sue allowed her to look. 'It *is* him. I saw him that day we went to the Healing Arts. Before I met Cecily and you in the Tea Room. He doesn't look too well, does he?'

Derek and the dark woman had made their way up the queue and were being shown to a table just behind and to one side of Sue, affording Sara a perfect view of Pauline's back and Derek's face, which was tired and unshaven. He looked

265

ravishingly unhappy.

'Must be the wife,' Sara mouthed across to Sue, as the dark woman, without looking at the menu, gave her order to the waiter who had pulled back her chair and was helping her into it. The trio's unvarying mezzoforte made eavesdropping out of the question, but from the frequent nodding and jerking movements of her head and Derek's mute middle-distance staring, it was clear that she was finding plenty to say, and in a vein that was deeply wounding to him. He was further sobered by the arrival of lemon tea for him and whipped hot chocolate and a Bath bun for her. In hushed, clipped tones Sara related all that she could see to Sue, who had no idea what to make of it but knew where her duty lay.

'Look, I think maybe I should go over to Larkhall. Do you mind? He was definitely meant to be with Cecily this weekend. I'm sure of that because she checked with me to make sure I wouldn't be there. Well, he's here, and that means Cecily's probably on her own. Look, *do* you mind? We could do a run on Monday morning; will you be up for a swim? Right, see you then. I *am* sorry, but I owe it to her, I know how she feels. I should just check.'

She stood up and with a weak grin gathered up her bags. 'And, er . . . Paul might have rung.'

Sara dismissed her generously and only afterwards noticed that her lovely Ray-Bans were still sitting on the tablecloth. She could give them back to her on Monday, which might even be, because she certainly did seem to be only loosely attached to her possessions, before she missed them. She sat on, slightly numbed by the sensation of having been caught up and dropped in the passing of Sue's emotional maelstrom. She tried to feel indignant. She had never exactly invited herself into Sue's confidence in the first place, but realised that she must have sent out the signal that she was prepared to be confided in. And she realised too that in this she had not been generous, but had herself been the needy one. She had indulged some need of her own to observe, since she could herself no longer feel, that tension that was stretched taut between these two incompatible people, the pull of their inarticulate wranglings and their Byzantine misunderstandings. It had been like watching two people, one blind and the other deaf, trying to knit with one needle each. And there was something else, something even more obvious and pitiful in this realisation, which was that no amount of vicarious interest in the furies and passions of others could ever restore the vital kick to her own life, in which it seemed the death of feeling had been so final. It really could not matter to anyone if she sat on and drowned her innards in another quart of coffee, discarded by someone with places to go and people to see.

The trio's last chords straggled into welcome silence and they trooped off the platform to a clatter of applause. Derek was using this little diversion to break off from listening to his wife, sitting back and clapping unnecessarily. The woman was looking round blankly, clearly not having heard a note. She was intent on resuming her monologue which, with the trio gone, Sara could now hear. So what *did* it matter if she had become an emotional parasite, feasting on the eavesdroppings of other people's agonies? She fixed her eyes on the folds of the pink and green window drapery and listened hard.

'. . . own fault because no one *would* be surprised to see *you* have a heart attack . . . gross . . . her all the way there, in fact . . . sorry for her, sitting there all miserable . . . black eyeliner, tears . . . down her face . . . ring *me* up at five a.m. *humiliating* . . . both of us . . . half the night . . . that place . . . oh, *well* out of it . . . comfortable cubicle.'

Derek's wife paused to spoon up some of the froth on her hot chocolate and Derek seized his chance.

'It wasn't comfortable. It was frightening. I was on my own in there and when I woke up there was no one to explain what was going on. I thought I was dying. I didn't dare move and I called out and nobody came. What *was* I supposed to think?'

'Don't ask for my sympathy. What about me? First *I* know is being called into the cubicle . . . young doctor . . . smug little . . . next bit would make me laugh if I hadn't been so *humiliated*.'

Derek sat back, looked over his shoulder then back at her and hissed, furious and imploring, 'Shut *up*.'

She had no intention of shutting up. She went on, raising her voice in a cruel impersonation. One or two people turned to look.

'Oh, you were brilliant. "Please be frank, doctor. How bad is it? No euphemisms. I want the truth." Remember saying that? Remember me and what's-her-name and the doctor round the bed? And him smirking, *smirking* and saying what you had was so rare they'd never seen another case in the entire hospital? But if you "followed advice" *you need not fear a recurrence*? Remember? God, *I'll* never

268

forget it.'

Derek's head was in his hands.

'Oh, and then the next bit was good. Your frightened little face and one hand creeping up to your armpit. "Oh, my God, what's happened? Have you operated? Why have you shaved my armpit?"'

She laughed without mercy. People at several tables were now listening more or less openly.

'And in comes the nurse with that kidney dish and says, "I'm afraid we've had to remove a lump, Mr Payne. It's big." Your face! And the registrar saying, "Oh, yes, I'm afraid it *was* big. But fortunately not malignant. A benign lump. A big, benign lump of toffee, in fact." Grinning all over his face! God! *Toffee*! A lump of chewed toffee in a kidney dish! I could have *killed* you.'

She stopped for breath and looked round. Her audience, trying to look nonchalant, were instantly shamed into resuming their own conversations. Sara studied the chandelier closely and a nervous peace was restored. Derek was scowling with concentration at the remains of his wife's bun while she produced a handkerchief and patted impatiently at her nose.

'Derek, I had a long think, sitting in that place half the night, and I've decided a few things. I've decided that I *will* stay with you, on the following conditions. First, and starting right now, you will lose weight. Second, after the way you've been carrying on, you owe me something, starting with a decent weekend. This one. So you are going to go to that silly little tart *now* and finish it once and for all, while I go and book a room at the Royal Crescent and have a rest. Then you can pick me up and take me to lunch at the Olive Tree. Salad for

269

you.'

She paused, searching for the means to inflict maximum damage. 'And then you can take me shopping, starting'—and for the first time a smile came into her voice—'at Droopy and Browns. Yes. And then? Well, tea perhaps. Nothing to eat for you. And later, dinner at, hmm, I think probably the Hole in the Wall. And then we'll see.'

Derek stared past her, trying to convey a lofty disassociation from his surroundings. His face had the faraway, other-worldly look of a defecating labrador.

But she had not finished. She raised her voice again. 'Because, Derek, I have had to drive for three hours in the middle of the night and sit for another two in Accident and Emergency, and *then* be ridiculed in front of the entire medical staff, all because my husband is a bloody idiot who has a panic attack and *hyperventilates* and *faints* and has to be *sedated* because when he's asleep in some floozy's bed a lump of toffee falls out of his mouth and gets stuck in his bloody *armpit*.'

She tipped back her head and drained the last of her chocolate. 'And consequently, Derek, none of the foregoing is negotiable. Understand?'

As far as Sara could tell, he did seem to.

CHAPTER TWENTY-SEVEN

When he was able to sit up he looked round the room and saw that most things had been broken. He believed he remembered them both falling hard against the shelves, scattering all the books and

270

papers and the boxes and pots which now littered the floor. A table had been overturned and two of its legs broken, and the television set lay screen side down with a deep crack where the back was now coming away. Water spread across the carpet from a smashed vase. The curtains had been ripped down from the wall and were strewn in a heap with their poles, knocked from their hooks, lying across. He noticed the small dark drops that had been sprayed up the wall from his own nose, where one of the man's first blows had landed. He touched his nose gingerly and satisfied himself that it was not broken. Looking down at his chest he saw that there was a lot of blood, his own blood, on his clothes. But his jacket was dark, and nobody, even if they noticed the stains, would guess they were blood.

Looking around once more in the strange silence his eyes took in the man lying on his back on the crumpled bed. Lie there, pig, it's your own fault. He had had to struggle hard. He had not known what strength he possessed until he had had to stop him, until saving his own life had meant ending his, as it had turned out. But he had been right to defend what was his. He had been right to be angry with the man for pretending to help him and then trying to strip him of everything he had. But he had killed him. And then there were all the other things that would catch up with him now. All the other things. He must cover everything up, at least get everything covered up for long enough to get away. The only thing was to get away. He must get away now, even though it was daylight outside. He felt huge distaste at the thought of waiting in the room until dark. He was surprised at how

271

clearly he could think, and how separate and remote he felt from the events of the past few days, separate even from the pain that he was now feeling mainly in his ribs, his raw hands and his swollen face. He stretched his body carefully as he gathered up the curtains. The poles were not broken and he replaced them easily on the wall brackets. Then he draped the curtains over the poles and pulled the material across to conceal the destruction from the outside. Next he went into the kitchen to clean the blood from his face. It was when he heard the splash of water from the tap that he realised he had a raging thirst. He turned his face up and drank greedily from the flow. The water hitting his dry throat helped him control the shaking of his hands. Back in the room he picked out his things from the wreckage. He would take only his one bag. He would take only his own stuff and leave the rest; he would leave the gun. Lock the door. Keep the curtains pulled across. Walk. Think. The van would be no use. Walk past the van. Stop shaking. Keep walking. Get to the edge of the trees. Keep down, keep calm and think.

CHAPTER TWENTY-EIGHT

In answer to Sara's enquiry, the junior assistant at the health spa declared that Sue had not come in.

'Mever so sorry, Miss Selkirk. I think she must be ill.'

'Oh. It's just that I was meant to be running with her this morning. Did she leave a message?'

But she had not left a message; in fact she had

not phoned at all.

'Mind you, *I'd* of rung if it was me,' he said primly. 'Definitely. Doesn't take much to ring, does it? Just to let you know.'

'She must have forgotten about the run. Does Paul know how she is?' Sara asked.

'Mever so sorry, can't ask Paul. 'S'Paul's long weekend off. Don't think he's on again till tomorrow breakfast. Sorry. I would definitely of rung, if it was me.'

Remembering Sue's suspicion about things being stolen at Fortune Park, she thought better of leaving the sunglasses at the desk. They could easily be lifted from behind the counter when the staff were busy.

In the early evening she telephoned Olivia. 'It's nothing urgent, but I've got Sue's sunglasses. She left them in the Pump Room on Saturday and I was going to give her them today. Anyway, could you tell her I've got them safe? Is she better? And how's Edwin?'

Olivia hadn't seen her since Saturday. 'I did think she'd be staying for a bit but I really only ever half expect her. She tends to come and go. I thought it was all off with Paul, at least it looked that way on Saturday morning. Obviously I picked up the wrong end of the stick. If she's not with him, she'll be at Larkhall. And Edwin's fine.'

'Yes, all right, I'll try her there. Oh, by the way,' Sara said. 'Who's Churchill? When we had tea together, Edwin said something about Churchill and I couldn't work out what he meant. I don't think it was Winston. Do you know what he meant?'

'Churchill?' Olivia thought for a few moments.

'Oh, *Churchill*. Churchill is the firm that installed his stairlift. Churchill's Stairlifts, as endorsed by Dame Thora Hird, I think I remember. That's all. He loved your visit, by the way. Would you come again? Could you perhaps manage lunch on Wednesday? He usually has a sandwich around one.'

'Love to,' Sara said. 'Actually our last conversation got interrupted and there are things I want to talk to him about. Wednesday's fine. Give him my love.'

She tried the Larkhall number and got no reply, so it was likely that Sue was with Paul, making the most of one of their doomed new starts. They might even have slipped off somewhere for a day or two in the glow of reconciliation, Sue simply sneaking a day off work because she was, for once, having a lovely time.

CHAPTER TWENTY-NINE

The next day Andrew pedalled up through Northend feeling the heat of his row with Valerie cool as he went higher. The row had come on unexpectedly, and he was still feeling a mild surprise, not just at the way it had arisen but at its unprecedented conclusion. If anything, things had been going just marginally better, probably because work had been keeping him away from home. And Valerie had actually encouraged him to make love to her last weekend, had quite actively given him to understand that she would allow it, and he had begun to imagine the start of a new and happier phase for them. He had understood, although as a man he accepted that he could never completely understand, that motherhood was the most demanding, difficult, exhausting and debilitating thing that any woman could undertake. Valerie had not only told him this but amply demonstrated the truth of it as well. But on Saturday night she had actually suggested that if he wanted to 'get physical' then that would be acceptable to her. It had been such a long time since she had used the phrase that he had almost forgotten how much he disliked it.

In the event, the knowledge that Valerie was not the woman he wanted to make love with had made it unthinkable that he 'got physical', but it had led him to wonder, with the youngest approaching her sixth birthday, if Valerie might now be getting over the post-natal depression that she said her GP, a *man*, had failed to diagnose, and to hope that after more than five years of uninterrupted nights she might be starting to feel less permanently fatigued. Most of all he had hoped that he might soon be allowed to come out from under the cloud of reproach that had hung over him ever since he had first begun to oblige Valerie by reliably impregnating her with the children she had insisted she wanted. She always referred to them as 'her' children, and they were, all three of them. He was sometimes not sure if he quite liked them, with their adept pleading for things, although he loved them with his whole heart.

But the real reason for Valerie's offer of compliance on Saturday night had become clear first thing this morning, when the lorry had rolled up. He had gone out and told the driver that there was a mistake. But the driver had his delivery

275

address and delivery time, and would not be deflected.

'I've got it down here, so I'm obligated, see? You'll have to ring them up if you want to query it. Office opens at ten. I'm not authorised, see?'

So he had been unable to prevent the driver from dumping seventy concrete paving slabs, three hundredweight of cement and half a ton of sharp sand in their back garden. Valerie had been taking the children to school and when she got back he had already been on the telephone to arrange for the whole lot to be picked up again, reloaded on to the lorry and taken back to Homebase. With an unctuous smile that had instantly made him wary, Valerie had explained that it was she who had placed the order. Materials, patio, for the building of, the task she had allotted him for August, designating all his leave, his free weekends and his evenings for its completion. Without asking him. Because she wanted a patio.

He pedalled on. *'But I don't want a patio,'* he had said. *'I don't want a concrete, suburban patio with white plastic tubs of patio roses and floral patio furniture and all this pathetic pretence that we are a happy, spontaneous, nice little nuclear patio family.'*

She hadn't understood, or had pretended not to. She had given him that condescending oh-men-what-do-they-know smile. 'It'll be lovely for barbecues,' she'd said, in her that's-settled-then voice.

'For fuck's sake,' he had shouted. *'Why won't you listen? Do you think that what is wrong with us is going to be fixed by a fucking patio? With a barbecue and a few burgers from fucking Sainsbury's?'*

'Oh, you snob. You disgusting *snob,'* she had

276

screamed.

And that was when it had got really ugly. But somewhere in the midst of the torrent of her enraged abuse, which had ranged from his coldness, his snobby tastes, his stupid job, his horrible cello and that smug snobby bitch in St Catherine, he had realised, with a sensation that made him half believe he was floating, that she was probably right, and that he did not care what she thought of him. He had been smiling when she finally stopped shouting, and then he had simply left the house to go to his lesson. Cycling up Northend, he was a happy man. He knew he shouldn't be, that he should not be able to walk out of fourteen years of marriage and, when it came to it, would not do so unscathed. But the guilt and pain could wait. They would come, no doubt, with the logistics and operational difficulties of splitting the household, but the decision to leave, the decision itself had a kind of clarity which was making him happy. He realised now that he had been living for a long time with the vague knowledge that the thing with Valerie could not go on indefinitely. There would be no more rows of today's sort because he had left her, although, of course, he still had to move out.

Sara had tidied up the hut in preparation for Andrew's arrival, but was unprepared for him and the way he seemed to be glowing. They exchanged the usual commiserations about the heat, which privately each of them enjoyed rather than otherwise and then Andrew assumed control of the lesson. He wanted to play something right through before Sara commented. Today he was not in any mood, he said, laughing, to be interrupted. He was in the mood to make a statement.

'Right,' she said, a little taken aback. 'I won't even bring the Strad up. You're on your own.' With Sara following, he carried the Peresson up to the hut and settled himself on a chair on the gravel in the shade. She, finding him so unafraid musically and every other way, realised that he could probably, at this moment, lead her anywhere. She could not take her eyes off him. Was it to do with the four-square boldness of the music, Beethoven's Variations on Handel's 'See the Conqu'ring Hero Comes', that made him seem taller and stronger? As he played she sang in the missing piano part where it was needed, watching his face and acknowledging properly for the first time that when animated and well, Andrew had a brilliance that outshone his conventional handsomeness, and that his brilliance was becoming hard to resist. Today he was as unstoppable as the music itself, attacking the wonderful Allegretto theme as if it were the music which was to be conqu'red, which of course in a way it was. Or perhaps it was she he was setting out to conquer, in which case, at any rate today, there would be no struggle. She found herself wondering how long he could stay.

From the pocket of Andrew's jacket on the ground, the mobile phone blurted insultingly through the music.

'Poole,' Andrew said brusquely. They looked at each other, unsmiling, as he listened. Sara got up and gently lifted the cello and bow away from him. The person at the other end had a lot to say. Andrew continued his gaze, betraying nothing, then rose and walked away a little distance, still listening.

Eventually he said, 'Right. I'll get over there now,' and snapped down the aerial. He looked across the valley for a brief second before turning to speak. He had gone rather white.

'I have to get over to Fortune Park and I've only got the bike. A body's been found. A man. Can you give me a lift?'

Sara turned left at the crossroads on the edge of Colerne to take the main entrance to Fortune Park. Nearing the hotel at the end of the long avenue she saw the fluttering orange tape of a police cordon and a single police officer, who ushered them past the hotel front, past the greenhouses and the walled garden, round to the rear car park which served the health spa and the beauty salon. There were many more police officers here and as she swung the car to a clumsy stop she could see that their attention was concentrated on the grass in front of Paul's French window. With a cry she sprang from the car and ran towards it across the gravel. Andrew caught up with her easily and took a painful hold of her upper arm. He led her into the shade of one of the massive chestnut trees.

'I know who it is, I know him,' was all she could say. 'I know him, I do, I *know* him,' she repeated. Andrew took hold of her other arm and turned her to face him.

'Wait here,' he said harshly. 'Don't come any closer. Wait here.'

She watched him stride off through the sharp stripes of light and shadow cast across the lawn by the high trees, and pushed her knuckles against her teeth to try to stop the shivering. Andrew stopped by the white screen that had already been erected over the French window. His arrival drew the

279

attention of almost everyone at the scene and an earnest conversation began between Andrew, a uniformed policeman, another man in ordinary clothes and someone else, the scene of crime officer or the pathologist, in white overalls and boots. She waited until it was unbearable. With a sudden, almost involuntary movement she made off towards the unattended other door, the main back door that led into the hallway of Paul's little flat. She walked slowly by on the other side of the trees, assuming that she would at any moment be stopped by an imperious Oi! or that the door, when she got there, would be locked. She lifted the latch, walked straight into the empty hall and seeing that the door on the left into Paul's room was closed, she simply turned the handle and opened it, almost hoping that a grown-up would come and put a stop to what she was doing.

She stopped on the threshold as if she had walked into a wall. The smell filled her nose and poured into her mouth, stuck in her throat and hit her stomach like a punch. She was swamped like a baby under a fur coat of putrefaction. She stared, gulping dumbly, taking in the tumbled boxes, the strewn and broken objects, the bedclothes on the floor and finally the astonished, angry faces of Andrew and God knew how many other people, before she had to turn and stumble back out into the sunlight. But even as she was being copiously sick on the gravel she realised with relief that the grey-haired, heavy corpse sprawled on the bed, with cheeks like burst fruit, was not Paul.

CHAPTER THIRTY

By the time Andrew telephoned much later, Sara no longer felt sick and he was no longer angry.

'I was very angry,' he said, 'but I'm sorry if I was a bit hard on you.'

'You *were* hard on me,' she said, recalling how he had pulled her upright when she had barely stopped retching and ordered her off the premises, shouting at her, not caring how she was shaking or how sick she felt. 'You were horrible.'

'Are you all right now?' he asked, contrite.

'Yes, I'm all right. I'm just glad it wasn't Paul. And I suppose I'm sorry, too. I shouldn't have done it.' She hesitated. 'I can't *stand* anyone seeing me be sick. I can't believe you've seen me being sick. I hate it. I'm really *embarrassed.*' It occurred to her that she would be much less upset if he had happened to catch her dancing naked. Not displeased, if she were honest.

'Don't be silly. I hardly noticed,' he said. 'Anyway, I always picture you playing the cello, usually in sunshine up at the hut. So don't worry about that.' The truth was that having seen Valerie through three pregnancies, he was a dab hand with vomiting women. A nostalgia bubble containing his young, vulnerable and newly pregnant wife rose to the top of his mind and floated momentarily, before it was burst abruptly by Sara's voice.

'So who was it? And where is Paul?'

'A man who was staying at the hotel. He'd been dead at least two days. Last seen at breakfast on Sunday morning, so it looks as though he was killed later that day. Strangled. He was French. Apparently he knew your friend Paul; they did a bit of business together in the antiques line.'

Sara drew in her breath sharply. 'Bernard. Bernard, isn't it?'

'You are extraordinary. Yes, Bernard Rameau. Anything else I should know?'

'But Paul. Where *is* Paul?' she asked.

'That's what I would like to know. There's a search on for Paul. We're very keen to speak to him. He didn't turn up for work this morning. That's why the body was found. One of the other staff went over to see if he was in his room, looked through a crack in the curtains, thinking it was odd they were drawn in the first place, and called us. Things aren't looking too rosy for Paul. Any idea where he might be, then?'

'He has friends in Bristol, but I don't know who they are.'

'Oh, yes, we've got those. We got a couple of names from his colleagues in the hotel. Names the Bristol police were familiar with, it turns out. Paul hasn't been over there all week, though, and he wouldn't risk it now. He was in with a pretty rough crowd. Housebreaking—professionals, not kids. Going after good stuff. A lot of what he was passing on to Bernard Rameau was almost certainly stolen.'

'*Oh!* Are you sure? I mean, are you sure he knew? I would *never* have thought that of him. He seemed so . . . well, not nice exactly, but you know, not *criminal*. His girlfriend—Sue—she's not a bit criminal. You don't think . . . Have you spoken to her? She might be able to help you,' she said, 'although she told me once he kept her rather in

282

the dark about his friends. Drove her mad, actually.'

'Yes, we've got her name. Haven't found her yet, either at the aunt's or the landlady's. Any suggestions?'

'Well,' Sara said, 'I wouldn't *assume* they're together, though they might be.' She told Andrew briefly about Sue and her triumphant dismissal of Paul. 'She was more determined than I've ever seen her. But he could have brought her round, I suppose.' Paul's skills in that department would be masterly. 'Yes, he could easily have done that, thinking about it.' She paused. 'There's got to be a connection, hasn't there? With Matthew Sawyer? You know Paul was working at the Assembly Rooms that night, don't you? *Must* be a connection.'

Andrew exhaled dramatically. 'Well, I don't know what, and I've been wondering, of course. I really can't see what. Paul was interviewed and eliminated from the Sawyer enquiry. He was seen leaving the Pump Room before Sawyer was killed. The girlfriend produced the alibi; that could be dodgy, of course. But there's no motive, and no evidence to suggest a connection, but we'll check it all again. Frankly I'm more interested in getting him for this. It looks very likely that he and his French friend had a fight over something and Paul went too far. There's no record of violence, no record at all in fact, but it happens. He might get away with manslaughter. But we need to find him.'

He paused again. 'Look, I really am sorry you had to be involved. You wouldn't have been if I hadn't made you drive me over in the first place. You must have had a bad shock. Are you sure

283

you're all right? I mean, would you like me to come over? To be with you? Wouldn't you like someone with you?'

'No, no, I'm fine. Really, I'm perfectly all right. I'm fine. I'm going to have a long bath and go to bed,' she said at once, her refusal of any offered comfort so habitual as to be a reflex.

'Right. Probably just what you need,' he said brightly, hiding his disappointment. 'Ring me if you need me. And mind you lock up now,' he added, just to hear her laugh.

Only afterwards did Sara realise that she no longer wanted to protect herself from the danger that came with the prospect of comfort from Andrew. All right, he was married, but just the same it would have been lovely to see him, lovely if it had turned out that he stayed. She lay in her bath and went over the conversation, recalling all the bits that had made her feel the familiar risky pleasure of being both attracted and attractive. Up until now, it had been all the more risky and pleasurable because, since Andrew was married, she had been assuming that the whole thing would exist only in their heads. In fact lately it had begun to take up rather a lot of space in hers, enough to dislodge any insight into her harmless but slightly pathetic habit of fantasising about unavailable men.

It was certainly a shame about being sick. As she remembered his remark about picturing her playing the cello, she remembered also that the hut doors were still wide open and the Peresson cello still up there, probably still lying on the grass beside his chair. They had simply left everything where it was when Andrew's urgent call had

284

summoned them away. She calculated that it was doubtful if the insurance would cover damage sustained during a damp night out of doors. She sighed and as she slid under the bathwater to rinse off her shampoo, her hair floated out around her like dark weed in a stream.

*   *   *

It was well after midnight when she put on espadrilles and walked slowly up the path in the moonlight. Proper moonlight had been one of the delightful surprises of living here. Moonlight and owls did not exist in the modern orange sodium-skied cities where she had mainly lived, and they had consequently faded from her imagination or had drifted into the realm of things half remembered from old-fashioned children's classics. Things like midnight forays along moonlit paths, the owl hoot as a signal of danger; until she had come here these had been lodged affectionately in the same mental category as Aertex shirts, Mother's homemade scones and mops of dark unruly curls. There was still something exciting about such a clear, starry night and the moonlight, something that made her pause to look round with a happy tingle in her body that reminded her of when she was about twelve years old. Tonight the full moon shining across the valley transformed the garden into a theatre in which every ordinary thing, unexpectedly shoved on stage, was suddenly and mysteriously beautified. Pale things soaked in the light and gleamed in the air. She could see the calico of the garden umbrella shining over on the far side by the pond. Her white bathrobe was suddenly a shimmering gown and the towel round her head a silk turban in the Turkish style. She was the woman in white. She stopped and stretched out her arms into the night, watching the light animate her long, strong hands into the graceful, pearly appendages of some romantically consumptive heroine. Pushing back one sleeve as far as the elbow, she made a shadow swan with a sadly fractured neck against the moonlight on the path, and then with her other arm made another, which came and attacked it. Then they kissed and flew away. She laughed, slightly madly. She turned her outstretched wrists and flexed her fingers with the prosaic thought that she hadn't played all day. She should do some hard practice tomorrow; a proper work-out for her arms and hands, and then some Beethoven. She might get out those Handel variations herself; she had been reminded how wonderful they were. James might like to do the piano part.

The man on the velvet chaise-longue had opened his eyes, shaking himself out of a confused dream of falling branches, boxes and leaves, into another in which a menacing white figure was advancing towards him. But he was awake. At first he was transfixed with disbelief at the sight of the tall silent figure under the stars, swathed in white from the top of its awful domed head to the hem of its long robe. Then it had started to rise, moving smoothly towards him. It stopped and stretched out its long arms and he stared as they turned and twisted, the fingers practising their grip, ready to envelop him. The figure advanced a little and stopped again. And he had seen, quite sick with horror, how the pale hands were reaching out and

286

the fingers were curling. Soon the figure would move upwards once more, rise silently up towards him, its arms would encircle him and the white fingers would close round his throat, cutting off his screams . . . He knew no name that he could give this spectre but everything he had ever heard in childhood about the avenging spirits of the restless dead came into his mind. So they were not just stories thought up to frighten little boys. He now knew them to be true. And he knew that the spirit's authority to take his life, for the life he had taken, was irresistible and also just. More with the realisation that he deserved to be dead than with the knowledge that he soon would be, he shrank into an abject, embryonic curl on the chaise-longue and hid his face. Shame rose and suffocated him.

As Sara dawdled up the path, Edwin came to her mind. She tried singing the long, eerie first phrase of Eternal Source of Light Divine, thinking, has it come to this? Here she was, actually 'chanting cold hymns to the pale, fruitless moon', the fate with which poor Helena (or was it Hermia?) had been threatened. She pursued her memory of the quotation and thought she remembered the preceding lines:

> Therefore know thy heart, examine well thy desires,
> Whether thou couldst endure the ancient livery of a nun
> For aye to be in shady cloister 'mured,
> Chanting cold hymns to the pale, fruitless etc . . .

She shivered at such a midsummer night's dream, until the thought of Andrew stole over her as a sudden and overwhelming physical need, flooding her with warmth, melting the icy vision and the last of her resistance. She would let it happen. *Ring me if you need me*.

She switched to a ta-ta, tarum rendition of 'Who Were You With Last Night?'. Improvising a little tap dance to go with it she carried on up the path, 'out in the pale moonlight', creating flashes of light as her white bathrobe flapped round her knees. From above, the moonbeams threw down the shadows of bitter-scented blackcurrant bushes across her path.

When he dared look again he saw that the avenging spirit was indeed moving closer. But instead of the smooth and silent glide he had seen earlier, it now seemed to be almost bouncing and it was making noises. More than that, his incredulous ears were telling him that the noise was some silly song and now his eyes were taking in that his tall avenging spirit was only a woman in a white robe with a white towel round her head. Two days of sleeping rough with little food, coupled with all that had gone before, had temporarily robbed him of reason. His relief was closely followed by panic as he realised that she was still coming closer and would reach the hut in a very short time. The zigzag of the path was leading her away from him but he knew that a short distance ahead the path made a hairpin turn back towards the hut and then led in a straight upward-sloping line directly to the door. In a few seconds she would take the turn on the path and he would be trapped in the hut as she walked towards it. He had only a few seconds. Glad that he had resisted the temptation to take off his shoes, he slipped quietly off the chaise-longue, gripped his bag and paused only long enough at the door to be sure that he could still see her back walking away from him towards the turn in the path. He darted round the side of the hut and crouched behind it, terrified in case the demented woman's singing had not drowned out the slight scrape of his feet on the gravel.

This is proper lunacy, she thought, slowing to a standstill in front of the hut and looking out again at the moon. If anyone could see me now I would be locked up. She carried one chair back into the hut and came back for Andrew's. She sat down and picked up the cello, conscious that it had been Andrew's limbs which had embraced it last. She drew the instrument to her. Better just to see how much it had suffered from hours lying on the ground. She pulled the towel off her damp head so that she would be able to hear, and drew the bow over the strings. She found that it was an impossibility for her to leave it like that, so crazily untuned, even though of course she was not going to play, it being after midnight and she in her dressing-gown out in the garden. It would be lunacy of course, but she must just tune up.

Behind the hut the man could sense that she had stopped moving about and hoped that she had now gone away. The drone of the bow across the strings made his heart thump with fear. It had been rash of him to stay here. This afternoon, coming across the wide-open hut with chairs out and that musical instrument on the grass, it had been obvious that someone would be coming back. But the chaise-longue had been the nearest to a bed that he had seen for two nights and he was exhausted. He could at least lie down without letting himself fall asleep.

289

From up here he would see anyone approaching from below in plenty of time to get away. He had, of course, fallen asleep, but had woken of his own accord much later, towards nine in the evening. It was surely safe now to stay till morning, nobody would be coming now. He had not reckoned on some crazy woman stealing up in the middle of the night.

All the same, she wondered if she could do it again. She had managed the Bach for Edwin, had got through it without faltering at least, although it had been hardly a performance. And thinking about it, to hear Andrew play like that today had made her feel that a piece of tinder in her was now dry and waiting for its spark. Andrew, who had never performed in public in his life, had been playing for her, drawing her both to himself and to the music, showing her how it was done, how to be, once more, fearless. There's only me here now, me and the moon, she thought. I'll play it again, for the moon, and for the owls and the foxes. And for Edwin, because he deserved better. I'll play the D Minor again. She began to play the second of the six Bach cello suites, the pieces which are the ultimate test, the pieces that Casals practised for twelve years before considering them ready for performance. Remember, she thought, not to barge into it, it's not Rachmaninov. Really, this is the wrong instrument for this, I should have the Strad. Never mind, reserve the tone, let's have a bit of taste. I will try to play it. I'll play it for this garden and for the valley. Without fear. And she played on.

She made him nervous. He considered the idea of shoving her into the hut and bolting the door. It would be easy to rush up behind her, he'd be on top of her as soon as she heard him. She was not very big or even properly dressed so that even if she struggled, which he did not anticipate, it would be over very quickly. It was a nice-looking house, there would be proper food around, and there was the car. She would not be able to report the car stolen until someone let her out, probably in the morning. He could safely drive all night and dump it somewhere very early. It would get him all the way to the Channel.

The notes were coming back to her easily enough; of course she had never quite forgotten. Memory never had been the problem. It was all coming back as the sound rose up from the urgent, moving conjunction of string and bow. It was taking her now, the indestructible and monumental rhythm. It hovered across the lavender and fruit bushes, the roses, the medlars and the apple trees and floated higher, up above the garden and out over the roof of her house below. Where to now, the straining, restless sound? She would go with it to its end, giving it all her courage and all her power. She could feel it, hear it, almost see the music rising as she swayed in obedience to her bow. She could send it higher still. Edwin, can you hear? I am playing for you. And although I am playing quite softly you will hear it because it is rising up into the wide sky and coming to you across the rooftops and fields and rivers and bridges and right in at your high window at the top of Bathwick Hill, and Edwin, I know you will hear it. Can you hear it, Edwin, can you hear it and can you feel the fire in this music, as I think I now can?

But somehow, as she played on, he could not

291

find the moment to rush out at her, catch her unawares and silence her. He had to find the right moment, but the music seemed to be filling each moment in a way he could not explain, but knew he had to be governed by. And as he waited he began not to hear, but to listen. He found that he wanted the music to go on. He was still going to do it but he would not be any rougher than was necessary, and he would have to wait until she stopped playing.

Now the music almost had the advantage of her. It was as if the knowledge required to play it was passing from her head and ears and fingers and arms, which knew every note, every deft turn of the bow, every shift of fingering and every last accidental, into some other part of her, the part holding the cipher that could turn the notes into music. She could hardly hold it. It had been so long, but it was coming back. She was getting it now, that feeling that she was only fully remembering the music after she heard it, as if it was not quite she who was playing. It was someone just infinitesimally ahead of her, a someone else who was yet a part of her, to whom she was listening and saying yes, that is right, that is *it*. She laughed and turned her head up to the sky. Edwin, this is what I meant. We have to let the notes go, and then we play music. This is how it is meant to be. It is music, it is not just notes, any more than the sky is just space. It is music, I am playing music again. She played on, until the piece came to the end in its full-hearted, sweeping finality and with it a triumphant shout which was her own voice. She dropped her bow gently on the grass and, still straddling the instrument, stretched her legs like an exhausted lover. Silence filled the garden. She bowed her head and the tears which ran from her eyes splashed on to the wood and trickled down the polished front of the instrument. Matteo, I also played for you, she said quietly. It was also for you. She wept for a long time.

With the sound of her crying, his strength simply leaked out of him and he had known that he could not harm her. Already too much harm had been done. Tears rose in his eyes for her, for himself and the mess he had made of his life, and for the life he had taken, and as his tears fell, he remembered again all the childhood tales of the unquiet dead and wept for all the poor, lost souls wandering the night skies between this world and the next.

Now she could feel the cold creeping in through the soles of her wet shoes and a rustle of wind made her shiver. The grief which had taken hold of her was subsiding and leaving in its place a soft, clear calm and a kind of bemused gratitude. Why now? Why now, after more than a year, should she be able to weep for him, and for the first time be able to play, really play again? Perhaps it was not the timing that really mattered so much as time itself. She was peaceful. She put away the chair, bolted the hut and carried the cello down the path. Above her the trees swayed in the warm wind. Soon, the weather would break.

The man was glad to see her go. He watched until she disappeared and saw the light go on in an upstairs room. He waited longer just to be on the safe side. He had no idea what he was dealing with. He was puzzled and annoyed with himself. It had been stupid to think he could make it here. He had to get back to France, take a hold of himself, think.

The police would be looking for him, but he had money, he would manage it. He waited until the upstairs light went out and then stole silently down the path. The keys were not in the car and anyway, she would probably hear it being driven away. But he caught sight of the unlocked bike and lost no time in pedalling off into the darkness further up the valley.

CHAPTER THIRTY-ONE

Sara woke at dawn with the conviction that last night she had been absurd. Lying in bed, she felt an acute anxiety that what had happened might, in daylight, turn out to be rather less or perhaps not at all momentous, and that what she had believed out in the garden to be the triumphant scaling of a barrier might yet turn out to have been a trick of the moon. If she were to pick up a cello now, she might find that the deadening mastery of technique was once again in control, once again camouflaging the fact that since Matteo she had been able to play not like an artist but as an operator, turning out, at best, a few expressive clichés and stage emotions. She showered and dressed slowly. This was the day she was seeing Edwin for lunch, and she wanted nothing more than to be able to sit with him again and tell him that she was indeed, really and truly all right, that she had shifted the boulder out of her stream as he had said she would. Perhaps she would play for him again. But she could not trust any impression formed under a full moon.

In the music room she sat down and began. She

294

warmed up, and began to play the second cello suite, nervously. But her heart was beating hard because through the imperfections she was hearing the music in the old way again. She thought she knew what the music was saying and also knew with a wild burst of happiness that she wanted to play it and play it and play it, working until she had exhausted all the ways she could find of saying it. She thought of how, in this room, Matteo would work obsessively at the piano, going over scores, listening to recordings, often working into the night because the music and the possibilities of what he might do with it had so excited him. At those times he had been so absorbed and happy, and looking round the room that was still his, Sara surprised herself by finding that she was happy too, remembering. She found herself crying, recalling Edwin's phrase about the gift, and remembering Matteo's.

Much later she took her coffee up to the table by the pond which was now unpleasantly dull in the daylight. The dragonflies had gone. The sun's glare was muffled behind clouds and the air was heavy with damp heat. There was something else that Edwin had said about a gift. A gift of love. And slowly, sipping her coffee and hoping for the return of the dragonflies, Sara began to understand.

When she thought she had made sense of everything, she tried unsuccessfully to ring Andrew. *Ring me if you need me.* That's what he'd said, she thought furiously, and now she did, and he had gone and switched off his mobile.

*   *   *

By lunchtime the clouds had solidified and lay like a warm lid over the city. Edwin was not in the garden, probably because the weather was uncertain, but the French window into Olivia's study was open. Serena must be in the kitchen. Feeling that, but for Edwin, she would much rather be somewhere else, Sara made her way across the grass and stepped inside. Because she was expecting the study to be empty, she started at the slight movement from the chair in the corner.

'Oh, I didn't see you,' she gasped. 'I didn't think you'd be here, on a weekday.'

Olivia looked up from her glass. 'Sorry if I gave you a fright. I'm sorry, I forgot you were coming today. Come into the kitchen. I'm having a drink. Join me.'

Sara followed her into the kitchen and stood while Olivia took an opened bottle of white wine from the fridge and fetched another glass. Her eyes took in another bottle over by the sink. And here's one she emptied earlier, she thought. She certainly had started early.

'Of course you won't have heard. I'm afraid that yesterday—' Olivia began, when they had sat down at the table in the window.

But Sara could not bear to hear Olivia's appalled account of the body in Paul's room. 'I have,' she interrupted. 'I have heard, so I do know. Andrew was having a lesson when he got the call, so I took him to Fortune Park.'

'Oh,' said Olivia, apparently uncurious. She sipped at her drink.

Sara had no choice but to go on. 'I've been thinking, and I know as well that Paul didn't do it. Kill that Frenchman, I mean.'

'Oh.'

'He couldn't have. Or rather, he wouldn't have. For one thing, he wouldn't have used his hands. Not in that way, I mean,' she said. She took a deep breath, feeling unprepared. Should she even try to express what she was sure of but could only dimly and imperfectly explain?

'The hands,' she blurted. 'Paul's hands. He has hands that are too . . . fine. I don't mean not strong enough, but I don't know what else to call it. He couldn't strangle someone.'

'I know what you mean,' Olivia murmured, still seeming only half interested, 'but it doesn't amount to a defence. And in any case, I don't think it helps Paul.'

'No,' said Sara, 'it doesn't help him. But the main reason it doesn't help is the same reason that we both know Paul didn't do it. We know Paul didn't kill Bernard, because Paul didn't kill Matthew Sawyer that way.'

Olivia looked wearily out of the window. 'What makes you think Paul killed Matthew Sawyer?' she asked, without surprise.

Sara hesitated. There was simply not enough time to give proper consideration to the question of whether or not it was wise to say any more. She had to go on.

'Edwin's offering of love, I suppose,' she said. Olivia looked back at her, apparently bemused. 'Edwin's stairlift. He called it "an offering of love". At first I thought he just meant from you to him. But then there was the other thing he said. "Remember Churchill." I didn't know what he was on about at first.'

She stopped. What *did* she actually know? She

297

had pieced together a hypothesis based on the utterances of an oxygen-deprived octogenarian. It would be possible, and much more comfortable, to backtrack now, this minute, out of the whole conversation and leave things well alone. But that would mean dismissing Edwin's words as senile babble and she could not do that. It was Edwin who had coerced her gently into playing the Bach suite, the piece she had been playing when she had first encountered the terrifying block, and he had known precisely what he was doing. She would not deny his wisdom. And she was probably in too deep already.

'"Remember Churchill." When I asked you, you said he meant the people who made the lift.' Olivia nodded. 'But the words kept coming back to me. Remember Churchill. It didn't make any sense. So I went over the other things he'd said that afternoon and then I knew. He didn't mean Churchills who made the lift. He meant Frank Churchill in *Emma*, didn't he? Jane Austen's Churchill. The piano in *Emma*, the "offering of love" to Jane Fairfax, who was so cool and impenetrable, remember? It's a while since I read it. But Frank Churchill suddenly went off to London pretending it was to get his hair cut, when he was really arranging to have the piano sent anonymously to Jane Fairfax. She loved music, and played so well and they were secretly in love. That was what was in Edwin's mind when he said to remember Churchill.'

'Sara—' Olivia interrupted.

'So that was what made me see. I remembered Paul going off mysteriously to London,' Sara went on, and she could not resist saying, 'For piano, read stairlift. Frank Churchill: Paul. You: Jane. I'm right,

298

aren't I?' Not that it was funny in the least.

'Sara—'

'He's in love with you, isn't he? I should have seen it when I came to supper that night, but of course I didn't. And when I saw his room. That ticking material instead of curtains—blue and white stripes, like here. Everything so tidy, simple. A few flowers. People can't usually help liking the same things as the person they're in love with. And if they can't be with them, they try to have the person's atmosphere around them by having the same things.' She thought of the music room in Medlar Cottage. 'I do know.'

She looked enquiringly at Olivia, who did not respond.

'And it was Paul who paid for the stairlift, wasn't it, because he adored you. You had to make it appear that you could afford the stairlift anyway, with or without the grant that Matthew Sawyer stopped you getting. And Paul couldn't let it be known that he was paying for it. He must have spent everything he'd saved, mustn't he? That's what he was doing in London that day. I suppose he had to go in person and pay in cash, make it look like an anonymous gift, so there was no invoice with his name and address, just the address here. Did you ask him to do it, or was it his idea?'

She paused and took a large sip from her glass. Olivia had given up trying to say anything and was staring at the table.

Sara said quietly, 'Of course you don't have to tell me, and perhaps you're not going to speak to me at all, but I don't think Matthew Sawyer was killed just because of the grant.'

There was no response, so Sara went on, 'You

299

see, I think somehow it had turned up. How did that happen? It did turn up, didn't it—the Hackett Collection?'

Olivia looked at her, astonished. 'What makes you think that?'

Sara motioned towards the study. 'The boxes. I saw the shoes that day I came to supper, remember? In one of those grey conservation boxes. I saw the same sort of boxes in Paul's room yesterday, scattered all over the floor. Only for a second. And I saw a little pair of scissors and other things too; a satin pincushion, I think. A silver needlecase.'

She waited to see if Olivia was going to come forward with a denial before she went on.

'Then I remembered Sue saying that Bernard was selling English antiques in Paris. Was he by any chance selling off the Hackett Collection as well?'

Olivia looked at Sara, who was staring back with a look not of condemnation but of impertinent curiosity. Sarcastically, Olivia said, 'Well, you do get around, I'll say that much. First at the scene of the crime again. Look, if you're so certain that Paul's a murderer, then what are you doing here? Why haven't you gone to the police?' She waved an arm in the direction of the door. 'Suppose Paul's here? What's to stop him doing the same to you, to keep you quiet?'

Sara shifted in her chair and was unable to prevent herself from looking round. 'Because I don't think you'd allow it,' she said simply, turning back to Olivia. She waited. They both drank some more.

'So did Paul sell the stuff to Bernard for you?' She felt like an irritating child who will not leave

300

off asking awkward questions.

Olivia closed her eyes and nodded. 'I'll tell you, since you're so nosy. It won't make any difference. You've guessed a lot of it, anyhow.'

She refilled their glasses.

'The collection turned up soon after I was made acting director, about three years ago. It was quite extraordinary. I got a call one day from the manager of a branch bank in Warminster. This chap was new, he sounded about eighteen. They were converting the basement and getting rid of the old vault. They'd found some boxes marked Bath Museums. He said they would fit in the boot of a car, so I went over, and do you know, when I got there, I still thought he was about eighteen.'

She sniggered drily. 'It was awful, really. A nice little Victorian Gothic branch bank, and they were drilling away at the façade so they could fit in a line of cash machines. Inside they were doing out the whole place in pink and grey, artificial weeping figs in round white pots everywhere, you know? They must have ripped out lovely old panelling to do it. And he was so pleased with himself. He had some awful phrase for it: expanded customer facilities or something. Ghastly.'

Sara smiled, a little puzzled that in the circumstances Olivia seemed able to enjoy telling the story.

'He had no paperwork to say what was in the boxes. There were three of them, flat packing cases, tied with string and sealed. Filthy, marked Property of Bath Museums. He just wanted rid of them. He thought I might know what they were, but he didn't really care as long as I took them away. They didn't need vaults in a branch bank now, he said, everything was on computer. I just signed a receipt for them and took them.'

She sighed again. 'Then things just seemed to turn out in a funny way. I had these boxes in the car. I had no idea what was in them so I took them home; it was quite late by then. When I opened them I found the Hackett Collection. Obviously it had been taken out of Bath before the bomb in the Circus—lots of stuff was—and then it must have just got lost. The museum's paperwork, anything that would have recorded where it had gone to, was destroyed by the bomb. And then I noticed that the bank manager had tucked the receipt under the string of one of the boxes. He'd actually given me back the receipt instead of keeping it, so there was no record that the bank had ever had it. Obviously too busy thinking about his expanded customers and their facilities.'

She cast her eyes heavenwards and she and Sara exchanged a headshake. Honestly, bank managers these days. Again it struck Sara as odd that everything had become so *conversational*. Didn't Olivia realise that she was incriminating herself? Or should she seriously worry that the reason for Olivia's calm was that she herself was going to be silenced before she had a chance to go to the police? Perhaps she should drop a hint—a lie, in fact—that Andrew knew where she was and what she was doing.

'The museum had no extra secure storage available, so the boxes hung around here for a bit. It's bending the rules, but they were safer here. And anyway, I was the boss.'

She smiled. 'That might have been it, but then other things happened. Just after that Dad, Edwin,

302

got worse. I'd been looking after him, going back at lunchtime and so on, but he needed someone here all the time. So we had to get a day nurse. That was when I promised him I would never let him go into a home. And money was incredibly tight because I was still being paid my old salary and I was expecting to be upgraded to director level.'

Her lips tightened. 'When I agreed to be acting director, I was helping them out of a hole. I knew it would take them a while to sort out my new salary and I was very patient. There was no question that I should've been put on the director's scale and I assumed it would be backdated. And in the end they took more than six months over it, and they decided not to upgrade me. They just "enhanced" my old salary by an *insulting* amount and refused to backdate it. They regarded the first six months as an "induction period" payable at the old salary.'

'But that's monstrous. Didn't you have a union or anything?'

'Oh, yes. I should have contested it. I was angry enough. Frankly, though, I was just too damn exhausted and I had so many other things to worry about. The job was demanding, and I didn't think I'd be able to keep things going at home.'

She sighed and Sara saw how easily a look of deep tiredness took over her face.

'Soon after that Paul appeared on the scene. He and Sue seemed very happy at first. Then one day he came round on his own. I was in the study having a cry. I told him how worried I was about money and he couldn't really understand at first; my salary seemed such a lot to him. And I didn't actually need much. I was short of about just over five hundred pounds a month on average. So I

303

explained it all and Paul just looked round and said, "Why don't you sell some of this stuff?" There were Hackett pieces all over the desk, you see. And I said, "You don't understand, they're not mine." And he just said, "I know." And then he took me completely by surprise. He kissed me.'

She gave an abashed smile. A younger woman might have simpered, but Olivia frowned and drank some more wine.

'I didn't let it go any further than that, although it was difficult. I've never been so flattered in my life. He said he was in love with me, if you can believe that, and that he was glad I needed help, because it meant there was something he could do for me. I could trust him and he'd keep me and Edwin safe. And to his own cost, he has.'

Sara was nonplussed by the unnatural neatness of her confession. She said, 'So that was that? Paul just sold things off then, gradually, to bring in a bit more money?'

'Yes. Of course they were sold in France. The collection was documented in this country and these collectors are very knowledgeable, some of them. It would have been too risky to sell here. Paul saw that.'

Sara had almost reached the bottom of her glass and suddenly felt a little woozy. Christ, she's poisoned me, she thought wildly. She's poisoning both of us. That bottle was already open. Frascati, is it always as sharp-tasting as that? She knows the game's up so she's doing herself in and she's taking me with her. That's why she's telling me all this. Get out of here, *get out*. Yet she was glued to her seat. She stared helplessly out of the window as a nauseous sweat washed through her.

304

Olivia grew animated in her defence. 'And there was a certain justice in it, you know, or I couldn't have done it. The collection wasn't even meant to exist any more, remember? It had been de-accessioned anyway, so who actually owned it? Can you tell me that? And I was furious, after the way they behaved over my salary. So why shouldn't I take it, when they wouldn't pay me what the job was worth? It wasn't for me, it wasn't greed. Do you understand?'

Sara nodded as Olivia swallowed from her glass. Hold on, she thought, Olivia's not looking too bad on it, and she's had much more than I've had. Then she reflected that she had gone to bed after one o'clock in the morning, got up again shortly after five and played the cello for nearly four hours. Then she had had a bath, and her planned rest up in the garden with a strong cup of coffee had turned out to be anything but relaxing, once her mind had started working. After that she had spent a frustrating and unsuccessful half-hour trying to get hold of Andrew by telephone before she had had to leave to keep her lunch date with Edwin. Somehow in the midst of all that breakfast had been forgotten.

'There was another thing. I had researched quite a bit into the Hackett family. They were wealthy. Steel mill owners in Birmingham. The parents moved to Wiltshire for the cleaner air, for the daughter's sake. She had tuberculosis. She was the collector, Eugenia Hackett. She was an invalid all her life and her needlework was apparently wonderful. She got interested in needlework tools through that and started the collection when she was still a girl. Eventually she couldn't even sew

305

any more and the collecting took over. People used to go to her. She lived to be fifty-three, longer than anyone expected, and by the time she died her collection was very large and important, as these things go.'

But what was the point Olivia was making?

'Don't you see? If I had just handed the collection back to the museum, what good would that have done anyone? It would probably never even have gone on display, which was what Miss Hackett wanted. I can't help feeling that she'd approve of what I did. Those pieces were sold to other collectors, like her, and the money was all going to another invalid, someone who suffered just like her. So that he could have the care he needed. Don't you see?'

There was a silence. As far as it went, Sara did see, but still.

'I didn't *deprive* anyone of anything. I just sold pieces from the collection carefully, only two or three at a time. They fetch high prices, some of those tiny things. I remember there was a box made out of a walnut, a real, polished walnut, mounted in gold with a tiny hinge between the two halves of the shell.'

Olivia was doing it again. Her eyes were lit up now with the enthusiasm of the expert, seemingly indifferent to the trouble she was in.

'Inside it was padded in crimson velvet, with places for scissors, needles, thimble and spools, all in gold. So tiny and so perfect. That alone made nearly a thousand pounds. Imagine, a walnut.'

Where did she think she was? *The Antiques Roadshow*?

'I sold just enough to make the extra for Edwin's

306

nursing. Then after a time he needed night nursing too, so I sold a bit more. I reckoned even so there was a few more years' worth, just about enough to see him out.'

Sara was momentarily tempted to surrender to the pathos of the story until the 'but still' of the whole thing reasserted itself in her mind. Matthew Sawyer was dead. Matthew Sawyer had been deprived of something. Olivia seemed quite able to overlook that. And apart from murder, her astute husbandry of her 'assets' should not blind them to the fact that it had been theft on quite a scale. If I had any sense, Sara thought, I would stop this right here and go and get Andrew. But she had to know if she was right.

She said, 'Olivia, it was a mistake, wasn't it? You made a mistake over that memo, didn't you? The memo Matthew Sawyer sent you that afternoon about the Hackett Collection. It wasn't about the collection, it was about the catalogue, wasn't it? What did it say? "MS needs urgent updating." You thought it was his initials, that he was on to you and was demanding more information. But I think he meant MS as in manuscript. He meant that the manuscript needed updating. He should have said improving or restoring, but he wrote it carelessly, in a hurry. He was talking about the catalogue, and he *didn't* know about the collection turning up.'

The silence went on long enough for Sara to begin to imagine perhaps she had not heard her. Then Olivia spoke, looking out at a sky laden with heat and as white and thick as lard. Her tone of voice hardened.

'On the day he died he told me that the Terry Trust wasn't going to give Edwin a stairlift. He almost said don't bother. Send him to a home to die, he said, more or less. You should have heard him. He'd got so much, he'd got so much damn money and I needed such a little amount to make a huge difference to Edwin. So much depended on that grant, though it was only for five thousand pounds. He was so stinking rich, and so *complacent*.'

She swallowed a mouthful of Frascati and gave a bitter laugh. 'Needless to say, *he* was being paid the proper salary. Straight on to the director's scale, on appointment. And still ambitious, had his eye on the top job, I think. And his wife has *real* money. Most of that afternoon I was trying to work out if I could sell enough Hackett pieces for the stairlift and still not run out while Edwin needed nursing. I was on the verge of tears all day. I worked out what I could get for my own things—you know, the things in the drawing room—although contemporary work fetches less than you'd think. I'd promised Edwin the lift. He thought this might be his last summer, and he was desperate to spend it in the garden. Then I got the memo, when the Hackett Collection was on my mind anyway, and I just jumped to the conclusion that Matthew had somehow found out about the bank in Warminster and would soon be on to me. So as well as refusing us the lift he was about to take away even the little I had. Just that little bit I was managing to get for Edwin's care. And if I'd gone to prison, what would have happened to Edwin?'

Sara pictured it. Olivia's cool exterior hiding the near panic she must have felt at her own and Edwin's world falling apart, her realisation that if Matthew Sawyer were just stopped, then she would remain a respected professional curator and Edwin could live out his days in safety. The necessity of acting quickly, finding Paul, telling him of their danger, the hurried planning of how, where and when Paul would end Matthew Sawyer's life.

'It wasn't until the Friday a week later I read his file copy of the memo. That's when I noticed George behaving oddly. That's why I asked you to supper: I thought you might know if he knew anything, or help me find out.'

'I didn't though, did I?'

'No, you were useless, and really quite irritating,' Olivia said.

She was quite drunk now, and openly hostile.

'I expect you're quite pleased with yourself, aren't you? Clever little Sara solves the Hackett racket?' She laughed weakly, but was nearer to tears than laughter.

Sara said slowly, 'But the murder. Paul murdered Matthew Sawyer, didn't he? What about that?'

Olivia gave her a steady, unfriendly gaze. 'Matthew Sawyer. Bernard Whatever-his-name-is. They're both dead. Everyone dies some time, why the song and dance? And what makes you so sure it was Paul? Or not Paul? You've nothing to go on. *I* didn't say he killed Matthew. The police don't think he did. There's no evidence that he did.'

'Somehow, though,' Sara said quietly, knowing that she was making Olivia even angrier, 'I feel sure that he *did* kill Matthew Sawyer. I don't know—yet—where the murder of the other man fits in. I'm only sure that Paul killed Sawyer, and that you know he did. Only I can't see how.'

'Feel as sure as you like. You can't prove

309

anything against Paul. I haven't told you anything. Everything I've told you comes down to me. *I* stole the Hackett Collection. All right, Paul handled stolen goods. But you can't prove anything else. And I've told you too much already.'

Sara felt utterly confused. First Olivia had been recklessly forthcoming about what she had done. Now the shutters were down and there was no point in pursuing it further.

Trying not to sound angry herself she said, 'Olivia, I don't understand. You've told me such a lot. But you know much, much more about all this. Why hold back now?'

Olivia stared at her blankly and then her face crumpled. 'You really don't get it, do you? Paul still has his life ahead of him, if he can get away. I'll certainly never see him again. And I don't give a damn what happens to me now. It doesn't matter any more. Why else would I have told you?'

Sara was suddenly aware of the awful stillness in the house above them.

Olivia sobbed, 'Dad, Edwin, he died last night.'

CHAPTER THIRTY-TWO

Sara was not sure how she got home, but she had been glad to get away. She had left Olivia crying at the table, insisting angrily that she wanted nothing, nothing at all, but for Sara to go. She telephoned Andrew again. His mobile was still switched off. She rang the police station and was put through to Bridger.

'Chief Inspector Poole's on special leave this

afternoon. He has a family matter to attend to. Can I help?'

But it was Andrew Sara had to speak to. 'No, I'll get him another time. Thank you.'

Special leave sounded like a funeral, but Andrew had been in such high spirits only yesterday—it had been only *yesterday*—and hadn't mentioned anyone dying. If it was a funeral, would Bridger not just have said that? Was one of the children ill? Run over? Somehow, special leave sounded as if it was for something a bit more planned than that. She decided to risk it and rang his home number. She got Valerie.

'Hello. Look, I'm terribly sorry to bother you at home, but I wondered if I could possibly speak to Andrew for a minute? I hope it's not a bad time. It's Sara Selkirk speaking.'

Valerie was breathing in and out heavily and sounded close enough, as well as sufficiently angry, to bite Sara's ear off. 'I don't believe this. Couldn't you have waited?'

'Oh, look, I'm sorry. I just hoped it wasn't a bad time. I am *sorry*—'

'You've got a bloody nerve! You know perfectly well what you're doing! You couldn't wait another minute to get your hands on him, could you! You whore!'

Before Sara could gather any sort of reply she heard Andrew's voice in the background, raised in anger. Still holding the receiver close, Valerie was shouting back at him. 'Oh, so it's not true, is it! You lying bastard! Don't tell me now you're not having an affair! You tell your bloody tart she's welcome— you liar! You filthy liar!'

Sara quietly replaced the telephone. Within a

311

minute it rang. On the third ring, she lifted the receiver no more than an inch and dropped it back into its cradle. She was shaking and tearful, smouldering with grievance, and suddenly overwhelmed by a huge fatigue. Wearily, she collapsed on to the deep sofa in the dark drawing room and acknowledged the enormous injustice she felt, less for Valerie's accusation which, given a little more time, might easily have been deserved if not altogether accurate, but more for having only so briefly known and then lost the sweet, wise Edwin.

She had been so excited about seeing him today. She had wanted to play for him again, properly. She had been going to tell him what had really happened in Paris. He knew only what the music press had said, and they had talked only of a nervous breakdown. A natural reaction, everyone said, to the tragic and untimely death of Matteo Becker two months previously. Delayed grief. She had wanted to tell Edwin that it had not been quite as simple as that. She had never told anyone that just after that first Christmas in Medlar Cottage Matteo had seemed quieter, a little unwell, and that she had been almost pleased. Perhaps he was going to slow down a little and enjoy being at home more. The first time he complained of the pain in his side she had just come off the telephone, making arrangements for her series of three concerts in London, Dublin and Cardiff. She had poked him in the stomach and teased him for over-eating. She had told him to drink lots of water and keep off the wine when he was in Australia, where he was going in four days. If it doesn't go away, see a doctor. If you can spare the time. When he was

312

leaving for the airport he had said wistfully, unaccountably, 'Sara, come with me?' and of course he had been joking, she was playing at the South Bank the very next day. She had ignored the faint look of fragility in his face and they had been laughing as they kissed goodbye. On the plane his appendix had burst. When the plane landed seven hours later, he had been taken to a hospital where they had been unable to prevent the onset of septicaemia. Five days later he had died.

After the funeral, she had gone on with her engagements. People were amazed at her strength. She had carried on until Paris, when she had simply stopped in the middle of the second Bach cello suite, frozen in mid-phrase. In the awful shocked silence of the hall, the only sound had, eventually, been her own footsteps as she left the platform. And she had not really played in public since, but had withdrawn into her life, bowing under the burden of her guilt and all the sympathy and all the kind understanding of people who understood nothing. But Edwin had understood something. He had known that after such damage, recovery is slow, but that perhaps she had spent enough time waiting. She looked out and saw over the valley the low sky, clogged with rainclouds, grief-laden, and she buried her face. Even if I had been on that plane, Matteo, I could not have saved you. Till the end of my life I shall wish I had seen how ill you were and stopped you going, but it was not my fault. It was not my fault you died. When the telephone rang again she did not answer it.

*   *   *

313

She was wakened by the cat springing into her lap. She had an idea that it was early evening, but the drawing room was darker than felt right. Against the horizon, banks of bruise-coloured cloud were building steeply, and across the lime tree meadow a shadowy pink light shimmered with the dangerous glow of imminent thunder. It was only just after five but as dark as a winter afternoon. She made tea and switched on lamps, intending this time to be gentler in the nursing of her grief. She rested. The thunder came and with it hard, perpendicular rain. Just before seven the telephone rang again.

'I've been trying to call you,' Andrew said. 'I've moved out.'

'Oh, I see.' She hoped that he was not going to go into the telephone call with Valerie, the thought of which still upset her to the point of nausea.

He said, 'I'm really sorry about . . . earlier. She got the wrong end of the stick entirely.'

Sara would give him no help. 'Quite. You might want to tell Valerie that I rang you about the case.'

He went on, 'Right. Only she insists on having the bike. It's hers really. I'll have to come and get it. I left it under that big tree in your drive yesterday.'

'The what? Oh, I forgot all about the bike. It'll be soaking wet. It's still where you left it,' she said. She walked with the telephone to the side window of the drawing room and looked down the drive to the copper beech tree at the end. As she stood rather stupidly looking at the place where the bike had been, there was another roll of thunder.

'It's gone,' she said flatly. 'I'm really sorry. I suppose I should have brought it in. No hope of getting it back, I suppose?'

'None. Never mind.'

'Look, I've got some things to tell you about the case. I think I know who might have done it. Although I can't work out how,' she said.

'I appreciate it, Sara, but this isn't a good time. Please don't add to the theories about *who*. What we need is the why and how, and something that will stand up in court. Oh, bugger it. Bugger Valerie's bike. I should have locked it. I was too excited about playing the Beethoven for you yesterday. Too excited about leaving my wife. Serves me right.'

'Anyway, you couldn't have ridden it home in this,' she said. 'Where are you staying now, anyway?'

'I'm in a B and B till the weekend, then I'm moving into a flat in Combe Down. The house of one of the Victim Support clients. She's a widow, got burgled last year. She's giving me the ground floor. Quite chuffed to have a DCI on the premises, so the rent's low. It's only temporary, until the house is sold. Look, Sara, about Valerie . . .'

She was simply not going to listen. She said, 'Don't. It doesn't matter. I'm sorry about the bike. You couldn't have got it in the car anyway, could you? There isn't a roof-rack. Look, there *are* some things I've got to tell you—'

'No, I'd have had to take the front wheel off. Bloody nuisance really, but of course she wanted it,' Andrew said. 'What I'd like is one of those great little folding bikes, you know the ones? I don't suppose I'll be spending money on bikes for a while now, though. Valerie's—'

Sara broke in rapidly. 'We've got to go to Fortune Park. They haven't moved anything, have

315

they? Meet me there. I'll tell you why when I see you. *Go*, Andrew, I'll see you there.'

* * *

Andrew's car drew up alongside hers in the car park. Through the pelting rain Sara saw his dark form loom towards her passenger door, open it and land heavily beside her, chilling the car with his large, outdoors wetness. He hadn't bothered with a coat and his hair was dripping.

'What's this about?'

They walked through the rain under Sara's large umbrella to the hotel entrance where she lingered under the porch while Andrew went in alone. The hotel manager had been warned that the DCI was looking in, but he was none the less surprised to see Chief Inspector Poole in wet-through, off-duty clothes, asking for the key to the flat. He'd been given to understand that the police had finished at the scene. He handed over the key without volunteering to accompany him, and watched him set off back into the rain.

As soon as Andrew had unlocked the door Sara darted into the hallway of the flat, towards the bike propped against the wall. Thinking she was about to touch it he had been on the point of calling out a warning, but she had already turned away and was saying, 'Yes. That's it. Come on.' She was excited and looked about to fling her arms round him.

'The car's clammy,' Sara said when they came out. 'Let's walk.'

They wandered under the dripping chestnut trees towards the avenue, while Sara related her conversation with Olivia. He listened, resisting the urge to hurry her. The rain did not let up and Andrew, holding the umbrella over them, noticed how the pale pink of the material had given Sara's skin, shiny from the rain, the glow of a child's.

'So just where does this get us?' he asked finally. 'All right, the Hackett Collection was being sold off. I don't yet see it gets us anywhere. And just what are we doing here? What's a bike got to do with it?'

'Remember, Olivia's admitted that she was angry with Matthew Sawyer about being turned down by the Terry Trust. And she's admitted that she and Paul were selling the Hackett Collection. She as good as admitted that she jumped to the wrong conclusion when she read Sawyer's memo. If she did, it's quite easy to see that she would want Matthew Sawyer stopped.'

'But she didn't admit that, did she? *You* said she must have misread the memo. And misreading a memo, even if she did, is not an admission of murder.'

'Yes, but listen. She was angry and upset over the stairlift. Suppose then she gets the memo, reads it and misunderstands it, thinks there's no time to waste and gets Paul to kill him that night. Then she has to go on as normal, of course, so she takes up as acting director on the Monday, shaken but calm, show must go on, all that. But on the Friday of that week Mrs Trowels comes back to work, and two things emerge. First, Matthew Sawyer is a more thorough administrator than Olivia gave him credit for. The memo was handwritten on plain paper when he was down in the Guildhall archive and just bunged into the internal mail. The last thing that Olivia expected was that he *photocopied* it at the

Guildhall and sent the *photocopy* back to the Circus for Mrs Trowels to file in his Bring Forward file for him to follow up. So one, there's a copy, and two, Olivia reads it again in a calmer frame of mind and sees her mistake.'

The rain pattered harder on the cotton of the umbrella and a flash of lightning, far off, was followed by thunder. 'And that was when she nearly panicked. First of all she feels genuinely awful. Sawyer's been killed for nothing, it was all a stupid mistake, and so then she feels terrible about his widow and all that. So you see her grief, which was real, also stopped her being suspected. And then, because George is clearly fretting about something, she starts worrying in case he saw anything. She starts wondering if he had maybe come back for some reason. But of course she just has to brazen it out, talk about the memo as if it had all been crystal clear to her from the beginning. And the reason she asked me to supper was because she thought I was well placed to winkle anything out of George and because she guessed you might be talking to me about the case. I didn't notice anything at the time about Paul, anything worth mentioning. I did see them glance at each other, and I thought she was just signalling him to pour more wine. I didn't suspect her for a moment.'

'And I'm not sure I suspect her now,' said Andrew, shivering slightly. 'But go on. Let's hear how it was done.'

Sara had allowed herself to be led away from the chestnut trees and into the walled garden, where the smell of wet catmint rose around them through the cold rain.

'Right. Olivia's at the Assembly Rooms with

318

Sawyer, for the opening of the alternative healing thing. Then she's due at the Pump Room. Sawyer's going there too, to do the rounds and lock up. And Paul's working at the Assembly Rooms, remember. So she explains it all to him and they work out that Paul should get to the Pump Room and do it there, because Sawyer will be the last person in the building. It'll have to be done with one of Paul's knives. You know chefs all have their own knives. Paul's got a set, although of course by the time I saw them, at Olivia's supper, the one he killed Matthew Sawyer with had been replaced. So Olivia goes to the Pump Room dinner and leaves early, gets home and goes up to see the night nurse and Edwin. She leaves them upstairs and says she's going to bed. Paul finishes at the Assembly Rooms and goes round to the Pump Room on the pretext of seeing if help is needed. He's trying to impress Coldstreams, remember, looking to further his career, so it's quite natural. But I bet if you check you'll find he'd never done it before.'

Sara looked at Andrew, a little triumphantly. He looked back, thinking how wrong he had been, up until this moment, to assume that women looking unbelievably sexy in the rain was something you only saw in films.

'He chains his bike to the railings in Abbey Churchyard, instead of taking it round to the staff entrance on Stall Street. Then he milled about helping for a bit, and just after eleven he quietly checked that the little office was still unlocked and that it was empty. James and I had both left by then, so our stuff had gone. I suppose if we hadn't he would have found another office—there are several little rooms only used in the daytime. And

319

he checked that the Stall Street door could still be opened from the outside and then he left by the front door, the one that always has a doorman on it. That way he says a proper goodnight to Matthew Sawyer, who's seeing people off, and he's sure that he has been seen leaving.'

'Or could it be because his bike's just outside, chained to the railings?'

'Ah, but he's only put his bike there to *make* that look the reason. Don't you see? So he cycled off, but then, you see, he went back round to Stall Street and slipped back in and hid in the office. And it's a *folding* bike, Andrew, so he could bring it in with him. We established that, didn't I?'

She looked so cheeky and pleased with herself that he thought he was going to kiss her. Instead he said, 'And he hid there until everyone had gone, is that it?'

'Everyone except Matthew Sawyer. From the Stall Street lobby you can go down the back stairs and out to the Great Bath, can't you? So he went down, probably when the last of the kitchen staff left and it went quiet. Now, he must have realised that it would be dangerous to kill Sawyer out by the Great Bath. It's too open. And if there was a struggle there would be noise, and anyone outside the building on the other side of the wall would be able to hear. They could even end up fighting in the water. Just in front of the spring overflow was a better place because it was inside and also it was dark. And there's the noise of the water.'

Andrew nodded. His hair was drying now, Sara noticed, and going a little fluffy. She wanted to touch it. She stared at the place between the base of his throat and the top of his chest, where dark hairs lay just under the top shirt button. She wanted to reach under his damp sweater and pull it over his head, hauling his shirt off with it.

Andrew said, 'I think you're overlooking how messy these things are. You said they hadn't planned it before that evening. How would he deal with the problem of heavily bloodstained clothes? He could hardly walk through the streets or cycle off, even late at night, drenched in blood.'

'Oh, I quite agree, he couldn't have. He couldn't have dealt with bloodstained clothes. He was in his chef's clothes: checked trousers, apron and T-shirt. He wouldn't have a change of clothes with him. He would just have a carrier bag or something for the apron and his knives.'

'Well, doesn't your hypothesis fall apart then? You *agree* he couldn't deal with bloodstained clothes?'

'Oh, yes,' Sara said, 'and he must have realised it too, so he took his clothes *off*. He took them off and put them somewhere well out of the way. He was naked.' She dwelt just slightly on the mental picture, and then substituted Andrew for Paul for a brief, private moment.

'Bet he kept his socks on,' said Andrew, jealously. 'A bloodstained footprint could have identified him almost as conclusively as a fingerprint. We didn't find any.'

'There's more than one possibility there, I think. He might have kept socks on, or'—she could not help smiling as she spoke—'he might have halved his carrier bag and sellotaped his feet up in the two halves. There would be sellotape in the booking office. Or he could have washed the flagstones down afterwards—plenty of water.'

Andrew laughed.

'After everyone had left, he must have shouted or called for help, anything to bring Sawyer down to investigate. Sawyer would be thinking that somebody from the dinner had got drunk and passed out or something. If it occurred to him at all, he would know that there were enough people there unpartnered for someone to disappear and be assumed to have gone home. And when he investigates, maybe even leans over the railing, suddenly there's a naked, terrifying savage behind him with a knife. A Celtic ghost, a soldier of Sulis, carrying out the wishes of the goddess. "May my enemy become as liquid as water" or something like it.'

She shuddered. 'In fact, I hope the poor man never knew what hit him.'

'Then what?' Andrew was concentrating hard now.

'When he was sure Sawyer was dead, he just left him there, hanging over the railing, dripping blood into the water that runs into the Roman drain and away. But of course he must have been covered in blood himself.'

She leaned forward under the umbrella. 'So he went out to the Great Bath and just walked into the water and washed himself clean.'

There was silence except for the rain. Andrew said, 'That's outrageous.'

Sara nodded. 'He threw the knife in too, of course. Then he dried himself off with his T-shirt, got dressed, and took the keys from the body. After that he just went back upstairs, retrieved his bike and his apron and the rest of his knives. I should think he locked the Abbey Churchyard door from the inside and left from the Stall Street door. It's quieter. Then he just rides off.'

'Back to Fortune Park? And what about the alarm?'

'No, *no*,' Sara said, almost crossly. 'Remember it was just after midnight by then. Sawyer was killed around midnight at the earliest. Say it was around twenty past, he couldn't have got back to Fortune Park, on the bike, before two o'clock in the morning. No, he went to Olivia's. He went in by the garden gate and she would be waiting for him in the study. They left the same way, with the night nurse assuming that Olivia was in bed. Olivia drove him back to Fortune Park. That was what puzzled me, you see: she drives a Citroen AX—far too small to take a bike. I didn't think of a folding one. It would take less than half an hour, and she would drop him off before the entrance so he could unfold the bike and cycle up to his door and arrive suitably puffed.'

'And he arrived back there before one o'clock, which is when he would have arrived if he'd left the Pump Room at quarter past eleven to cycle home.'

'Exactly. So his movements at the time of the murder appear to be accounted for, since he couldn't actually have an alibi.'

Andrew pondered this for a time. They had reached the end of the rose walk, and were standing by a pretty wooden bench under an arbour of yellow climbing roses. The bench was sodden, too wet to sit down. By silent consent they moved away, back down between the dripping rose beds.

'There is, of course, not a shred of evidence to support this.'

323

'Well, no, but there are things that are difficult to explain if it didn't happen that way.'

'Such as?'

Sara sighed, as if Andrew were being just a tiny bit dim. Again he found himself wanting, at the very least, to kiss her. 'Sue confirmed that he arrived at about quarter to one. She waited up for him. When he came in, she said his hair was damp.'

'So what? It had been raining.'

'Yes. It was raining at about ten thirty. I remember because that was when I left and I had to get across to Manvers Street with the cello and all my stuff in the rain. But it stopped about ten to twelve, didn't it? If Paul had left to cycle home at quarter past eleven his hair would have got wet, but it would have been bone dry long before he arrived near one o'clock, even long hair like his would have dried completely as he cycled. And it was damp. And I think the reason it was damp was because he had been immersed in the Roman Bath less than an hour before, washing off Matthew Sawyer's blood.'

'Oh, Sara. I wonder. I wonder. And the alarm?' Andrew murmured.

She went on, 'I think they realised in the car that there were loose ends.' She took a deep breath and stopped. 'I think,' she said, 'that Matthew Sawyer had the memo on him. When I saw Olivia and Sawyer at the Assembly Rooms they were arguing. There was a piece of paper and she was objecting to something in it. When she stalked off she practically shoved the paper at him. I thought it was all to do with his speech, that he'd ignored all her briefing notes or something.'

Andrew turned to face her. 'And you think it was

the memo.'

'Yes. You see, I don't think she'd briefed him at all. He hadn't a clue; she couldn't have. I think she spent the entire time before the opening, when she was meant to be briefing him, arguing about the Terry Trust's decision. And maybe Sawyer wanted to discuss the Hackett memo as well, and I guess she wouldn't let him get a word in. A pity, because then she would have realised that she had nothing to fear and he'd still be alive. At any rate, after the murder Olivia had to get back into the Pump Room, and I think it was to retrieve the memo from Sawyer's pocket. Of course at that stage she didn't realise that there was a copy. But she couldn't just saunter into the Pump Room at half past one in the morning, even with the keys, could she?'

'So what do you think she did instead?'

'She's your jogger,' Sara said, walking on. 'She went back home, went in by the study, and put on Sue's track suit and trainers, because she didn't have any of that kind of thing herself. Plenty of people jog at night, and with the hood up she wouldn't be recognised. But there were people around, the ones the shop security videos showed. Drunks on the benches, and those teenagers. She had no option but to go round and round the town until the coast was clear. It was about twenty to three before the area was completely deserted.'

'And then?'

'She let herself in and went down to the body, where Paul had told her she'd find it. She got the memo. But she found another piece of paper too, the one that Matthew Sawyer took from the attendants' room, with all the security codes on it.

325

Then she must have wondered about another thing. Fingerprints on the body. So she heaved him over the side into the water, certain that he'll lie there for hours and prints will be washed away. Then, I think she must have realised that she'd got all the security codes in her hand. Now, remember what we said ages ago about the building being locked and alarmed? Why had the murderer bothered to do it at all?'

Andrew nodded.

'There wasn't any good reason. Except the reason the building is locked every night: to safeguard the objects.'

Andrew frowned.

'You see? Of *all* people, Olivia is the only one who would be incapable of leaving the building unsecured. You've seen what a professional she is. She's a senior curator, she really cares about the objects. Even'—Sara pre-empted Andrew's objection—'yes, even the ones she was flogging for personal gain. It mattered to her, you know. Anyway, suppose for now she'd got the codes in her hand.'

Andrew nodded.

'She would see that she could safeguard the museum and possibly at the same time throw the investigation if she set the alarm using Matthew's code. She might even have thought that she could create a bit of confusion about the time of death. She wouldn't have had long to think about it. I reckon she just did it, threw the keys over the wall into the Great Bath and jogged home. Next day she got rid of the track suit and shoes and bought a replacement knife for Paul.'

'What makes you so sure it was Olivia? It could

326

have been Sue, protecting Paul. Perhaps they were all in it together,' Andrew said. There was a dispiriting lack of evidence.

'Remember what you said when you'd seen her on the Sunday? What was wrong with her, because she could hardly walk? That was the result of about three hours' jogging when she wasn't in training. You would be in agony for days. When I went running on Monday after two weeks off because of the hot weather, I felt a bit of stiffness the next day, but nothing like Olivia. She would really have suffered. And Sue lost a pair of trainers and a track suit recently. Olivia would know that Sue was vague enough about things like that just to moan about it for a bit and then replace them.'

They stopped again. Andrew placed a hand on Sara's shoulder and caressed it gently as he spoke. 'Sara, it's an amazing, intelligent, fabulous construction, and it's all plausible. But no jury would entertain it for a minute. I'm sorry. You could even be right down to every detail, but on the basis of the evidence, we couldn't convict anyone.'

Over Andrew's shoulder Sara could see the rain plopping in deep splashes into the rectangular pond at the far end of the garden.

'I know,' she said, sighing, dipping her head to one side so that her cheek gently stroked, just once, against his hand. He caressed the warm skin of her neck. As he slid his fingers into her hair and pulled her head gently towards his, she said, looking at him, 'Let's go back.'

He knew what she was asking, and his face tightened as he sighed and let his hand drop.

'I want to. You know I want to, but I can't. I still have to look into all this,' he said roughly. 'It can't

327

wait. I'll have to bring Olivia Passmore in for questioning. Look, you'd better go home. You do understand, don't you? It can't just be left.'

Sara almost gasped at the rejection. 'On the contrary, it can. Leaving it is precisely what we should do,' she said, taking the umbrella from him. 'Just leave it. The whole thing,' she added bitterly, over her shoulder, walking back towards the car park and leaving Andrew in the rain.

CHAPTER THIRTY-THREE

On the journey back, mesmerised by the squeak and swing of the windscreen wipers, Sara was almost overwhelmed by weariness. Over the long high stretch of road across Bannerdown, rain lashed the car. More thunder followed her and lightning not far away tore out of the sky and zapped the fields on the edge of the horizon. This was too much: too much weather, too much murder, too much for one day and much too much Andrew. She was too much in the open. She drove on, longing to be home. She would organise the usual spinsterish armoury against rejection: a hot bath, the fire, some wine, an early night. She found herself wondering what was on telly.

Olivia was in the kitchen. As Sara walked numbly in by the back door she saw her, standing in exactly the same spot where James had stood not long ago to chop onions, while she had watched from a chair on the other side of the table. From the stillness around her, Sara was sure that she had not just arrived. She had been standing there, in a drenched raincoat, waiting.

'It was open.'

Olivia seemed to have sobered up. Her face had been washed pink and white by the storm and looked attractively feverish. It was easy to see how such a face, suggesting a tragic and beautiful soul, would entrap a passionate and much younger man.

'I'm always forgetting to lock up.' Sara could not think of much else to say. 'I've just been back to Fortune Park.'

Olivia gave a short, disgusted sigh. 'Waste of time. Paul didn't kill Bernard. But you'll never find him. He's gone.'

'Where to?' Sara asked mildly.

Olivia ignored the question. 'He had to get away. He didn't do it, but he'd never be able to explain who did without opening up the whole thing. Not just me, not just the Hackett pieces. The police will investigate Bernard and it won't take them long to find out about some of his other little dealings.'

Sara had no idea what she meant.

'Immigrants. He was bringing in illegal immigrants from Paris. Not many, only one at a time, and not every trip. Paul didn't like it, but there wasn't much he could do. They were going to be sent back to West Africa. The ones who spoke English wanted to come here. Bernard usually dumped them before he arrived in Bath, but this one was ill. He was from Senegal. So Bernard had to bring him and hide him in Paul's room. When Paul was away there was a fight about money or something, the man killed Bernard and disappeared. Paul got back on Sunday night and found Bernard's body. He had to get away. He rang me late on Monday night. He was desperate, he

329

was sleeping rough. He rang me to say goodbye.'

'Where is he now?'

Olivia snorted. 'I don't know. A long way away, I hope. What makes you think I'd tell you, anyway? That's not what I came for.'

'Shall I take your coat?'

Olivia shook her head.

'Want to sit down?' Sara asked.

Olivia did not respond.

'Well? May I ask why you are here?' Whatever it was, Sara hoped it would not take long.

'They haven't seen her at work since Friday. Where is she?'

Sara shook her head. 'You mean Sue, I guess? I really don't know. I was expecting to see her on Monday myself, remember? I rang you.'

'You know where she is,' Olivia said tightly. 'She's told you not to tell me, I suppose.'

'Why should she do that?' Sara asked.

Again she was ignored. 'I've been trying to ring her all day, to tell her about Edwin, and there's been no reply. I've just been round to Larkhall and the house is empty. I rang the next-door bell, and they said nobody had been there since the weekend. I thought she'd be here. I've no idea where she is.' She looked angrily at Sara. '*I'm* her aunt, not you.' She began to hiss. 'I'm sick of the way you've been quietly muscling in. It's *my* family, not yours.'

'Of course it's your family,' Sara began. 'I haven't tried to—'

'Shut up! Don't think I don't see! First taking over Sue, then all that muscling in on Edwin. *My* father,' she said savagely.

'I know,' Sara protested. 'Look, *you* invited me

330

to meet Edwin. I don't know what you mean. We had a wonderful time, that day.'

'Don't! As if I hadn't heard enough! Don't you realise,' she said, 'I've heard nothing else from Edwin, for days, his *last* days, except how wonderful you are? That wonderful talent? "Oh, Livy, isn't it strange that my own daughter never had any?" When I've spent *years* caring for him and worrying and doing anything to keep him at home? It's so unfair!' She dissolved into tears and brought a sodden handkerchief from her pocket.

Sara wanted to reach out and touch her, but instead she said, 'Oh, that *is* unfair. I'm sorry. I wouldn't have wanted that. He did understand that you did everything for him, you know. He told me.' She moved over to the wine rack. 'Let's have a drink. Always helps, I find. Don't you?'

'Don't patronise me! You know nothing about it! Nothing! You've got the lot, haven't you? Everything! And you're so bloody smug and patronising—you make me sick!'

'Olivia, you're very upset just now—'

'You even had to have a go with Paul, didn't you? That night at my house, you would have had his clothes off, wouldn't you? He *loved* it, of course—he was flattered. And that stunt, cutting your finger, just to get his attention.'

Perhaps she wasn't quite sober. A glass of wine would make her worse. The sooner she could get her to leave, the better. Sara's indignation rose.

'Look, come *on*. That's so silly. Cut my finger on purpose? I'm a cellist, for God's sake. Look, Olivia, sit down for a minute. Did you drive here? Shall I get a taxi for you?'

She walked round the table and gently placed

331

her left hand on Olivia's right arm, to guide her to a chair.

Olivia's arm flew up, recoiling as if she had been burned. She grabbed Sara's wrist. 'Don't touch me!' she yelled, digging her fingers in.

Sara gasped. 'Olivia! Let me go!'

Olivia's only response was to bang the back of Sara's hand down on the table, with horrible, unexpected strength.

She was breathing ferociously, but sounded calm. 'A cellist, are you? That's not what I've heard. A cellist who can't play?' Sara was trying uselessly with her right hand to loosen the grip of Olivia's fingers. 'I'm not letting go. You may as well stop that. You'll only do yourself more damage.'

Sara saw that Olivia, with her left hand, was drawing the largest knife from the wooden block on the table. With her free hand she reached for Olivia's hair and at the same time tried to find the breath to scream. The prick of the knife in the fleshy base of her thumb reduced her scream to a terrified whimper.

'Oh, don't, don't, don't—'

'Did you know I was left-handed?' Olivia asked conversationally. 'Very strongly left-handed. So I never could, you see, master any musical instrument. Never got anywhere. But I wasn't unmusical—I longed to be able to play.'

Sara had started to shake and could scarcely find words. 'Please, please, Olivia . . .'

'Still,' Olivia said smoothly, 'it's quite handy. I can do *lots* of things with my left hand.' On the word 'lots' she gave another stab with the knife into the base of Sara's thumb. She howled as the skin was punctured.

'Oh, yes. *Lots* of things. *Lots* and *lots* and *lots* and *lots*.'

Blood was now running from her hand on to the table. At the sight of it Sara screwed her eyes tight and her head swam. She thought she might be sick. As she fought against hysteria, her moans came in great gulps.

'Olivia, stop, stop—let go, please . . .'

'Shut up,' Olivia said, through her teeth. 'I haven't even hurt you yet.' She lifted the knife and laid it across Sara's small bare wrist, where every vein and tendon that fed the hand stood out, exposed. The knife blade sat on her skin.

'Where is she?'

'Olivia, I don't know. I don't know. I really don't.' Her legs were not going to hold her up much longer. 'Oh, please, *please* let me go, don't hurt me, don't hurt me. I don't know where she is.' Great snivelling gulps broke from her.

'Oh, stop fussing. You're not going to die. It's nearly impossible to die from a severed wrist, did you know that? It's quite difficult to cut through veins. It's the tendons that come off worst. Here. And here.' She tapped instructively on the wrist with the flat of the knife as she spoke. Sara had to squeeze her legs tight to stop herself from peeing with terror. She knew how sharp the knife was. The merest slicing motion against her wrist and she would never be able to play again.

'All that talent, and all that fuss to Edwin about not being able to play. You deserve to be shown what it's *really* like not to be able to play. Now'— the knife blade was tickling her wrist now—'where is my niece?'

Sara's grasp of the present swam away, and her

333

mind slowly filled with the huge, ugly certainty that after this day her life would go on, but without purpose.

'She doesn't know.' The sound came from the doorway. In the fraction of the second during which both women were transfixed by Andrew's voice, he walked into the kitchen.

'She doesn't know.' He paused. 'But you do seem rather anxious to find out, I must say.'

Although Olivia was silent with shock, her hold on Sara's wrist, and on the knife, did not slacken.

'Andrew, Andrew, make her stop. Make her stop, please, please—' Sara's voice gave out in frightened sobs.

'I want to know where my niece is. I'm worried about her. Don't come a step closer, or I'll do it. I *will*,' Olivia said.

'She will, she will, Andrew. Oh, please, please help me.' Sara was leaning across the table, her legs having almost given way.

Andrew paused, considering. He said gravely, 'I think perhaps you should be worried, Miss Passmore, but not for the reasons you think.' Olivia looked at him with alarm and lowered her eyes to the table. She made sure of the grip of the knife in her hand.

'We are conducting a search for Paul Rose. We have reason to believe that Mr Rose is involved in the murder of Bernard Rameau, whose body was found in his room yesterday. He had been killed some time on Sunday. We also suspect that Paul is connected with the murder of Matthew Sawyer.'

Sara whined.

'Sara, be quiet.' Andrew's voice was harsh. He went on, 'I'm very much afraid, Miss Passmore,

334

that Mr Rose was not acting alone. He had an accomplice.'

Olivia considered this, tapping distrustfully on Sara's wrist with the flat of the blade.

'Miss Passmore, I'm sorry to say that it looks very much as if your niece is involved. She was clearly working with him and they are certainly together now. I am hopeful that it will not be too long before they are apprehended. Mr Rose is an unpredictable man.'

'You're wrong,' Olivia said, raising the knife. 'Sue is not with him. I'm sure she's not. *She* knows where she is.' She tightened her hold on Sara's wrist. 'I want her reported as missing. I want some help to find her. Her grandfather's dead, and I haven't even been able to tell her.'

Andrew smiled sympathetically, ignoring Sara's low moans. 'You're upset. It's very difficult to take in, I know. It's the last thing you want to think. But she is quite clearly implicated, I'm afraid. We can prove that Paul Rose is a murderer. Your niece may actually have been involved in the . . . violence as well, but she is certainly an accessory. Very unpleasant, I agree.'

Olivia, wild-eyed, raised her voice. 'Look, my niece is not involved. I *know* she isn't. Wherever Paul is, that's not the issue. Don't you understand what I'm telling you? She is not involved!' Her breathing was coming in angry gasps. Sara sank her head on to the table, unable to control her gulping.

Andrew gave a complacent tut and shook his head. He thought for a moment. 'Well, I have to say, I hope you're right. If she genuinely isn't involved, then I hope for her own sake she *isn't* with him.'

335

'What do you mean?'

Andrew said gravely, 'Miss Passmore, I have been trying to tell you. Paul Rose is a dangerous man. Both he and your niece disappeared some time over the weekend. I am quite sure they are together and that they are in this whole thing together. Paul Rose certainly was not acting alone when he killed Matthew Sawyer. However, if the person who helped Mr Rose was someone *other* than your niece, then the only reason that Mr Rose could have her with him is because he suspects she knows things that might implicate him. He may even have abducted her. If she really is innocent then I would say she is in serious danger.'

Olivia said faintly, 'But her landlady's gone as well. Her car hasn't been seen for days. Only Sue's old banger is still there.'

'I'm afraid that worries me even more,' Andrew said. 'Mr Rose would find a car very useful, especially if its owner had been taken along. No car reported missing, you see? And there's no shortage of remote places that he could drive to, possibly with them in the boot.'

His voice softened. 'He's young, isn't he? If he thought he could possibly start all over again, perhaps back in France, he'd do anything he had to to get away with it. I suppose you know he's been dealing in stolen property? His associates are known housebreakers. Paul's been selling stuff hand over fist to this Rameau fellow. You see, he'll do anything he thinks he can get away with'—he looked gravely at Olivia—'including disposing of your niece and her landlady.'

Andrew allowed Olivia to ponder this for a few seconds and then said, falsely cheerful, 'On the

336

other hand, perhaps the landlady's just away on her own somewhere for a few days. Did she have a job? Oh, she did? I see. That is a bit more unusual. Oh, look, I'm sorry. It is upsetting, especially on top of your sad loss. My condolences, by the way. I'm so sorry, but there's very little that I can do about your niece until we have proper grounds for believing her innocent. If we had those, we would of course step up the search considerably. If we thought we had an abduction on our hands, you see, rather than two murder suspects. All comes down to resources, you see?'

Olivia was sobbing openly. Andrew stepped forward and with utter simplicity removed the knife from her hand. Sara withdrew her hand from Olivia's limp fingers and sank into a chair, still shaking. She covered her face with her hands and rocked to and fro, moaning, as blood from the puncture wounds on her thumb smeared her cheeks and made them sticky. She was aware of Andrew's voice, intoning the words of the statutory caution and arrest, followed by brief words on his mobile phone.

Olivia had her face in her handkerchief and was saying, 'I'll tell you everything. I want to tell you everything. Paul did kill Matthew Sawyer. I wasn't there. I drove him back to Fortune Park with his bike in the car and went back to the Pump Room. I had to get something. I locked up. I'll make a statement. He didn't kill the Frenchman. It was the immigrant, the Senegalese man. I'll tell you everything, only please find her. Sue's done nothing wrong. She's the only one I've got left. I'll tell you everything, but you must find her.'

Bridger and a WDC arrived within fifteen

337

minutes. The WDC took Olivia, handcuffed, out to the car. Sara refused to have a doctor called but allowed her cuts, numerous but trivial, to be dressed. Then, seeking the comfort of hot water, she stood under a scalding shower and afterwards got dressed in clean clothes. When she came downstairs Andrew poured her a large brandy which she downed almost in one. With Olivia out of the house, she had been able to stop shaking, but she was still a bad colour and inclined to tremble.

'Miss Selkirk won't be fit to make a statement before tomorrow. And I'm still on special leave, Bridger,' Andrew said, 'so you can deal with this tonight. I'll be in in the morning. Find out everything she knows about an illegal immigrant, Senegalese, who was hiding at Rose's place. He's our chief suspect for the Rameau killing. And get everything you can from her about the Sawyer murder. We should get a guilty plea on an accessory charge. And I want due consideration to be shown. As soon as you've got a full statement, let her off the hook about the niece.'

In the hall, following the lull after the door closed, Andrew wrapped his arms round Sara. She allowed herself to sink against the warmth of his body, smelling his skin, anticipating the feel of it.

'Oh, God,' he said into her hair, 'I've got you. Got you at last. I only went halfway to Olivia's house, you know. I turned round and came here. I had to see you. I love you, Sara. I want you.'

Sara's legs became unreliable once again. She giggled, partly from the brandy and partly because she was enjoying the idea that Andrew was easily strong enough to lift her and actually carry her upstairs, should her legs give way completely. To hell with the sexual politics. She was giving herself up to the sensation of his hands and of his warm skin and his mouth, and feeling with complete happiness the growing hardness of his body against her. The nerve of the man. He seemed to think he could just undress her right here in the hall, and he was right. She tugged at the zip of his jeans and as he twisted to help her get him out of them, she had the mundane thought that perhaps this time she should just lock the door, in case Bridger came back. Before Andrew had her shirt off. Where the hell was the key? Ah, yes, the hook in the cupboard. On the hook.

'What did you mean, "let her off the hook about the niece"?' she asked suddenly, drawing away.

Andrew moved a strand of hair away from her face and kissed her eyelids. His hands delved back into her shirt and slipped round her breasts.

'Doesn't matter now.'

'Andrew?'

He took a deep breath and pulled her close to him again. 'Okay. I knew,' he said softly, looking at her, with one finger tracing a line down her nose and across her lips. 'We sent out the registration of the landlady's car yesterday afternoon. I was interested in the connection with Sue, so I put out a call. We got a check in Perthshire this morning. Vehicle owner and one female passenger, Sue Harman. Cecily Smith has walked out of her job, and decided to go away for a few days, and Sue went with her. So I knew they were quite safe. Wherever Paul is, he's alone.'

He kissed her again, lightly, thoughtfully. 'I'm sorry. But we need to find him. And the Senegalese man. And don't you think she rather wanted to unload the whole story? Thank you for what you did.'

He kissed her properly.

'You mean you made all that up? All that time you were standing there, with my wrist under that knife, you knew where Sue was?'

'But I won't get a conviction in this case without Olivia Passmore's confession. And I won't get to Paul without her co-operation. I had to put her under a bit of pressure.'

'With my wrist under a knife? She could have destroyed my hand. She could have—'

'I don't think she would have. Look, I am sorry. I had to do it though, don't you see?'

He looked at her, worried, trying to make her see. 'You *must* see.'

'You *knew*. All the time she had my hand, you could have stopped her. You were *bargaining* with my hand.' She looked at her hand, where a little blood was seeping from under the bandage. 'Look, I'm bleeding again,' she added prosaically.

'Sara, I wouldn't have let her hurt you. I love you.'

'But if she had, suppose she had? And you kept on at her, knowing.' She was going to choke on the truth of it.

'Come on,' he said, gently taking her hand. 'Let's sort you out. We need to get that under running water.'

She pushed him away, almost sadly, and started doing up the buttons on her shirt. 'Go back to your wife, Andrew.'

'I've left my wife. I don't want my wife, I want you. Look, let me help you, you'll drip on the carpet—'

'I can do it myself.'

'Sara—'

'You should go back to your wife, you know. But go, anyway.'

She locked the door behind him, even though, this time, he had not paused long enough to remind her to do so.

CHAPTER THIRTY-FOUR

Derek had taken to bouncing on the balls of his feet. He had always worn good English shoes, polished to resemble varnished wood, but now, instead of planting his feet with the permanence and immovability of two small matching items of mahogany furniture, he had lately begun, when talking on the telephone or taking assembly, to swing a little, and then to bounce. He enjoyed the private flexing of his buttocks that this involved, now that there were five pounds or so less of them. Only another four and a half stone to go.

He was bouncing now, killing a bit of time in the station before he walked with a confident swing down to the Guildhall for his interview. He'd thought it better to come by train and avoid any panic over parking, although it had meant leaving enough time for the train to be delayed or cancelled, and now of course he was early. How did he look? He had left home certain that he was immaculately dressed, so it was a little disconcerting the way that woman seemed to be staring at him. He stared back and shamed her into looking away. Probably waiting herself, although

341

not for an interview. Been shopping, judging by the three carrier bags with Jigsaw and Square written on them. Nice dress, black linen it looked like, nice body. Nice hair. She was strolling about now, pretending to read the wall posters, and turning back in his direction. It was the face that was really amazing, because of her eyes, which were so large, blue-green and magnetically strong that he had to give a little cough and look at his watch. Watch it, Derek, he warned himself, you're only five days into your promise to Pauline; at least try to make it to the end of the week before entertaining adulterous thoughts.

People were trickling through now from the London train and the woman was almost running.

'Robin!'

The grey, curly-haired man with red-rimmed glasses to whom she was calling stopped dead, to the annoyance of the people behind him, and held out his arms.

'You're a darling to come just like this,' she said a few seconds later, coming out from the grip of his bear hug. She was obviously too pleased to see him to lower her voice. 'When I rang this morning I didn't expect you to get on the next train.'

He was beaming back at her.

'Actually, I had to cancel lunch with the artist formerly known as Nigel,' he said in a loud, gleeful whisper. 'But I had to come, there's so much to talk over, lots to plan. Simon still wants you for the Dvořák before he leaves Birmingham, Nagano keeps asking. Can you still play something for me later, even with the bandage? And listen now, I know you said it's not serious, but I know a very good man and I think you should just go and see

342

him, just for me.'

'Robin, it's nothing, only scratches, honestly. Haven't time to bother with it. I'm beginning to think about doing the Brahms sonatas again. What do you think?'

Robin sighed happily and shook his head. 'Darling Sara, I think you're as stubborn and wonderful as ever, and it's plain tragic that I'm fifty-eight and happily married. Let's have tea. Why don't I take you to the Pump Room?'

'No, not the Pump Room'—she was laughing as she led him out of the station—'absolutely not the Pump Room. Let's go somewhere else.'

The man was obviously puzzled. But the woman he called Sara was obviously not going to be drawn into the private reasons behind her distaste for the Pump Room, and Derek, watching her go, silently concurred with her opinion and felt the passing of a kindred spirit.

EPILOGUE

Two lives were lost in the second Channel Tunnel fire. When the heat had abated sufficiently to allow the crews to reach the scene, they found the same powdered concrete and fused metal in steaming confused heaps and also, this time, two carbonised male skeletons. It had been, as a spokesman said, deeply traumatic for everyone concerned. The thirty-eight passengers had been in the restaurant car at the front of the train when the alarm was given and smoke had begun to appear. Everyone had been very frightened but remained calm, except for that one man. Only that one driver had panicked and lost control and it had been surprising because he was a regular, a French lorry driver who knew the tunnel well and had always seemed a calm, easy-going sort of character. The stewards had been quite unable either to understand or to calm his incoherent shouting, and it was when they had been busy trying to reassure the other passengers and issue the smoke hoods that he had broken through the emergency door and run off. To the horror of those watching he had bolted down the tunnel in the direction of the fire instead of towards the escape tunnel a few metres further up. Of course it later became clear why, when firemen recovered the other body, that of the driver's illicit passenger, crouched in the cab of the lorry.

The French lorry was identified easily enough from the paperwork on the English side and so, consequently, was the driver, Thierry Langlais, who collapsed in the tunnel trying to reach his hitch-hiker and never got home. But the passenger who had died in his hiding place became something of a difficulty. He had had no ticket to travel, and whether any spoonful of the ashes around him could once have been a passport was impossible to tell. A search of dental records was fruitless. No one came forward to report that their student son had failed to telephone, no wife or lover or acquaintance of any kind made any enquiry whatsoever. The police rather perfunctorily traced the lorry's regular journey of the week before, starting from Agen on Saturday, arriving in Bristol on Sunday, leaving Bristol on Tuesday for its two destinations in London, then back via the tunnel on the night of Thursday 24 July, the night of the fire. The driver could have picked up a hitch-hiker anywhere on the way.

If anyone had thought to prompt them, some of the regular drivers using the overnight lay-by and burger van on the A46 Bath road just off Junction 18 of the M4 might have been able to remember seeing a man, who had seemed to come out of nowhere, approach the cab of the French lorry that pulled in during the evening of Tuesday 22 July. There were one or two who might have identified the lorry as Thierry's, because Thierry more often than not pulled in for a burger on his haul back from Bristol. They might, if they had noticed, have been able to recall that as Thierry had jumped down from the cab, he and the man had talked for a few moments. Then the man had waited by the cab while Thierry had gone to get burgers at the mobile van at the end of the lay-by, where he had remarked that he had a French-speaking hitch-hiker to relieve the boredom of the journey home. And although it had been too dark, and the man too far away to say with certainty whether he had been white or black, one of them might have remembered that the man had climbed up into the passenger seat as Thierry had stepped up at the driver's side and driven off. But no one did ask them. Police officers on both sides of the Channel checked their missing persons lists regularly at first, then less assiduously and finally not at all. They bemoaned with their colleagues the lack of resources for conducting such searches, thought privately that he was probably a foreign national, and hoped, when they thought about it at all, that relatives would eventually come forward.

The passenger could not be allowed to remain a difficulty indefinitely. Because his clothes, his belongings and the seat he had been trapped in had smelted into his soft body, all that remained after his fierce and unofficed cremation were his bones, sunken under a soldified ooze of molten vinyl and tacky with human tar. With the tenderness of archaeologists the fire crew had chipped his skeleton out intact from the encrusted fusion of wet clinker, tied a number round the black twig of a toe bone and placed it in a box labelled 'Male: 30–40 yrs: 1m 79cm: Not identified'.

All through the rest of the summer he lay in the mortuary. At the end of September he was removed to a room at the end of a corridor in the basement where it was quiet, where the human traffic of relatives, undertakers, mortuary attendants, pathologists and police had all but ceased. There, the only noise was the faint hum of the refrigeration system that kept the room in perpetual winter, and there, wrapped in frosty white paper, he was placed in a vacant drawer alongside other, seldom-opened drawers, in which lay the bodies of other unclaimed and unmourned people.

348